CHILD OF TULATHNE

CHILD of TULATHNE

LILA SAMSON

Edited: Hannah Van Vels Ausbury
Cover Art and Design: Lila Samson
Formatting and Illustrations: Lila Samson
Map of Zekhar: Lila Samson

First Edition Printing, 2024

ISBN: 979-8-9906103-3-0 (Hardcover–Dust Jacket)
ISBN: 979-8-9906103-1-6 (Hardcover–Case Laminate)
ISBN: 979-8-9906103-0-9 (Paperback)
ISBN: 979-8-9906103-2-3 (eBook)

LCCN: 2024915058

For my father, Tim, who first introduced me to a fantasy fellowship, and inspired me to write my own.

Pronunciation Guide

Aleksander - *Ah-lek-sahn-der*

Alesathne - *Ah-less-ath-nay*

Aoife – *Ee-fah*

Bozkei - *Bo-z-kay*

Brevindun - *Breh-vin-dunn*

Bunc - *Bunk*

Caliphus - *Cal-ih-fuss*

Caoimhe - *Keev-ah*

Carissa - *Car-i-sah*

Ceileh - *Ch-ey-lah*

Clauden - *Clod-en*

Demir - *Deh-meer*

D'orde - *De-ord*

Dzera - *Dzh-ehr-ah*

Edrun - *Ed-run*

Elmere - *El-meer*

Elspeth - *El-spe-th*

Ethingar - *Eth-in-gaar*

Farnich - *Far-neech*

Fazhia - *Fah-z-ee-ah*

Genoise – *Gen-oh-eez*

Halkin - *Hal-kin*

Hatenepta - *Hah-ten-ehpt-ah*

Homunculi - *Ho-mun-cu-lie*

Iscah - *Iss-cah*

Janek - *Yahn-ekh*

Kasajb - *Kahs-ay-eeb*

Kallendrine - *Cal-en-drine*

Kutsalyot - *Koot-sahl-ee-oht*

Lauklin - *Lawk-lynn*

Lenore - *Leh-nor*

Mekartlim - *Meh-kart-leem*

Ölmesuz - *Ool-mesh-ooz*

Orzei - *Or-zay*

Posheica – *Posh-ih-cah*

Pozhontec - *Pah-zh-on-tek*

Revla - *Rev-lah*

Rodzjiek - *Ro-dzh-yek*

Rodzjiekim - *Ro-dzh-yek-eem*

Saoirse - *Seer-sha*

Satie-Hak - *Sah-ti-ay Haak*

Toprazi - *Tohp-rah-zee*

Tulathne - *Too-lath-nay*

Varek - *Var-ehk*

Wythane - *Why-thay-n*

Zekhar – *Zeh-khar*

Zekharyan – *Zeh-khar-ee-an*

Ziva - *Zee-vah*

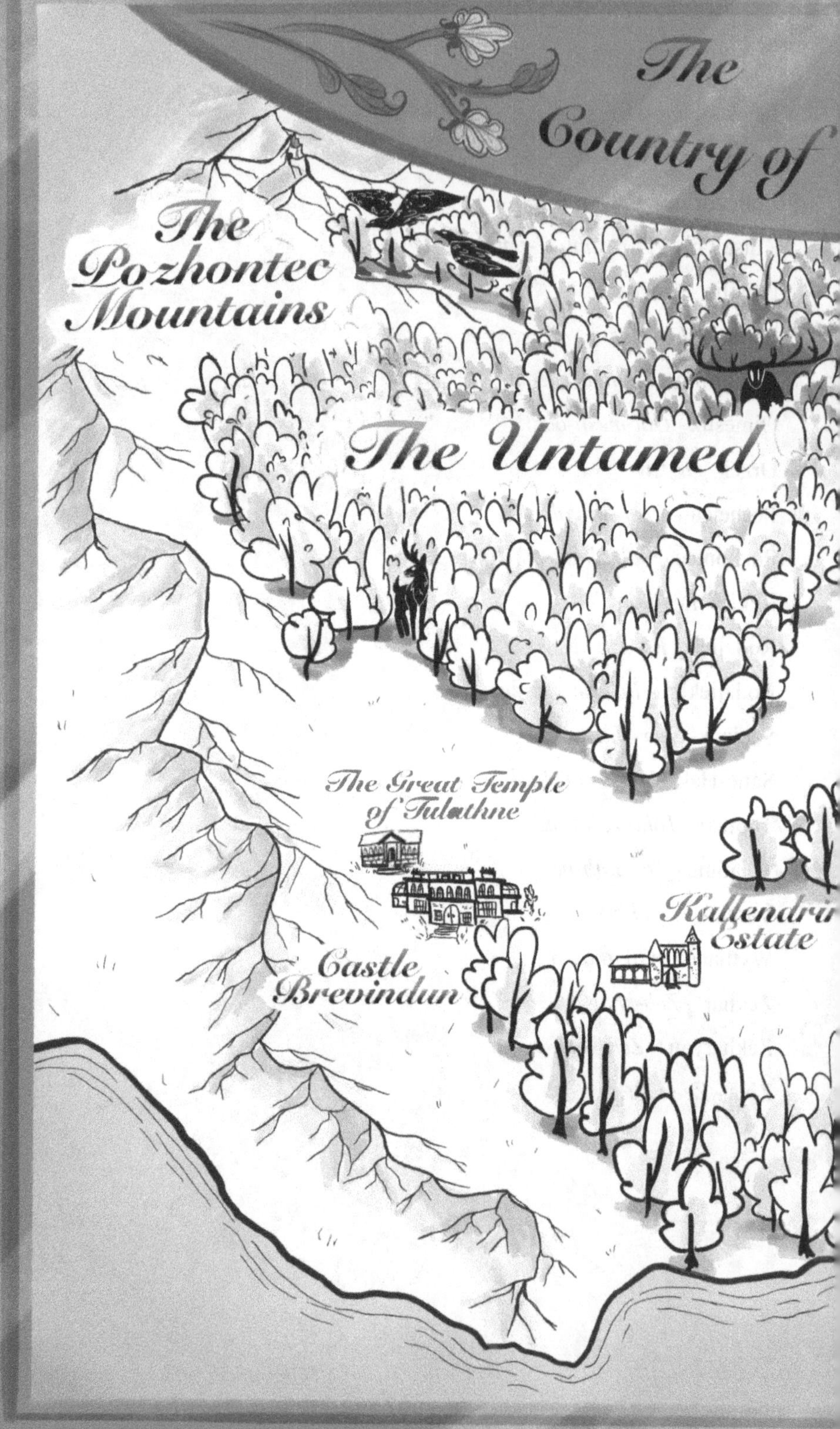

The Country of
The Pozhontec Mountains
The Untamed
The Great Temple of Tulathne
Castle Brevindun
Kallendrir Estate

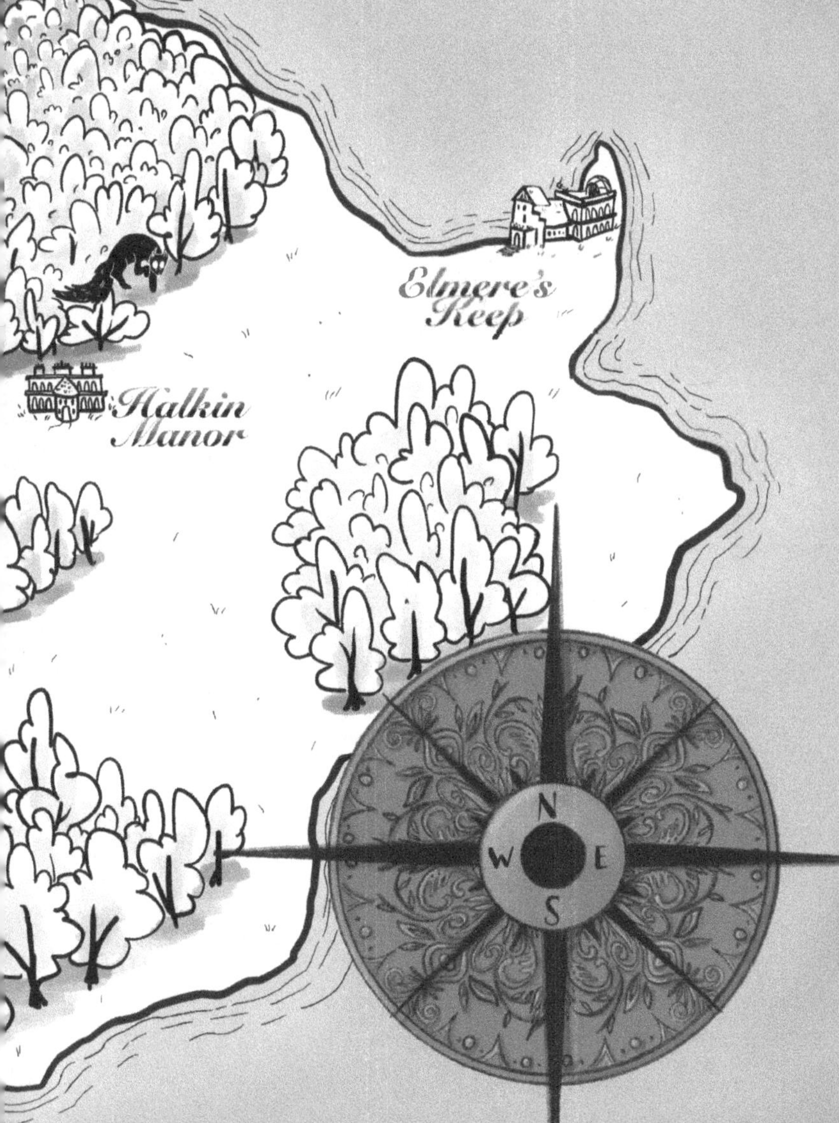

ZEKHAR
Elmere's Keep
Halkin Manor
N
W
E
S

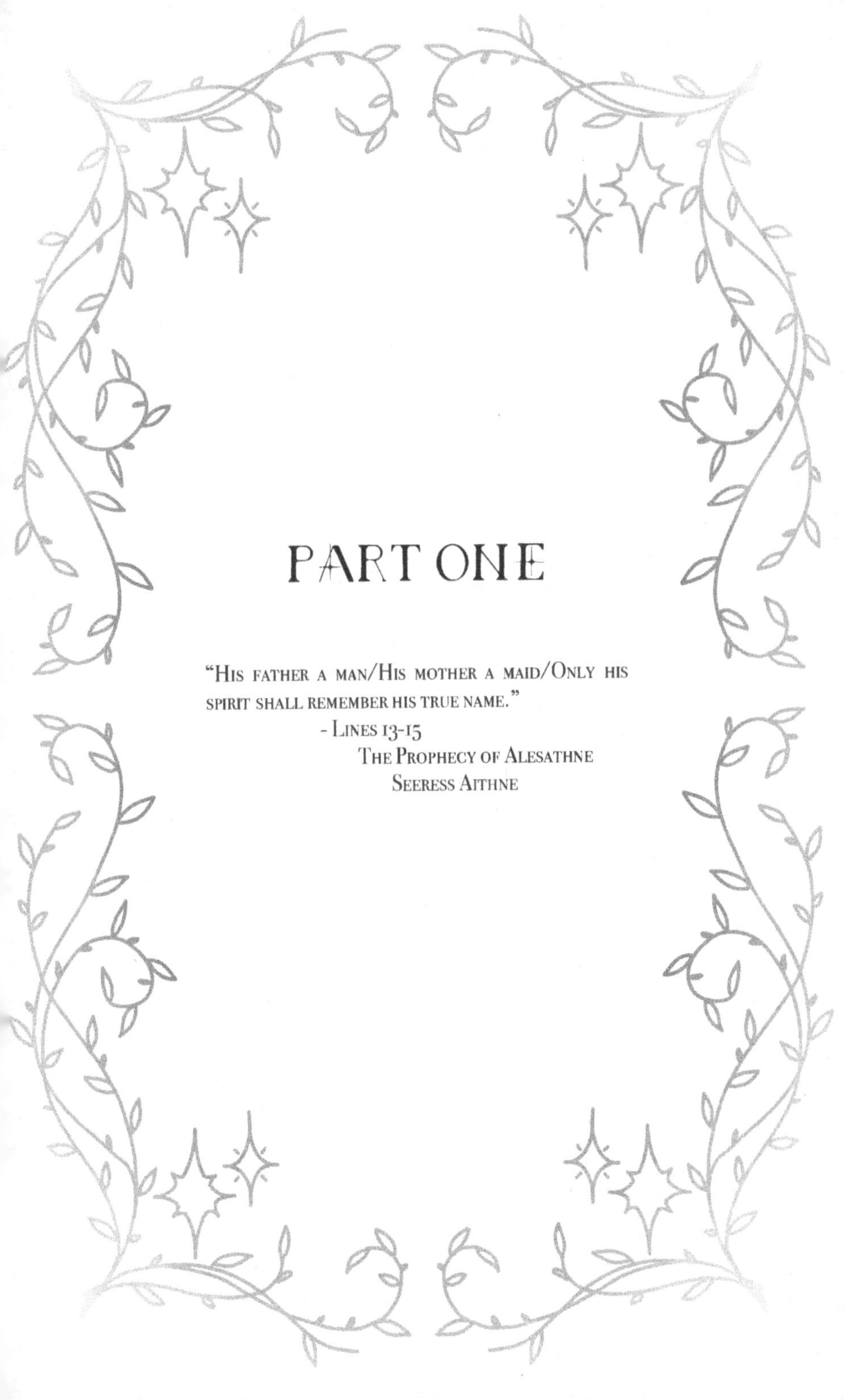

PART ONE

"His father a man/His mother a maid/Only his spirit shall remember his true name."
- Lines 13-15
The Prophecy of Alesathne
Seeress Aithne

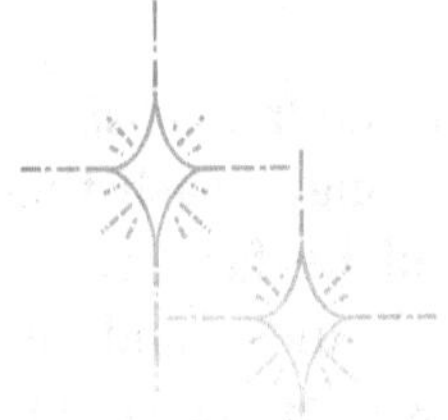

PROLOGUE

ABOVE THE HOUSE IN THE VALLEY, just past the edge of the forest, were two stars. These stars had names, though no one asked what they were. On this night, they were completely unconcerned with what was happening on the earth below and didn't care that no one knew them personally. They danced around one another, enjoying this evening of company and reunion after centuries of separation, wandering alone and lost through the cosmos.

The screams issuing from that house in the valley didn't matter to them either, though they certainly heard them. There, on the midwife bricks, was not a woman they necessarily cared for, nor was she someone they knew.

She clenched her sister's and mother's hands, knuckles white, arms shaking. One midwife pressed gently on her hips, offering a breath of relief between contractions, while the other pressed lightly on her stomach, feeling for the baby. Her hair had been neatly braided back by her aunt, who now sat in the corner, weaving a bracelet for the child from red and black thread, whispering prayers into it—petitioning the goddess to watch over the child, bless them, give them strength, love, and a good life full of beautiful sunsets, happy memories, and a purpose.

Outside the door sat the father, spooning a small amount of salt and spice onto his tongue each time his wife screamed in agony. His coughs echoed, his face screwed up. The father of this new father patted his shoulder and reminded him that she's going through much worse; he could handle a salty, spicy spoonful.

Just as he ate another, the shouts inside the room rose. They became too loud too fast. The spoon clattered, forgotten, to the boards of the kitchen, and he rushed towards the closed bedroom door.

Unexpected silence hit the moment his hands touched the door handle. From beyond came the sounds of his wife gasping for breath, crying, and sighing. Soft voices crooned praises, and then—

He pushed open the door at the sound, not worrying about decorum. Rushing to his wife, on her hands and knees on the floor, he lifted her tired face to his and planted a kiss on her forehead. Her shaking arms took him into a tight embrace before she was pried away by the midwives and laid back on a bed to have her stomach massaged back into place. The grunts and yells resumed, but the original cause was busy in the arms of his new grandmother, fussing as she wiped fluid from his nose and eyes. Taking the end of her braid, she danced it over his face. The sensation caused him to pause. Sparkling blue eyes blinked up at her, pupils large and straining in the sudden bright light.

A laugh brightened her voice, and she announced that he opened his eyes, that he was breathing and healthy and blessed.

The red string now fastened around his wrist, the child squirmed and whimpered. He only settled when he was placed in the arms of his mother.

In the heavens, the stars halted their dance, wispy tendrils of celestial hands reaching out to clutch one another. A shared gasp filled the small space above the earth.

Nearly a millennia had passed since they'd seen one another last, but for good reason, as their own memories came rushing back bursting with images of war, heartbreak, and at the beginning of it all, a deep, painful betrayal.

Just a half hour's walk from the village, the wise woman bolted out of bed, catching the two dancing stars as the cries of a newborn still echoed from her dreams.

Within hours, she was racing through the thin forest, cloak held tightly over her hunched form. In her hand was a budding twig of rowan, wrapped with copper and bells. It jingled as she ran, the calls and cries from her vision mixing with panting as she pushed herself around fallen trees and rocks—till she found that small hut, a garden out front, and knocked.

The moment the father answered, his face lit up.

He called to his wife, racing from the front door, trusting the woman to follow him in. She sat in the bed, bathed in candlelight. Their son slept in her arms.

No, the father realized. Not his son.

So much more than his son.

He called to his wife, and when she looked up, only a moment passed before her eyes widened. They glistened with fresh tears as she looked down at her newborn. Neither of them said anything. Neither of them dared speak the name the wise woman knew belonged to the child. The name they all knew belonged to him.

She was the first to speak. Muttered prayers in an older dialect mixed with the jingling branch as she waved it over the babe's bundled form. "Alesathne," the old woman whispered, kneeling beside the bed.

The baby blinked stiffly, still swollen and sensitive to the light. A soft coo echoed through the room.

She smiled. "Welcome back."

Chapter

ONE

*T*HERE WAS REALLY NOTHING THE YOUNG man could do except sit against the wall, tailbone aching, waiting for the right pair of shoes to click down the steps. Tassels at the bottom of a tapestry brushed the top of his shoulders. They tickled the nape of his neck normally covered by a collar, a scarf, or a gorget. One day, when he was around the age of nine, he'd spent hours staring at it. It was an ornate tapestry, with shimmering threads and hand-stitched prayers in the border of the piece. At the center hung an image of a woman. With flowing black hair and a face concealed by a veil, She held in one outstretched hand a sword and in the other a hoe. The portrait glowed with silver threads behind Her head and golden threads around Her feet.

He'd often wondered what it would be like to talk to Her—*really* talk to the goddess, not just kneel in the temple or at the oratory in the corner of his bedroom, separated from the rest of the space by a screen painted with a pattern of stars and flowers.

Servants ran by, some offering a nod, others too busy in their tasks balancing vases overflowing with flowers or gathering swaths of fabric against their chests so they wouldn't sweep along the immaculate floor.

Orders echoed up and down the hall, and Mrs. Buckneel, the

woman who had acted as the royal wet nurse over twenty years ago and had since graduated to manager of the castle, was the cause of all of them. Usually one could count on the queen herself to be found standing beside Mrs. Buckneel or at the very least running in and out to check on proceedings—that was, when she wasn't busy herself. Today, she certainly was. The midsummer celebration was in two nights, and as the capital of Zehkar and the home of the royal family, Castle Brevindun was unequivocally the place to host it.

One maid, around his age, placed her vase on the floor beside a statue of King Clauden's father, the late King Tepes. Hands on her hips, she heaved an incensed sigh and flicked a blossom of jasmine that stuck out at her, lips and brows scrunched in a grimace.

Another passed, bumping her with her hip and muttering something with such speed and ferocity, Aleksander had no time to make out what was said.

The servant girl's eyes landed on him in that moment. Her cheeks went scarlet with embarrassment. "Sorry, Champion Wythane," she heaved, picking up the vase and trotting down the hall double-speed.

A smile curved his lip as the maid retreated. Though he had done nothing to earn the title, it made his chest swell ever so slightly with pride. Here he was, a boy born to a small family in the forests at the foot of the Pozhontec Mountains, just south enough to be civilized and just north enough to be familiar with the Untamed and all the stories about it—and he was a Champion.

No, not just *a* champion. *The* Champion.

Discomfort tugged at his stomach. It always did when he thought about his title for too long. He'd won no battles, had not calmed diplomatic disputes—had just been born under the right stars.

Finally, the *click click click* of heels bounding down the stairs met his ears and he pushed himself to his feet, leaving behind his thoughts around his position. Legs groaning, back aching, he shoved his shoulder blades back and cracked the spot right between them before assuming a stance of practiced casualty, one hand resting on his leg and the other on the sword strapped to his hip.

Down the stairs raced the woman he'd been waiting for. Her long blonde hair was tied up in an ornate style that made use of her wild curls, adorned with pins of pearl and ruby and sapphire. Two ringlets, one on each side of her face, fell just above her collarbones, bouncing in time with her stuttering sprint down the staircase. Pale green eyes lit up as they met his, falling the moment she spotted the sword.

"Don't say it," he started.

"You're going to get someone killed, Aleksander," she huffed, stopping before him. The velvet gown pulled taut against her chest as she stretched her arms, straining even more as she took a deep breath. Her brows scrunched towards one another, creasing her upturned nose. "God-*dess*, this dress is tight."

"I'm not going to get someone killed by just wearing my sword, Carissa." He turned with her, starting towards the foyer.

"What happened to the carefree boy I've known all these years? I swear, ever since you turned fifteen you're taking this much more seriously than is necessary." Her step faltered, and he caught her hand. "Thank you. But honestly, why not leave it in your room just once?"

"I've left it in my room plenty of times."

"Not this year. And not when we leave the castle. I've never seen you in the city without it."

He rolled his eyes. "When we're in the city, I'm your guard. Do you know what that means, Carissa? I have to be able to guard you."

"Oh, cut the formalities. You just wanna look handsome and roguish for all the ladies we'll meet in town." She checked his shoulder with hers, hard. A broad grin split her face. "I understand."

He lunged to return the bump with a much more forceful shove, but the older, taller of the two—who also just happened to be trained in twelve different dance styles—sidestepped the blow with frustrating agility.

She threw her head back in a raucous laugh.

As much as his ears burned, Carissa's suggestion couldn't have been further from the truth. It actually was as simple as he said. Everyone recognized Aoife, the antique arming sword that adorned his side with her oiled leather grip and gold filigreed pommel, glistening with inlaid rubies and mother-of-pearl. Though the capital city of Brewith was full of supporters of the crown and danger was often the farthest thing from Aleksander's mind, he couldn't ignore the nagging he felt when he considered leaving Aoife in his room.

Blinking into the sun, they stepped down towards a waiting carriage.

"We aren't walking?" Aleksander asked, eyeing their driver, Bunc, and the two mares pawing the stone.

"No," Carissa sighed dejectedly. "Janek is worried the heat and the exercise will make me ill."

He took her hand in his, assisting her into the carriage. His eyes widened. "Are you...?" He didn't know how to ask if she was pregnant. After growing up with her, it was strange to picture the twelve-year-old he first met as a mother, even though she'd been married for the last four years.

She shook her head, answering before the question was even voiced. "No, I don't think so. At least, I don't feel like I am. Either way, you know the struggles my mother had." A sad smile took to her face as she slid along the velvet cushions. "Janek doesn't want me to go through the same. Which I appreciate."

Taking a seat across from her, he tapped the window behind him and the carriage lurched forward. Carissa leaned her head against the door, staring out at the world that passed by. Her eyes began to fade, growing distant and clouded in the midday sun.

"What is it?" Aleksander asked.

She jumped at the suddenness of his voice, took a deep breath as her eyes roved his face, and leaned back against the door. "I had another vision this morning. Before I took breakfast."

His brows furrowed. "What did you see this time?"

Carissa was not just the princess. She was the called the Eyes of Time by the priestesses. Among all the women of the temple, there were only five who had visions. All were lauded as blessed by Tulathne, pure in heart and mind, learned in Her ways. To be gifted with such divine sight was rare; yet, from the time she was eight, Carissa's visions rivaled theirs for accuracy and frequency. Even Saoirse, the oldest priestess in service, whose words were considered those of the goddess Herself, had praised Carissa's skills.

She adjusted in her seat and smoothed her skirt. "It's...hard to describe. I saw creatures, the likes of which we've never encountered before, amassing on a field of lilies and chrysanthemums. I saw you, of course." She nodded at his sword. "Aoife. There were people helping you. One of them you fought back-to-back with. They had sharp teeth. Wore shining armor. They wielded shadow and flame like one wields a whip." A shudder slid down her spine, causing her to roll her shoulders as goosebumps prickled along her arms. "Frankly, I'm glad they were terrifying. They seemed formidable. Strong."

As he listened, his face contorted more and more.

"The sky turned from blue to red to black, and you were lost to the ground turning in on itself, as was the person you fought with." Carissa shook her head, a curl falling free at her neck. "It's wildly dramatic, isn't it?" She turned her eyes out towards the world beyond the glass. A deep sigh whispered from her lips. "And I have absolutely no clue what it means."

Aleksander turned the description over in his head. The voice of Caoimhe, a priestess and his teacher for the last five years, replaced his own as he picked the vision apart.

She had seen a battle, clearly. He wasn't alone, there were allies, and one of them was incredibly skilled in whatever battle art they knew. The flame and shadow could be anything from actual fire and darkness to simply meaning their sword stung like a flame and they stole life like the night steals the sun. The ground turning in was difficult too. Literal options battled against symbolic—a cave in, or a rockslide, or perhaps just a misstep on his part, either with his own two feet or in terms of a decision.

One thing had come from years of listening to her visions: he'd accepted they'd never be clear and understandable until they were in the thick of it.

Noise rising in the town drew their attention, and both turned to peer from the carriage windows.

Preparations for the solstice were fully underway. The frantic, busy pace of the town matched what Aleksander experienced within the castle. Carts of streamers, banners, and fancy hanging lanterns moved into every open space on the road they could find, desperate to get where they needed to go. Someone shouted about the carriage, and all heads within a ten-foot radius spun. People began to close in on the carriage, pointing and shouting, kissing the wheels, crying out to Aleksander with praises. In the capital, when a royal carriage passed by, it was hardly ever cause for excitement. But when it was this carriage, one owned specifically by the princess and used by her and the Champion, excitement overtook even the most placid of onlookers.

Ten years of this. Exactly ten last week. Ten years of listening to common folk laud him as a god, of listening to the priestesses remind him of who he is and what he is meant to do. Ten years of Carissa's husband Janek—and before him Captain Poranek—reminding him that his skill on the battlefield will eventually decide the fate for not only Zekhar, but the whole of the continent, the whole of the world.

After ten years—where first he was overwhelmed, then exhausted, then used to it—he did what he always did. His right hand rested on his heart, and he nodded, a soft smile on his face. A long, slow tug on his heart radiated pain through his chest.

It was strange to be the Champion, but that didn't mean he didn't want to hold that title. No, there was no grief in that sentiment. There was only grief in seeing the people—Ölmesuz and Zekharyan alike—begging him for help, for support, for blessings and peace and security.

After ten years, one thing had not changed.

He was still so desperate to give that to them, and so lost as to how.

Chapter
TWO

NOTHING IN THE MODISTE'S SHOP INTERESTED him, not even remotely. While Carissa had been whisked away by the modiste herself, the two babbling on about color choices, fabric selection, if Carissa was looking for a custom order or a pre-made gown, and more, Aleksander resigned himself to study the different gowns in the room and see which colors worked with the palette of his doublet the best.

His fingers danced through the jewels dripping off a gown on display—regal, with a rich red-purple fabric pinned in the way of the Ölmesuz so that the wearer's arms were bare, as well as their back, draped with gems and metal which had been hammered and cut just so in order to make it seem as if the neckline itself was growing the crystals.

"Lovely, isn't it?" a voice purred behind him.

A jolt of panic shot down his spine and he jumped, turning to see a woman who glowed as though she herself was hammered from a sheet of bronze. Her ears, sticking out from the sides of her head and drooping with the weight of multiple piercings and adornments, twitched as she smiled.

Some likened Ölmesuz ears to that of a cow, and in this moment, he understood why.

"My apologies, Champion. I did not mean to startle you."

Aleksander nodded. "No, I'm alright."

Clear, red eyes trained on him. The thick lashes framing them didn't even twitch with a withheld blink. Instead they stayed still, wide and fixated.

He shifted on his feet, glancing back at the dress. "Did...did you make this?"

She nodded, eyes fluttering closed as a smile grew between her cheeks. "I did. It was a challenge I gave myself to make something that would appeal to both my people and yours. Your women have very strange preferences."

The jewels twinkled against one another as he ran a finger through them again. "Well, they do like fancy rocks."

A shining laugh. "We all do."

Hand dropping to rest on the hilt of his sword, he extended the other to her. "What's your name?"

She took his hand, arching her tall form down to touch the back of it to her forehead. "Satie-Hak, your holiness."

He winced. There was nothing new about the title. He was, and had been for a while, very well aware he was the Sword of Ages; the Sword of Ages, Champion of Tulathne, the Blessed One —so many things. Being called "Champion" was strange, but being called "holy" felt wrong. He did not feel worthy of being placed on the same level as his goddess.

"Wonderful to meet you, Lady Satie-Hak."

Gently folding her hands together behind her back, her eyes lifted to perceive the people in the town beyond the thin pane of glass. "Ah, it seems your followers have found you," she laughed.

Turning, Aleksander first saw his own shining blue eyes in the window. Blinking past them, however, was a group of three young women, all wearing simple garb, their hair tied up as though they'd just recently gotten out of the fields to the north or away from their looms and wheels.

Their eyes lit up when they met his.

Shouts of "he looked at me!" and "oh hello, Sir Wythane!" and even more high-pitched, giddy calls rattled against the glass. The girls hardly looked at him anymore, instead taking in one another and clasping hands, jumping up and down before sprinting away.

Flush burned at his ears and cheeks.

When he turned around, Satie-Hak had her hands folded tightly and her eyes averted. "Sorry," he muttered. "I wish they wouldn't do that."

She shook her head, plastering a smile. "No, don't worry, my lord Champion."

A bell rang and they both turned. The woman entering was Zekharyan. She had her long brown hair pulled back from her face with two beaded braids falling before her ears, a nervous expression on her face.

Satie-Hak's face lit up. "Lyra!" Outstretched arms welcomed the patron.

Lyra smiled. Aleksander couldn't ignore the way her eyes kept darting back to his, each moment punctuated by a split moment of panic.

"It's so good to see you!" Satie-Hak said, standing back to take in the woman. "I was wondering if you'd ever come back. I'll get that gown for you."

Lyra nodded wordlessly as the Ölmesuz scampered into the back. Her dark eyes found Aleksander's and she offered a short smile and a stiff curtsey. "Your holiness."

He nodded back to her. "Ma'am."

Shifting on her feet, Lyra eventually forced herself to walk around the store and peer at various garments. Weathered fingers hovered above embroidery, beading, silks. She was about as old as Aleksander guessed his mother would be, with her eyes and cheeks just starting to show signs of age. Those eyes darted back to him now, and she turned abruptly, dropping into a low curtsey. "My lord, might I have a moment of your time?"

Aleksander's heart stuttered. "Of course," he said, voice strained.

At the words, the woman rushed forward and took his hands, dropping to her knees. Her mouth opened to say something, but she stopped. It took every bit of control Aleksander had not to let his discomfort show on his face.

"My lord." She pressed the backs of his hands on to her forehead. "My daughter is ill. She has just turned seventeen, and she has a fiancé, and she's loyal to our Lady. She prays for your safety and honors Tulathne in the temple as much as she can." Lifting her head, her eyes shone with tears. "Your Mother is the Lady of Balances, of give and take. I've already lost one child. Please, do not let me lose another. Let her thrive. Let her live. Let me see her live."

Tears burned in the back of Aleksander's throat.

The grip on his hands tightened.

"I've spent all I can on treatments. We've seen Ölmesuz, Mekartlim, and Zekharyan healers, and we have no money to visit the Rodzjiek healers in the city. She's set to be married on the solstice next year. Please... You are our last hope."

Grief flooded Aleksander. This wasn't the first time someone had approached him with the desire for healing, for help, for protection. As the reincarnation of Alesathne, they thought he held some sort of godly power. That he could rewrite fate and control even the most out-of-control circumstances.

And every time he wished violently, deep in his heart, that he had that power.

His first instinct was to ask her what she wanted him to do. He wasn't a healer, but he knew healers—good healers too, who could actually help her daughter. Maybe.

But no. It was never that simple. He knew she, like all the others, hoped against hope that he did, indeed, have those powers Alesathne did. To heal the sick. Restore the injured. Some even claimed he could raise the dead.

So he knelt down before her. Her eyes widened at the movement. It was unfitting for a lord to kneel to the position of a commoner. But with each beat of his heart, something deep inside him, something not born of Alesathne or the years he'd spent in the palace, reminded him that he was just like her. Like all of them.

He smiled softly. "First, let me say that I hear you. And I am so sorry for what you've endured."

She stifled a sob.

"I know this is not what you want to hear"—his throat closed—"but I am no healer. Regardless, I am still who I am. What's your daughter's name?"

"Clair" came the choked syllable. "Her name is Clair."

Aleksander nodded. "I'll keep her in my heart and in my words when I next speak to my Mother. She is understanding, our Lady. I have faith that your prayers and mine will be heard."

Still crying, she stood, with Aleksander's help. Stiff hands swiped at her tears, leaving red patches on her cheeks where she pressed too hard.

All of his guilt, his pain, sunk deep into his gut. "Here." Before he knew what he was doing, he dug into the satchel on his hip. The light leather armor he wore creaked as he moved. It was mostly for show. To remind people of who he was, what he could do. His fingers found a soft velvet pouch. It jingled when he touched it.

"There are about seventy pieces of silver in here," he said, placing it into her hand. "There's a very good Rodzjiek healer in Brewith. She services the palace. Her name is Zvezda z'Brewita. I've had many a bone set by her, and the queen herself has survived many illnesses by her hand. Go to her, tell her you were sent by Alesathne." The name was thick on his tongue, but he continued. "Be well, and have faith."

Lyra stared at the coin pouch in her hand, unblinking. Slowly, she looked up to him and shook her head almost invisibly. "I can't take this."

"You can, and you will."

She looked back down at the coin pouch, fingers trembling as they ran over the soft blue velvet.

Aleksander's stomach flipped. *Please,* he thought. *Please just take it.*

After a moment, she nodded. "Thank you, my lord Champion." Her voice broke on the words. "Thank you."

As he nodded, Satie-Hak came from the back with the

woman's gown. It was a wedding dress. She took it, passed a handful of silver over to the seamstress, and left. As she passed by, she clutched the purse and gave Aleksander and earnest nod.

The bell over the door rang out, signaling her departure, and Aleksander felt he was going to melt under the tension running through his body. He could never do much to help, but something was better than nothing. At least, that's what he told himself when the guilt gnawed at him in the wee hours of the night.

"Aleksander!"

Carissa danced in, clothed in a gown that was supposedly the latest fashions from their neighbors across the sea in Ethingar. Arms out, she spun slowly, shifting her hips to show off the various intricate layers of fabric that now clothed her person.

He blinked himself back to reality, forcing that awful swirling sensation down. Anything to draw him away from the realities he didn't want to face.

For a moment he worried he'd never be ready to face them.

"Well?" Carissa asked, arms extended in what she definitely intended to be an artistic pose but looked rather silly. "What do you think? Isn't it gorgeous?"

It was, Aleksander had to admit, a beautiful dress. Just...not on her. The full layers of the skirt nearly swallowed her whole. By the look in her eyes, it was clear she was aware of it as well, but didn't want to say it. A glance between her and Satie-Hak, who was also eagerly awaiting his opinion, and he cleared his throat.

"It's a nice dress, but...Carissa, don't you think it's a little... much? Especially for one night? I mean, honestly I can't imagine any event this would be a good gown for unless it was a party in Ethingar itself."

The princess's face fell, but only slightly. "That's what I was thinking you'd say."

Satie-Hak bowed gently. "Your Esteemed Highness, if I may..."

Carissa nodded, encouraging her to continue.

The two chattered on for what felt like hours to Aleksander, but was most definitely a few minutes at most. They discussed her hair, what elements of herself she'd like to draw attention to, all the things that make a dress into an impression. "These layers here make it seem as if one hip is constantly raised and the other lowered, as if you're standing unevenly."

Aleksander couldn't take his eyes from an elegant silk gown in the corner, decorated with lace. It looked all too similar to the one Lyra had left with.

"It doesn't define your waist, and as for your eyes...Miss, your natural green eyes are completely ignored in such a colorful ensemble. And what a lovely shade of green they are too, like old-man's beard that grows in the verdant forests of your kingdom."

"Hm...you've a point there," Carissa said, fussing with her hair. The movement drew Aleksander's attention back and pushed his thought away. She shook her head. "No, you're right. This is not the right dress. I wanted something beautiful and unique but...Ethingar was not the choice I should have made."

"We'll find something else, Your Highness. In time for tomorrow."

Carissa's eyebrows bunched up. "Are you sure? That can't be enough time for you—"

"How about this one?" Aleksander gestured to the gown he was inspecting earlier—the shimmering eggplant silk, glowing with rubies and gold.

Carissa's eyes lit up. A large smile broke her painted lips. "That's *exactly* it."

THREE

WORD CRASHED AGAINST SHIELD, AGAIN AND again. Strafing to the side, Aleksander deflected an incoming blow, planted his feet, and knocked the sword from his opponent's hand. Held at a point, Aoife's shimmering blade angled neatly towards Janek's neck.

Chest heaving, the captain of the guard's lips parted into an impressed smile. "Smooth work. Take a break, Aleksander."

Aoife dropped from ready and drew a thin line in the dirt as Aleksander made his way over to the water station at the side of the pit. His shoulders burned, vibrations continuing to ring in his fingers from the impact of sword on shield. "Will you be joining us tonight, Janek?" He drained his cup in a single gulp.

"Why wouldn't I?" His friend joined him, patting his shoulder before getting his own cup. Water sloshed around when gestured to the boy before drinking. "Carissa showed me the gown you helped her pick out. I never imagined you as one with such an eye for fashion, Champion."

Aleksander laughed. "Oh yes, I'm actually thinking about abandoning my role as the Sword and running off to live a secluded life in the Pozhontecs. Did you not hear Clauden screaming up and down the halls that the future of Zekhar is doomed?"

Their laughter softened and both paused to take a drink of water. It was hot from the day and the stones around it that somehow seemed to trap and amplify whatever the midsummer sun was giving them.

Stone scraped against wood as Janek leaned against the table, his full weight pushing it back a few inches. Broad shouldered, standing about a head taller than Aleksander, Janek had always managed to have a casual air about him, even when something was weighing on his mind.

Especially when something was weighing on his mind.

A moment passed and Aleksander debated whether or not he really wanted to ask Janek what was wrong. There was a lot going on. The castle was in full decorating swing from sunrise yesterday to this very moment, as well as housing some of the dignitaries that traveled for the solstice, the questions about who should escort princess Carissa; should it be her husband, or the boy she's meant to be seen as a team with; Seer and Sword. And then there was Janek's own troubles—not that he had any great issues weighing on him, but Carissa's visions had been waking her up at night. First ones about her and Janek, then ones about her country, and finally the one he told Aleksander the day before.

But this was Janek. The two had known each other for eight years, and there had never been anything between them to suggest that asking if Janek was okay would be crossing a line. Especially when his face was one of clearly practiced ease, one that Aleksander had watched him perfect.

He heaved a deep sigh, keeping the man in the corner of his vision while he scanned the empty training ring. "So." Aleksander raised the cup once more. "What's wrong?"

Janek's dark eyes darted over for a moment. "Wrong? Nothing's wrong."

"You weren't hitting as hard as you usually do. And your eyebrows are stuck in a little mountain on your forehead. What's wrong?"

A deep sigh issued from his chest. "Nothing."

Aleksander pushed off from the table, eyeing him. "See, that 'nothing' I *know* is something. Do I need to ask again?"

"Carissa had another vision," he said slowly.

"Oh." Aleksander kicked at the dirt. "I know."

"You know? She told you?"

"It was about me, wasn't it?" Confusion bit into Aleksander's mind. What if there was another vision she didn't tell him about? Maybe one that was worse, one that didn't end with him getting swallowed in a hole in the ground—whatever that meant—but instead implied his death or the destruction of Zekhar?

"Yes," Janek said, and Aleksander breathed a sigh of relief. "I just didn't think she'd tell you. She was deeply distraught." Anxiety swirled in the lake-like depths extending behind his eyes. "You're like a brother to her, y'know."

A sick weight nestled into Aleksander's stomach. "I know."

"And she thinks it could foreshadow disaster for you. I sat up with her most of the night trying to figure it out, and when she wasn't trying to figure out what it meant, we just lay there in silence until she brought it up again."

"But the prophecy won't come about for another few years," Aleksander insisted. "I'm only fifteen. None of my past lives have been as young as me when their duties needed to be carried out. I've got another decade ahead of me, at least."

A hand dragged down Janek's face. "Perhaps. But we don't know that it won't be different this time. Truth be told, I fear I haven't done a good enough job training you."

"You've done great," Aleksander said, brandishing Aoife with a flourish. "I'll never know a scratch thanks to your tutelage."

A soft smile broke his friend's abruptly exhausted visage. "Thank you, Aleksander." Wind flowed through the arena; swirling, dancing cyclones of dust settled in their hair and clothes and stuck to the sweat not yet evaporated from their exposed skin. "Go inside and wash." Janek flicked at his nostrils, voice soft and low. "The party is in a few hours. We wouldn't want you to show up all sweaty and gross and in those linens."

The Champion laughed. "I don't even know what I'm going to

wear, Janek."

"You've seen Carissa's dress. You're escorting her, so be sure you wear a color that doesn't match it but complements it. That way it'll show you're a team but you're also individual people." He couldn't hide the smirk on his face.

"Carissa told you to say that, didn't she?"

Janek laughed, clapping a hand on his shoulder. "Of course she did. But when it comes down to it, you are the Sword of Ages. Nothing anyone says or does will diminish that."

"No," Aleksander laughed. "I guess not."

There was always someone ready to remind him that his role as the Sword of Ages was serious. He came here when he was five, gathered by King Clauden and the head priestess Saoirse. They questioned his parents, the midwives, the wise woman of his village—what her name was, he couldn't remember anymore no matter how hard he tried. The memory lingered as him standing on the lawn before the small cottage, his parents waving goodbye—only for it to be abruptly cut off by a hand thrusting a sword at him, grip first.

Regardless of the fact that his parents seemed like they were so willing to let him go, he tried to remember the times his mom rocked him after a nightmare, what her voice sounded like as she sang. Or the feeling of his dad's hands on his, showing him how to flick the fishing rod to catch something from the river. They were proud of him. Proud of themselves for bringing him into the world. Part of him wondered if either of them ever regretted giving him up.

Even as he learned his history, his identity, he couldn't help but wonder if they'd ever seen him as anything more than Alesathne, son of Tulathne. If he'd ever been just *their* son.

Knowing his identity was never a point of nervousness, despite it all. In fact, over the years, it became...mundane. Normal. A simple truth of life, no different from the fact that he loved spiced fermented cabbage, drank water, and breathed air.

Being Alesathne had its perks, but Aleksander couldn't deny how, sometimes, having those perks felt wrong and strange.

"You should escort her," Aleksander said, taking his armor off and neatly stowing it in his bag. "You are her husband."

They'd had an arranged marriage, the engagement finalized when they were merely five and seven, long before Aleksander himself had entered the picture. Though he would be in the wrong to not acknowledge that, although it was not their choice, they were a perfect pair who truly were in love. They balanced one another in a way he never thought possible.

"Yes," Janek sighed. "But let's think about this critically. I'm her husband, but what role do I play? In the eyes of the people, I formed an alliance between my family and hers, secured an income for my sisters whether they are married or not, and *one day*, I will be the queen's consort. You?" That dark, sincere gaze scanned Aleksander's face. An expression like regret passed over it. Only for a moment.

He smiled. "You, Aleksander, are the Sword of Tulathne come back to save us. That is of much greater importance to the people. Yes, my wife and I will rule them...but you'll save them." After a moment, he shrugged and laughed. It was an unnerving, hollow sound that set Aleksander's blood on edge. "Besides, the country would much rather see a young, handsome man alongside their future queen than me."

"Only because you're not the Chosen One," Aleksander joked.

There was no humor in Janek's eyes when he responded. "Exactly."

FOUR

*I*MAGES OF WARRIORS—ALEKSANDER'S PAST LIVES—danced on the ceiling above in a scattering array of candlelight reflected off the great, meticulously looped and hammered chandeliers overhead, hung with diamonds that shimmered and twinkled lightly in the breeze coming in from the great open windows. The men stayed eternally depicted in various scenarios —dancing, holding Aoife aloft, bowing in prayer surrounded by birch and rowan trees, leading an army, slaying a swarming dark evil with red eyes, battling creatures that did not have much definition in their appearance. They appeared as grey, red, and brown jumbled blobs—swarming, standing in a formation, lying dead.

A courtier had stopped him earlier in the night after she noticed him staring at the paintings. "Do you have any memories, Lord Alesathne?" she'd asked. "Anything left of those lives before?"

Aleksander didn't have the heart to tell her he didn't. Her eyes were too bright, too curious. She was older, with greying hair, and he'd remembered her from his vow ceremony five years back. She'd been one of the first to make an offering to Tulathne in thanks. So he shrugged and told her he had memories that felt like dreams and dreams that felt like memories—which wasn't a lie—and that he wasn't sure which were real and which were fake anymore. The courtier nodded, patted his arm, and left. Still his eyes danced over the paintings. Admittedly, whenever he was in this room, he could hardly tear his eyes from them.

Despite the lord before him chattering on, none of the words were directed to him, and Aleksander found his gaze drifting from the paintings themselves to the writing curling around and between each scene. Some of it was in Zekharyan, others in a much older version of the language he'd long ago accepted he'd never be able to read or understand, much to the priestess's chagrin. Though, from decades, perhaps centuries, of sun and smoke and cleaning, even the modern Zekharyan written in small letters had begun to fade into the red, orange, green, and gold ribbons acting as frames.

Noise rumbled all around Aleksander. Laughter, names being called from one end of the hall to the other, declarations of good news and of treaties that were met with a hearty "hear hear!" from anyone within earshot. Restless fingers drummed on Aoife's pommel.

Carissa burst into laughter at Aleksander's side, tossing her head back and placing a hand on his bicep, partially to steady herself and partially as a cue for Aleksander to laugh.

Which he did.

"That's absolutely hilarious!" Carissa managed to get out between body-shaking guffaws. Aleksander couldn't help but feel like she was trying just a touch too hard to be liked by the emissaries before them.

Lord Terrell, however, seemed to completely believe it. He puffed up his chest and laughed with her, sweeping aside the ornate coat he wore. It was trimmed with his signature motif—a climbing vine pattern that matched the ribbon going up the side of his pants. "Yes, Your Highness, I suppose it is."

The laughter died and Carissa let out a long sigh, wiping her lower lashes with the pad of her thumb. "Well, as delightful as it is to hear all your stories, I find myself rather parched and a touch hungry." Her gaze alighted on Aleksander. "The food, then?"

Offering his arm, he nodded. "If that is your wish, my lady." A nod to the lord. "Lord Terrell."

Lord Terrell responded with a deep bow. "As usual, my good Champion, your presence is enlightening and your company inspiring. It's an honor to speak with you."

Aleksander felt this would be a good time to smile and nod, perhaps thank Terrell for his flattery, but his cheeks were already hurting from all the smiling he had been doing. He settled for a nod and a "yes, of course" as a response.

Outstretched hands and muttered apologies on his behalf and the princess's were offered to all those he dissuaded while on their way to the table laden with decadent catered foods. Servants stood behind it ready to mix or plate whatever a person requested. All Carissa needed to do when she approached was smile and nod towards the table. The man behind it flashed a smile and got to work fixing something up and passing it over to her. She took a deep drink of the fizzing pink liquid, gesturing for something to be given to Aleksander.

He smiled softly, waiting for the woman to hand him a glass. The water shone clear as crystal in the light of the many candles and lamps. Fresh raspberries and slices of lemon bobbed in it. Without warning, Carissa popped a cookie in her mouth and spun on her heel, walking at an impossible pace through the crowd. The sudden shift startled Aleksander; he stumbled to follow her.

"Where are we going?"

"The terrace," she said sternly. "I need fresh air."

Her shoulders were tense, one arm straight at her side and the other holding the cocktail pressed close to her chest. The rich gown swayed behind her as she walked, trailing along the polished parquet, the jewels twinkling in the fading sunlight along the low, scooped back. They wove through a ballroom full of lords and ladies swaying in ornate garments, all pinks and blues and golds to celebrate the longest night of the year, with what some called the prettiest sunset. Unmarried women wore flower wreaths on their heads, streaming with white and gold ribbons, and unmarried men wore boutonnieres of fresh wildflowers. As much as this was a holiday and an evening for celebrating the turn of the seasons and the world, as well as forming and strengthening connections with other courtiers from neighboring countries, no one could deny that the two solstices also worked as the greatest matchmaking events of the year.

A rush of twilight air fluttered around Aleksander, wafting the scents of the garden into the great hall. Pink painted the tops of the hedges, making the lilies dotted around them glow even whiter than they were. Chrysanthemums, hyacinths, and lilacs weaved through them, forming waves of color and texture leading to the hedges finely clipped into multi-pointed orbs. Starbursts, supposedly, though they hardly resembled stars.

Carissa stopped, hand on her hip, drink to her lips, staring out at the coming darkness.

Behind her by only a few steps, hand now gripping his sword, was Aleksander. He waited until she heaved out a deep sigh before speaking. "What's going on, Carissa?"

She didn't answer right away. She drained the rest of her glass and dropped her hand before turning. Her cheeks were pale and her eyes darting around in a way Aleksander was too familiar with.

Sand and dust shifted beneath his boots. A glance to Carissa, a glance towards the door. "Do I need to get Janek?"

"No," she said. "Just...give me a minute." Her eyes rolled back in her head, becoming much too still. The necklace resting just below her clavicle rose and fell with her breathing, catching the sun at different angles, scattering it back into his eyes. He blinked it away, watching her closely until she opened her eyes once more. A weight seemed to descend on her shoulders, and the glass began to slip from her thin fingers.

Aleksander dove forward, gently raising her wrist and taking the cup from her.

"Thank you," she said softly. Her eyelids hung over her eyes, heavy and tired.

"What did you see?" he asked quietly.

She shook her head. "Mostly what I told you before, but..." Slumping onto a stone bench nearby, she leaned forward and rested her chin in her hands. A long pause hung between them, and Aleksander debated taking a seat himself if she would take so long to speak.

"Do you remember," Carissa finally began, voice as distant as her gaze, "when we were kids? We were in the temple, looking at the tapestries. And I pointed at one and said, 'This is the one we'll have to watch out for.'"

"The one depicting the Champion surrounded by five people, standing on a bluff?"

Carissa nodded. "I got a feeling when I looked at it," she said, sitting straight. "A sort of icy shock up my spine. I felt it in the ballroom, talking to Lord Terrell. That's why I excused us." A hand wildly gestured to where she stood a moment ago. "There... there I saw something worse. But...different. I don't know what it meant. I don't want to speak on it, not yet." The jewels on her gown twinkled as one with her jewelry as she shot to her feet. "I may be wrong. I hope I'm wrong." Her bright eyes met his, and she smiled. "I'm going back in to dance with my husband. He may not accompany me, but I was still able to convince him to show up."

Aleksander appraised her. All tension left her body, and what was left was the normal Carissa. At least, to those who didn't know her. To people aside from him and Janek.

"You've been having a lot more visions than normal recently." The softness in his voice startled him. He sounded... scared. But no, of course he wasn't scared. He was the Sword of Ages. Alesathne doesn't get scared. "Do you think there's... something they're trying to tell you?"

"Every vision's purpose is to tell me something, Aleksander. That's all they're good for." The princess shook her head, walking towards the edge of the flowerbed. Her gaze lingered on a lily. "You know as well as I that they're never straightforward though.

This time more than ever. Whatever the message is... I don't think it's good." She straightened, spinning to face him. "Or maybe I'm reading it all wrong."

The wind shifted, sending a chill across Aleksander's neck and ruffling his hair. The longer pieces dipped below his brows, brushing his eyelashes. One hand rose to sweep them away. "Carissa," he said. "If you're not feeling alright, you can excuse yourself. You're going to be queen next year. People won't balk at you taking a moment for yourself."

Carissa dismissed the thought with a wave. "No, I'm fine, Aleksander. Thank you." Her eyes drifted over his shoulder. The sun had long since met the horizon, now nearly hidden by it. The last rays of light set fire to wisping, curling strands of hair that escaped her meticulous style. Some of that brightness caught in her eyes too. "I'm going in before the bonfires are lit, but it seems *you* have someone who'd like to talk to you."

Turning to see what Carissa was looking at, Aleksander found a young woman standing by the door. Her dark curls cascaded over her shoulders and contrasted to the elegant golden gown that draped to the floor. Intricate orange embroidery shone along the hem and the neckline, and on her head sat a wreath of daisies and larkspur.

"Lady Elmere." Aleksander jerked himself into much too deep a bow. "A pleasure to see you this evening."

Chapter

FIVE

GENOISE ELMERE, DAUGHTER OF LORD EDRUN Elmere, had been friends with Aleksander ever since a winter solstice party when he was ten. It was a pitch-coated night that had followed a sunless day, and Aleksander had just taken his formal vow to Tulathne, to serve Her and honor and worship Her, in all things and thoughts and actions. To be an image of Her on earth. To bring pride to Her name and Her son's soul.

So many people wanted to congratulate him. He'd never met most of them until that moment, and he hadn't seen them since. Many hands clasped his shoulders, patted his back, raised toasts in his honor, and gave drunken offerings of wine and food to the goddess. He had escaped the noise and chaos and gone into the main hallway full of tapestries and statues. Genoise was eleven and not yet lady of her house when she decided she wanted to explore the palace on her own and stumbled upon one tapestry that was whispering and breathing.

Behind it was a small cubbyhole that was once a servants' entrance but had since been closed. Aleksander sat on the floor, a deck of cards he'd retrieved from his room on the floor before him. She joined him, and they split a plate of sweets she'd kept in her hand the whole time.

In the faded light, backlit by firelight and the moon, Genoise almost glowed as she smiled when Aleksander's eyes met hers. It was small, but bright.

Aleksander felt a blush creep into his cheeks.

Carissa gently dragged a hand down his arm as she passed. "Have a good evening." When her back was to Lady Elmere, face entirely turned to be visible by Aleksander only, she wiggled her eyebrows. The gentle smile she'd held expanded rapidly into a giddy grin.

His cheeks burned even more.

Genoise watched as Carissa slipped past her inside, offering a quick curtsey and the proper deference before taking a step forward. "Good to see you, Aleksander."

Aleksander's tongue seemed to stick to the roof of his mouth. Every word he could say flew through his mind like he was scribbling it on parchment, only to be scratched out. It was all he could do not to stutter as he cleared his throat and greeted her. "You seem well, Genoise."

"I am. Thank you." She nodded enthusiastically, the flowers on her head bouncing.

And there they stood, staring at one another, silent anxiety buzzing in the air between them.This was what their conversations were now. One would find the other at whatever solstice or court event brought them together. They'd offer a few words back and forth about the small things—how her riding lessons are going, how his training is advancing, how their families are, the weather—and eventually they'd sit in silence together, waiting. A few more moments would breeze by until someone broke the calm with a joke or a new piece of court news or something else they'd learned, and the two would begin to gossip and laugh like old friends.

At the moment, however, Genoise wordlessly swept over to the bench Carissa had perched on moments before, and Aleksander joined her, adjusting his sword so it didn't pull on his belt.

She inhaled deeply. She didn't look at him.

"I heard there was a Rodzjiek soldier joining your father's

ranks," he said quietly.

"Oh yes. She's been in training a while. She only just got promoted. D'orde is our age too, and kind of scarily strong. She's here tonight, actually." Genoise checked over her shoulder, leaning towards the door, as though she could see her among the throng. Turning back, she scanned his face and smirked. "Not as skilled as you though."

Joy burbled in his chest, and there it was, the laugh that meant they were still friends. "Please," he scoffed. "You've never seen me fight."

"Oh no, but I've heard the stories. Shattering dummies in half with a single swing?" She exhaled sharply. "Bushes better watch out."

"Hey, you try swinging a sword around for a day and let me know how easy it is to slice one of those in half."

Before they'd even taken notice, an hour had passed by, full of chatter about anything and everything their minds could dredge up to discuss. Court politics, gossip, the rumors of the Mekartlim losing their land to Rodzjiekim and contemplating what would be better—war with the fire-wielders or taking their people into the mountains where they'd face new challenges like the Orzei themselves. That said nothing of the creatures that the Rodzjiekim told stories.

Around them, the night darkened. The sun fully dipped behind the curve of the earth and the only light left was that which streamed out through windows and doors on to the terrace and its garden; it paired with the moonlight and made the flowers in Genoise's hair shimmer.

Perhaps Aleksander was wrong—perhaps the whole country was. It could not be him who was blessed by the goddess. No, in this moment, it was not him, but this girl beside him with her rosy cheeks, deep eyes, and contagious smile.

Genoise's eyes creased shut with a laugh and his heart stuttered in its pace.

Balance could be brought to the world by her mere glance, he figured, if only she chose to look upon the right people, in the right place, at the right time.

She leaned on his arm, cackling at the concept of those people with wings disappearing for good. As if no one would see them soaring through the skies or the massive eagles that favored them. A wave of energy flooded through Aleksander, warming his cheeks, his ears, his chest. He became very aware of the pressure on his sleeve as she gripped his forearm, head tossing forward in a laugh.

Despite the sudden awareness and hesitancy he felt, he leaned into her, his own laugh joining hers.

Moments like this were what helped him get through the holidays. There was always someone ready to remind him of who he was, but it was only Genoise who could help him forget.

There were times he wished he could be with her outside of the solstice celebrations. They could visit one another's estates, go for tea—whatever it was people who called on one another did. He'd fear, on occasion, that this wasn't real. That she wasn't who he thought she was, that who she played at the solstice was just one of the many masks she wore, the same kind he'd seen Carissa don and doff at will.

Yet, even with those worries, he caught the way her cheeks rose when she smiled at him, how her shoulders dropped from their proper, pushed-back position, and maybe, just maybe, Genoise was only herself when hiding on a terrace, a darkened sitting room, or behind a tapestry—when she was with him.

Without a plan on what to say next, he opened his mouth, trusting the words to come as they needed. Part of him was reaching for the word "dance." They'd never danced at one of these events before, but in this moment, he couldn't help but notice the desire to take her hand and lead her onto the floor.

As he inhaled to speak, his mind blanked. Nothing came but a small prickling along his neck. His mouth hung half open, eyes blinking rapidly. The breeze. It was...wrong.

A shiver crawled up his back. It was different than the evening air that swirled around them, chilled drastically from the full sun he had stood in hours earlier. He bolted up, Genoise's laugh cutting off abruptly as her support left and she caught herself on the stone bench. Aoife's grip was already in his hand.

Something was *very* wrong.

A sickening scent wafted through the flowers, like rotting meat and metal. His breathing sped up, and he peered out at the line where the tops of the hedges met the dark sky, just barely glowing with what was left from the sun as it finished dipping beneath the horizon.

The warmth in his chest froze into a sick, creeping, poisonous sensation, crawling along his bones and his veins. Goosebumps popped up along his neck and arms, down his back.

"Lady Elmere, go inside." The words fought to get out of his throat, thick, heavy. Desperate.

She fixed him with an aghast stare. "Pardon me, your *holiness*, but I was having a good time out here with you and I would like—"

"Genoise." Turning around to face her, he noted the way she startled when their eyes met. It sent that sick feeling straight to his gut, but he continued, voice wavering more than he wished it would. "There is something wrong. Get inside, find Carissa or Queen Lenore or the king—anyone. Tell them to send Janek and the first regiment to the west side of the garden. Now."

Genoise nodded, those large eyes growing ever wider as she took in his concern. His fear.

A horrible, tearing, guttural screech rose above the sounds of the festivities coming from inside, and both Genoise and Aleksander jumped. His eyes fixed on the hedge before them, thirty paces away, where the screech had turned to a gurgling rumble.

Behind him was the telltale clicking of a lady's shoes racing along the stone of the terrace.

He was alone now.

Aleksander's eyes shot from side to side, scanning the hedges for any sense of what was happening, what was on its way to him.

The lovely hedge the groundskeepers had spent hours

shaping and styling rustled, branches inside being snapped and twisted in audible, harsh, careless movements. A path was clearing. Aoife swished as she left the scabbard at his hip, the sharpness of her blade glinting a promised threat in the haunting mix of moonlight and firelight.

A hand reached through the branches, and he jolted back a step.

Gnarled, knobby fingers topped with cracked nails broke apart the branches, tearing a hole for the rest of the body to follow through.

Bulging, yellowed eyes swiveled around in a grotesque face comprised of sharp, gnashing teeth and skin that seemed to be patched together, holding to the cobbled bones by sheer will. A too-long tongue darted out from the teeth, flicking and writhing before being brought back into the gaping maw.

Aleksander sucked in a breath, his heart racing, stomach turning at the vile sight.

The emaciated body stumbled out onto the polished stones of the terrace, and those roving eyes found the boy with the blade much faster than he would have liked. Another screech tore from the creature's mouth.

Aleksander fought to keep Aoife steady.

For a moment, it felt as though Aleksander had been thrown from his body and was watching from above; his situation sank into his gut in one immense fearful, hopeless wave. The embroidered navy doublet, the ceremonial sword belt, the lack of armor—Aleksander's heart sank with the realization that he was very vulnerable.

And this creature was very, very hungry.

A sharp swallow clawed its way down his throat, his heart beating against the bone bars of his ribcage.

Some dark, thick mist snorted out of its mouth, followed by a hissed sort of horrid language.

The Sword blinked, and when the split second of blindness ended, his body flooded with panic.

It lunged.

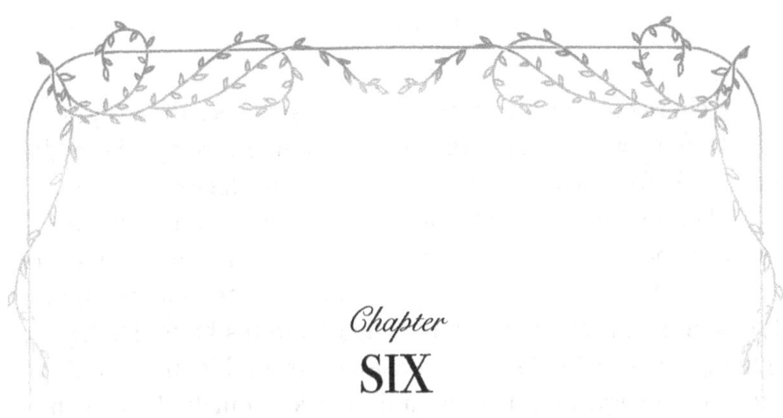

Chapter
SIX

THOSE RANCID, BROKEN, FILTHY NAILS DROVE right for his face. Aleksander dove to the side, the claws passing by at a hair's breadth. Bringing Aoife around, he dropped her heavy and fast on the creature's neck. A sickening crack and snap echoed through the terrace. The large head on the too-thin neck rolled onto the stones, foul black blood spraying over his doublet.

The tip of his sword rested on the stone, right at the midpoint of the slice. The creature's body lay to one side, the head on the other.

His stomach churned, and he fought down the food that threatened to come back up.

That same chill washed over him again. And again. Stronger too. Vibrations rocked up and down his arms, his fingers tingling and burning.

Get ahold of yourself, get ahold *of yourself.* The words thundered over and over through the pounding in his ears.

Now was not the time to let this kill get to his head.

Goddess, he killed it.

He...*killed.*

Goosebumps spread out over his body, his back, his legs, his arms. Every inch of him rejected the concept.

A chorus of those guttural screams came over the hedges.

Aoife scraped against the stones, trailing through the puddle of ichor before raising to readiness beside his face once more.

Aleksander did not like the way his arms felt, not one bit. In training, he'd get tired and shake, but that was after hours. This shaking, this prickling, it went deeper. It felt as though thousands of zaps were coming right from his bone. He tried to ignore the drastic lack of sensation from his fingers to his stomach. Everything buzzed, and he cast a quick glance behind him to see if the backup he requested was on its way.

If Genoise had done as he said.

It wasn't likely. They were friends, but that didn't change the fact that she was just a courtier. She'd never been taught to hold a sword or still her mind before battle—although the latter was proving difficult for Aleksander as the zapping became sharper, he was the one trained for this, not her. He was familiar with preparing for a fight. Even though all his previous fights were just against Janek, or a dummy, or another guard.

Even though this was different.

Another hard swallow forced its way down his throat.

The branches rustled again, and this time he saw a face through the gap rended into the hedge. It looked similar to the first one.

That one had been easy to kill.

To his right, more hedges rustled. He spun, glancing between that spot and the one coming from the first direction launched through the brush with a snarl.

A scream tore from his throat and he threw himself forward, catching one of the creature's claws on the blade and severing a finger. It howled in pain, gnashing at him with teeth. A dark mist flowed from its throat, heavy and thick.

He backed up, too worried about what that might be or what it might do to risk close proximity.

From the other bushes, another figure vaulted towards him.

He planted his foot in the first creature's chest and spun, getting caught by the other's claws. They were at least four inches long, sticking from a thick hand of rotting meat and tendons. It was much sturdier than the last. Wild bloodshot eyes were locked on him, and it parried nearly every attack he made.

The one he'd kicked aside was rising now.

Aleksander sucked in a deep breath, drawing on every element of training he could. Thrust, swipe, parry, kick, spin, thrust, swipe, parry, parry, dodge. His breath panted heavy and hot from his gaping mouth, hair sticking to his forehead.

One strong swipe and he heard that same crack as before. The one with the too-big, bulging eyes fell. The bushes rustled and his heart dropped into his gut.

"Someone come help me!" The words tore from his throat, a scream louder and more painful than he expected. With it came a violent, desperate pounding from behind his ribcage.

The taller, stronger creature lunged again, and he drove his sword perfectly into its open, growling mouth. The blood-red eyes rolled back in its head, and its arms slackened as it fell.

He pulled his sword free just in time to swing at another one crashing through the once-immaculate garden, but a sword came down before his and cleaved into the creature's head.

More and more poured in, shoving past him, past those who joined him in silence, swords raised.

Screams sounded from behind, in the ballroom still full of guests and dignitaries.

"Go!" The shout came from beside him. "Protect my wife!"

Janek swung at another coming from the brush and charged towards two more.

Aleksander turned at the order, blood thrumming through his ears. The entire ballroom, moments earlier decorated and stately, complete with a band in the corner and a busy dance floor, was chaos. Only a few managed to get through the soldiers that had begun to funnel out the door and fan around the building—but even one would have caused a panic.

At first glance, Aleksander counted seven in the din.

Adjusting his grip on his sword, Aleksander surged forward to one poised to sink its teeth into the throat of a decorated man

—the captain of the guard, Aleksander realized, from their neighbors in Revla. The creature's claws dug deep into his chest and arm.

The man did not have his sword.

This was to be a party after all.

Pain shot through Aleksander's chest as he raised Aoife. He couldn't imagine the uselessness the captain felt. To have a job such as his and not have his weapon when he is most needed.

His sword swung down, catching the thing's arm and slicing it clean off. The howl of pain it let out as it turned on him was deafening. Another swing, and Aoife was lodged in its ribcage. Blood dripped down the blade and onto the cross guard, weaving through all the ornate etchings and cracks around inlaid pearls and rubies. It scraped along bone, and flying free, the creature fell.

The captain lay on the floor, unmoving, his eyes roving the ceiling. His breath came in sharp, inconsistent pants.

"Someone help the wounded!" Aleksander yelled, kneeling by his side and pressing a hand to the claw wounds that seemed like they would never stop bleeding.

An Ölmesuz woman rushed over and gathered her shimmering robin's egg skirts and packed it into the wound without another question. Her hand rested on his chest, silver hair falling from the ornate updo it had been pinned into. Blood began to weave into the fine silk fabric. She glanced at it, then at Aleksander, and nodded.

With a nod in return, he stood to survey the scene.

So many had broken in. Not just the original seven, but many more than that were already lying dead by the hand of a soldier or a servant with a well-placed knife stroke.

Over by one of the large open floor-to-ceiling windows, Aleksander caught a flash of auburn curls swish through the air as the young woman, decorated in her officer's uniform, swung her sword down. The blade crunched into the creature's skull and lodged there. He turned away, swallowing the bile in his throat.

One man in the corner screamed as he watched the creatures tear into a woman near him. Their teeth ripped a hole open in her arm before dropping the mess of fabric and flesh as another sunk its teeth into her throat. The creature tore it free with an ease and swiftness that seemed entirely wrong. Another creature, one of the large ones, lunged towards the dais, where the venerable King Clauden fended it off with his greatsword.

The royal was much stronger than Aleksander. Standing nearly two heads taller, his chosen weapon was an ornate greatsword with an eagle-head pommel. During times of peace, it was displayed above the throne on the dais. It had been there since before Aleksander ever set foot in the castle. A scream tore from his throat, thundering through the room. One slash, and a wound opened on the creature's chest, long and deep. A puddle of black blood began to form at its feet. The blade was in the air again, and when it came down, it cleaved into the creature's head. It twitched, then went still. Clauden grabbed it by the throat and wrenched his blade free with an awful squelch. Before Aleksander even could trace his movements, he'd bounded off the dais and charged at one making its way for the boy.

He slid behind the king, readying his own sword.

"Go to the far wall!" Clauden shouted over his shoulder. His long hair had fallen in front of his eyes, the crown on his head cockeyed, but Aleksander was still able to follow his glance to a group of courtiers cornered by two of the devils.

The king's words were muffled, like he was trying to shout over a violent coastal storm, but the waves rolled onto the beach at three feet tall and were simply too loud.

Still, Aleksander nodded, focusing on the shapes his lips made beneath his thick beard, and darted across the room.

Get ahold of yourself, he repeated, the words thundering in his mind with every footfall.

He needed to focus. These unfamiliar sensations were hurting his awareness. It could cause his death if he wasn't careful.

You are Alesathne, he reminded himself. *You are not made to break.*

Aoife was in the air above one, and he swung it down. The blade caught in its shoulder, and with a deep breath he shoved it forward to the ground and levered the hilt down, severing its arm from its body.

The screech it made caused the other to turn, and taking advantage of the opening, the other courtiers fled. Some tripped over one another, and the one in the middle glanced between the easy, fleeing prey, and the predator that had just severed its friend's arm.

Beneath Aleksander, the creature writhed, nails clawing, teeth gnashing, desperately trying to get free. Angling Aoife so her pommel faced the sky, he drove her point down and into the back of its neck.

It stilled instantly.

That one action seemed to be enough for the other monster to make a decision. It roared, foamed spit dripping from its mouth, and lunged.

Aleksander ducked under it, and when he attempted to get up, he found himself shoved onto his back, the wind whooshing from his lungs and seizing his diaphragm.

The gnashing teeth were inches from his face, held at bay by the sharp edge of his blade.

It pressed further. He set his jaw.

This would hurt.

His palm pressed against the blade, pushing it further into the creature's neck so it caught just enough. It sliced deep and fast, for being as old as the world itself, supposedly, the legendary sword was surprisingly sharp.

Nausea lurched in his throat as his attacker's blood dripped into his face.

The sleeve of his doublet warmed as his own blood ran from a fresh wound on his palm, and he released the blade just long enough to grab a clump of thin, stringy hair atop the creature's head and pull it further into the blade.

A slam reverberated through his arm as his hand, still

holding the creature's head, fell against the parquet.

He pushed the body off of him and stood.

Outside was finally calm, with only a few soldiers picking off stragglers and taking care of the few that remained inside the castle.

Carissa, still on the dais, kicked one in the chest and raised a dagger.

Aleksander rushed forward, skewering it through the chest before she had to use it. Black blood spurted on to her gown and she covered her mouth, gagging at the putrid smell.

With a crackling gurgle, it fell from his sword and landed in a wet thump on the floor.

The band had silenced long ago, but without the chatter of courtiers and diplomats or the ringing of blades and screams of guests, the silence buzzed in Aleksander's ears.

It was more deafening than any cry he'd heard during the attack.

Aoife fell from his shaking fingers and clattered onto the floor.

Janek strode in, his fine suit stained and his hair hanging, covered with sweat and blood, in his face.

"What..." Aleksander's tongue was thick in his mouth, the words struggling to get to his throat. "What was that?"

Janek shook his head. "I don't know. But..." A glance to his wife as his words fell silent. Her dress swept along the steps glistening with red and black blood, smearing it along the marble and staining the hem further. Curls fell in her face. The elaborate updo she'd had her hair in was lopsided and fallen. "Carissa?"

No words left her lips as wide, glistening eyes scanned the scene. "Dear goddess," she finally gasped, taking in the myriad of creature corpses, strewn with the occasional Zekharyan and or Ölmesuz individual. Nine losses total.

Far too many.

"Hear me," she called. All eyes still in the room turned to her. The princess's voice shattered with every word she spoke. "The guests must return to their rooms or their carriages. You"—she met the eyes of an older soldier whose beautiful suit had been entirely destroyed by claws and his own blood—"call the healers. Don't move the injured. Just stay with them. The rest of you, clear the bodies of those *things*, burn them in a pyre. And call in the priestesses." Her watery eyes drifted to Aleksander. "My good Champion, go to your room and don your ritual garb. We have dead to bury this evening."

He nodded, a slow move that dipped his hair into this eyes. "Yes, Your Highness." He moved to leave, but a vice closed around his bicep and pulled him back. His fist raised and he swung, throwing his body back to get free. Lord Terrell's hand retreated, both of them flying into the air in surrender. Panic laced his sweaty, ichor-splattered face. There were no wounds to him, none that Aleksander could see, but the lord was visibly shaken. How could he not be?

"It's just me, your holiness," Terrell rasped. "It's alright. You're alright." His eyes, wide and crazed, did not leave the boy's face. A slow finger pointed to the sword laying in the middle of the floor.

"Don't leave your weapon, my lord Champion."

Entirely void of what to say, how to respond, Aleksander swallowed hard.

Something in Terrell's eyes shifted. He offered a reassuring nod.

In four long strides, Aleksander scooped up Aoife and sheathed her back at his hip. He shook, entirely unaware of his feet hitting the floor as he blindly followed the path he had traveled hundreds of times back to his room.

Chapter

SEVEN

TREMORS CONTINUED UP HIS ARMS, THROUGH his body, and to his legs as he looked down on himself, seated at the end of his bed. The plush red comforter stuck to his left hand, still weeping blood from the slash he'd delivered there. He did his best to wipe it off on his doublet. Dark ichor smeared with his own, and he leaned forward, forehead in his one good hand.

Curtains swayed in the cool night breeze coming in from his open window.

What *happened*?

Aleksander's mind ran through every detail of the event. The festival had been so normal. He'd been with Carissa, talking to everyone they could. They got a drink. Then he was with Genoise in the garden.

His stomach dropped.

Genoise. Did she get out?

But then...*they* came. What even were they? Aleksander had never seen anything like them, not in folklore classes or on tapestries. They weren't like any creatures from the Untamed or from any neighboring country. But beyond that they just felt so... wrong.

The blobs of grey, red, and brown painted on the ceiling of the hall sprang to mind. A great weight settled on his shoulders.

I guess this isn't the first time I've gone through this.

That weight wrapped around him, like arms encircling his, a hand smoothing his hair. There was no malice in it. In fact, one could almost consider it comforting, if it weren't for the images that flashed in his mind next. Images of war, of tragedy. Events that happened once, long ago. Events he knew were meant to happen again.

He wasn't the first. He wouldn't be the last. And this was certainly just the beginning.

The thing that bothered him most, however, was the gnawing feeling in his chest, and the churning in his stomach.

Something was missing.

He took a moment to run his awareness down his body, checking for wounds he hadn't noticed or any foreign sensation within himself.

No, nothing was gone. Yet there was that *ache*. That awful, awful ache. No concept he dredged up from the recesses of his mind or the past few years of his life made any connection to it.

So he focused on it, right in the center of his chest, and closed his eyes.

"You can be here," he whispered, as if the feeling could hear him. "It's okay."

His eyes opened, heavy and raw from silent tears he didn't remember crying, and drifted to the small tapestry of Tulathne on his wall. It was similar to the one in the great hall, but in this one she gestured to the sky and out to the viewer. The realm of spirit and the physical realm. Again, a depiction of balance. A reminder of who *he* was.

In the last ten years, he'd studied in the temple and in the sparring ring who he was meant to be. What he was called to do. He bowed back when people revered him with titles like "Champion" or "his holiness." He'd studied his past lives. He'd dreamed of the day that he'd finally rise to his station, grab his destiny with both hands, and wield it like the sword it was. Tulathne had been there every step of the way. She was with him in the sparring ring, in the temple. He knew it; he felt Her. Her spirit feeding into his, giving him strength.

But this time...

This time, there was nothing. Each swing delivered, each drop of blood drawn, every wet thump of a head or an arm or a body hitting the floor—he'd felt *nothing*.

Nothing but that awful ache and the coldness that still hadn't left his bones.

He'd never killed before. Never watched life actually leave something's eyes because of his sword. But today he did. Five times. Close enough for them to breathe on him. Close enough for them to get their blood on his clothes, in his face.

Oh goddess, his face.

He ran to the pot in the corner and threw himself over it.

Aleksander heaved and heaved, ridding himself first of any blood he had swallowed, then his dinner, then nothing over and over and over, as though the images now burned into his mind and the actions he'd committed could be purged from him in the same physical way.

When he was done, he raised his head and fixed on the tapestry of Tulathne hanging on the wall.

"My lady," he croaked. A warm shudder crossed over his back, and he sighed a deep, relieved sigh. There was that presence he'd missed. "I am sorry I come to you in this state." He spit into the pot. "I am sorry I could not serve as your son well enough. I didn't see it coming." Goosebumps grew in a wave down his back and arms. "Thank you for preserving me and my family. Give Carissa the guidance she needs. Give me the words to say and the strength to bury those lost this evening." The shaking through his body slowly started to fade, arms and legs turning to jelly. "Prepare me...for next time. Steel my soul and my mind."

Words faded in his mind, his patchwork prayer dissolving into the candlelight evening.

When his legs solidified once more, he pushed himself to standing and went about his business. The pitcher on his vanity ran cold over the slice he'd delivered into his palm, water streaming into the basin turning red. A strip of linen was all he had to wrap it with. He scrubbed his face, his hair, his neck. Once bandaged and clean, his shaking hands roved the garments hanging in his closet before they found the robes he'd only worn a few times.

They were soft, silken, and glistened with gold threads on a pale blue background that could easily be mistaken for white at a passing glance. The bloodied clothes now piled in the corner, he left, robe sweeping behind him, Aoife strapped over it.

He shouldn't wear her with the robes.

He knew that.

But that weight still rested on his shoulders.

THE AIR IN THE MEETING hall was thick with anxious energy. Curtains on the far wall were drawn shut so no one was entirely sure how long they'd been there, nor what time of day it was. The only light came from sconces on the wall across from where Aleksander sat at the polished mahogany table, flickering from their freshly poured filled oil jars.

Ten people had taken various places around the table. More than Aleksander had expected, and yet in a way, fewer.

King Clauden Wythane and Queen Lenore Wythane rested in side-by-side thrones at the head of the table, glistening with polished leather, oiled wood, and inlaid gold details. Next to them, across from Aleksander, sat Carissa, Janek, an older man Aleksander was sure he'd met before, and the three dukes of the kingdom that made up Clauden's inner circle of advisors: Duke Kallendrine, with his salt-and-pepper hair combed back perfectly to complement his meticulously trimmed beard; Duke Halkin, an older man with short silver wisps of hair and deep eye bags; and Duke Elmere, Genoise's father, with the same dark, mysterious countenance as his daughter.

The last at the table, seated directly beside Aleksander and to the immediate left of Queen Lenore, was the head priestess of the Great Temple, Caoimhe. The last sat slumped back in her tall chair, draping grey fabric hanging loosely from the arms resting on the sides of her chair. Her hood, embroidered carefully with images of stars and words of the vow she took to Tulathne when she was thirteen, was pulled back to rest on her shoulders and show off the circlet on her forehead of woven silver and set red jasper stones. Her dark hair gathered in the collar of her robe. Beneath her usually bright, usually cheerful eyes, two dark purple bags drooped. The shade accentuated the red in her eyes.

Aleksander was sure she hadn't stopped crying since she'd been brought into the ballroom to view the bodies.

That's one thing he'd always liked about Caoimhe. No matter what the circumstances, the nature of the life lost, Caoimhe would mourn it. Even a bug.

One of Aleksander's most vivid memories of his studies in the temple was a time he got startled by a spider on his desk and hit it with his quill. It killed it, but didn't crush it. She'd picked it up with her bare hands, cupping it close to her face with tears in her eyes, apologizing for the injustice done to the poor creature.

For a woman moved by the seemingly inconsequential passing of a spider, spending the night burying nine people she'd known, worshiped with, and befriended was certain to be much, much more devastating.

Aleksander reached a hand out to the woman next to him, gently taking hers and offering a reassuring squeeze.

Steel eyes slid to him, and for a mere moment, a smile shifted her dry lips.

She squeezed back.

They'd overseen the funeral together, burying them in simple pine boxes decorated to the nines with strings of polished stones and crystals, fresh cut pine boughs, and rowan branches.

Caoimhe had hardly been able to get through the liturgy.

"Sister Caoimhe?"

The name startled her and she dropped Aleksander's hand. Sitting straighter, she found Clauden's eyes. "Sorry, yes, Your

Majesty?"

Despite his intimidating height and stern exterior, the king's eyes softened, offering momentary sympathy to Caoimhe for what she had to do and how it wore on her. "I was asking if the seers in the temple have had any premonition of this."

Clearing her throat, she shook her head. "No. No, we had no warning. The only thing our seers have been noting is the simple, obvious fact that Their forces are gathering, and Alesathne's time once again arises."

Lenore rose slowly, ring-adorned fingers splaying across the polished hardwood to brace herself as she leaned forward. Similar to her daughter, she had bright eyes, thick lashes, and long golden hair, though hers she wore in a thick braid adorned with ribbons, an old Zekharyan style. It fell over her shoulder, pooling on the polished wood. Her voice was even when she asked, "What exactly have they seen, Caoimhe?"

"Nothing much. A darkening sky, Aleksander on a battle field, the rumble of distant thunder. He..." She trailed off. "I can recite the oracle our great Mother Saoirse received from the goddess, but it's not a nice oracle." At this, her eyes slid to Aleksander.

Not nice for him. That's what she meant.

Whatever Saoirse saw, whatever she was told... It did not offer much hope of a smooth way forward.

"I'll be fine," he reassured her with a smile. "What was it?"

Adjusting herself so her forearms and hands rested flat on the table, she lost herself in the table's reflection. In memory. "I don't remember the exact words, but it was something like... like..." She closed her eyes.

> *Blue to red and sky to sea*
> *And both shall fall to darkness.*
> *Two paths open before the Champion,*
> *One with fault, the other blameless.*
>
> *Bid him take care for his soul I shall test,*

To find his true mettle in time.
Strength and loyalty go hand in hand,
For these are the ties that bind.

From the corners of Zekhar desperate cries will fly,
Begging and bowing and scraping for notice
As over them the clouds catch fire,
And all becomes truly hopeless.

The Sword of Age may fall to age,
So inspect the foundation you claim.
Perhaps you will wish to forget your personage,
But do not forget your name.

Four spirits shall stand where once there were five.
A single choice shall see them all fall.
There is but one chance, My son, My sky.
You determine the fate of them all.

Most people at the table shifted, eyes downcast, absorbing the words. Saoirse was the oldest woman at the temple, serving as an oracle and seer since before even Caoimhe's birth. Carissa may have been the Voice of the Goddess, but *Saoirse...* Saoirse was revered as much as the gods themselves. When she spoke, everyone listened. And today, there was certainly something to be heard.

"So the Scourge *is* coming," Carissa said quietly.

PART TWO

"And of the Accursed/A creature wrought from pain/Who rose sword to heaven/And slandered the name/Of our Great Lady/Our Balancer, our Keeper/This Accursed shall too be revived/Shall too remain fit for the reaper."
- Lines 16-23
The Prophecy of Alesathne
Seeress Aithne

Chapter

EIGHT

HERE IT WAS. THE NAME NO one spoke of in all his years in the castle. The Scourge of Tulathne. The Cursebringer. The Death of a Thousand Ages.

As Aleksander was meant to bring back justice and order as the chosen Champion of Tulathne, the Scourge's sole purpose was to upend that. Out of everything Aleksander had learned about his duty as the Sword, knowledge of the Scourge was one of the topics that was discussed the least. They were whispered about in old stories, prophecies, never named by anything other than their titles. No one ever even talked about who they were. Each Sword had a record of their lives, their origin as a farmer's son, a knight, a carriage driver. But no one ever spoke of the Scourge, other than how they had been killed.

Part of him always wondered if his teachers didn't talk about them because they didn't know, or if they feared discussion of the Scourge would bring them back quicker.

During such a time of peace as he grew up in, he couldn't blame them if it was out of fear.

Around the table, every person was silent. All eyes stared off into space. Hands held chins, rubbed foreheads, wrung together...until one person deigned to break the silence.

"Well, can't say I'm surprised they're back already," the old man said. He was Ölmesuz. That much was clear by the telltale, unnatural gold-brown of his eyes that seemed almost banded as the candlelight flickered over them and the cattle-like ears that drooped through the dark hair pulled back away from his face. Those ears twitched as he thought. He raised a hand stretched with rough, dark grey-tan skin and marred with pale scars that could easily have been centuries old. He ran it over his chin, scratching at his beard. "Their followers aren't stupid enough to make such a bold move when they have no proof of the Scourge's birth. Their army isn't ready yet, but their followers are starting to build one. That's for sure."

Aleksander's heart jumped into his throat. The notion crossed his mind just for a moment, but it worried him enough that his breathing became stilted, punctuated by heavy exhales. Not only was the Scourge here, but those forces that attacked the previous night were controlled by the people following them, not the Scourge itself. Those creatures weren't many and they weren't even of the Scourge themself—and he'd still been so shaken he couldn't sleep.

So shaken, in fact, that he missed his prayers that morning. He knew it drew him further from the goddess. That simple fact tore into his soul. Still, he was wholly unable of making himself kneel before that tapestry in his room. He couldn't even stand the thought of his legs pressing into the plush velvet of the kneeler.

"Champion Wythane," a different voice interjected. It tore Aleksander from his spiraling thoughts, and his eyes focused on the Duke Elmere as he leaned forward. "My daughter speaks very highly of you."

Aleksander blinked. "And I of her, my lord duke."

"By her words, I've been led to believe you're an intelligent, levelheaded boy." His hands clasped together under his freshly shaven chin. Warm eyes held Aleksander in their gaze. "You fight well?"

Aleksander glanced between Carissa, Janek, and Clauden before answering. "Yes, sir. I fight as well as I can for my age and size."

The Ölmesuz rolled his eyes. A shock of frustration ran through Aleksander, entirely unbidden and unexpected. He willed his face into stillness. There was no use in sneering at this stranger.

Duke Elmere nodded. "Then, as...threatening as that oracle may sound—the fact that it needs to be brought into our lives in the first place is worrying, I don't ignore that—I, for one, have faith in you."

A soft murmur rippled through the others. Murmurs of agreement. Carissa met Aleksander's eyes and gave a soft smile.

"You are a strong young man, in spirit and in body. Yes, the Scourge is on its way," he continued, "or is already here, in some opinions, but I, for one, believe that the only person to truly end this all is you. What happened at the festival yesterday was awful, but it was the start of much worse. If we do not act now, we will be in even more dire straits. Caoimhe, what does the prophecy call for? What are our next steps?"

The priestess's hands twisted together as she turned over the questions in her mind. Aleksander couldn't help but stare, waiting for her to speak, waiting for her to tell them what to do. But it wasn't her who spoke. It was the *other* woman who had spent most of her life training in the temple. The woman who was set to inherit the throne within the next year...should the coming war not destroy it.

"I had a vision," she said softly. "Most of you in this room know about it"—a nod to her parents, to Janek, to the Ölmesuz man—"but it brought to mind another vision I had years ago. I saw..." She shifted in her seat, clearing her throat and lifting a hand to fiddle with her small silver pendant, etched with the same image of Tulathne contained on the tapestry in Aleksander's room. Fear twisted her delicate features. "I saw a lot of things I do not wish to speak on here. I don't want them to be real. Perhaps if I keep those details to myself, the goddess will take pity and re-weave the strands of fate She's already started to spin. But I do know that Aleksander was not alone."

Janek took her hand, rubbing his thumb along the back of it. A worried smile flitted over her lips for a mere moment.

"There were five spirits with him. Five which I believe Saoirse has seen too."

"She has. However, the future is not set in stone," Caoimhe said, nodding at Carissa's words. "Even Saoirse says so. When we have visions, we see only one possible outcome. The oracles we receive can be interpreted in many different ways." Her eyes turned to Aleksander once more. "It is clear some at this table believe my sister's words to you foretell a great challenge you will face, one where you may lose if you take the wrong step." A smile parted her lips now. "But I choose to believe the goddess says it as a means to encourage you. To tell you there is a path before you that will lead to victory, and you will not be alone as you walk it."

"Or the path has always been leading towards destruction and She's just warning everyone," the strange man said.

"That is certainly an option," Caoimhe said, shooting a glare in his direction. "I disagree, however."

"Regardless"—he shifted in his seat, hand resting lazily on the table as he leaned back on the conditioned leather—"the Scourge's allies are growing and becoming brazen. What do you suggest to mitigate that?"

"We begin by gathering our own allies," Lenore said. "Simple as that."

"Aleksander needs to find the person who summoned them," Carissa whispered. Her eyes were hidden in her head now, Janek's hand on her shoulder and another on her thigh. With a deep exhale, the color returned to her cheeks. Her eyes rolled to peer out from beneath fluttering lashes. "I keep seeing a...a building process. There are mages who make these homunculi, and their magic is therefore woven into the life of their creatures. They are not summoned. They're made, and that means we can find the person who created them and remove them from this equation." Her eyes scanned the table, all seated there listening intently. "Someone created those creatures, and we must move to find and stop them and others like them before they do too much damage and create too strong an army."

"You know what those were?" Aleksander asked. "I've never seen them before."

She nodded. "I was...*gifted*...a dream last night. After the funeral. It was of Lord Anders the Bright"—a gesture towards Aleksander—"your previous life. He was the one who called them homunculi. The magic that brings them to life is... Well, it's never done for good."

"He cannot go out alone, Carissa," Lenore said softly. Her eyes met his, and he knew she'd seen how he was after the fight. "Not only is he truly untested in real battle. Those few in the garden proved to be too much for him. Champion he may be, but that does not mean he is not still a child. An untested, castle-fed child."

"I am the Champion," he spat, the shaking returning to his fingers as fear transformed into anger, defensiveness. "A few of these *homunculi* will not be the end of me."

"Then why did that small attack on the solstice upset you so?" Lenore's lips pressed tightly together. A long sigh exhaled through her nose. "Child." She said the word slowly. "I do not say this in any way to suggest that I doubt your ability. I say this to simply state the fact that you have not killed before. Not until yesterday. And it's different when it's real, when your life is actually in danger. Not only will this journey to find the sorcerer responsible be perilous, but if you go alone, you will have no one to watch your back. Even the best soldiers in our regiment need others looking out for them."

Every muscle in his body tensed in frustration, yet he forced his hands to stretch out on his thighs, willing calm into his forearms and up thought the rest of his body. Lenore's words hit a chord with him, but they were true.

"The tapestry had five people," Carissa said, drawing the myriad attentions back to the topic of finding companions for Aleksander. "I am one of them, I know that. I knew that the moment I saw it as a child. There are four more. All warriors."

"I will give you one from my regiment," Lord Elmere said. "I know just the one."

"And I." Duke Kallendrine nodded along, leaning forward and pushing aside his notebook, now full of scribbled notes. "I have a new man at my estate. A Mekartlim. He's strong, skilled, and loyal. When I return home, I will find him and tell him of this honored role he's being offered."

All eyes turned to the third lord—Duke Halkin. He shrugged. "I'll find someone, if you need."

"Allow me to come choose them," Aleksander said. "The vision Her Highness and Mother Saoirse had identified five specific spirits. If there was any importance in that, Tulathne guide me, I'll come to your demesne and meet the finest soldiers you have. The goddess will be sure to find the right soldier to join me."

Halkin's beady eyes ran over Aleksander's face before he gave a single approving nod.

The remainder of the meeting was spent mulling over travel plans, who was going where and when, what to do to find the person who started all of this in the first place. Carissa, so sure she was the seeress in the tapestry, promised to devote her time to tracking down any traces of magic she could. Janek confided not all the flesh burned and promised that he would have some of the servants bottle up whatever was left so that his wife might be able to track their creator's signature.

Aleksander was the last to remain at the table when everyone else had stood, conversation drifting away from important issues to well wishes and goodbyes. The wood of the table was cool under his hands as he pushed his chair away. A hand landed on his shoulder.

"My young Champion." The voice was soft, and he quickly discovered it belonged to Caoimhe. She stared down at him with concern flitting through her otherwise vacant eyes. "Mother Saoirse says this will not be easy for you. Remember your footing, always."

"What do you mean by that?"

"The oracle, remember?" Her hand withdrew, and she folded them together, starting towards the door. "Inspect your foundation. Choose the right path."

For the first time, that line sunk in. It brought with it memories of the vision Carissa had days prior—of him falling into a void as the earth swallowed him, turning in on itself.

Carissa had seen the same thing Saoirse did, just from a different angle. Carisa got the visions, however warped they might have been, and Saoirse heard the narration from the goddess Herself.

He nodded. His hands were leaden in his lap. A once-full stomach, happy with the succulent dinner he'd eaten hours ago, now felt hollow and empty, churning against itself. Aleksander smiled. "Thank you, Caoimhe. I'm sure the goddess will watch my steps."

She stopped, hand on the frame, casting one last glance his way. "I certainly hope so."

FOR THE SECOND NIGHT IN a row, Aleksander could not sleep. Exhaustion weighed on his body, begging him to close his eyes. Even when he did, nothing happened. The curtains around his bed fluttered in the evening breeze. Outside, owls hooted. A pressure built in his chest, in his throat. He wanted to scream. He needed to let out this ache that clawed up his throat. There was no way this was happening. No Sword had ever been this young before. All of them met their destinies well after their twentieth year, the oldest being in his early forties. Nothing about this convinced Aleksander the Scourge was here now. Nothing about this could be true.

He blew out a deep breath, staring up at the canopy above his bed, the gathered fabrics and the portions of light and shadow they created.

Cold shocked through his feet when he planted them on the

floor. He shrugged on a tunic and retrieved Aoife from his bedside. The trunk she usually sat in, velvet interior shaped to the sword, was closed across the room. He hadn't used it the last two nights. Ever since the burials on the solstice, Aoife had leaned against the table beside his bed, right below an oil lamp he kept burning low through to morning.

Barefoot, he padded down the hall to the great hall. The parquet was clean now, scrubbed within an inch of its life so that it glistened, perfectly polished, in the moonlight. No trace of the black or red blood that had been spilt there.

Vases full of flowers and immaculately groomed trees had been left in their places. No one had moved them since the solstice, and for once, Aleksander was glad an element of that night remained. They added life to the room.

He made sure he didn't look close enough to see the blood splattered on the moon-like jasmine petals.

Aleksander walked to the dead middle of the room and lay down, staring up at the murals he'd seen hundreds of times, acknowledged as him—or, at least, a version of him. Now he was looking at them through a whole new lens. One past Sword held a head in his hand, another rode over a field of homunculi corpses on a golden horse, another battled a shadowy figure with red eyes.

This was his future.

Battles he'd have to relive, to some extent, until he would get to come home a victor. Until he would get to rest for whatever remained of his life.

Would it truly be worth it?

The thought made Aleksander sick. Of course it would be worth it. Of course he'd live, of course he'd make everything better, of course...

I could run.

Not an option.

His heart thundered in his chest. His hand fell along his side, fingering the carved details on Aoife's sheath. Was there truly any way of getting out of this?

Tulathne would not give me a task I could not bear.

"Trying to figure out what will be required of you?" Janek stood in the doorway, arms crossed.

Aleksander blew out a sharp breath. "No. I know what is required of me."

"Trying to figure a way out of it then?"

His head whipped towards his friend, scrambling to his elbows. "Why would you—"

The young man held a hand up. "Calm down. I'm not here to judge or blame you for that. I would think the same thing were I in your position."

The racing heart in Aleksander's chest slowed. It had been so overworked in the last few days, the boy had moments when he worried it would burst. But now, as his friend slowly crossed through the room to him and he lay back on the wood to stare at the paintings, he felt calm. Truly calm.

Silence radiated through the room.

"Magic is not easy for us, you know."

By "us," he meant humans.

By "us," he meant Carissa.

"I know," Aleksander said. "But if anyone can do it, it's her."

"She's exhausted, Aleksander. She's having one or more visions daily. I'm...I'm worried." A deep sigh flew from his chest, dripping with all the concern and love Aleksander expected to hear. "She'll try and try to find anything she can until she collapses. Until she destroys herself."

The following silence made a fuzzy kind of sound in Aleksander's ears.

Beneath him, the parquet finally began to warm to his flesh.

"Promise me you'll make her rest. Promise me you'll take care of her."

At this, Aleksander sat up. "What? Are you not coming with us?"

Janek shook his head. His eyes never left the ceiling.

"But...why? You're the most skilled warrior we have! Carissa needs you. I need you!"

"I'm not, actually."

Aleksander's brows crunched together over his nose. "Who's better than you?"

"That man at the table, the Ölmesuz," Janek said, eyes dancing over the murals on the ceiling. "Varek Kasajb. Trust me, he's the better choice. He has about a thousand years to him, with a service record and generations of endorsements from Zekharyan kings to match."

Aleksander lay back down. "This all started happening so fast. I feel like I don't have time to breathe." He paused. "I just want to run."

"It'll feel like that for a while. For a long while. But eventually, it'll mellow, and you'll feel like yourself again."

"Who says I don't feel like myself?"

His friend laughed. It bounced off the wood and stone in the room, rattling the ribs in Aleksander's chest. "No one has to say anything. Anyone can see it in the way you handled yourself in that meeting. You're royal and holy. You know that. I *know* you know that. You've never been one to defend it before, but you did in there."

Wind whistled past outside, and Aleksander's head snapped towards it. Janek silently reached out, placing a hand on his and patting it a few times.

A deep breath expanded his lungs.

This happened before. This has happened before, and it has never ended poorly.

An exhale echoed into the room.

The path was opening before him. He would be careful as he walked it. He would not run. He would not make the Champion into a coward. The Sword was not a coward.

Another inhale.

Aleksander was not a coward.

Another exhale.

No matter how badly he wished he was.

I N THE HALLWAYS, THE TORCHES STILL burned. It was much too early for Aleksander's liking when Ziva had knocked on his door and thrown open his curtains to the still-dark sky beyond. She'd chided him for sleeping in, though this was the earliest he'd woken in years, set out clothes for him, eyed the sheathed sword that lay beside him in bed, and left with a swish of her skirts.

Aleksander had not slept much.

Following his discussion with Janek, he'd managed to return to his bedroom and find some semblance of comfort, but any time he slipped too close to sleep, he would jolt awake with images of the homunculi swirling around him, teeth gnashing and claws scraping. Once, he swore one had crawled into his room and onto his bed, poised to strike. He couldn't move, and when he did, his room was empty and the blade of his sword swished into nothingness. Now, his legs kicked between the sheets, face pressed into his pillow and another one held against his chest. On the other side of his pillow, lay Aoife.

It was a comfort, keeping her there. Even if he knew it was a childish choice.

The only light came from the candle Ziva had left for him, resting on the window sill.

Why he was supposed to get up this early, he had no clue. But after the events of the past few days, he doubted he'd ever get much sleep again.

Donning the clothes laid out for him—a thick, good quality doublet that was the color of pines in the winter and structured pants to match—he sat before the mirror and combed back his hair. With each pull through the short, mousy brown locks, he muttered a prayer.

Tulathne protect me.
Guard my mind and all in it.
Tulathne protect me.

The eyes staring back at him in the mirror were fading as he recited the prayer over and over, begging for sleep, for rest, for comfort.

Let me find comfort in you.
Guard my head and all in it.
Tulathne protect me.

He set the bone comb down on the table with a *clack* and stood to retrieve Aoife and strap her to his hips. A glance around the room, and his eyes caught once again on the tapestry of his goddess. It struck him then. He may not see Her likeness in this way ever again. If he really was being sent away today, there was no telling what he'd encounter. No telling what would happen. A weight sank into his gut.

I do not want to go, he thought.

But he still sheathed Aoife at his side, still knelt in the oratory and offered a quick prayer for safety and guidance, still glanced at the room one last time before closing the door. The hallways themselves were all nearly silent, save for the scratching and skittering of mice that seemed to always be awake and exploring the insides of the castle walls. His boots clicked and scuffed along the stone. His shadow followed, cast by flickering torches across the walls, dancing over the decor hanging between them.

Blinking into the darkness, Aleksander's eyes adjusted and he was gifted just enough visual clarity to navigate the winding stairwell, whose railing was old and nicked and smoothed down to near perfection from decades and maybe even centuries of hands sliding along it. On and on it stretched until eventually the stairs leveled out into solid ground and Aleksander walked into the corridor that led to the main hall. More torches lit the walls, the guards stationed in even placements down the hall giving Aleksander a mere nod as he passed by. Occasionally, a nod in the direction he must go. One such guard even pulled aside the curtains for him to go into the main hall.

Four people waited along the wall, just to the side of the tapestry Aleksander had sat beneath days earlier.

"Aleksander!" Clauden's face lit up, tired as it was.

The man he was speaking to turned, and those critical golden eyes fixed on him. Today, he was clad differently, no longer in court attire, pressed and embroidered and egregiously expensive, but instead in simple clothes and dark leather armor. A battle-worn sword sat at his hip. A smirk appeared, and he spoke first.

"Glad the god-child had humbled himself enough to join us so early."

Aleksander's gut twisted at the comment."I have no problem waking up early, I'll have you know," he spat.

The man chuckled, pushing himself from the wall he'd been leaning on and dropping one hand to rest on his hilt. He was nearly a head taller than the king. The calm slope to his shoulders did nothing to dissuade the primal panic growing in Aleksander's chest.

"Varek." The king's voice was low, warning.

Varek.

"Of course, my king." The Ölmesuz crossed a hand over his heart and bowed low. "Good morning, my liege, I do hope you've gotten your beauty sleep. We've a full schedule for you today."

"You must be the warrior Janek told me about," Aleksander said, catching his friend's eye as he said his name. Janek gave a strong nod, not leaving his place of support against the wall. The sureness in his gaze made Aleksander stretch out his hand to the man. "I've heard little of you, but what I have heard is surely impressive. A pleasure."

Varek's dark eyebrows shot up, a smile curving his lips. He straightened his back and Aleksander fought to keep his hand steady. The man stood two heads above Aleksander. All Ölmesuz were tall—that much was fact. But standing face to face with a man who towered even over the king? That was nearly enough to make the Champion himself stumble back a step or two.

Still, the large, scarred hand clapped around his and gave it a strong shake. "A pleasure, I'm sure," he purred back. The leather armor he wore creaked as he moved.

Carissa's voice broke through the flickering of flame and the short, shallow breaths Aleksander had been trying desperately to deepen and slow, even as Varek's hand clasped tighter and his feral grin grew wider. "Now that Aleksander is here, we may leave the castle and perform the rites before we go."

"Go?" Varek dropped Aleksander's hand as the boy spun away from him. "Go where?"

"On our journey to collect the others." A tired, somewhat worried smile slipped her lips. "And hopefully find the sorcerer who attacked the solstice. Now's a good a time as any. The trail will still be fresh...if there is one."

Aleksander blinked. "Wait, we're going now?" The thought had crossed his mind, true. But actually hearing it, so early in the morning, so earnestly from his friend's mouth... It suddenly made Aleksander aware of all that he was going to miss in Castle Brevindun and all he still wanted to do before his life's purpose came to fruition. "I...I thought we'd have more time... I thought *I'd* have more time. I've hardly prepared. I haven't trained enough. I—" He swallowed hard. "I wanted to dance at the solstice."

It sounded so stupid to him now. But that didn't stop him from wanting it. From realizing he missed his opportunity to do so.

"Wow," Varek said. "We'd better call the Scourge and let them know they're too early. I'm sure the person set on the destruction of Zekhar will take your desire to *dance* seriously."

A large, soft hand rested on his shoulder. "I know, boy." Clauden turned Aleksander ever so slightly so he could look the young man in the eyes. The smile he wore was one of hope. Of courage. Of certainty that this was the right choice. "We're asking a lot of you. But you're ready. I know you are."

"I'll be the judge of that," Varek snorted and tapped Aleksander's shoulder with the back of his knuckles. Slow steps backward distanced the two as he spoke. "I'm not the only one folks have been talking about. Chopping straw-filled dummies in half? My, my, I'd better watch my step around you, your holiness."

A spin on his heel towards the double doors he shoved open, one hand on each, with almost no effort. They slammed behind him

Distaste brewed in Aleksander's stomach.

"I don't like him," he muttered.

"He's a tough character," King Clauden said softly. "I know it well. But he's an indispensable fighter. Smart too. And loyal to the crown. Varek served our family back when the First King was on the throne."

"Aside from that"—Janek shrugged—"he's admittedly a bitter old man. His Majesty had to bribe him to join this quest and none of us are sure he won't abandon it, but he's one of the best we have. A little bit of risk for a lot of reward, as they say."

"Let's worry about this later, shall we?" Carissa's hands wrung together so tightly they came apart red and raw. "We've the ceremony, and a long journey to Duke Kallendrine's land."

The group began walking, and Aleksander tripped over his own feet to keep pace with them. "We're going to Kallendrine's land first? Why not Elmere or Halkin? Their lands are farther than Kallendrine's. Does it not make more sense to go to the farthest and work our way home?"

"The farther from home we get without allies, the more lost we are in an emergency," Carissa said. Her steps were sure, her back straight. The woman he saw two days ago, jumping down the grand palace steps with a hairstyle that took hours and a truly regal gown, now felt foreign as she now walked beside him. Her curls were braided back and wound around her head tightly, exposing ears that held single diamond studs. Her gown was not velvet or muslin, nor was there any trace of lace on it. The dress she wore now was tight to her torso and arms, made of sturdy, dark red corduroy. Not much was on it in way of detailing, save for a thin border of embroidered gold leaves around her neck and wrists.

Most of all, however, the look in her eyes was not one Aleksander had ever seen.

She looked...angry. Scared. Determined.

Beside her, Janek mirrored the expression.

"That makes sense," Aleksander said, shifting his gaze to the doors before them.

The large oak slabs swung open and Caoimhe lifted her head, smiling at them.

"Caoimhe!" Aleksander shouted, bounding towards her with a sudden burst of energy. Taking her hands in his, he pressed them against his forehead in a bow. "Good morning, my lady."

"Good morning, Aleksander." Her voice was steady, if not softer than usual. "You prepare to take your first of many journeys. How do you feel?"

"I feel...nervous," he admitted quickly. "This happened all so fast."

"We were all told it would come on suddenly," she said, nodding. "Good, though, that it happens now." Her eyes drifted to the sky, where the sliver of moon still shone and the constellations were yet discernible, despite the growing dawn. "The moon rests in the heart of the Balances."

Aleksander was just able to make out the shape of a hand holding a scale. The constellation that had represented Tulathne for ages—long before she was known by the Zekharyan name.

"She blesses this departure. Not only are you beginning this journey with the moon's new life, but in her star-home, as well. She has not only chosen this day. And with that, you will not fail." With a smile, Caoimhe turned back to Aleksander, removing a scroll from her robes. "I also have this, for you. A reminder." She held his gaze, nodding slowly. "Watch your steps, my lord Champion. Heed Her guidance."

"Of course." Aleksander took the scroll and stuffed it into his belt. He didn't need to look at it to know what it was; Caoimhe's words were enough. As much as she believed the oracle was meant for good, Aleksander's stomach churned at the thought of it. There was a strong chance he'd never open the scroll.

He half debated throwing it into the first river they passed.

"Shall we get started?" Carissa said, stepping off the stone staircase to the grass beside where a large bronze dish had been set alight with tinder and fragrant herbs. It perfumed the air wish a sharp, heady scent, smoke swirling and disappearing into the dark sky.

Carissa's gentle hand on Aleksander's arm guided him to the brazier alongside Caoimhe. The priestess chanted a few words in old Zekharyan, tossing in a hard resin that snapped and popped in the heat of the coals and the flames.

Carissa and Aleksander took turns wafting the smoke into their hair, watching for images in dancing blaze rising from the embers.

Just before the ritual should have ended, Caoimhe turned to Aleksander and asked him to raise his hands.

His brow furrowed. "Why?"

"I have something to ask of Tulathne in regards to you, young lord. Please." She gestured, and he lifted his hands, palms up. All three closed their eyes. "Good goddess, take this, the soul of Your son, the soul of our Champion, into Your care, as You do all your children on this earth. Grant sanctity to Your true son, the one of Your soul. He has not studied as I have, but he is of You more than Your earthly servants ever will be."

Aleksander's eyes shot open.

This can't be what I think it is.

Eyes still closed, Caoimhe continued. "Bestow the power of Your spirit upon him, that he may act in Your name as son, servant, and Champion. This I ask of you, this I say." Her eyes opened and found his immediately.

Somehow, she did not appear shocked to find him looking at her, nor did she exhibit shock at his own panicked expression

"Repeat after me."

Aleksander did not move or speak. His eyes stayed trained on hers, heart racing.

"I, Aleksander Wythane, soul of Alesathne, son of Tulathne, Champion of the Goddess and Sword of Ages, take upon myself the divine order of the Lady of Balance."

His lips did not move.

The flames sputtered and Caoimhe shot the brazier a look as if she were addressing the goddess Herself. Her chilled eyes slid back to Aleksander. "Say it."

And take on the role of a priest? Swear myself not only as her Champion, but as her attendant for life as well?

"No," he said softly.

The whole world seemed to drop silent.

Carissa cleared her throat. "Aleksander, you must say it. We cannot have you go on this quest unordained."

"Why?" His head whipped to face his friend. "We all know what life a priest lives. It's the one I've been living all this time, minus the combat training." His heart beat fiercely in his chest. "I can't—I *will* not live the rest of my life in the temple, leading services and weddings and studying the holy texts, bowing and scraping to a goddess I already serve. She *knows* I serve her." He nodded to the brazier. "*You* know I serve Her." He nodded to the pair of women. "Or did that vow I took when I was ten mean nothing?"

At this, the two paused. A look was shared between them, a look Aleksander was not familiar with, nor was he given time to discern the meaning.

The vow he'd taken five years ago had been complex. It had required oil being painted over his brow, along his collarbone, and on each of his hands. He'd had to memorize and recite a long prayer and an even longer oath, promising himself fully to the service of Tulathne as Her Champion, as Her hand in the world, that each step he took would be willed by Her. He'd eaten a roasted lamb in her honor, washing it down with rich wine that made him dizzy despite the fact that he was much too young. He'd danced the night away with courtiers and chatted with lords until he'd had enough. Was that day and all that led up to it a lie?

The fire in the brazier flared.

"Was it all a lie?" His voice was quiet.

"No," Caoimhe said sharply. "Of course not."

"Then I don't need to do this."

"Yes, you do," Caoimhe snapped.

Aleksander shook his head. "You told me the Swords get to live normal lives after they fulfill their role. I'm going to live a normal life, Caoimhe."

The priestess's eyes flickered. "Aleksander, do you truly believe you'll get a normal life?"

The flames in the bronze dish flickered impatiently.

A strong snap echoed, and Carissa and Caoimhe jumped.

Aleksander just stood and stared into the flames, a recurring chant of *I can't, I can't, I can't* repeating in his head. Caoimhe's gaze grew desperate, glancing between the snapping flames which seemed to grow with every moment of Aleksander's refusal, and the boy himself.

"Far be it from me to interject," a low voice, one Aleksander had gotten very familiar with very quickly, echoed from the cobblestones at the bottom of the hill where a carriage was waiting. Varek stared up at them. "But this is stupid. I saw his prior vow ceremony. It was more encompassing and earnest than this," his hand waved wildly at the image before him. "He's covered, and you know it. He may not be a priest, but he's just as holy as you my lady, if not more so. Your goddess sees that, I'm sure. She's let him last this long."

Caoimhe shifted, not daring to look at the man shouting up from the street.

Aleksander took a few steps closer to the brazier, staring into it so intently he could feel the heat on the back of his eyes. Sucking in a deep breath, he prayed he wouldn't stutter. "I,

Aleksander Wythane, Sword of Ages, Champion and Chosen of Tulathne, establish here and now that my vow stands. I serve my lady with all I am. Each step is guided by you, each word placed in my mouth by you. Grant me your strength and your protection as you always have."

Aleksander could have sworn he saw a woman's face smiling back at him as the brazier roared into a pyre. The snapping of the flames was nearly deafening. Caoimhe and Carissa stuttered back a few steps, away from the flames that licked out in their directions. After a final burst, it shrunk down and fizzled out into ash.

A low whistle broke the silence. "I guess your goddess agrees."

TEN

"GODS, WHAT EVEN WAS THAT?" VAREK tapped Aleksander's calf with his boot as he slid around the stumbling fighter. "I've seen children fight better, Aleksander."

Aleksander regained his footing in the dirt, squaring off once more. Sweat dripped down his neck. His hair was already plastered to his forehead. The decision to leave in the early morning had been smart. It wasn't hot when they left. The first time they'd stopped, Varek had run him through a number of drills to inspect his fighting style and offer uncensored critique of Aleksander's form, speed, even the way he drew his sword. The pair had only just begun to break a sweat then. Now, hours later, the small clearing they'd pulled into off the road was reeking of men and metal.

Varek gave Aleksander an appraising look and shrugged. "Well, younger children."

The leather on Aoife's grip would surely press new lines into Aleksander's hand from how tightly he held it.

"Are you done antagonizing him?" Carissa asked from her seat beside the carriage, not bothering to look up from the sticks and parchment she was analyzing.

They had stopped an hour prior to feed and water the horses beneath the open sky. Ever prepared to do her work anywhere and everywhere, the princess had quickly pulled out her small trunk of magical items—and mundane tools to make notes on what she'd found.

A strong sigh huffed from the man, his shoulders slumping and feet slipping from their fighting stance. "It's part of the fun, Carissa. Let an old man enjoy his life sometimes."

Aleksander bolted for Varek, swinging his sword with such force he stumbled back as he parried one blow after another. When the final hit sent them stumbling apart from one another, he barked out a laugh and gestured to the boy with his sword.

"See? That's what I wanted." Varek rested the flat of his blade over his shoulder and nodded. "We're done for now. Go sit."

Aleksander's nose scrunched up. It felt like all they had been doing was rest. He still had a good few fights left in him. He hefted his sword in his hand, weighing the options of challenging the Ölmesuz again or putting Aoife down for a moment.

Varek began to walk to the carriage to retrieve the water skin, chattering over his shoulder. "You manage to hold off your anger well enough, but it's not always anger that they play on. Mostly it's fear. And keep watching your tells. They've gotten more obvious as the day's gone on."

The mouth of the water skin pressed into Aleksander's hand. "What tells?" he grumbled.

"The same tells I told you about this morning. The little"—he mimed holding a sword and flicked his wrist a few times—"the twitching you do with the sword before you swing? That's gotten so obvious I could pick it out in the darkness of a cave." He pointed to a log. "Sit."

He wanted to argue, but Aleksander did as he said and slumped down beside Carissa, resigning to grinding his teeth together as he inspected her progress. Four sticks balanced in her hand, inscribed with runes and letters he was wholly unfamiliar with. The parchment beside her was filled with scribbles—some in Zekharyan, others in that strange carved language.

Varek took a few long drinks from his own water skin, some of it sloshing down his beard.

Aleksander frowned. How could a man act in such a way before a princess?

Said man let out a long, satisfied sigh before propping himself on his knees before the lady and her makeshift table. A long finger pointed at the papers. "So, what's all this?"

"This, Varek, is how I will find out who created those homunculi." Flipping the paper around, she pointed at a few different sections of it. "I've already run tests on the flesh last night, before we left. The rune sticks are common among mages. We use them to let the magic communicate with us. It organizes it where it needs to go, and we discern what it's telling us. I was thinking about finding a way to have the rune sticks tell me where the homunculi originated from, but I'm not sure if that's possible. I don't know magic well enough to do that." With one hand, she held the paper to the top of the trunk and opened it, selecting a small vial of clearly rotting flesh. "Using this... somehow...I should be able to make the runes tell me where to go or discern a sorcerer's signature." She stared at the vial. "I'm... not quite sure how to use it yet. But I'll figure it out. I have many books with me that I can use for reference."

"Hm." Varek nodded, eyes trained on the papers. "Why not just use an identification spell? Or try scrying? Isn't that something you mages do?"

Tired, wide eyes blinked at the papers as he pointed. Carissa pursed her lips as he continued.

"Use the flesh you have leftover as a net of some sort, to catch the energy you need. The bowl and the runes can still be useful for tracing the source—"

"You're right," Carissa said, holding her hand up. "I could. But that would only bring up what kind of magic wove it together. We know already it's not the kind mages work with. Anything more than that won't help us. I wouldn't be able to get anything from those spells that we could actually use. The bowl and the runes could work to point the general direction, maybe, but without a way to connect it to the magic in the flesh, I'm still at a loss." She shook the vial. "If there even is magic left in this." She leaned over the trunk and began scribbling things out. "But if I found a way to alter the components...maybe extract the essence of the flesh? This could work."

She spun it to face Varek again and he shook his head, correcting a few elements of her notes before reminding her that this kind of magic wasn't common and often was only wielded by those who spent decades studying the arcane arts. Breaking apart a spell, extracting the core of it—it could hurt her if she wasn't ready. Not to mention the fact that they were dealing with creatures made in ways even the most skilled of mages were untrained in. It would take a lot of time. And a lot of trial and error.

Aleksander leaned back, staring up at the sky.

Birds flitted overhead, distracting him from the conversation happening beside him. It was beyond him, anyways. Despite his years of training alongside Carissa, there was a reason he had never truly become a religious scholar like she did. It just didn't click in his brain, all those combinations and components and history and intention you have to weave together to be able to work with magic as a Zekharyan. There had to be equal give and take, which was the cause for so many specific components for any one spell, or else it wouldn't work, or it could backfire. Or, in severe cases, the mage could die. Ölmesuz understood magic like they understood the stars. If it wasn't clear by the centuries of scholars whose names and discoveries echoed through history, it was made clear by the ready assistance offered by Varek, who looked at Carissa's notes as though he were reading a child's nursery rhyme.

Aleksander's eyes fluttered shut, and he stretched his tired legs out before him.

The silence was comforting. The birds had stopped chirping, the horses stopped their crunching on their feed and their quiet, nickering chatter to one another. Even Varek and Carissa had stopped—

As soon as his eyes had closed, Aleksander's eyes were open again, staring into the dead sky.

He hadn't fallen asleep. That much was certain. The clouds were almost in the same position as they were before.

But everything had stopped.

He lifted his head slowly, finding Carissa watching the tree line, her breath so shallow it looked as though she'd turned entirely to a statue. Varek, on the other hand, was slowly rising from his crouch, sword sliding almost silently along the grass.

"What is it?" Aleksander whispered, sitting up as slowly as he could, scanning the area for Aoife—who lay an uncomfortable foot away from his fingertips, albeit against the same log he'd been using as a pillow moments ago.

Varek lifted a hand to silence him, his ears twitching as he zeroed in on the sound. The broad sword raised to ready beside him, Varek dropped into a fighting stance, feet wide, center low.

That's when Aleksander heard it. The ever-so-imperceptible whisper of leather against leaves.

"Mekartlim! Get down!" Varek swung his sword up, and a clash echoed over their heads. Steel hit steel and soon the flurry of feathers that had appeared above them like a blanket was navigating the small clearing, wings moving in dizzying, distracting patterns as the man attached to them evaded and attacked Varek.

"Aleksander!" Carissa shrieked, jumping to her feet and throwing a panicked point at the edge of the trees.

Snatching his sword, Aleksander spun just in time to deflect a blow from another man. His hair was cut short, much shorter than Aleksander's. He wasn't Mekartlim. If the lack of wings wasn't enough of a cue, there was no individual among those winged people on earth who would deface their hair with that short of a style.

This second man wheeled back, circling and preparing for yet another attack, when Aleksander struck first, landing a blow across his midsection. The armor there prevented him from drawing blood, but the strained, loud exhale told Aleksander he had succeeded in knocking the wind from him. His sure steps turned into stumbles as he blinked rapidly, gasping in an attempt to regain what had been stolen from him.

Mere inches away, a wing snapped open. Aleksander stumbled a few steps to the side, thrown by the wind. A sword was on his throat in seconds.

If he's here, with his sword at my throat—

The man's pale yellow irises locked on Aleksander's, pressing closer.

Where is Varek?

Aoife raised a few inches, and the soldier's blade pressed in, still biting cold and harsh against his throat. The man's lip raised in a snarl. "Don't even think about it." He rustled his wings. "You forget, I've got weapons on my back that could snap your lady's neck in a second."

Carissa blinked suddenly, eyes darting from a scene Aleksander did not have the vantage point for and the scene he was a part of...and then to the strong bone structure of the wing before her, poised to knock her head to a deadly angle in the span of a single breath.

His grip on Aoife loosened, then tightened. This was his duty, to protect her. He could not fail in that. If he did, then what good would he truly be to anyone else? To Zekhar?

To Tulathne?

Then, the man threatening him fell still. Tension froze in his arms, his wings. Panting breaths turned stilted and shallow.

Carissa's eyes were wide.

It was Varek's voice that broke the silence, as low and dark as the depths of hell itself.

"If you value that short life of yours, Lieutenant Polat, you'll drop the sword from Champion Wythane's neck and greet us like the guests we are, instead of intruding highwaymen."

Over the Mekartlim man's shoulder, a flash of silver caught Aleksander's eye. A telltale squeak of metal on leather made its way through the thundering of Aleksander's pulse in his ears. "Or if you'd prefer, I can drop you here and now."

The man's head drifted down enough to give Aleksander a glimpse of the venom held in Varek's stare. It seemed as though the old man was poised to burst into flame.

"Well?" he snarled, pressing his blade further towards the man's neck. "I'm waiting."

Chapter

ELEVEN

ALEKSANDER HAD BEEN PACING BACK AND forth for what felt like hours. "This isn't right," he muttered, hands tucked tight under his arms. "How can he not know who we are!"

Varek leaned on the bars of their shared cell, head hung low. He didn't give Aleksander a response.

After Varek's outright threat to the lieutenant, the other soldier had gotten up and done a similar move with his sword against Varek's neck. With no choice but to listen, they crowded into the carriage along with their driver who now sat in the corner of the cell. The human soldier drove them the rest of the way to Kallendrine's estate with the Mekartlim flying overhead. Then, they were dumped in the prison—Aleksander, Varek, and their driver Bunc to one cell; across the way sat Carissa in a cell of her own.

Throwing himself against the bars, Aleksander threw a hand out towards her. "You're the crown princess, for Tulathne's sake! How do they not know who you are?"

She sat straight on the bed in her cell, inclining her head in his direction. "They've never met me. Handing them my papers means nothing at this time. I could very well be a fake."

"Who would want to impersonate you?"

"Who would want to destroy the solstice festival?" Varek's

voice was low. "I get it. You've lived in the palace, probably never had to sit on a bed like that in your life." Aleksander's eyes flicked towards the thing sticking out of the wall that could barely be considered a bed. Varek continued, "This is your first time in a cell. As someone who's been in one before: shut up. Being loud and angry will only make it worse, kid. Her Highness has shown her papers, Bunc has shown his, your complaining isn't going to change their minds."

"We just need to wait until Lord Kallendrine shows up. He will be able to clear it all." Carissa's voice wavered, but her appearance did not. Her nose scrunched almost imperceptibly, and Aleksander knew it was her trying not to yell.

"And what if Kallendrine doesn't show up?" he pressed.

"Then we figure it out," she hissed.

Aleksander slumped against the wall. The fabric of his doublet caught and scratched against the rough stone as he slid down to sit. Everything about the dungeon was cold. The walls, the cots, and the air flowing in through the vents at the top of the room, so thin he could only get his first three fingers through. Mere hours ago he had been waiting for them to get back in the carriage and the shade so he could stop sweating. Now here he was, desperate for the hint of warmth felt only by wiggling a few fingers through the hole in the wall.

"Get your hand out of there," Varek snapped. "You have no clue what's on the other side."

"Sunlight," Aleksander said. "I know there's sunlight and warmth. I'm freezing in here, aren't you?"

"I've been told I'm a veritable furnace, so no." The man turned away, leaning on the wall beside Aleksander.

"And who said that? Surely there's no one willing to share a bed with you."

Aleksander wasn't sure why he said it. Perhaps it was the cold. The misfortune of their situation. The whole rotten day, frankly. From waking early, to the botched ritual on the lawn, to the ambush in the forest during training, nothing in the day had done anything to give him any semblance of comfort.

The words weren't intentional. But he couldn't take them back once he'd said them. Even if he wanted to.

His new trainer's eyes narrowed to slits, jaw clenched. "Watch what you say, *boy*. I could help you get better at fighting, but I could just as easily end this all here and now. Let the Scourge win." Something flared behind his eyes—it nearly shoved Aleksander back from him. "If you catch my meaning."

The air between them grew thick, heavy. This man could be older than the country, and Aleksander wouldn't be any the wiser. Who knew how many wars he had fought in, how much blood was on his hands?

Aleksander's throat closed and his back bumped the cold stone wall.

"No one is threatening or berating anyone," Carissa said, blowing out a long breath and standing from her position on the bed. "Varek, leave him alone."

His eyes did not shift to her. "Lady Wythane, you'd do well to remember the bargain your father struck with me. I believe it may give you the peace needed to allow me to do whatever I please."

"Whatever you please, as long as it doesn't involve threatening the only hope for my people—and your people, you'll remember. Possibly the hope of all on the continent, truly. The world even." Her slender fingers wrapped around the iron bars, turning white as she spoke. "You would also do well to remember the woman you are speaking to will be your queen before the next summer solstice."

"If your father does as he says. But who knows, wartime may shift Clauden's priorities." Varek huffed a bitter sigh, tension straining in his neck, up to his jaw. "The Kutsalyot know your people take advantage of the situations they find themselves in. He may not see you fit to rule during such a crisis. May delay your ascension. Trust me, Your Highness"—he spat the word like a curse—"it wouldn't be the first time a king of your line has gone back on his word."

The sunlight that broke through the crack Aleksander had

wiggled his fingers through moments before wavered, and Varek retreated to the single bed in the cell. It creaked under his weight as he sat, back to the stone wall, eyes fluttering shut.

In this particular moment, Aleksander did not know what to do. There was movement in other parts of the dungeon, as well as outside. Carissa seemed resigned to be resting on the bars, one pressing a line from her hair down her nose. And Varek— there was no way he would try to sit next to Varek after that incident.

So, he did the next best thing, and slumped along the wall, landing in a standing puddle of rainwater.

"Oh *goddess*," Aleksander said, shaking off his hands and bolting to his feet. The seat of his pants was soaked with a viscous water likened to that one would find directly beneath a layer of pond scum. The velvet was now slimy, and the draft flowing through the dungeon cooled him immediately. He resigned to sit a few feet to the left the puddle and lean his head against the wall.

A creak echoed through the hallway.

Varek was on his feet before Aleksander had time to process the man's movement, leaning against the bars and scanning down the hallway for any trace of who made the sound.

"Varek," a silken voice drawled. "I see you're still getting yourself into trouble, aren't you?"

Varek raised his head, a slight smile on his lips. "Is that who I think it is?"

"Of course it is, you monster. Do you truly think I'd leave this world without seeing you again?"

A woman stepped into view between the two cells. Her hair was the color of molten gold, and it flowed like it too, all the way down to the floor where it was tied up ever so slightly with an intricate silver band. Her eyes scanned the pair of them before flitting across the hall to acknowledge Carissa. The gown she wore seemed to be woven from moonlight itself, gathering and draping in a way that reminded Aleksander of all the tapestries and depictions of the other goddesses of old. It pooled on the floor, shimmering as she bowed.

"Your Highness, I apologize for the inconvenience." Raising her head, the woman nodded as she took a step towards the bars. "We offer our deepest condolences and ask that you join me, the Lord and Lady Kallendrine, and Sir Polat in the dining room for an early supper. You all must be so tired from the journey."

Carissa's cell door swung open and she stepped out slowly, eyeing the woman—and then eyeing Varek. "How do you two know each other?"

The woman herself glanced at Varek, and Aleksander noted the expression she gave him. It was not one he had expected—a look insinuating a lost love or perhaps a still-burning flame that never got fanned. No, instead he caught the way her eyebrows rose unevenly, the way her lips pursed, and her eyes appraised him steadily. This was the face of someone who often opposed him, but not in a truly awful way—perhaps a family member of sorts. It nearly elicited the same response from Aleksander that a specific look from Queen Lenore, that kind of motherly, disappointed expression he'd caught only a few times.

Almost.

She smiled, bejeweled ears twinkling as she cocked her head to the side. "We have had many run-ins throughout our centuries on this earth. I daresay without my influence, he would not have agreed to help you."

"Oh please, Fazhia," Varek spat, not unkindly. "You cannot say that your influence truly changed me that much."

"I disagree. The Varek I met all those years ago wouldn't be caught *dead* even near a worshipper of Tulathne. Much less would he choose to be alive and *helping* Her son."

The cell door swung open, and Aleksander stood. He made sure to do slowly. For some unknown reason, he had convinced himself that rising from his slumped, dejected position in the cell slowly would offer more credence in the eyes of the court here.

Bunc, who had been leaning in the corner the whole time nervously tapping his foot, straightened and looked at the woman expectantly.

Fazhia stepped aside, gesturing for him to exit.

Bunc took advantage of the moment and sprinted up the stairs.

Varek grunted, shrugged, and nodded to her. "I suppose I do have you to thank for softening my heart to the Zekharyan *hira*."

By the way Fazhia's nostrils flared and her lips pursed ever so slightly, Aleksander knew that whatever "*hira*" was in their language, it was not something that should be attributed to a goddess.

"But you forget—I was serving the Zekharyan crown long before you were. And maybe, just maybe, I have something serving me out of this whole arrangement." Standing tall, Varek cracked the spot between his shoulder blades and stood aside, gesturing for Aleksander to leave before him. "After you, your *holiness*."

He took a step, and the wet fabric sticking to his backside and legs was all he could think about. Not only was it incredibly uncomfortable, but here he was in the demesne of a lord he respected—a lord who respected *him*—and he appeared as though he were a child who had wet himself the moment anything remotely worrying happened.

Nonetheless, he offered a bow to Fazhia, who slowly, eagerly returned it before rising to her full height, which happened to be two heads above Aleksander.

Her sapphire eyes glowed. "It is truly an honor to meet you, Son of my Lady."

His brow furrowed. "You follow Tulathne?"

She nodded, gesturing for the three to follow her. "In all my years, I've been fortunate enough that my travels allowed me to experience many religions and all the changes they've made to themselves throughout the centuries. The Goddess of Balance was always one I held dear to my heart. I've been a loyal servant of hers for over a hundred and eighty years now."

"And a pariah of our people for nearly as long," Varek said, a particular, chiming lightness in his voice.

Despite the comment, she smiled wider. "Varek is the

furthest thing from a religious man you'll find, yet he still jabs at me for choosing to leave the Mother and our Honored Dead."

The soldier raised his hands in defense. "I may think the Kutsalyot are just an excuse to make sure we remember people, but I would be an idiot if I didn't admit that in times of desperation, a few of my prayers have been answered. That's all I'm saying."

"I've made peace with the fact that most Ölmesuz will not appreciate my decision. But there are some that"—she glanced at Varek—"while they don't understand it, still recognize me as one of their own."

"There were times when we stole and hunted for the other at the risk of our very lives," Varek said, gently patting a hand on her arm. "You're one of mine whether I want you or not."

Fazhia laughed, and the rest of the walk up the staircase was in near silence, save for the passing comment or question asked by either Carissa to Fazhia or Fazhia to Carissa. Eventually, evening light streamed in through tall windows that opened to a portico full of flowers, vines, lanterns—and a long, ornate table.

A man stood abruptly as they entered. This man Aleksander knew.

The Duke Kallendrine nodded, a bright smile on his face doing little to hide the embarrassment peeking through. "My dear Princess Wythane! And young Lord Wythane, as well. Welcome, welcome!" His dark eyes caught Varek, and he paused. "Ah yes. I remember being told it was not Sir Unwin accompanying you, but a different fellow. I believe we met at the council meeting, Sir—"

"Varek," he answered, not taking the extended hand. "Just Varek."

Duke Kallendrine dropped his hand quickly, clearing his throat and meeting Carissa's eyes. "I am truly sorry, my lady, for the misunderstanding in the woods. But you must admit, Lieutenant Polat is a skilled, swift fighter."

Carissa smiled ever so slightly. "I would be remiss if I did not admit I was truly frightened for my life, my lord."

A thunderous rustle of feathers echoed through the portico, and the aforementioned man dropped to a place beside the table, tucking his wings in and bowing low. His dark hair slipped over his shoulder, braided meticulously to keep it out of his face in the way that most Mekartlim did. Eyes as pale as freshly tilled earth rose to meet theirs, dark features glowing with the setting sun.

If it were not for the way he'd attacked them hours earlier, Aleksander would have approached him and introduced himself.

As it stood, he crossed his arms and waited for the man to speak.

Chapter

TWELVE

"MY GOOD LADY, I MUST APOLOGIZE for the violence done to your attendants, and the violence threatened to you." He stood tall, hand to his heart. "It was not my intention to cause undue harm. With the situation that happened at the solstice gathering, and with my lord informing me of your wish that I attend you, I've taken great lengths to secure the estate and the surrounding lands the Kallendrine family oversees."

He was eloquent. Earnest. A part of Aleksander's anger towards the man cooled, and he placed his hand on his heart, bowing slightly. "Sir Polat," he started, unaware of where his tongue was taking him. "Thank you for the apology. We appreciate how seriously you're taking this. Though"—he straightened—"neither of us are Her Highness's attendants. You must have heard your lord address us. This is Varek. I am Sir Aleksander Wythane, Champion of Tulathne." Any fear abated in his chest. He raised his chin higher and lifted his hand to rest it upon Aoife...where it instead fell to his side.

Right, they'd taken their weapons.

He brushed his hand on his pants, resting it awkwardly on his hip. "When you address me and my companions, use our proper titles."

The man blinked, hand dropping to his side. "My deepest

apologies." A smile. "But in the future, if you want people to see you and respect you as the man of noble standing that you are, I ask that you offer deference and understanding to someone who is new to court and new to your ways. It will get you a lot farther with the people who could actually help you as you take on your duties."

Aleksander took in the man and his words, and with it, guilt. Polat was right. Of course he was. How could Aleksander have talked to him in such a way? After the years of classes where he learned about the importance of decorum and respect when meeting anyone—not just members of the court—how could he have gone so against this newcomer so quickly?

He cleared his throat. "No, I should apologize," he said, "It was rude of me to talk to you like that. It's... Today has been awful, honestly. And the dungeon didn't help."

The smile gracing Polat's dark features widened, crinkling in the corners of his eyes. "I appreciate your apology, my lord Champion."

Lord Kallendrine exhaled sharply, gesturing for the three to take their seats at the table. Fazhia took her seat, joined by another woman who introduced herself as Lady Kallendrine. She pulled out her chair with slow movements. Her tan skin shimmered with a dusting of gold on her cheeks and nose. Beside her sat her husband, and at his right hand sat Piran, Kallendrine's advisor. Bunc joined them at the table too, not long after Sir Polat had managed to maneuver his wings around the high back of his chair, and they were finally able to begin eating.

Before them rested a lavish meal of roasted turkey, sweet potatoes, rosemary bread with decadent butter, and a variety of summer vegetables. Aleksander carefully raised his fork, mouth watering at the meal usually reserved for fall where it was often paired with a thick, rich squash soup, and took a bite as carefully and mannerly as he could, though his stomach had been rumbling all day and this surely was exactly what he needed.

Carissa ate a faster then he did, shoving a fork into her mouth and chewing rapidly before swallowing to answer whatever question was asked of her.

Fazhia's movements were measured, as were the other members of her court, and Aleksander was surprised to see Varek not only eating slowly but carefully, wiping gravy and butter from his beard with a napkin, resting said napkin on his lap, and generally behaving unlike the man who scarfed down a plate of eggs earlier in the day and, when pressed about the yolk remnants in his mustache, said that he was "saving them for later."

The conversation over the food began lazily, with discussion of their travels, what has happened so far in them, how the king and queen fare, how the royal court has managed after the solstice event—then, into more pressing matters. What is being done? What is the plan? Yes, Duke Kallendrine has begun to gather his forces. Yes, they will be ready to march on command. Yes, he's in communication with the other nobles of Zekhar. No, there are no suspects yet. No, the general public does not know.

All of this talk turned what was a delicious, satisfying meal to roiling nausea. Aleksander pushed away his plate, half eaten, and sipped lightly on the water given to him.

It didn't take long for everyone to stop their eating as well, and begin a deep discussion of The Plan. As Carissa explained, everything suddenly became very clear: she didn't exactly have one.

"I've been working on a spell that will help. Problem is, I'm not very well versed in magic. I've been studying, but I'm still just a novice. But while I work on it, we will be making our way around to the other dukes that were at the council. Keep our eyes open for anything that may be amiss, that may lead us to the sorcerer responsible." Her hands flailed wildly as she searched for the words. "You know, if there's any strange group activity, any uptick in crime, any...any bodies going missing from the graveyards. That kind of thing. Then, once we have our evidence and have visited Dukes Halkin and Elmere..." She shrugged. "We all go and kill the culprit."

Those present mulled over her words, nodding and tapping

out thought diagrams on the table with fingers in the air with a fork.

Eventually, Lady Kallendrine spoke up. "So, your plan is—and do forgive me if I come off as rude, Your Highness—to go around, gather a team, and hope your skills as a novice mage are enough to find the individual who killed nine courtiers?"

Silence reigned at the table.

Lady Kallendrine shook her head, running a hand down the thick brown waves streaked with gold that fell over her shoulder. "I don't doubt your abilities, Princess, but these people are evil. Awful. They don't want to be found, and it won't be easy to do so. What are your plans after, if this works? And if it doesn't, what do you plan to do then?"

"Carissa is a skilled seer, and yes, she's only a novice, but she knows what she's doing," Aleksander found himself saying. "If we fail, we fail. We go back to the palace and work with the mages and priestesses there to figure it out. And if we succeed, then we go back to the castle and plan our next steps." He shifted uncomfortably. "I think all of us are aware that any action taken now could spark a war."

"If you find a Crafter, they may be able to give or create tools that would help you," Fazhia said, shifting to the only other Ölmesuz at the table. She gave no comment on Aleksander's words, nor did she appear to have heard them at all. "Have you any word on Sameen?"

Varek shook his head slowly. "Not since the fire that nearly took down Jazeira."

"Jazeira?" The duke said. "That town hasn't seen a fire since..."

"It's been around eighty years, yes." Fazhia nodded at Varek. "I was worried he got lost to the fire. If before that was the last time you or I have had contact with him..." She trailed off, tears welling in her eyes. "I'll prepare a space for him."

Varek's eyes steeled. "We lose contact with one another all the time. Look at us, Fazhia, this is the first time I've seen you in, what, seventy-five years? We have no proof he's gone." He looked back at Aleksander, then to Carissa. His voice was so steady, so sure, so demanding. Yet, there it was in his eyes. The unmistakable glimmer of fear. It was gone before Aleksander was sure he even saw it. "There are more Crafters than just Sameen, and Your Highness would do well to find one. I can help you in the mean time, but I never studied. All I know I learned from..." Darkness settled over his face. The intensity fled from his gaze, replaced with blank grief. "I learned from someone much smarter than me."

Fazhia looked down at her hands.

"No matter," he said. "My knowledge of magic is rudimentary. As much as it comes easily to all Ölmesuz, I do not know if I can help you well enough."

Carissa nodded. "Very well, we will add finding a Crafter to our itinerary."

The rest of the conversation hashed out where they will stop, how and where they will assemble their forces, and open lines of communication—it was decided that a raven and perhaps a revival of kulning, the art of singing lilting, peaking tones from mountain to mountain, would be the safest bet. Coded, of course. Most regiments of the Zekharyan military had at least one woman whose voice was high enough to properly deliver the messages.

Dessert was brought out and was, surprisingly, devoured. Despite the heavy air at the table and the discussion leaning towards topics only ever brought up during a war, there was a lightness about it. The sweet lemon tarts were appreciated, and by the end of the meal, everyone was wiping powdered sugar from their lips and laughing as they exchanged stories.

Even Varek had a half smile that broke open for the occasional chuckle at things Aleksander said. He even surprised Aleksander with a clap on the shoulder and an approving nod.

The laughter faded. Over the table, a mood of quiet contentment settled. For a moment, they weren't on a journey or fearing the oncoming war. Everyone there was just enjoying a dinner with friends—as much of a friend as anyone at this table was to one another. Some sat quietly, sipping their wine, and others had turned to one another to engage in their own small discussions. The lieutenant—who had insisted very early on that everyone simply call him by his first name, Demir—turned to Varek as Aleksander finished his dessert.

"I am truly sorry, sir, for the way I treated you when we first encountered one another."

Aleksander smiled at his formality. Even after hours of food and discussion, the soldier kept his speech proper.

Varek waved it away. "Don't even think about it. You were impressive out there. I never considered Mekartlim could use their wings in battle, but they make an incredibly effective weapon. You stunned me well, whether it was intentional or not. My ears are still ringing."

A smile broke Demir's face wide open, so much so he seemed to glow from the inside out. "Thank you! You see, I never knew what to do with them when I was in training here—normally Mekartlim train to fight in the sky, and even then, most of us use bows for distance—then, I opened them one day and sent my opponent flying. I was more careful after that, of course, but I figured in the moment of a true fight it would come in handy, and believe me, it has."

"If I were you, I'd worry someone would try to slice them," Aleksander said, his eyes roving the gold-brown feathers shifting around the back of the chair.

Demir shrugged. "I won't pretend I don't hold that same fear. But when it comes down to it, you're bound to walk away from every fight a little wounded. Wings heal just like any other part of the body, so I don't think there is anything to fear. If it breaks my wings, it could have broken my arm. But it'll be better with rest and care."

There was an unexpected warmth and brevity about the man. Years of training with Janek taught him that most experienced fighters were gruff, or at least reserved. Varek went even further and solidified to Aleksander that the more wars you fight in, the longer you live, and the more scrapes you endure, the harsher you get. Yet, here was Demir before him, smiling and laughing and asking Carissa about how she and Janek met.

Aleksander immediately decided that he liked Demir, and was very pleased that it seemed Demir liked him as well.

Lord Kallendrine stretched his arms above his head and bowed out his chest. "Well," he said, exhaling a long, deep breath, "I daresay it is time for us to all rest. How soon must you get on the road?"

Carissa opened her mouth to answer.

"Surely not so soon you cannot stay the evening? I have plenty of guest rooms. Please, let us all spend the evening resting and recovering. We shall gather tomorrow morning to finalize the conscription of Demir to your cause, and then you shall be on your way."

"That sounds great," Aleksander blurted, not giving any of his travel companions time to say anything to the contrary.

The lord and lady smiled broadly, and it wasn't long before Aleksander was brought into a private room with a hot bath placed before fluttering curtains. The crisp air of evening brushed over his closed eyes as he soaked in the tub. Moment by moment, the stress lacing his muscles faded away, only to be replaced by the pain brought on by overworking himself. Despite training nearly every day for the last few years of his life, Varek had put him through the wringer in the last few hours.

After drying off and bandaging the wound on his hand which had finally begun to form a thick scab, he moved from the warm, perfumed bath to a warm, perfumed bed. His freshly moisturized face pressed against a soft, downy pillow. Trapped within it were all the wonderful scents of evening air. All the worries of the day danced in his mind, but as he inhaled that fresh scent of mist and dew that only seemed to coalesce in the blue hours of the morning or the dark of night, it all melted away.

"Tulathne," he muttered softly, snuggling into his blankets, "my Lady of Balances, Peacekeeper, I ask that you guard my dreams tonight. Give me no omens. Give me no nightmares. Let me sleep."

With all the pain his body held, he still managed to find comfort in the soft mattress. A weight draped over him, feeling as though a blanket were laid over him by the goddess Herself, endowed with peace and comfort.

For the first night since the solstice, Aleksander slept without Aoife beside his bed.

UNTIL WE MEET

Chapter

THIRTEEN

*I*T WAS NOT A SERVANT ENTERING the room, not Janek throwing him from his bed, not a plate of breakfast set down on the table beside him, smelling of rich spices and succulent cuts of meat. No, it was the birdsong. The music echoed in from his open window on a cold breeze. They were loud. So very loud, and singing an immensely complicated song, all as one.

Aleksander's eyelashes fluttered over his hazy gaze, clearing just enough so he could take in the beauty of the sun hitting the trees right outside his window. It glowed that brilliant green-yellow that is usually reserved for late spring or early fall—the bookends of summer, not the immediate middle of it.

He made a move to get up, but found himself glued to the bed. His legs were leaden, as were his hands. They seemed to sink into the mattress, and no matter how hard he tried to lift them or even wiggle a finger or toe, he couldn't move.

That cold, panicked chill ran up his spine. Cold swirled through his stomach. His heart raced.

Why can't I move?

And that was when he saw it. The image in the corner of his room. A woman with long dark hair, a veil over her face. Nearly a copy of every image he'd seen of Tulathne yet...different.

Somehow so different, and so very wrong.

"My Lady?" he asked quietly.

She stared at him through the veil. That chill creeped over him again. The veiled head tilted to the side. "You mistake me," she said. A thousand voices spoke at once, whispering, screaming, muddling together into a wave that swept over his prone body. "Though I understand why."

A sensation tugged his vision to the other side of the room and his eyes adjusted to the image he saw tucked into the early morning shadows in the corner. There stood another woman, with glowing red eyes and a form obscured mostly by dark mist. No, not obscured—she *was* the mist. Her head cocked at the same angle as the goddess's had earlier, she took a step towards him.

The birdsong was so, *so* loud.

A dream. This was a dream. An awful, terrible dream made from all he'd ever seen about his destiny, his identity. That was not Tulathne in the corner or...maybe it was, at least a version of Her. One he feared, one that didn't reach out to help him. Like the solstice, when he'd fought without feeling that rush of...what? Rush of what? Was it Her presence? He always said it was but... this cold, awful chill. This is what he felt that night. Not Her.

And the other figure.

His eyes turned to it—just his eyes, his head was weighted as solidly as his body.

That was the Scourge. He was sure of it. Every painting of them had been a version of that swirling form of darkness before him. So cruel, so awful. No source of light, of warmth.

Would those birds just be quiet so he could *think*?

He had to wake up... He had to.

The Scourge opened their mouth to say something, but what came out was garbled whispering and screaming. It turned his throat raw, and he felt as though the blood vessels in his face were about to burst.

Tulathne reached for him as well, those pale hands belonging to ghosts and specters, reaching from the beyond, reaching to fit a claw into his ankle and drag him there as well.

This was not right.

Nothing about this was right.

"Stop," he whispered. His voice was hoarse. As if he'd been screaming for hours. "Stop, get back."

But both specters kept approaching, and when Tulathne's mouth opened behind her veil, the thousand voices that had once spoken in unison earlier began to cry out their own warnings. Begging him to flee, to run, to fight, to stay, to end the Scourge while he could—to end everything.

Tears tracked down his cheeks.

The birds grew louder.

"Give him space!" Varek's voice boomed through the room, somehow breaking whatever shackles held him to the sheets.

Aleksander flew up from his bed, chest heaving as though he'd run from the highest peak in the mountains all the way to the capital and back. That chill situated on the base of his skull, down into his spine. Goddess, how it made him sick.

Sucking down breath after breath, he scanned the room. It was light out. It was much lighter than he had seen in his dream.

Or was it a dream? If it was later in the day, then...

No, it was a dream.

It had to be a dream.

Aleksander dragged his hands down his face, fighting back the sobs and screams clawing into his chest. A thin hand rested on his knee. Carissa's wedding band sparkled through the cracks in his fingers.

"Aleksander?" Her voice was quiet. Distant.

"I'm fine," he said. His hands dropped to his blanket. "I'm fine."

"What happened?" Fazhia spoke now. "You were... We thought you were dying."

The sickening, leeching chill slithered down his spine. He twitched, wriggling in an attempt to get it out for good...and then it was. It was gone. But something remained. Rather, it left an emptiness behind. The lack of it was so tangible, so strange.

Aleksander paused. What was it, that its absence could be felt so strongly? And what was it to *him*, that its absence somehow felt worse than its presence?

Still, Aleksander shook his head and pushed himself to the left side of the bed where he could stand. "I'm fine. Just a bad dream. When are we leaving?"

It was only now that he took in the faces around him. Carissa still sat on the other side of his bed, leaning halfway across the crumpled duvet as though she'd half a mind to crawl after him. Fazhia stood by the door, with a very concerned Duke Kallendrine and Lieutenant Polat—Demir, he reminded himself. His gaze fell on them, and they shrunk back. Only Demir stayed steady in his footing, matching Aleksander's stare. There was something, he realized, that had truly startled them. Whether it was something about his countenance now or when he was locked in that horrible dream, he didn't know. But it wasn't something they needed to figure out right now.

Before him stood Varek, his face a stoic mask, lips pressed thin beneath his mustache.

"I'm fine, Varek," he said.

An eyebrow twitched upward for a mere moment before the man took a deep breath and nodded. "Alright. If you say so." A glance around the room, and he waved his hand. "All of you out. We'll meet in the portico. I'll be sure our Champion is ready."

When no one moved, a churning growl fitted itself into Aleksander's throat. "Go!" he barked. "He said to go!"

They jumped, uneasy steps hemming between staying while he was clearly distressed or respecting the order barked at them, but eventually, slowly, all made their ways out into the hall.

A hand rested on Aleksander's shoulder. It was larger, heavier, and warmer than Carissa's had been on his leg, and as Carissa shuffled past and disappeared in to the hall with the others, he realized it was Varek whose fingers were ever so slightly pressing a rhythm not unlike a heartbeat into his clavicle.

Aleksander shoved him away, taking a few steps towards the door as it closed. "I don't need you here either." He raised a shaking hand and pushed it shut the rest of the way.

"Just get dressed" was all he said.

The boy watched as Varek laid out some fresh clothes for the journey ahead atop the blankets. Beside them, laid down with great care, shining in the daylight, was Aoife. The distance between them was covered in two strides. Her metal was cold beneath his hands, but warmed quickly. A heavy, necessary sigh issued from his chest. The tension remaining in his shoulders dripped down his arms, and Aoife suddenly felt much heavier.

"I also found this," Varek said, handing a rolled parchment to him. "Looks important."

Taking it in his empty hand, Aleksander did his best to unroll it. There, written in black ink and flourished letters, was Saoirse's prophecy. Just as he'd assumed.

Aleksander swallowed hard and rolled it back up, tucking the reminder into a loop on Aoife's scabbard. "Thanks."

Varek raised an eyebrow. "You're not going to read it?"

"Why should I? I already know what it says." His grip tightened around the scabbard. The parchment crunched beneath his fingers. "I don't need to be reminded that I'm responsible for everyone. I already know that."

"Hm" was all he got as a reply. He didn't watch as Aleksander raised the sword to his face, pressing his thumb against the paper and forming a deep fold along one of the sides, nearly flattening it. "You don't need to keep it," Varek finally said. "I'm not going to tell anyone if you burn it or throw it out the window."

Now it was Aleksander's turn to raise his brows. "How do I know you're not lying? Not trying to get me to disrespect Carissa and the other seeresses?"

"I don't have any care for them," Varek spat, his head snapping from the blankets he'd busied himself straightening. "And I certainly don't have any care for their words, whether they claim they're from a goddess or not." His shoulders rose with a deep breath. "If you want, I'll burn it."

"No." The response came quickly. Panic shot to Aleksander's

fingertips. "No, if anyone is going to burn it, it's me."

His heart raced. He didn't want to burn it. The oracle scared him. He'd be a fool to say otherwise. But the thought of letting it go...

Aleksander shook his head. "And I'm *not* going to burn it."

Fear and anger buzzed in the air between them. Finally, Varek huffed, waving his hand and turning back to the blankets and pillows he'd already put back in place. "Put your clothes on." Varek didn't look at Aleksander as he spoke. "And don't worry about telling anyone what your dream was about. Dreams are for the dreamer, not their friends."

"I don't want to talk about it." Aleksander slipped off the tunic he'd worn to sleep and shrugged into the fresh shirt and a new doublet—blue and brown and gold lay nicely against the cream sleeves gathered to puff at his wrists.

"I *just* said you don't have to." At this, Varek stood straight and took in Aleksander as he fitted the sword around his hips. Between glancing up at the Ölmesuz and down at his belt, Aleksander caught flickers of some deep emotion through Varek's eyes. Backlit by the sun, it seemed he would have been a better fit for Aleksander's role. It gave him a godly halo around his head, and his eyes held drops of sunlight in them as was. Yet around them were lines brought on from centuries of fighting and slow aging. And exhaustion. The bags beneath Varek's eyes were unmistakable. Aleksander had seen them on Janek or Carissa or his teachers often as he grew.

"Did you sleep?" Aleksander asked. "Last night?"

"The beds were so comfortable, how could I not?"

But Varek blinked, his jaw flexing and puffing the sides of his beard momentarily.

There was a part of Aleksander that wanted to sit on the bed, ask Varek to do the same, and tell him all about what had happened in his dream. He wasn't kind like Clauden or even understanding like Lenore. But Aleksander found himself fighting not to ask why Varek didn't sleep, to tell him why his own night had been so fitful and restless.

Varek's lips were pressed together sternly, his brows low over his eyes.

So he simply patted Aoife, offered Varek a bitter smile, and said, "I'm ready now."

◊ ✳ ◊

THE SUN WAS ALREADY HIGH in the sky when they made their way back to the portico. Exactly how late in the day, Aleksander didn't know. But the way the sun had started to slink too close to the mountains in the distance told him enough. They'd be on the road in the dark tonight, that much was certain. Demir stood beside their readied carriage. A priestess of Tulathne—one Aleksander had never met before—stood with him. She smiled, bowed, and gestured for him to join them.

"What is this?" He stepped forward tentatively.

"We are blessing Sir Polat in the way of Tulathne and binding him to your service." Her voice was a low melody. Her words rumbled through Aleksander's bones.

"Oh." His cheeks warmed. "We don't need a ceremony for that. Demir already agreed." His eyes flitted to the soldier with his wings shifting behind him. "You did *want* to join us, right?"

"My lord asked me to partake in an important quest for the fate of all our peoples. Serving the son of his goddess directly." A smile broke his face. "How could I not want to join?"

Aleksander blinked. Was it *that* easy for him? This was what Aleksander was destined for and had been preparing for all his life. He was proud of who he was, but if the night after the Solstice attack had shown him anything it was the simple fact that, Alesathne or not, he had moments where he wished he hadn't been found those ten years ago and brought to Castle Brevindun.

Concern rippled through his mind in a soft wave. How could the man before him say yes to such a job so easily? So free of concern or fear?

Brushing those thoughts aside, Aleksander nodded and stepped forward, plastering a smile to his face. This was the man he'd shared a meal with last night. A man who, despite only knowing him for a few hours, had shown Aleksander kindness and guidance, as well as his own awareness of his shortcomings. Any fear he felt wasn't logical. It was the remains of his dream, casting a warped lens over the world.

"Alright," Aleksander said. "Let's begin then."

Chapter

FOURTEEN

AFTER AN OFFERING AND A SHORT prayer the priestess turned to them, dark cheeks raising and creasing her eyes in a bright, genuine smile. Her eyes squinted so much, it appeared as though they were entirely made of sparkling night sky. A sturdy hand extended, shimmering with jewelry. "May I have your sword, my lord Champion?"

Aleksander obliged, unsheathing Aoife and handing it to her.

"And yours, Sir Polat?"

Demir did the same. His sword was similar in size and style to Varek's, with dark metal and even darker wrappings on the grip. Up the fuller, however, were intricate, ornate carvings of feathers and leaves, as well as something written in a language Aleksander couldn't read.

"Wow," he breathed softly.

"Beautiful, isn't she?" Demir's smile grew. "My sister inscribed a saying on it for me in an older version of our language. It says, '*Her Zaman Rüzgarla.*'"

"What does that mean?"

"Always with the wind. It's a blessing given to Mekartlim before their first flights without a parent or instructor supervising them." Demir's pale eyes glistened as he took in the inscription. "She had this done because serving Lord Kallendrine

—and now you—is the first time I'm doing something without my community."

Even the priestess's voice was soft when she said, "That's lovely, Sir Polat."

Demir nodded his thanks.

Balancing the two swords in one hand, she draped a woven band around them and asked the two to hold to the ends. With their grip, the loop tightened and the swords clinked softly as they were tugged closer together. "Repeat after me. I, Sir Aleksander Wythane—"

"I, Sir Aleksander Wythane."

"Sword of Ages and Champion of Tulathne—"

"Sword of Ages and Champion of Tulathne."

And so it went until he had recited the entire vow.

"I, Aleksander Wythane, the Sword of Ages and Champion of Tulathne, swear today to guide you in the light of the goddess, on the fields of battle and off. You are my charge and I am yours. My body is your shield, my arm your sword. This I swear, and promise you my sword."

When he was done, it was Demir's turn.

He straightened, adjusted his wings so they fell open ever so slightly, steadying his form and emphasizing the intensity in his eyes as he gazed down at the Champion, and recited, "I, Demir Chilik Polat, Blessed of the Orzei and loyal servant to Lord Kallendrine, swear today to follow you in the light of the goddess, on the fields of battle and off. You are my charge and I am yours. My body is your shield, my arm your weapon. This I swear, and promise you my sword."

They pulled on the ends of the woven band, and the swords spun until both of their hilts were again facing the owners. Aleksander took Aoife, Demir took the hilt of his sword, and the wrap fell to the ground. A smile alighted the priestess's lips. She placed a hand on each of their shoulders and offered a prayer to Tulathne for their safety and guidance.

With that and nothing more, they were off.

Bunc was in the driver seat with a pack of sweets given by

Fazhia as an apology for all the stress caused to him. He guided the carriage through the town and back onto the main road, now heading north towards the land belonging to Duke Cavan Halkin. Above them flew Demir, circling back every now and then to report on what he saw.

Aleksander had never considered how helpful it would be to have someone with a view from the air until they had someone periodically swooping down to give updates on the state of the weather, oncoming carriages, towns they were set to pass, and so forth.

Through the afternoon, Aleksander watched the man flying as best he could out of the small window in the cart. As the sun had just begun to set, Bunc pulled the caravan off the path to a small grove with an old well. He and Demir took to watering and feeding the horses, Carissa lit a lantern and situated herself away from the fire so she could focus on her spell work. Even Varek chose rest instead of slicing at air and running the same fighting form over and over again. He sat himself down at the fire, his sword detached from his belt, and opened up a small book he'd kept in his pocket, squinting down at the words in the fading light.

Aleksander nestled down a few feet away, Aoife still at his hip.

Varek cast a sideways glance to the boy. "You're really attached to that sword, aren't ya?"

"It's been used by all the Champions before me," he said. "Of course I am."

The man chuckled softly. "Sure." It was a harsh sound, that laugh. The kind of laugh that insinuated he thought Aleksander's attachment to such an object was silly. That, perhaps, the history behind it was silly.

He opened his mouth to counter Varek, to ask what, exactly, was so funny about what he'd said, but the man's eyes just scanned through the book in his hands. He didn't offer Aleksander so much as a second glance.

So, Aleksander closed his mouth and leaned back onto the

roll he'd nestled in a patch of creeping Charlie and crab grass. Overhead, clouds painted bright pinks and golds floated by. A great shadow passed through, and a gasp came from another member of the group. Aleksander's head shot up just in time to watch Demir rocket into the sky, his wings beating furiously to propel him faster and faster towards whatever he'd seen.

"What the hell got into him?" Varek muttered, squinting at the man that had now become a dot in the twilight.

No one answered as a giant shape exploded from the clouds, pumping its wings and diving down to meet Demir.

"By the gods," Bunc whispered, his hands frozen on the rope as he pulled up a bucket. "I never thought I'd see one."

Aleksander felt as if his head were floating. A cry echoed out from the creature as it met Demir, the two spiraling around each other. "Is that...?"

"An Orzei," Varek finished. The most earnest smile Aleksander had ever seen appeared on his lips. "Yes it is."

The giant eagle spun through the clouds, looping around Demir, flying over and under and around the small speck of a man. Demir's entire wingspan was equal to just one of the creatures wings. Yet, as massive and formidable as the eagle was, Aleksander found himself smiling too.

The pair flitted around one another before Demir hovered for a moment, the Orzei taking off into the higher clouds, continuing its path west to the mountains. Slowly, the man came back down. His dark cheeks flushed, eyes glowing, and hair rustled, Aleksander finally understood the stories of the Mekartlim he'd heard as a child—how they were wild, fierce, and at one point, worshipped as spirits of the wind.

Aleksander wasn't sure people were right to stop calling them that.

Demir flashed a large smile. "Her name is Defne. She's just passing through before roosting in the Pozhontec peaks."

Varek grinned wildly. "I never get tired of seeing them."

Smoothing his hair, Demir laughed, gazing skyward once more. "I never get tired of flying with them."

◊ ✳ ◊

CRICKETS BEGAN TO LILT THEIR songs into the night air, stars dancing overhead. Night herself swirled through the trees and into the camp like a thick ink. The trees somehow seemed to take in all the light they could, standing as black sentinels with spindly arms, and the void of the forest beyond them darkened even still.

"You want to talk about that dream?" Varek's voice was so low, Aleksander didn't know if he'd actually heard him at first or if he'd imagined it.

But his eyes scanned to the man beside him and found his book hanging limply from his hand, an inquisitive expression aimed right at him.

Aleksander shifted. "No."

"Was it a vision?"

"No, I don't get visions, I'm not... No, look, I told you, I don't want to talk about it." He rolled over, staring into the brush that danced with shadows of varying greys.

"And that's okay. I'm just asking if there's anything useful in it. Anything that might help her." Varek nodded towards Carissa. The princess's hand was buried in her hair, tearing it from the braid that had fallen down her back and sending frizzy puffs of curl dancing in the wind between her lantern and her notes.

She hadn't had a vision at all yesterday. None that Aleksander had seen or been told about, at least. Today, she'd only had one which had resulted in a shake of her head and the simple statement of "same as last time." Never mind that she thumbed the pendant of Tulathne around her neck with furrowed brows and pursed lips. Never mind she hadn't eaten all day.

Never mind she stared, now, at her pages, hands smudged with ink, actually *trying* to have a vision. She said she needed more clarity, and that's how she got it.

It only made Aleksander's gut twinge and his heart race whenever he heard the scratching of her ink pen's nib against the parchment. Anxiety spiked in his chest each time she blew out a quiet curse.

"Have you noticed anything I haven't?" he asked softly.

Varek shook his head. "No. But if she keeps up with this, we're all screwed."

"What do you mean by that?"

"I mean"—he leaned towards Aleksander, lowering his voice even more—"if she keeps up at this, we're going to be clear out of luck because the only person with magic knowledge and skill is going to be sick and possibly entirely out of commission." Another glance towards Carissa. Aleksander followed suit. There she sat, adjusting her arms and shoving her hair out of her face again, again, again. She blew out a sigh, dipped her pen, and scribbled something down that mere moments later, after scanning the whole paper, she scratched out with a screwed-up lip.

"My lady." Demir paused near her on his walk to the fire.

She didn't look up at him.

"My lady," he repeated, dropping to a knee before her, "It's time for you to rest."

"No thank you, Demir. I'm working." Her tone was clipped, bordering on harsh.

If it bothered the Mekartlim, he didn't show it, save for the slight tensing of his wings. His hand slid onto her wrist, gently pulling it away from the paper and twining his fingers with hers. "You know, you remind me of my sister. She has such a strong sense of duty. And an unshakable work ethic. Let me guess, if you have something you need to do, you will forgo all other things—even those like food and water—until you get it done. Am I right?"

"We need information and we need it now." At this, she met his gaze. "Who is to say we will even get until the next morning to plan? There could be an attack anywhere in the country right this moment—"

"And even if there is, you won't be able to help, because you haven't found anything and we're at a random waypoint on the road. Delaying a few hours for sleep will not change anything, Your Highness." Whether Carissa noticed him reach for the pen or not, she didn't react. A small smile flashed across his face as he removed the writing from her fingers, a smile meant to reassure her, and placed it back in the case situated beside the lantern. "Do you want anything to drink, my lady?"

Her eyelashes fluttered and she sighed. "Have we any tea?"

His wings drooped ever so slightly, the bottom feathers curling gently against the dirt. A smile flashed across his face. "Yes," he said softly, "we do. I'll get you a cup." Standing, he offered her his hand. She took it, and together they walked towards the fire where he had laid his bedroll. "Rest here a moment. I'll get a kettle and some tea."

She slumped as though she'd been dropped, knees folding in on themselves and hand splaying out to the sides just in time to catch her. Her head bobbed. "Thank you, Demir."

He brushed some of the unruly curls from her eyes before patting her shoulder and moving towards the carriage. Varek tossed a glance to Aleksander with a quick nod in approval. He groaned as he pushed himself up, momentarily seeming as old as he was, and joined Demir at the carriage. Aleksander watched the man go, speaking in hushed tones with the Mekartlim as they worked together to prepare Carissa a cup of tea. A loud yawn came from across the fire, and he looked back to see the princess already curling up.

"Are you doing alright?"

She opened her eyes momentarily before pulling Demir's blanket over her shoulders. "I will be."

"Any visions? I mean, any that you haven't already told me about?"

"No." She shook her head the best she could. "No visions, no breakthroughs, and none of the test spells I've done have worked."

"Maybe we should listen to Fazhia's advice and wait to find a

Crafter." At this, Aleksander yawned himself, so greatly that his eyes began to water. "I'm beat. Is there anything you want before I inevitably fall asleep?"

"Janek," she said, not opening her eyes this time. "I want my Janek."

Chapter

FIFTEEN

ALEKSANDER DID NOT SLEEP MUCH THAT night. It wasn't that he didn't try—he did, even as Carissa fell asleep moments before Demir brought over the kettle to set beside the fire, even as Demir adjusted the blankets around her and drank the tea that was supposed to be for her. Even as Varek fell asleep and Bunc began snoring.

There was a moment in the night where he rolled over. Varek was awake on watch and Demir had fallen asleep on the bare ground next to Carissa and his bedroll. "Did I sleep?" he'd asked the man.

Varek had glanced his way, shrugged, and said, "I suppose."

More moments like that happened. He'd fall asleep, wake up feeling as though no time had passed, and eventually the sky was brightening.

Waking up once and for all, his limbs were heavy, almost buzzing with the fitful rest he'd endured. In each joint was a stiffness he'd never endured before. It hurt just to breathe.

Demir still snoozed beside Carissa. His wings twitched as he dreamt, still staying rather tucked in despite having to lay on the ground. It looked uncomfortable, that angle they were at, one up in the air and the other curled up and nearly flattened against the ground. Yet, he slept steadily and deeply.

"Are you up for the day now? Or are you still trying to sleep? Oh, and before you ask, your lordship, yes, you did. For the hundredth time, yes."

Aleksander turned to find Varek sitting by Carissa's trunk going over her notes. He pushed himself to his feet. A very long, big stretch drew a groan from him. In response, Carissa grunted and curled deeper into the blankets she'd wrapped around herself.

"Find anything interesting, Varek?" His body felt as though it were moving for the first time as he approached Varek.

The Ölmesuz shrugged. "She's not entirely lost, so that's something." He pointed to scribbles as he spoke. All the letters blurred together to Aleksander. It was as if the writing didn't want to be read. "She keeps scribbling out ideas that I could have told her were stupid." A flash of a glare towards the sleeping princess. "And she's supposedly the pride of the Temple."

"She is," Aleksander snapped.

"Yeah, yeah. Oh, here—one of them made the piece she'd worked with fall to ash. And when she tried to rework the spell, it had a similar outcome. That's why this is all scratched out. She's resigned to not use any incantations similar to that or with these components in them." Again, pointing to scribbles Aleksander was entirely unable to decipher. "So far, it seems like these notes are all she deems useful." He rotated the paper so Aleksander could see. "At least she's got that right."

Stars had been placed next to only three notes:

Incantations useless, try ~~*sorying?*~~ *Rodzjíek method?*

Connect other components must connect to flesh.

Channel through visions?

Aleksander nodded along, as if he understood a word of it. Of course, there were a few words he did actually understand. Just not in this context.

Varek continued, "If we find a Crafter, there's a very good chance she'd be able to acquire tools that either preserve the flesh, amplify her magic, or both. Either way, it will allow for further study and more trustworthy results."

"Snooping on my notes, are we?" The drowsy chiding drew both their attentions to the lady now sitting up beside the fire that had died hours before.

"We're just looking at how far you've come in the last day." Aleksander surveyed her. The drooping shoulders, messy hair, and bags beneath her eyes did not comfort him much, if at all. "Did you sleep at all when we were in Lord Kallendrine's estate? These look like you've spent hours on them."

Carissa shrugged, picking a leaf from her hair. "I slept enough."

Aleksander pressed his lips into a thin line. When Carissa said she slept enough, that means she worked until her eyes crossed or her last candle burnt out. No wonder she fell asleep so suddenly yesterday.

"Hmm," said Varek, scooping up her papers and placing them in the notebook she'd torn them from. "Well, I do hope you slept enough last night. We're likely going to be stopping in the next town we pass today and traveling tonight. I'd like to get most of the way to Halkin's land if we can. If we could even get there before nightfall, that would be ideal. We've managed to cut time by going around most towns, if we keep doing that—for the most part—we should make good time."

She nodded, standing and nearly tripping over the soldier sleeping behind her. "Has he been there all night?"

Varek nodded, eyebrows raised. "Wanted to make sure you actually slept, he said. He'd made you tea too. In case you'd woken up."

A soft smile graced her lips, and she knelt to stoke the embers. "I could boil water on these, right?" she asked after a moment.

"I suppose," Varek said. "They look hot enough."

That was all she needed to tug the teapot free from the carriage, fill it with water, and get it over the rippling coals. Despite Varek and Bunc's shared itch to get back on the road as soon as possible, the sun climbed farther from the eastern horizon and they all sat around on their bedrolls, sipping the tea the princess had put into all of their hands. Demir took his with an embarrassed smile and muttered his thanks, as well as an apology for not getting her tea soon enough last night. Carissa waved it off and assured him it was alright.

Aleksander was, frankly, glad for the moment of peace before they started their journey for the day. His bones ached, his head pounded, and his eyes were blurred—but with the tea, he had a moment to calm his racing heart and mind and *exist*.

By the time their things were packed up and Demir was bowing to those remaining on the ground before shooting into the sky to resume his aerial patrol, Aleksander actually felt somewhat ready for the day. There was a different air around those in the carriage now that Demir was with them and Carissa had slept. Gone were her long stares out the window or the huffs of annoyance as the notebook bounced in her lap and her quill smudged a line where she did not want one. Now, in the jostling carriage, her paper and quill were nowhere to be seen, and when she did stare out the window, it was to watch an animal or a particularly beautiful tree. No, instead of her stress radiating distraction and tension into the bones of her companions, they actually just...talked. Carissa and Aleksander talked, and for the first time in days, he saw his friend in her eyes, not the woman she'd been—stuck in her work, harsh and neglectful not only to those wanting to help her, but to herself.

Their conversation drifted from their travels, the intriguing birds they'd seen flitting about the canopies they'd stoped beneath, and eventually to what they want to do once they get back to the castle.

Carissa waved her hand. "Beyond everything else, I'd like to sleep in my own bed. With Janek. I... You wouldn't understand, but once you get so used to having another person there, sleeping alone is difficult. Uncomfortable." A wistful smile slid across her lips. "What about you? What are your big plans?"

Aleksander did not quite know how to answer, but he fished something out. Whether it was truly at the forefront of his mind didn't matter. "I want to dance at the winter solstice," he said, smiling. "I didn't get to at the summer solstice. I wasn't lying when I'd said I really wanted to."

A single eyebrow rose. "Oh? Do you have someone you want to dance with?" Carissa's grin turned mischievous. She sat back and scanned his posture, his expression. "Is there a young lady at court that has caught the attention of the Champion?"

Beside them, Varek—who, until now, had been entirely silent —scoffed.

Doing his best to snuff out the blush creeping up his neck and into his cheeks and ears, Aleksander shook his head and swallowed hard. "No, I just want to dance."

"I bet it's young Lady Elmere, isn't it?" Carissa leaned forward. "I've seen her seeking you out every single solstice since you were what, twelve?"

"Ten," he said, then wished he hadn't.

"Aha!" Face lit up, she shook a pointer finger at him. "I was right!" She was nearly bouncing in her seat. "You *do* like her!"

"She's just nice, is all," Aleksander insisted, tucking himself further into his doublet's collar, if that were ever possible. "I haven't danced much, and I know that if I do dance, she would be a gracious partner since we're...friends."

He hesitated on that word. Despite the fact that he and Genoise had indeed grown close over the years and shared a friendly acquaintance, he still didn't know if it was proper to call her a friend. Over the years, he'd become familiar with the way Carissa would switch personalities during court events and with him—even between him and Janek. Some part of him, no matter how sure he was that Genoise was being authentic with him, couldn't help but remind him that she is a lady. A capital "L" lady, with a title and land and a role to fulfill. A lady from a well-off family. Sure he was the Sword of Ages, but what pull did that really have?

An awful ball of anxiety gnawed inside his chest at the notion.

If anything, it would make her more likely to try to get on his good side.

Aleksander shook the thought from his head and shrugged, pressing his forehead against the glass of the door, staring out as the trees and bushes pranced by. A large shadow swooped overhead, and looking up, there was Demir, circling to check on the carriage before shooting off with swift wingbeats to scout ahead. Leaning back, Carissa's gaze was still focused on the soldier soaring through the sky. Aleksander shot a glance at Varek.

The man's face was tight, contorted. He studied Carissa, brows furrowed, lips flat. A sideways glance, with which he saw Aleksander watching him, and his face shifted—not relaxed, but not tense in the same way he was before. His gaze refocused on the trees out the window.

Aleksander decided he'd ask Varek about that later.

That was, until Varek raised a hand and rapped on the roof. The carriage jolted to a halt, and he opened the door. "Alright, kid, come with me."

"What?" Confused and not even wanting to follow, Aleksander still toppled out of the cab, adjusting Aoife on his hip as he straightened. The summer sun beat down on his doublet. Its heat became unbearable in a matter of moments.

"We haven't been working you, your holiness." He tied his hair up and took off the doublet he wore—a dark grey with maroon stitching. Flashing a grin, he patted Aleksander's shoulder just a touch too hard. "I doubt the goddess would want her son to be a pampered palace brat. No, you're a Champion, aren't you?" Then to Bunc, he shouted, "Drive on! We'll run after you."

At this, whatever kindness had been building towards the Ölmesuz disappeared entirely. "Oh, come *on*, Varek!"

Still, the carriage jolted forward, Carissa slamming the door shut with a grin. "Have fun!"

Varek instantly took to his pace, but for Aleksander...

Running had never been easy for him. When he was a child, he'd had a few friends that also lived on the outskirts of town. They'd often make up games in the forests, build forts from fallen sticks and rocks. One day he'd been running. He couldn't remember if he was chasing someone of if they were chasing him, but he collapsed and gasped for air, unable to get even the smallest gulp into his lungs. One of his friends saw and ran to the village to get the healer there. His other friend was just as scared as he was. By the time the healer got there, his vision was blurred and his throat raw. She immediately made a steam pot with various herbs and stuck his head over it for a half hour, until he could finally breathe in and out in steady, normal breaths.

Watching Varek and the carriage get smaller and smaller, oh, how pungent the smell of the leaves and mushrooms from all those years ago was in his nose.

A slow, deep breath. A quick prayer to Tulathne. Aleksander leaned forward and took off after the group.

Demir circled overhead, forgoing his scouting ahead in favor of watching over Aleksander as he stumbled and gasped and continuously reminded himself what Janek told him—in through the nose, out through the mouth, it helps his lungs take oxygen in slower.

But goddess, he felt like he had no air at all.

Some act of mercy appeared ahead. It seemed they were not as far off from the village set before Duke Halkin's estate as Varek had thought. Buildings rose in the distance, breaking the trees and culminating with a large parapet belonging to the very top of Halkin's manor.

"You've got this!" a shout echoed.

Glancing up, there was Demir, keeping time with him. At least, he was doing his best. The wingbeats were slow, with a lot of gliding between them as to ensure that no one man pulled ahead of the other.

A bright smile lit his face, and he nodded at Aleksander.

"Keep going!"

Keep going, Aleksander thought between gasps. His vision began to cloud, and he blinked hard to clear it. *If I keep going, I'm going to die.*

His steps slowed, each footfall heavier than the last, until he fell onto his hands and knees, straining for any semblance of air. The dusty ground beneath him puffed with each exhale. It didn't help, all that dirt and sand getting into his mouth, nose, and eyes.

"Is there a healer?" Demir shouted, his boots dropping to the earth beside Aleksander.

"He'll be fine," Varek snapped, "Get up, kid."

"Varek, he can't breathe."

"He's tired, that's all."

"Varek!" Demir's voice boomed louder than Aleksander ever expected the man would be capable of. "I've seen this before. His throat and lungs are constricting. We need a healer or he will die."

Their words became farther and farther away. Aleksander's face hurt from the veins beneath it full to near bursting, his eyes straining to be free from his skin and his skull. With every inhale, his throat narrowed more and more.

Darkness began to creep into the corners of his vision.

No, no, not like this, he thought. *Alesathne would not die like this. I cannot die like this.*

Two hands hoisted him up, and he was looking Varek in the face. His mouth opened to say something, but it was that moment that Aleksander saw nothing at all.

Chapter

SIXTEEN

OH, HOW HE MISSED THAT SMELL. The throbbing in his head, the burning in his throat—all of it was almost worth it for the moments he got to spend inhaling that glorious, pungent steam.

Two hands held him up, and as his eyes fluttered open, sore and wet from tears and gathering dew, he made out the dark cloth draped over his head and the pot before him, still bubbling.

"His breaths are slow! And deep!" a woman shouted.

Aleksander took another long, slow inhale, and the hands shifted on his chest.

"Come help me. I can't hold him much longer."

Stiff, heavy arms hung at his sides, yet he managed to hoist them up and rest on his knees. "I've got it," he croaked, sucking in a wheezing breath that made him cough. "Thank you."

"Oh, praise the Bozkei," she muttered, falling to her knees beside him and peeking her own head into the steam tent. Large, expressive eyes blinked up at him, set in a round face with rich, tan skin. When she smiled, fangs peeked out from her lips. "Stay here. Take deep breaths. I'll be back in a moment."

And with that, she disappeared.

Footsteps echoed in the invisible space around him, as well as the clattering of bottles, a squeak of a door hinge, and muffled whispers and voices. Carissa's whispers he picked out almost instantly—hushed, quick, with lot of staccatos for emphasis. He'd been on the receiving end of such whispers many a time growing up. There was no mistaking her voice. The other one, the whispers conversing with Carissa's—those were harder to decipher. The voice was slow, smooth, quiet. A creak of leather and the shifting of weight on boots; the person cleared their throat, and he knew immediately. Varek.

Aleksander closed his eyes and tried not to think about the man for too long.

He was the reason Aleksander was incapacitated, after all.

"I'm back," the mystery woman said, lifting the blanket from his head. The cool, dry air of her cottage nearly stung his flushed cheeks. Steam gathered and dripped off of his bangs and onto his nose. He was clammy, hot, and uncomfortable, but his lungs were relaxed and his breathing was normal, if not still a mite raspy.

She held something out to him, the creases framing her eyes growing deeper as she smiled. "Chew on this. It'll help."

The small root piece she pinched between thumb and forefinger looked relatively boring. There were no tendrils coming off of it, nor were there crevices full of dirt. In fact, it looked like it had just been washed, and maybe even peeled as the flesh seemed too smooth to have come directly from the earth. So, he did as she said. The moment he bit down, bittersweet oil slid down his throat. He coughed, but managed to keep the root in his mouth.

"It's an acquired taste. I should have warned you." Her dark eyes flitted over his shoulder—to meet Varek's or Carissa's, Aleksander presumed. She nodded. "He should be well enough to travel soon. Would you like me to prepare sachets you can use to help him if this should occur again while on your journey?"

Aleksander glanced back. He had heard wrong. It was not Carissa and Varek. It was Carissa and Varek *and* Demir. All of them, standing, whispering, waiting.

Carissa's lips pressed into a thin line, and she nodded,

fingers tight around her goddess's pendant. "Yes, thank you, Madam Nelka."

The healer nodded and curtsied. Her long, intricately embroidered skirt bunched into a pile on the ground where flowers climbing up from the hem became nothing more than a jumble of colors. Beaded bracelets clinked as she rushed into a side room.

The rustling of fabrics and the twinkling sound of glass being handled resumed.

Before Aleksander could speak, Varek stepped forward, face stern.

The boy's mind raced with possible responses to whatever Varek had to say. "Sorry I couldn't keep up; I was too busy dying," or "You don't get to lecture me; you almost killed me." Whatever Varek planned to say, the rage building in Aleksander's chest was ready to fly in response.

Leather creaked as Varek knelt, eyes on Aleksander's. "I am deeply sorry" was all he said.

Aleksander's chest cooled. Of all the comments he was expecting, an apology was not one of them.

"I was unaware of your condition, and I put you in danger. That is inexcusable. Forgive me." His head bowed forward.

It felt like a joke, the apology. Scenarios raced through Aleksander's head of the hundreds of other times Varek should have apologized but didn't. Why was this any different?

Varek knelt there, face still downcast, silent.

Aleksander found himself nodding. "Yeah," he croaked. "Of course."

Not meeting his gaze, Varek nodded and rose. "Thank you."

"Well," Carissa interjected before either man could speak further, clasping her hands together tightly and holding them to her chest. "The good thing is that we're almost at Duke Halkin's estate. We'll be there before nightfall, and then we can be on our way and travel through the night, should everything else go according to plan."

"Wait." At this, Aleksander fully turned in his chair to match

Carissa. "We're not staying the night? What about finding the sorcerer? Don't you need more time to work on your spells and notes and…whatever else you need?"

The princess shifted from foot to foot. "I am not having any visions. Nor a breakthrough. We…" She exhaled sharply.

Disgust flipped Aleksander's guts.

He was a horrible person. Here was this woman standing before him, a childhood friend, practically family—regardless of the circumstances that brought them together—and he had the audacity to ask her to push herself further so they would have even a sliver more of a chance to find the sorcerer. How could he act as if he didn't promise Janek he'd look after her and encourage her to care for herself? As if he hadn't sat and watched Demir talk Carissa down so she could rest?

As if he hadn't thanked the stars and any god listening that someone was able to get through to her?

There was no way he could sit there and tell her to do exactly what he was advocating against the night before.

"I'm sorry," he said quickly, wiping a bead of either steam or sweat from trailing down the side of his face. "I'm just—"

"No," she said. "No, it's fine. I just… This isn't the best town. Duke Halkin warned me against that. We'd be better off on the road, trying to get to his estate, no matter our arrival time."

"Wait, it's a…" Aleksander shot a glance to the door Nelka had left through. "It's a bad town? How? Are we not safe here?"

She glanced at Demir and Varek, but the silent question remained unanswered as Nelka returned, a small trunk in her hands. "This should be more than enough for your journey. It has enough steam pouches to last you ten attacks, and I've put more of that root in there that he can chew on should he feel any tightening or shortness of breath, regardless of physical activity or not."

Carissa took it and nodded her thanks.

The healer's head bobbed, the scarf wrapped around it nearly glittering in the daylight filtering through the windows. At the end of her scarf—which was, in and of itself, halfway down her back—two braids poked out. Both were thick, tied off with leather strips that only served to enhance the rich dark brown of her hair.

Drying off as best he could and putting on a fresh tunic instead of the doublet, the group stepped outside and Demir guided everyone back to where Bunc was waiting, still in his seat, absently nibbling an apple. They put Aleksander's damaged doublet into the trunk at the back. It seemed in Nelka's haste to help him breathe she had cut it off him. Upon returning it, she apologized profusely and said that she would have done a better job with the ties were there not multiple people shouting at her all at once.

Just before climbing in, Aleksander's eye fell on a store. Inside was a small seating area, and off to the wall, a table nearly collapsing under the weight of hundreds of various pastries, breads, and general sweet treats.

After what happened, one scone in particular was making his mouth water. "Why can't we spend time here again?"

Carissa placed a hand on his back and gave a firm push towards the open carriage door. "It's not a place for people like us."

Now, that didn't sound right.

Aleksander frowned. "What do you mean, 'people like us?'"

Her face shriveled up, concern, hesitancy, and frustration mixing in her cheeks and turning them red. Carissa motioned for the men to help.

Both shrugged, but it was Demir who said, "Farnich is mainly Rodzjiekim and Ölmesuz. They don't worship Tulathne."

Alexsander's eyes narrowed. "Okay?"

"They don't believe in Her," Demir continued, staring pointedly at him. "If you follow my drift."

The Champion was about to shake his head when Varek sighed deeply. There was no sugar, no softness to his words as he spoke. "They don't believe in the Sword or the Scourge or anything that's happening, Aleksander. They believe you're a hoax, and that Carissa's father kidnapped a child to support his religious agenda."

While the words hit his ears, Aleksander hung with one hand off the roof, completely void of thought and full of confusion. "What?" he said, once the silence between them became too apparent.

Carissa pushed past him into the carriage and took her seat, fiddling with her ring. The pink of her cheeks had turned dark crimson and spread to her nose and ears. Angry lines broke her forehead between her brows.

Varek nodded. "The princess doesn't feel comfortable staying here if you two are seen as religious zealots or her family as kidnappers and liars."

"What about you two though?" Aleksander nodded to each of the men. "Are you not seen as religious zealots?"

A hearty laugh erupted from Varek, sending his body folding forward. Demir shook his head, a small smile on his face.

"You think we're religious zealots?" Varek laughed louder.

Carissa cast a nervous glance to the street. In case anyone was watching, drawn in by the spectacle Varek was creating.

Frustration clawed at Aleksander's shoulders, gripping tightly and folding his face up in doing so. Brows clenched tight together over his eyes, nose scrunched, and lips tight, he frowned. "It's a logical question."

"Take a look at us, kid," Varek said, gesturing between him and their new companion. "You really think I am going to be mistaken as a follower of Tulathne? Or Mr. My-Mom-was-an-Eagle over here?"

"Then why are you with us?" The question spit from his mouth, venomous.

They were wrong. They were wrong, and they were rude. Neither of them had any reason to be here if they thought all the prophecies were a lie...if they thought his life was a lie.

"We have records centuries back. 'And when time forgets/ When nations reset/ The Scourge shall rise again./ Be careful, oh Son, forget not what was done/ Raise up, Sword, against foe and friend.'" The line came back to him without prompting, echoed in his mind by Carissa, Lenore, and Caoimhe, from all his years in the temple.

Varek held up a hand, brow furrowing.

"We have our reasons, and the desire to serve your goddess is not necessarily one of them," Demir interjected. "If it comforts you, however, do know that I love Tulathne and find Her to be a most intriguing, gentle goddess, and it is an honor to serve Her beside you."

Aleksander's eyes flitted to Varek. "What about you?"

His left eyebrow arched, lids drawing low to half cover those golden irises. "That conversation is much too long, kid. And it's certainly not for the middle of a street. Just know I have my reasons as much as Demir does. As much as you do. And remember, I vowed to stand by both of you in this." He thrust a finger towards Carissa, then to Aleksander.

"But you have a bargain struck, so is this really loyalty? Besides, you don't think any of this is real," Aleksander said.

"Hold on, I didn't say that."

"But you don't, do you? You think we're making all this up?"

"Aleksander, take a breath. If it makes you feel any better, I don't think *you're* crazy." He bent forward ever so slightly. Hair fell before his eyes, creating curtains on both sides of his face. "But that aside, watch what you say to me. Like you just said, I made a deal with the royals. My loyalty can break whenever it needs to. But it won't unless I have good reason."

Aleksander fell silent. Not because of the threat, but because he...believed Varek. Those words cut deep. A scream still built up inside his chest and stomach, aching to be let out right in the Ölmesuz's face, aching to make him wince and flinch even a little; but under that, a small voice told him to let this rest, to pick it up later. It didn't matter if Varek believed all this like Aleksander did, what mattered is he was there with them.

As they all sat in the carriage and petered through the town, the new discovery that this was not a belief shared by everyone replayed in Aleksander's mind as he met the eyes of men and women, young and old, Rodzjiek and Ölmesuz and Zekharyan through the glass window in the carriage. Some looked at the carriage in awe, then at him with wonder. Perhaps they didn't even know who he was; they just knew he was important.

But others, they knew. He saw it in the way their eyes changed the moment they beheld his face. Some got angry, though he wasn't sure why—if it was at him, or towards the royal family, or at the rumor that he was kidnapped. Some were shocked, perhaps wondering why a man not welcomed by their society was traveling through the center of their town.

Then the carriage jolted to a stop to wait for traffic to clear. Aleksander took to scanning the passersby once more.

It was different, the way they looked at him here. And Aleksander was not quite sure how he felt about that.

A few people he made eye contact with pretended as though it never happened and continued raking their gaze over the carriage, the detail in the wheels, the fine, thin glass of the windows.

But one woman met his eyes and held him there. She was Ölmesuz. Old. Older than Varek, easily by a few centuries if not a few hundred. Her hair was grey and seemed to have lost its shine, though as the sunlight caught it, flashes of orange and green appeared as though it had once been a rich copper. Cut-emerald eyes sparkled out at him through wrinkles, and her drooping ears twitched when she noticed him watching her. A tongue swept out to wet dry lips, and her brows softened from their hardened expression.

Those eyes were not sparkling because they were cut from emerald—though everyone said Ölmesuz eyes were truly gemstones in and of themselves.

No, Aleksander knew that was just a turn of phrase. He knew that the moment the sparkling shifted and silent tears tracked down her cheeks.

Bunc clicked to the horses and the carriage lurched forward. The woman turned to keep her eyes on Aleksander. He turned too.

Just before she was out of view, her wrinkled lips shook as

she mouthed, "I'm so sorry."

Aleksander turned back slowly to the interior of the carriage. Carissa's furrowed brow studied the pedestrians, and Varek sat beside her, looking out the opposite window.

He could not bring himself back to reality quickly. Her eyes stuck in his mind like a brand, the flaming image of them vivid against the red-dark of his eyelids whenever he blinked. His pulse beat loud in his ears, his hands buzzing and shaking as he gripped tightly to the hem of his tunic.

The heart in his chest had never tried so desperately to shatter his ribs as it was doing this moment. So much so, in fact, that he had looked down, sure he would see the organ leaping through his skin with each beat.

When he raised his head again, he jumped at the sight of Varek watching him. His face was still aimed out the window, but in the corner of his eye, beneath dark lashes, those eyes—*like tiger's-eye*, Aleksander thought—were on him.

Aleksander shifted in his seat, tucking his hands beneath his thighs. He gave the man a large, bright smile. Without teeth.

Those eyes scanned over his face, head tilting momentarily before he nodded, expression unchanging, and returned to his own observations out the window.

The smile still hung between Aleksander's cheeks, but he was unaware of its presence.

Something within him had...shifted. He couldn't figure out what but the way that she regarded him—not as a god, not as a lord, and not as a warrior, but instead as just as Aleksander whether she knew his name or not—that was unexpected. The genuine emotion she'd expressed...

They believed it. Just as he believed all of this was real, all of these people firmly believed that it was a lie. That he was a victim.

I'm not a victim, Aleksander repeated in his head. Each breath became shorter, more desperate. *I am Alesathne. I was made for this. If I'm not...*

Varek glanced away and his eyebrows rose slowly, elegantly.

A slow, deliberate breath in, which Aleksander found himself mimicking. A visible, deep breath out. It fogged on the window. Varek caught his sleeve in his hand to wipe it away.

Aleksander exhaled too.

He swore he saw Varek smile.

Chapter

SEVENTEEN

"And these," said Duke Halkin, gesturing to the line of soldiers assembled in the training ring at the back of his estate, "are the lovely men and women of my guard that I've elected for you." He clasped his hands behind his back and puffed up his bony chest. "Please, take your time. Ask of them anything you require. They are all skilled in fighting, though some are faster than others and others are stronger than some."

Ten faces stared out at Aleksander. Through his exhausted haze, they all looked nearly the same, just with slight height differences and maybe different hair colors. Of course, it didn't help that all of them wore the same set of armor—dark, tarnished iron.

Every single one of them looked over their heads, as if the group stationed before them was not worthy enough to gaze upon the faces of the people they may possibly end up working and fighting alongside.

Duke Halkin gestured to Aleksander. "I know I said take your time, but don't hesitate to ask things of them, get things going. We have a few hours before they must be dismissed for—"

"All of you," Varek said, taking a step forward, "will pair off. Fight until one is disarmed. The winner will report back to me." He pointed at the first person in line, then at another further down. "You two, go." Another pairing—the third and the eighth. "Go." And another. He continued on until all were matched with a partner and had found a section of the training grounds with ample room to conduct a match. A loud cry of "fight!" broke over the ring, and soon the air was full of grunts and shouts and the reverberating clangs of metal on metal.

Varek strolled casually through the fray, with Aleksander close behind. The pair surveyed each fight. Halkin was right. These people were highly trained, but some were indeed faster than others. For those who weren't fast, they often made up for it with a heavy swing of their sword.

Still, despite the constant displays of skill and ferocity, no one stood out to Aleksander.

Varek called for a pair to stop and asked them both to leave the ring.

"Wait, why?" Aleksander said, glancing between the equally confused fighters and the man who ordered their departure. "They weren't done."

"And they wouldn't have been done for a while. Both of them telegraphed their attacks so openly that they were able to counter it before the strike was even delivered." Varek nodded to them. "You're done. Go back to your barracks or wherever it is you're meant to go."

A towering, hulking Zekharyan jutted her chin out from beneath her helmet, teeth grinding behind closed lips. Her shoulders went back in an attempt to get taller, as if she could compete with Varek's stature. As if she could challenge him.

"Don't even think about it," he snarled. "This is nothing against you. We need a specific fighter. And you just don't cut it."

She glanced in Aleksander's direction before her gaze followed Varek's hand moving towards the hilt of his sword. Her jaw clenched and a breath huffed into the air.

Yet, she sheathed her sword, slammed an armored fist to her heart, and bowed. "My lords," she said. The words were quick and angry before she spun on her heel and followed after her partner.

When Aleksander looked up, Varek was watching him.

"What?"

"You think that was a bad decision?" Varek asked, nodding after the pair as they disappeared behind a door to the soldier's quarters.

Aleksander watched them leave. The fight replayed in his mind. Varek had been right. Just watching, Aleksander saw the moves in his mind before they were executed. He knew exactly how the fight would be carried out. Almost as if it were scripted. To the untrained eye, it would look like both of them were fast, skilled fighters—and they were. But against a real opponent, one who would be watching for any tell, no matter how small...

"No," Aleksander said finally, stepping in front of him to continue his observation. "You were right."

Varek raised an eyebrow, that snide smirk turning up a corner of his mouth. "Finally able to admit that, are we?"

Aleksander didn't dare acknowledge that with a response, whether it was true or not.

◊ ✳ ◊

THE AFTERNOON WORE ON. HOUR after hour they worked the candidates. They ran laps, climbed ropes, deflected projectiles hurled by Demir. By the time the sun had paused above the mountains, everyone was tired and sweaty. Aside from hours of bumpy travel through the night and into the next morning, walking, talking, standing, and eliminating possible recruits had the group aching to get off their feet.

Well, Carissa and Aleksander were. Varek seemed as though he had another few days of walking, talking, standing, and yelling left in him.

"Time!" the gravely bass echoed over the arena. "Go on in. Your lord insists you eat. We will confer. Don't be surprised if some of you are never addressed by any of us again or if you get your rest time interrupted to show me more of what you can do."

Five soldiers remained on the field. Each slumped in their armor, not even jumping at Varek's barked order. The group nodded, bowed sloppily to Carissa and Aleksander, and shuffled inside.

Upon turning to face the rest of them, Varek ran a hand down his face, a loud, long sigh sputtering through his lips. "We're never going to find a worthy fighter from this pathetic lot." His eyes fixed on the land to the north. off into the unseeable distance, where the mountains dissolved into the sea. "Should we reach out to the lords past the Untamed? Or maybe some of the Ölmesuz nobles in the south. They may not care about the prophecies as much as you do, but I trust their soldiers more."

"Duke Halkin, he's... There are a lot of... My father trusts him. He has good soldiers," Carissa stumbled through her words, her voice weary.

Varek clucked his tongue. "Not good enough."

"Why don't we go inside, get something to drink, maybe something to eat, and pick this up once we've got clearer heads?" Demir's voice was like honey on a wound. Even Varek seemed calmed by the suggestion.

The old Ölmesuz nodded. His eyes drooped with the weight of the last few days. "If Her Highness agrees."

"I agree," Carissa said, rubbing the back of her neck. Areas on her pale blue dress were darkened where she'd sweat through, and strands of hair clung to her cheeks and forehead. "We've had a long night and an even longer day. If we're at such a grand demesne as Halkin's, we should take advantage of it."

Inside the manor, a vaulted ceiling with carved wooden beams was illuminated in soft golden light. The setting sun filtered through stained glass, inlaid in the ceiling, between joists. In the center of the great hall was a large, long table where soldiers, servants, and even Duke Halkin's sons congregated. The three of them elbowed one another, glancing at the group as they ambled in. Aleksander's eyes fixed on them, though theirs stayed firmly on Carissa.

For some nobles sons, the fact that the princess was married meant nothing. Marriages—especially royal ones—could be annulled and reforged in the blink of an eye. She caught their stares and snarled—actually snarled.

That seemed to be enough to dissuade them.

A quick glance around confirmed that the large spread in the center was not a table to sit at. Those were positioned at the sides of the hall.

Aleksander slowly watched as people made their way down the table, piling food on their plates, and peeling off to sit against the walls.

"An old custom," Aleksander found himself saying. "To make a table full of food that no one sits at. You're supposed to—"

"I've been to a *ceileh* before," Varek hissed, pushing past him. "I don't need to be taught like a child." He picked up an empty plate and slid in with the soldiers filing down the line, scooping food onto his plate as he went.

A hand squeezed Aleksander's. "He's just exhausted," Carissa said softly. "We all are."

"Even if he'd slept for three days straight, it won't change the fact that he doesn't like me."

"Doesn't like you?" Demir appeared on the other side of the princess. His wings twitched with the effort to keep them from sweeping the sandy floor. "Varek likes you well enough, Champion. He wouldn't be helping you if he didn't." His piercing eyes shifted to Carissa, hand hovering by her elbow, as if it was a punishable offense to touch her. "Why don't you take a seat, my lady? I'll get your food for you."

"No." Her nose scrunched up, eyes closing as she shook her head. "I can get my own food, Demir. You're the one who has actually been active today. You sit. What would you like—chicken or venison?"

Despite the war in his eyes where Aleksander saw him resign to not challenge her, a glowing smile appeared in response. "I'm a simple man, my lady. Venison reminds me of home."

"Then venison it is," she said, and marched to take a place in line.

Demir crossed his arms over his chest. "She's a good lady, your princess."

Aleksander nodded. If there was one thing he'd known about Carissa all his life in the castle, it was that she never allowed her station and privilege to get in the way of respect towards others. He'd seen one too many noblewomen treat a lower lord as trash. But never Carissa. "She really is. She's serious too. Go sit or she'll order me to force you into a chair."

He laughed, but obliged, selecting a place at a table along the wall with enough chairs for everyone and a few more for any stragglers looking for a place to sit. Aleksander joined him, trusting Carissa to get his food as well. He was proven correct when she returned, balancing one plate in each hand and one on her forearm, as though she had spent the last twenty-two years of her life being a barmaid instead of a princess and a mage.

Varek joined shortly after, a large pint of ale and plate piled high with meat and potatoes as his dinner.

Around them, chatter went on as normal. As he ate, Aleksander caught snippets of conversations around who was up for a promotion, a shift from regiment to regiment, a complete transition from demesne to demesne, and, of course, who was rumored to be secretly carrying on with whom. He even heard a few such rumors get confirmed. He stuck his nose into his water glass, holding it against his lips but not drinking as he felt his face flush.

"Mind if I sit?" a bright, confident voice asked over the table.

"Do you intend to hassle us about how we handled testing when it came to your comrades?" Varek said, shoving a forkful of venison, roasted potatoes, and carrots into his mouth.

"No, I intend to sit and eat my dinner," the woman bit back, placing her plate down without waiting for another response. "Are you always so rude to ladies?"

"He's usually rude to everyone," Aleksander said. He took a sip upon realizing how strange it must look to be sitting there, nose in his cup, not doing anything aside from...what, smelling the water? Once he swallowed, he finally lifted his gaze from the table.

The blush in his cheeks returned anew. He quickly looked back at his food.

She was young. At least, she looked young, which for an Ölmesuz could mean she was anywhere from twenty years old to a hundred and forty. Aside from her age, Aleksander was embarrassed to have his first thought about her be that she was rather pretty. Around her eyes fluttered thick, ice-white lashes, a strong, downturned nose, and freckled cheeks lifted in a soft smile.

He shifted in his seat and shut out the thought. No matter how old she was, this was not important. They were here to find a soldier, not blush at the first girl to smile at him.

Large amethyst eyes blinked at him, a shade he'd never seen on a person though it was supposedly a common one among the Ölmesuz. "You're the Champion, aren't you?"

Aleksander nodded, stabbing at his potatoes and not looking up. "Yep."

"You're looking for a warrior to join you. Duke Halkin announced as much this morning when we were assembling for breakfast."

"And why weren't *you* in the group?" Varek said, finally turning to her. His demeanor changed again, similar to how it shifted with Fazhia, but much less challenging. His brows relaxed from their scrunched position, and even his eyes seemed to lose some of their guardedness. Something deep welled up in them. Something...painful. In a moment, however, it all faded. Whatever he'd remembered or felt in that moment was gone, and the man Aleksander was used to returned. "You got a name?" he snapped. "Or are you just gonna pretend like you know us so you get some points with the guys in battalion?"

"My name is Iscah," she said. Her fork stabbed violently into a pile of green beans on her plate. "And I wasn't there because I'm not *in* the battalion, much less a solid enough soldier to be chosen from it to perform for you."

Aleksander's forehead crunched down to tough his nose as he studied her. It made sense. Despite the fact that she was partially clad in the same light plate as nearly everyone else in the hall, her hair, a metallic silver, was not short, nor was it tied up in a style worn by the women who did fight. It was arranged in a style similar to what he'd seen Carissa wear on occasion. There were braids coming from above her temples to the back of her head, where half her hair was gathered in a bun. The rest cascaded in shimmering waves down her back, and a few strands fell loose and brushed her cheeks. Her drooping ears were decorated in multiple piercings, some dangling and some even connected to others with a chain.

No, this was not the kind of woman who would be fighting.

"Why are you here then?"

She popped the green beans in her mouth, chewing thoughtfully. A glance towards Varek, Carissa, and finally she settled back on Aleksander. "I'm a soldier. I'm just not in the squad that handles most of the fighting. I'm in munitions and development. I'm a Crafter."

Chapter

EIGHTEEN

UKE HALKIN'S DARK EYES FLITTED BETWEEN them. "No," he said, the word almost a laugh. "*Absolutely* not. You cannot take my only Crafter. She's not a warrior." A pointed look to Aleksander. "You *asked* for a warrior."

"I can wield a sword," Iscah said, armor shifting as she leaned forward ever so slightly. "They said that's all I really need to know."

"Oh please," Halkin's chair smacked back against the stone wall as he sat. "We all know the stories of what's to come. We all know what's happened in the past. Do you seriously think, Crafter Hatenepta, that you would be able to handle it?"

"They think I can."

"But do *you*?"

Iscah's hands curled into fists at her sides. Her pale cheeks turned scarlet. Her voice was measured, but no less terrifying. "I do."

Halkin huffed. "You stay with me, and you are still a soldier. You still get the glory and you still get to serve when the war starts. If that's all you're after—"

"We need a Crafter," Carissa said, leaning on the table. "I don't care if you weren't expecting us to take her. We need her. And she's willing to serve us."

The tension in the room thickened. One could almost hear the creaking of the lord's vertebrae as his head slowly swiveled around to lock, once more, on Iscah. "You are?" The words sounded like a threat, low and poisonous.

Yet, Iscah nodded.

Carissa's arms bent, drawing her closer to the old Lord's worn face. "My lord duke," her words were a whispered trail of black smoke, filling the room with impending dread. A shiver traveled down Aleksander's spine. It wasn't the first time he'd heard it. When they were kids, it was the voice she'd used with him when he was younger and doing everything he could to piss her off. As they got older, it was the voice of a woman who, despite rank and skill, got underestimated at meetings. That voice reminded Aleksander she was not just Carissa, but the Eyes of Time—prophetess, mage, and ruler all rolled into a convenient, pretty package with curls the color of wheat. A smile broke her lips and Aleksander was surprised to find she hadn't grown fangs. "I am so close to finding out who it was that desecrated graves to create those homunculi, and I need a Crafter to supply me with tools that may amplify my skills and ensure a higher success rate." Her bright eyes grew eerily dark. "You wouldn't want to be the cause of another disaster, would you? I know my father—and my mother, actually—would be incredibly disappointed to find out that one of their trusted dukes was complicit in the murder of their people."

The duke's throat bobbed with a hard swallow.

"Now," she continued in that same tone, "I can either take her from you and inform my father that you refused a request from the princess of your country, to whose family you swore fealty, or you can allow us to observe her fighting, assure you she will be an asset and not a liability, and stand with us and a priestess to bless her and swear her to our cause, thus cementing yourself as a supporter of the Sword of Ages and loyal servant of Tulathne and all her many, mysterious ways."

A glance among all in the room, and Duke Halkin was ushering everyone out into the yard.

"We could go to the training ring," Varek said. Aleksander's boots shuffled along from rug, to polished stone, to uncut grass, echoed in Varek's own steps. "It's not far."

"You wish to test her fighting prowess?" Arms outstretched, Halkin spun beneath the starry sky. "Test her."

Around them, finely clipped hedges rose from beds of flowers.

Just the thought of an all-out fight had Aleksander's body nearly melting. The meal had been filling, but no amount of fine food would replace a lost night of sleep. Iscah drew her sword from its scabbard and stepped forward into the clearing between the group and where the lord of the demesne had stopped. Grass twisted beneath her heel as she spun to face whoever may challenge her. Aleksander sighed deeply, rolling his shoulders and stepping forward, only to find himself pulled back with a hard tug on the back of his doublet.

Without a word, Varek strode forward, sword already drawn.

"Alright," he growled, "let's see what you've got."

"Varek," Aleksander hissed, "are you sure you want to do this?"

"Better me than you." He glanced over his shoulder and tossed the boy a grin. The bags beneath his eyes were bordering on black. "We all know you've still got a ways to go, your holiness."

A panicked look passed between Carissa and Aleksander. Even Demir stepped forward as though he himself planned to stop Varek. Aleksander grabbed Demir's sleeve. He wasn't sure why. He was just as scared as everyone else that Varek would pound this poor girl into the dust and leave them not only without a Crafter but without aid from Duke Halkin. Or worse, that a tired Varek would be sloppy, and this girl would humiliate him. Neither of which were desirable outcomes.

Something, though...something deep in his chest tightened his fingers around the fabric and tugged the man back a step. It was that same something that kept his feet fixed to the ground. Demir's eyes caught his, wild and silently begging for Aleksander to let go. Pressing his lips together, Aleksander shook his head. "Let him go," he whispered.

Varek rolled his neck, stepping into a stance Aleksander had seen from the front more times than he could count on this trip—legs spaced, feet steady, knees bent, sword raised in one hand, the other hanging in midair before his face, ready to move however it needs to. His shoulders rose and fell with exhausted breaths.

Across the way, Iscah slid into a graceful mirror of Varek. Her brows drew low over her unblinking eyes, chest rising and falling in deep, uneven breaths. The blade of her sword shone in the moonlight as it lifted to her side—

Iron crashed into iron before Aleksander had time to register Varek's move. He had *never* gone that fast against Aleksander, to the point where his limbs and blade were almost a blur moving from point to point, his feet dancing around Iscah's.

Panic flooded anew through Aleksander's spine. Where he once stood on two solid legs, he had to pat his thighs to make sure they hadn't dissolved; they certainly felt like they had.

He wasn't just going to humiliate her—and forget about fearing for his safety or dignity.

Varek was going to *kill* her.

Iscah somehow managed to match her opponent's movements, countering and fluttering her way through the match. Her hair was a silver banner behind her, giving Aleksander something to track throughout the match. A laugh rose from the man beside him, and Aleksander's eyes fell on a truly mad Duke Halkin. His grin was broad, eyes wide with fear and pride and expectation not at all marred by any sort of true joy. Aleksander had never seen such a man, usually so refined and calculated in action and speech, so utterly feral and terrified before.

Through the fear, an odd swirl of joy bubbled in his chest. Heavy hands hung at his side, and Aleksander admitted to himself the fact that he was glad Varek was fighting. Aside from the exhaustion, he was glad it was the old Ölmesuz striking fear into the duke.

Huffs, grunts, and the occasional yell intermingled with slash after slash, hit after hit.

Aleksander's eyes finally isolated Varek, just barely able to keep up with his movements. His foot slid between Iscah's and caught an ankle, sending her stumbling away.

This is it. Aleksander's stomach turned. *I don't know if I can watch.*

Iscah's back was to Varek, her side unprotected as she flailed her non-sword arm in an attempt to regain the balance stolen from her.

But Varek didn't raise his sword. Didn't move it at all from the position it held just off to his side, pointed at the hedges. He shifted his back foot to his side, facing her head on as Iscah whirled around to him, her own sword ready and moving.

A chill ran through Aleksander.

He's...open.

Varek did nothing but slowly swing his sword forward.

The tip of Iscah's blade slid up along Varek's palm, drawing blood, catching the cross guard of that beautiful sword and flinging it away with a muted metallic clang. A rustle of grass cradled its fall.

Varek hadn't even tried to stop it.

Iscah, chest heaving, arm trembling, tucked her blade neatly under his chin.

The man's hands raised slowly as he lowered himself to his knees, eyes trained on the girl before him.

"Do you wish to swear yourself to our cause and company?" he asked quietly.

Rapid, heavy breaths were pouring from Iscah's snarl as her eyes flitted over the man before her. A single nod.

At that, Varek actually grinned. A true, honest, earnest grin, glowing with pride. "Spectacular."

NINETEEN

HE PRIESTESSES SERVING THE DEMESNE AND Farnich as the surrounding town showed up three strong, all with various elements to make the ritual all the more dramatic, all the more binding. The shortest one, a Zekharyan woman, carried a band similar to the one the priestess at Lord Kallendrine's estate had used to facilitate the bonding of Demir to the group. But the other two carried things not only unfamiliar to Aleksander, but entirely confusing.

The other Zekharyan, standing only a touch shorter than Carissa, carried in her hands a small box. When she opened it, Aleksander saw that inside was nothing but ash mixed with gold flakes. Before both of them had even produced their swords for the oath, she had dipped her thumb in the ashes and smeared one band over Iscah's brows and a swipe from the base of her nose to her chin. Aleksander had half a mind to protest, but allowed her to do the same. The ash was bitter in his mouth, sticking to his teeth and feeling both drying and smoothing along his tongue. All in all, a sensation and taste he'd preferred to do without.

The third was an Ölmesuz woman. Unlike the others, she did not wear the robes associated with those who had vowed their lives to Tulathne. No, instead she wore ornate, traditional

Ölmesuz clothing. The fabric of her gown was pale white, so light and thin it was a wonder it wasn't sheer. It draped over her shoulders and was held closed beneath her bust with a thick woven band of red, blue, and gold threads. It created a pattern reminiscent of reeds along a river, and was tied in such a way that a panel of it hung flat down her front, stopping around her knees and ending in tassels. A beaded necklace fanned out from her throat to her shoulders, jingling as she walked. In her hands, bedecked with rings and bangles, she brought forth a small jar.

Iscah smiled at her and closed her eyes.

The woman, a small smile playing at her own red-painted lips, unscrewed the jar and lifted it above Iscah's head. Tilting it ever so slightly, a stream of fragrant golden oil dripped a line down her scalp and into her hair.

"With the blessing of the Kutsalyot, and the ever watchful gaze of our Mother, I offer you health, prosperity, and protection. May you, Iscah Hatenepta, daughter of Miraz and Asenath, walk forward into a great journey. Your words shall be a light to the dark places, your presence a comfort to the fearful. Your heart will be with us, as all ours will be with you. May the Mother and all the Kutsalyot be between you and any harm, always and forever, until the day you return home to us."

When his new companion opened her eyes, Aleksander found tears tracking their way along Iscah's lower lashes.

"May time be a friend," she said softly.

Iscah nodded. "And may life be a joy."

After this, the woman—by this point he had acknowledged that she was not a priestess, but instead a holy woman from the Ölmesuz religion, a role for which he knew no title—turned to him and repeated the process, pouring the oil and reciting an altered version, devoid of the names of his parents or any mention of the Kutsalyot and the Mother—whoever that was. Instead, she substituted Tulathne, though the tightness in her jaw betrayed her opinion towards the goddess.

The oil was cool on his scalp and smelled of wildflowers and vanilla.

Her eyes met his, and she smiled. "May time be a friend, and your life a joy."

He nodded, not quite sure how to respond. A quiet "thank you" was all he managed, but it seemed to be enough. She stepped back, and the shorter of the two priestesses of Tulathne came forward, wrapping the swords in the way the other had done all those days ago. Aleksander recited his half with no guidance, and when it came time, Iscah needed little prodding before she recited hers.

"I, Iscah Hatenepta, Daughter of Time and loyal servant to Duke Halkin, swear today to follow you in the light of the goddess, on the fields of battle and off. You are my charge and I am yours. My body is your shield, my arm your weapon. This I swear, and promise you my service."

In contrast to her previous emotional response, Iscah's words seemed endlessly hollow as she recited the oath, though there was no malice in her tone. Aleksander saw in her eyes and the twitch of her smile that she was truly excited to join them.

His mind drifted back to the conversation earlier in the day.

Perhaps she was one who thought this was crazy. Here she was, joining them, but who knew what her *true* stance was? How much of this was her feeling obligated to join, and how much of it was her actually wanting to?

Regardless, her grin broadened as she took her sword back and sheathed it. A fist pressed against her heart. "I'm honored to embark on this quest with you," she said, bowing slightly. "If you'll allow, I'll gather my things and then we can depart."

"Of course," said Carissa, stepping forward to take Iscah's hand in hers. "If you wouldn't mind, might I see some of what you're working on? There may be some things we deign useful to us. Well, mostly me."

Iscah nodded. "Of course my lady. Come with me."

As the two retreated, the soft voice of the Ölmesuz holy woman floated over to Aleksander from the other side of the room. "With the blessing of the Kutsalyot, and the ever watchful gaze of our Mother, I offer you health, prosperity, and protection. May you..." She trailed off.

"Varek Kasajb."

"Varek Kasajb, son of..."

Aleksander turned to watch the interaction out of the corner of his eye. The pair stood by the wall, Varek's face barely concealing the fight happening in his mind. He shook his head, and she nodded.

"Varek Kasajb, child of those we've lost, continue forward on your journey. May your words be a light in the dark, your presence a comfort to the fearful. May you find the peace you seek, and may you bring peace to others. May the Mother and all the Kutsalyot be between you and any harm, always and forever, until the day you return home to them."

The oil dribbled onto his scalp and through his hair. This time, the woman did not smile as she returned the lid to the jar and set it aside. Her hands, simultaneously large and gentle, cupped his face and brought his eyes up to hers, though she stood nearly a head shorter than him, and spoke with deep earnestness. "May time be a friend, and the rest of your life a joy."

He nodded, closing his eyes as she pressed her forehead to his. Against his, her long, black hair seemed even darker. Quiet murmurings—perhaps another prayer?—floated from them, and when they parted, Varek's eyes were softer. "Thank you, *h'met'r*."

"Of course, my brother." She smiled now, a soft, sorrowful smile. "Is there anything else I can do for you while I'm here?"

A bitter smile flashed over his lips. "Not unless you can turn back time."

"No," she laughed lightly. "We were blessed by it, but I don't think I'm able tell the Great Stream to stop flowing."

Varek bade her goodbye, ran his hands through the oil in his hair and stroked it through his beard, and Aleksander noticed that the man actually had some grey in his hair. It was not pure, unmarred onyx; it was obsidian, scattered with quartz. His eyes met Aleksander's. The boy braced for a verbal lashing, perhaps a rude comment about how he shouldn't be eavesdropping or staring. But none came.

Varek straightened up and gestured to Aleksander's hair. "You're going to want to rub that in. Otherwise the heat from your scalp is going to drip it into your eyes, and trust me, it burns."

"Oh." Aleksander clumsily reached up after shifting Aoife to his other hand to wipe a small trail of oil that had begun to slide down his forehead. He slowly worked it in. The oil was thick and truly, fully coated his hair. Good thing it smelled divine. "Thanks," he said.

"Don't mention it."

The man walked out through the large doors and into the night, trotting down the steps in the direction of the stables. And there Aleksander stood, alone in the hall of a castle he'd never entered before, with more questions than he'd ever held in his mind at once, all begging to be answered.

He figured now was not the right time to ask.

Chapter

TWENTY

LEKSANDER ALMOST REGRETTED AGREEING TO RIDE in the coach with Carissa and Iscah instead of perching off the side or running along with it.

Almost.

Not only were they around the same age—Aleksander learned Iscah was only twenty-one, which was why her blessing from the *h'met'r* was about beginnings—but they couldn't have been more made to be friends if Aleksander and Janek had gotten together to craft one from clay for her. The moment they'd returned from Iscah's quarters and workshop and loaded in to the carriage, they'd been chatting as if they'd known one another all their lives. No topic was off-limits, though they mostly stuck to Carissa's personal life and Iscah's inventions. According to her, being a Crafter left little time for romance or even friendships.

At the moment, they held between them a board they used most nights on the road to prepare food. On it now rested Carissa's papers, an ink pot and dip pen, a vial of homunculi remains, and a small, golden object.

It looked the most like a sundial than anything else, as far as Aleksander was concerned—though he would be remiss to acknowledge the intense detail on it. Iscah told him it was a focus for Carissa, something she could use to channel the flow of magic. The face of the "sundial" was a gold plate, with inlaid agates and crystals, engraved with swirling designs and those same little runes carved into the sticks Carissa had. They now hung off a small bag on her belt. There was rarely a time she went without them, and Aleksander couldn't help but feel a slight twinge of concern every time he saw them dancing about her hip.

As far as he knew, the last day of travel had been unremarkable. No visions at all, though the Aramerk—as that was what Iscah called the sundial—was supposedly helping Carissa refine her powers. They'd pored over her notes for that entire day, save for when the carriage stopped for lunch or tea and they'd exchanged stories of their girlhood that were wrought with stupid decisions and the natural hubris all daughters of men who raised them with strength and tenacity possess.

Still, sitting across from her as she bowed her head over the notes, his eyes didn't leave the bags beneath hers or the dried blood on her lip from where she'd chewed it so hard she'd torn skin.

The carriage slowed to a stop, and Varek opened the door. His hair was wet with sweat from running the last few miles beside them, but other than that, the man wasn't really any worse for wear. He even offered a bow before speaking, though it became abruptly clear the bow was sarcastic. "My esteemed lord and ladies," he panted, "may I interest your sorry, pampered selves in getting up, stretching your legs, and assisting a poor old man with setting up camp for the night?"

"The poor old man just ran for an hour," Iscah drawled, not even giving him a look. "I think he can handle starting a fire on his own."

"Oh, you're gonna be fun." The door opened wider and he stepped aside. "Let's go."

Iscah's face scrunched up. She scooted closer to Carissa. "We're working. Have the Champion do it."

"I need all three of you. We've got work to do before Her Highness can settle in and continue her work." A cursory glance over the notes. "By the looks of things, you're getting close to figuring it out anyways."

When neither of the women moved, Aleksander slid across the seat towards the open door, doing his best to catch Iscah's attention with a bobbing head and unblinking gaze. He cleared his throat, and finally, she looked up. Her expression softened from the one with which she had met Varek, but annoyance still curled at her lip.

"Thank you for everything you're doing for Carissa," he said softly, anxiety building in his gut. "However, right now, if we want her to get any sleep, we need to make camp."

After a long, slow blink, Iscah puffed out a sigh. She shuffled the board across her lap and slid out of the carriage behind Aleksander. Carissa remained bent over her work and did not give either of them acknowledgement of their leaving other than shifting her legs wider to support the board on her own, without Iscah's assistance. Her fingers, stained with ink, fluttered over words and runes. The other arm draped over the board, fingers absently attempting to crack one another in the same way they'd been trying for the last few hours.

One thumb produced a sharp snap and she flexed her fingers out, letting them finally fall still.

"Oh," Varek huffed as Iscah dropped out of the cab behind Aleksander. "So when I tell you to do something, you don't listen, but when the *kid* asks, you'll drop everything to do as he says."

"The *kid* is at least respectful," she spat. Passing by Varek, she came only to his shoulder. Shorter and younger than the other Ölmesuz, Aleksander had expected her to be somewhat softer than she was. Her round features, bright smile, and lilting voice offered that notion when you first laid eyes on her. Yet from the moment they'd met, she often chose words and a tone that was much harsher.

Varek arched an eyebrow as she strode towards the patch of grass where he, Bunc, and Demir had already begun dumping their supplies.

"You could be nicer," Aleksander muttered, adjusting Aoife at his hip.

"I'm as nice as I need to be, your *holiness*." Varek leaned down and picked up a pack of dried meat, catching a slice between his teeth before burying it back in the box and digging through it for something else. Much of their fresh food had been eaten, and though they'd just been through a town, no one had thought to pick anything up. "Now give them a hand. I want to have dinner ready by the time the sun hits the peaks."

After an hour of gathering materials, arguing with Demir and Iscah about the proper way to light a fire and if the bedrolls had been placed too close, and helping Varek cut up a sack of potatoes, onions, and other various vegetables, the sun had indeed begun to creep behind the peaks and turn the sky. Thankfully, a pot of soup boiled over the flames.

Iscah leaned against the carriage. The door was open. The setting sun had warmed the carriage enough for Carissa to request the door be left open for air, but she herself had not moved. "Carissa, come eat. I'll move your things to a table where we can both continue to work once we're fed."

A quiet, muttered response turned the corners of Iscah's mouth down. "I'm not asking you. We need food if we're going to keep working."

"She's been alone for too long," Aleksander said, spooning some of the soup into a bowl for himself. Iscah's face tilted in his direction and he shrugged. "When she works alone for too long, she gets really deep into it and it's hard to get her to do anything else."

"Will you help me then?" Iscah said, tossing a hand in the direction of the princess still situated in the carriage.

With a sigh, Aleksander placed his soup on a rock and brushed his hands on his thighs, striding forward and doing his best to remember what Janek would always do to get her out of these fixated states.

As he rounded the door and his eyes fell on her, his heart sank. An hour or two had gone by, that was all, yet it looked as though she'd been awake and at work for days. The braided crown she'd tied her hair into that morning was almost entirely loosened, hair falling around her face and her neck in frizzy tendrils. The bags beneath her eyes were nothing compared to the red within them. He swore he could hear her eyelids click when she blinked. And worst of all, her cheeks—they were flushed redder than he'd ever seen.

"Carissa." His voice was low, warning. "Put aside the board. We're getting food."

"I'm not done, Aleksander," she muttered, fingers playing over the Aramerk, tapping the gems and tracing the swirls. Her eyes rolled back and her face drained of color.

His whole body ran as cold as death.

"Oh Mother!" Iscah gasped, lurching forward. "Carissa!"

"Stop." Aleksander just barely stopped her, hands on her shoulders, guiding her away from the carriage. "She's having a vision, but...she's gonna be fine. I... Iscah, I think the Aramerk is working." He swallowed hard. Carissa had visions all the time, but she never looked like this—so corpse-like, so drained. She was channeling her magic better, that much was for sure. But for mages it was a give-and-take.

His heart thudded in his ribcage. Carissa hadn't given anything, not that he knew of. That only meant disaster.

If mages did not give, then the Flow—magic itself, the living, breathing thing it was—would take.

What was he going to do? He never knew how to stop visions, no one did. He had to get that focus away from her, but would she even let him?

If only Janek were here. Or Caoimhe. Even Saoirse. Just someone who knew more about Carissa and magic than he did.

"I need to deal with this," he finally said.

And then, he felt it. That dark, curling chill at the base of his skull.

No.

Doing everything in his power to ignore it, Aleksander nearly tripped over his own feet to get back to her, and as he planted one knee on the bottom of the carriage, her eyes rolled back, her face bright red. A rattling inhale sent her coughing.

"Carissa," he crooned, reaching for the board. It slid from her fingers with ease. With it went the Aramerk. "It's time to rest, Carissa. Janek says it's time to rest."

Those bloodshot eyes caught his and she frowned. "I'm not dumb, Aleksander. I know he's not here."

"Doesn't matter that he told me to make sure you rest and take care of yourself," he shot back, reaching under her arms in an attempt to carry her out of the carriage.

"I'm. Not. Done," she hissed.

There was no strength in her arms as she tried to push him away.

"Yes, you are."

Backing out of the carriage, Iscah stood by to catch and support Carissa on her descent. She huffed out a strong curse as her feet stumbled in the grass, but nonetheless walked in the direction they led her.

"Is she alright?" Demir shouted. He stood at the edge of brush and trees. At the sight of Carissa's fall, the firewood he'd held tumbled into the brush and he launched a few feet off the ground to soar over to the group.

"She's exhausted," Aleksander said. "Too many visions, I think. I...I don't..."

"Soup."

Varek pressed a bowl into his hand with nothing but the one word.

Aleksander nodded his thanks and spooned some of it up to her lips. "Eat, Carissa."

Begrudgingly, she opened her mouth. Carrots crunched between her teeth and the tension fell from her shoulders. Shaking hands rose to take the bowl from him. "I can feed myself, thank you," she muttered. After a few more bites, she glanced at those assembled around her and frowned. "Go, I'm fine."

Varek was the first to back off, retreating to the other side of the fire and settling down to have his own bowl of soup. Iscah lingered, but with Demir's gentle arm around her, she allowed herself to be led off to her own bedroll beside his. The two sat, and Aleksander overheard her apologizing for Carissa's state.

"How many visions did you have?" The moment he asked it, he wished he hadn't.

She chewed lazily, swallowed, lifted the bowl to drink some broth, and sighed. "Eight."

In an instant the world fell away. All that was there was Carissa, Aleksander, and the yawning, humming void that opened around them.

Aleksander's breath became shallow and slow.

"Eight." He repeated the word as if that would somehow make it better. Make it make more sense. "In a few hours."

Carissa nodded. "The Aramerk works. I don't know how she made it, but it works. And I..." A sharp sigh. Her hand stopped stirring the spoon through the broth and vegetables, and she shook her head. "All I see, whenever I see anything, is...the same as I've always seen. Just slightly different. Every time." A bitter laugh. "And each time I hope there will be a great difference. Like it was a cruel joke, or...something. I kept going back in, sure the next vision would be more...clear. But none of them were."

The spoon scraped the bottom of the bowl and she brought more soup to her mouth.

He swallowed hard. "What do you see?"

"No." She shook her head all too quickly. "No, I'm not going there."

For the first time Aleksander could remember, he felt rage blooming behind his sternum. Not that anger that makes you want to scream or hit a wall, but the kind of absolute rage that makes your entire world go still. The kind that makes you wish you could burn it all down and start it over.

"That's it, I'm *done* with this, Carissa," he snapped.

Carissa blinked up at him, seemingly as stunned as he was.

All down his arms, his chest, even into his legs, Aleksander felt himself shaking. "Stop telling me you don't want to go there, you don't want to talk about it. If you keep doing this on your own, you may die. You came with us to *help* us, and so far all you're doing is isolating yourself and refusing to share your visions." His voice was rising now, getting louder than he ever dared to get. "I understand you don't like what you see, Car, but guess what, they're the only thing we have that gives us an edge up on this whole situation. So what—the mountains crumble, Varek turns into a demon, any of us dies... Who cares if what you see scares you! I think it's meant to." At this he leaned towards her, hands curled into fists on the packed grass. "You're our warning system from Tulathne Herself. She blessed you with this power, and you're spitting in her face by refusing to use it to help us. This is not something you have to do alone. It's not something you're even *supposed* to do alone! So cut the crap, get over your fear, and *tell me what you saw.*"

Her lip trembled, but at least she spoke. "If I say it, that makes it real."

"You *seeing* it makes it real." By the way her demeanor changed, Aleksander was well aware that this was serious, that it truly bothered her, deep in her core, to even see—much less how much it would disturb her to talk about. Still, he couldn't stop himself from pressing her further. "What. Did. You. See?"

A deep, long inhale. Her breath held as she placed the soup on the ground before her and folded her hands in her lap. Carissa did not look at Aleksander as she spoke.

"It starts as it did before. You and the five spirits, though most of them have faces now." Thin, stained fingers fiddled with the hem of her gown. "We are in a field. The Scourge's forces around us—the homunculi, mainly. And...one by one I watch as the flesh strips off our bones and joins them. I *see* it, Aleksander." Her eyes flicked up to his, shining with tears. "I watch as we are all flayed and turned into one of *them.*"

The crackling of the fire was the only thing punctuating her silence.

"In some of the visions you join us, getting flayed and turned into a homunculi, screaming all the while," she continued, looking back down at her hands. "But sometimes, like with this last vision..." She fanned out trembling fingers on her knees. Her laugh was humorless. Scared. "I have the *privilege* to watch as every corner of Zekhar is scorched. And do you want to know the real thing I don't want to see happen? The real reason I don't talk about this?"

Aleksander nodded.

He immediately wished he could take it back.

"As my country is burning and my people are screaming, I see the Scourge standing above it all." Her eyes flitted up, burning with rage and fear. "With *you*."

Chapter

TWENTY ONE

CARISSA'S WORDS HUNG IN THE AIR like smoke. The chill had not left Aleksander, and in the silence that followed the end of her statement, it only deepened its hold into his bones, along his spine, curling into his jaw and cheekbones. Around them, the field and the forest beyond were loud, but in that moment it was all as though Aleksander was hearing it through cotton. None of their companions had reacted.

And all she did was fix him with a stare and a furious snarl. "How's that for helping you with my gift?" She spit out the last word as though it, in and of itself, was poisonous.

He shook his head. "I...I don't know what to say."

"Ha, that's interesting, considering you had so much to say before I told you that most of my visions end with you either dying gruesomely or serving the Scourge." She turned away abruptly, picked up her bowl, and resumed eating. "Pardon me for hoping that the next vision will be better, that it will give me hope for us."

After that, she didn't move. Carissa just sat, hunched over her bowl on her bedroll, slowly eating and doing her best to slow her breathing.

Aleksander scooted back. She was done talking to him, that much was clear. He knew if he tried again, she'd probably grab

Aoife from his hip and slice his head off herself. But he couldn't just leave her. Was he the cause of this pain, yes, but...

No. This wasn't about his feelings. She needed space.

He stood, finally looking over at the others. Iscah's eyes were large. It crossed Aleksander's mind that she'd never seen Carissa have a vision before, much less share that it was one of immense tragedy. She leaned into Demir, a shaky hand over her lips. His face was drawn as he held her, lips pressed to the top of her head, despite the fact that his eyes were fixed on some place very, very far away. His wings twitched, and he blinked, glancing up at Aleksander.

"I'm...I'm not going to betray you," he whispered, his throat tightening. "I...I'd never."

Demir opened his mouth to speak, and closed it.

"Of course you wouldn't," Varek said quietly. "You're on the side of Tulathne. You're her son."

There was something in his tone that jabbed right in the tender spot of Aleksander's chest. "I *am*."

Varek's eyebrows raised. "Kid, I'm being serious. You've been raised for this your whole life. You're not going to side with the Scourge. We know that."

"Do you?" Aleksander asked, stepping closer. "Because the way that Demir doesn't want to look at me doesn't offer much comfort or hope." A weight settled in his stomach. The cold deepened, like fingers caressing his lungs, his stomach, his legs, spreading ice and nausea through his body.

That could not be his future.

"Eat some soup," Varek said, holding out a bowl. "We'll... we'll discuss this more in the morning. It doesn't change our plans. We're continuing to patrol the land, meet with Duke Elmere, and when you and the princess are feeling better, we're going to find and kill the sorcerer who started this."

Aleksander nodded, his arms and legs feeling like lead.

The bowl still extended, he took it and sat.

"Who knows?" he said softly. "Visions aren't an exact science."

Varek shook his head. "No, they're not."

Spooning the soup slowly into his mouth, Aleksander grabbed that notion with two hands and tucked it close to his core.

Visions aren't exact, he repeated over and over in his mind. *Visions are wrong all the time.*

The broth was warm as it slid down his throat.

These ones had to be.

THE STARS ABOVE HIM REALLY proved to test his knowledge of the constellations. After years of studying, of being so sure he knew exactly what they were and where they were, he found himself wishing he had Lenore's heavy, dusty, ink-stained astronomy book to double check his guesses. One of them, however, stood out. One he'd loved since he was a kid. There was no reason, none at least that he knew, but it was the one the he always found. And it brought such comfort to him whenever he did find it.

Now, it sat right above him. The most notable element of it was a cross of five stars, supposedly right were the constellation's head was. The Weaver, they called her. A bundle of stars that depicted a woman sitting at a loom. Creator of fates, controller of destinies. So entwined with them, in fact, that it was said stars joined and left the arrangement to herald coming events.

On this night, her appearance comforted Aleksander very little. After such a drastic confession from Carissa that her visions of this whole ordeal often ended with him dead or a traitor, his fate didn't seem so clear.

Usually, the Weaver reminded him that he'd be okay. It was in the Sword's destiny to survive, to conquer, to be a hero.

But maybe that was just the past Swords.

Was fate tied to a soul? Or just the lifetime the soul was placed into?

Around him, his companions slept. Iscah had bundled up with her head on Demir's lap, still distraught over what her creation had wrought. Varek himself had even knelt before her and reminded her that the Flow is volatile and greedy. It's why their people never wield it, even though they could. They just find ways to manage it. And she was indeed skilled in managing and controlling it.

She'd drifted off while occasionally muttering her apologies, her prayers to the Mother for forgiveness. They were answered by Demir's soft voice telling her over and over that what Carissa saw was not her fault. He'd fallen asleep leaning against the carriage wheel, fingers combing through Iscah's hair as she slept fitfully on his lap.

Blankets and grass rustled, snapping Aleksander's gaze from the twinkling tapestry overhead.

Aoife was already out of her sheath. He'd kept her out and at his side should anything truly go wrong. There was too much at stake, too many people to protect now. But as he raised the blade and pushed himself off of the rock he'd perched on, all he found was Carissa, rising from her bedroll and inching her way to the carriage.

"Go back to sleep," he said.

She froze, back to him, hands in tight, nervous fists at her side as though it was her father who had caught her sneaking out of the castle instead of a boy stopping her from destroying herself further. "I'm fine," she whispered. Her voice was tired, slow. "I just wanted to check my notes."

"You can check your notes in the morning." Aleksander's boots hit grass. "You need sleep."

Neither of them moved.

Around them, crickets chirped.

"Do you seriously think I'll betray you?"

He *hated* the way his voice broke. But it couldn't be helped. This was Carissa. She'd seen him train from the time he was five years old, witnessed his commitment and care firsthand. Witnessed his piety.

And yet, a few visions of him in a less-than-preferred situation, and she was entirely ready to point fingers and claim he was going to be a cause in the downfall and destruction of their homeland.

"Carissa."

"I don't know, Aleksander," she said softly. "I don't know."

"You know me," he hissed. "How can you truly look at me like this and tell me that you aren't sure whether I'll stay loyal to you, to Tulathne?"

At this, she turned. Exhaustion and whatever kind of magic-poisoning she'd undergone aside, she was the embodiment of desperation. Fingers twitching at her sides, brows knit together, mouth hanging open in a grimacing sob, she shook her head as tears rolled down her cheeks. "I can't. That's the problem, Aleksander. You're family. I can't say you'll betray us. I can hardly bring myself to remember the visions that suggest you will. But I've seen them, and I can't discount them."

In six long strides, he pulled her into a hug.

Her arms wrapped around him and she hung there on his shoulder, choking on her sobs.

"It won't happen," he said softly. "I won't let it."

"I can't lose you." Her tears soaked his shoulder, but he didn't let go. "I can't let that happen."

"It won't," he repeated.

And they stood there for a long moment, holding one another, crying. Comfort ran from his lips on a loop, reassuring Carissa that the Aleksander she knew, the Aleksander she grew up with, would never do such a thing. There had to be another explanation. Mother Saoirse herself said visions and prophecies have multiple interpretations. They just needed to find the right one.

After a while, Carissa took a deep breath and unhooked her fingers from his ribs, his shoulder. Sloppy hands swiped at her cheeks to dry her tears. "I'm...I'm going to go to bed," she said.

He nodded. "I think that's a good idea."

Together they hobbled back to her bedroll. She lay down, and

Aleksander lifted her blanket up over her shuddering body, tucking it around her shoulders and under her chin. As he rose to go, she caught his hand.

"Stay, please. For a minute."

A light tug down, and he knelt before her.

Weary eyes drifted up to his. Her lip quivered, warning of a new flood of tears. "I'm sorry," she croaked.

"Hey." He smoothed back her hair from her face, smiling as softly as he could, ignoring the thundering panic in his chest. "Everything is going to be okay."

She nodded, pulling his hand into her chest and closing her eyes.

Aleksander did her best to lay beside her, part of him feeling guilty for taking the space between her and the fire, but she was the one who had pulled him there in the first place. Finding a place to fit his head on the mat, he let his eyes flutter closed momentarily.

Soon, her breathing slowed, deepened. He wiggled his fingers free of hers, pressing a kiss to her temple.

It was strange, this reversal of roles.

He couldn't count all the times he'd been sick, injured, woken by a nightmare, or anything else of the sort where Carissa had stayed by his bed until he slept, holding his hand and stroking his hair. Her mother was *her* mother, not his. As much as Queen Lenore loved him and treated him like a son, there was a distance there he never understood, nor did she ever attempt to close. Carissa didn't even have to be asked before she filled that role for him.

Her eyelashes fluttered as she fell into a deeper sleep, and he walked over to Varek, kicking his boot.

A jolt and a grunt, and his eyes fluttered open to fix Aleksander with an annoyed stare.

"Watch change."

◊✳◊

C ARISSA DID NOT USE THE Aramerk the next day. Or the day after, as they continued their trek to their third stop, Lord Elmere's estate. Instead, her and Iscah talked, she rested, and there was even one time where she'd asked if she could try running alongside the carriage like Varek did on occasion. It was quite the sight to watch her tie up her gown, which by this point had a muddied hem and more than its fair share of sweat stains, and huff along behind the carriage as Bunc drove at a terribly slow pace.

After a few minutes, she called for him to stop, and she got back inside.

It was a true relief for Aleksander to see her acting normal again. She talked about how she was looking forward to the winter solstice, which was now only in a handful of months, and how excited she was for all of them to come. Of course she would have to check with her mother that there was room on the guest list for all of them, but they were all allies in the biggest conflict to grace her parents' rule. Even as far back as five generations, there had never been an incident quite like this, so she was sure they'd all be able to make room for them.

On the third day, most conversation had died down, and Aleksander was sore after training with Varek for hours that morning. The entire carriage shook as he threw himself onto a seat, and then shook again as Varek did the same beside him.

And there they all sat, starting their own private conversations amongst one another, glancing out the window, leaning their heads against the walls. Varek spent most of his time going over his notes for Aleksander, and Aleksander spent most of his time nodding along absently to whatever the man said, occasionally throwing in a "you're right," or an "understood."

Aleksander had to bite back a sigh when Varek reached the end of his very lengthy critique and the carriage was once again thrust into blissful silence.

Iscah scrunched her nose after a while. "I hope we get where we're going soon, or we at least find a town or a spring. I think we're all getting just a touch too ripe."

"That's a very nice way of telling us we stink, Iscah, thank you," Aleksander sighed.

"I'm not saying you *stink*," she said, "I just said I think we *all* stink a little." Her lips darted into a smile before she pressed them together and made a soft, repetitive popping sound, gazing around the space as though it was new to her.

Aleksander, personally, could not wait to never see the inside of this cart again.

"Is it too much to ask you to open a window?" Iscah finally said.

Varek obliged, popping the glass pane out and sliding it up into the ceiling. Fresh air blew through the car as the carriage rumbled along. Iscah took a long moment to savor it, relaxing back in her seat and allowing her eyes to drift shut.

She sat like that for a while, still as the carriage rumbled on, until her brows slowly drifted together, ears twitching as her eyes opened. "Do you smell that?" she asked, half crawling over Carissa to get to the window.

"No," Aleksander said, shifting just enough to have a more unobstructed view of the window.

A breeze blew in. Everyone in the carriage breathed deeply, glancing between one another, but there was nothing notable. It was fresh, clean, and warm like late summer air was, but—

Wait.

Aleksander's throat tightened as he inhaled again.

There *was* something. It was a thick scent, mostly obscured by the warmth of wildflowers in the sun, but it was there.

"Smoke," Varek said, opening the door and leaning out. "Demir!" he called.

The shadow circled and dropped low—just past Varek's head, Aleksander could see feathers come into view as Demir kept pace alongside the carriage. "Find out what it is." The door snapped shut and Varek nodded towards Aleksander and Iscah. "Get yourselves ready. We don't know what we're coming up on."

Even over rocks, the carriage didn't slow. Demir's shadow looped down, hovering by the driver, and then taking off again. The carriage lurched to a stop and Bunc knocked on the roof. "Everyone out!" he called.

Varek's were the first pair of boots to hit the grass, followed quickly by Carissa's, Iscah's, and Aleksander's.

As the Sword poked his head out of the door, the smell grew tenfold. Not only was it smoke. It was the stench of burned fabric, burned hair...burned meat. Those already on the road stood stock-still, gazing out ahead. Demir swooped down on the far end of the group just as Aleksander passed the door.

All the air left his lungs.

Before them, only a mile or so down the road, was a town.

Rather, it was the charred, smoldering bones of what *used* to be a town.

Chapter
TWENTY TWO

ALEKSANDER'S FEET MOVED BEFORE HE KNEW what he was doing. He shoved aside Carissa, Iscah—anyone who got in his way, and sprinted at full bore towards the burnt ruins. Shouts echoed behind him, overlapping calls for him to stop, come back, you'll hurt yourself, it's too far. And they were right. It was far. Moments into his run, his lungs began to seize and burn. His gasping, hitching breath blurred his vision as the strange mix of hyperventilation and oxygen-deprivation muddled his brain. Still, he ran.

There wasn't a great pyre of smoke going up. There wasn't an inferno engulfing the buildings. Not anymore, at least.

But the air was thick with what was left.

His foot caught on nothing and he stumbled forward, catching a large gulp of air that sent him into a choking, coughing fit. Aleksander forced his tongue to the roof of his mouth, exerting every ounce of control he had over his body to breathe steadily in and out his nose. Between the gasps and panicked, racing thoughts, he prayed to Tulathne, the Kutsalyot, the Mother—anyone who would listen, that he could get there before he collapsed.

Vision blurred and torso convulsing, he dropped to the earth.

The dusty, rocky road cut into his fingers, his palms, his knees.

A high-pitched whine sounded in his ears as he coughed. Blinking up at the town through tears... It was still so far. Two arms circled beneath his torso and he lifted entirely off the ground. A strong wind lapped at his cheeks, and through the panic, he realized he was flying.

Demir.

When the soldier set him down gently on the dirt, a pot just starting to give off steam was placed before him. Soft, firm hands held the sides of his head over the steam and a blanket was placed over his head, still smelling of dirt and smoke from the night before.

After a few inhales, his lungs shuddered back to their normal pace. His throat burned. But he was okay.

A firm hand rubbed circles on his back, singing lightly in a language he'd never heard, but elements of it reminded him of Ölmesuz slang Varek had thrown around. The melody rose and lowered, fluttered around certain notes, and altogether served to help him slow his breathing further. Something about it was like a lullaby. Were it not the middle of the day and were he not about to tip right into a pot of hot water, he would have given in and let it lull him to sleep.

"We can't just go around it. What if there are people who need help?" he heard Carissa argue.

"That town has been smoldering for days. You can tell by the smell." Varek, of course. "And we don't have enough supplies to help people even if there were any left."

"You can't be sure everyone is gone or dead."

"Like *ghen* I can," he snapped.

"We need to go," croaked Aleksander, lifting the blanket off his head and sitting up. Iscah's hand rested on his back, pressing slightly to encourage him to bend over and go back under the blanket. Aleksander chose to ignore it.

Carissa's face was pale, but for once it was not due to her exhaustion. Her hands shook at the sides of her dress, fingers carding through the folds and shuffling fabric against itself in a nervous tic he'd only seen her do a few times before—one of them being right before her wedding.

Varek's, on the other hand, was stone. Entirely unreadable, completely unchangeable.

"If not to help people," he continued, staring pointedly at the towering statue, "then to see whether it was caused by the Scourge or not. To see if we can learn things—" He broke off into coughs.

"That's why you ran?" Varek lifted a brow. "To see if the *Scourge* did it, not because—"

"I don't know why I ran, but that's not what we're talking about." He bowed his face over the pot and breathed in more steam. Once the catch in his throat felt sufficiently calmed, he sat up. "We need to go. If there're people there, we can help them and they may be able to give us the information we need—on how it started. And if not, then we just get to look for it ourselves."

A flare rose in his companion's eyes. Varek tensed his jaw... and sighed a deep, resolved sigh. "Fine. Get back in the carriage."

Aleksander got the seat by the window as everyone who was not flying or driving piled back in. It was open, and despite the enduring tightness in his lungs made worse from the smoke, his head hung out the window, hair flapping in the breeze around his forehead and against his cheekbones.

The ruins slowly drew close. When the two beautiful bays pulling their coach stepped onto the charred cobblestone, Bunc's quiet, fervent pleas for them to relax floated to Aleksander.

Varek was right. There was no way anyone was still here.

The horses stuttered back. Whinnies and stomping hooves pierced the air. The mares tossed their heads, trying to create distance between themselves and whatever horrors had taken place in the village.

"This is as far as they'll go," Bunc shouted. "If you wanna go in, you'll have to go on foot. I'm not stressing my girls out with this."

Aleksander nearly fell out of the door with the speed he opened it. But once his boots hit the road, stepping into a pile of ash, total control of his body vanished; he stood, petrified as the houses, the shops, the...bodies.

Everything was destroyed.

The lingering scent of burning flesh accosted his senses. Aleksander did his best to block it out by raising a sleeve over his nose, but it didn't do much. The back of his neck tingled. That chill he had grown used to over the last couple of days spread to his fingers.

Instinctively, he reached for Aoife.

As if there was anything here to fight.

As if there was anything here at all.

"Oh gods," Iscah breathed, stepping into place beside him. The usually bright expression was gone in favor of one that seemed to mimic Aleksander's own. Her jaw hung slack, brows drawn ever so slightly together just so they started to form a crease between them. Her blinks were uneven, slow. After a moment, she shook her head and turned on her heel, surveying their surroundings. "This is...awful."

"This is why I didn't want to come here," Varek said, leaning on the carriage. His voice was quiet, reverent—almost tender—as he spoke. "Not only is it a waste of time to sift through rubble, I wanted to avoid"—his hand extended, gesturing around them —"this. No matter how many like it I've seen, it's never fun."

His eyes fixed on a stone beneath his foot. He gave it a kick and watched as it tumbled along the path, curving off towards...

Varek blew a breath from pursed lips, averting his gaze. "Mother's sake," he breathed.

Aleksander swallowed his nausea and turned away from the tangled, scorched corpse the rock had rolled towards. He didn't let himself look at the hands.

The tiny hands.

All these people...

"Why...? What was the point of this?" Carissa took measured steps forward, hitching her skirt up in her fists, surveying the ground, the collapsed wooden frames, the rubble. At one point, she leaned over a body half hidden beneath a collapsed market stall, studying it in the way one would study a rock or a flower. She looked as though she would, in this situation, benefit from a magnifying glass. But at the end of it, she rose, shook her head, and swiped at her eyes. "This is awful." Her fists clenched at her side. "We should have *been* here."

"Stop with that right now," Varek snapped. "We had no way of knowing. Blaming ourselves isn't going to solve anything and it's not going to undo this either."

Finally, Aleksander got his feet to work. His boots shuffled forward, dragging scuffs through the charcoal beneath him, bringing him further into the town.

Rubble fell—the sound nearly made him jump out of his skin —but instead of a creature appearing from inside the pile of destroyed wood and stone, a vulture tilted his bare head at him, as if to ask if the man wielding a sword was truly afraid of a mere carrion bird.

His arm relaxed; his grip on Aoife did not.

"We should go. The sooner we get to Lord Elmere's estate, the sooner we learn what he knows about this, the sooner we get the fifth spirit, the sooner we can plan our next moves." Carissa was already starting to pick her way back to Bunc and the horses and the safety half an inch of painted wood and padded seats afforded when Varek grabbed her arm.

Demir fluttered forward to stand between Varek and Aleksander, sword at the ready.

"I heard something," Iscah said. Her sabatons clanked along the scorched earth as she jogged to join them. The long, drooping ears, still adorned with all sorts of piercings, twitched.

"Me too." Varek's voice was low, almost so low Aleksander couldn't hear.

But there was something he could hear. Something everyone could hear, which was undoubtedly what Varek and Iscah picked up on prior.

Breathing.

Horrible, ragged, wheezing breathing.

But above that was movement. Things falling in the distance

to their…left? No, right. No—no, it *was* their left.

Aleksander spun, Aoife out in front of him.

"Fix your stance." The comment was so natural for Varek, he didn't even bother to call out to Aleksander beforehand, much less look at him as he said it.

Despite the annoyance brought on by the unsolicited advice, Aleksander obeyed. His frame locked, strong and prepared for whatever would come at them.

They wouldn't destroy a town just to create some homunculi, would they?

He shook the thought from his head. No, the sorcerer was awful, and they served the Scourge who was even more so, but even they wouldn't stoop to such a level.

The scuffling, rattling, and wheezing got louder. Closer. A shiver ran down Aleksander's spine.

Right?

A swish of a sword leaving a scabbard, and Varek strode forward to the doorway of a collapsed store, the sign still half there, if mostly burned away. The rest of it crumbled as he pushed it aside to clear a path.

If the tightness from running earlier had been inhibiting Aleksander's breathing, it didn't matter in this moment. He was holding his breath regardless.

For what seemed like eternity, Varek peered in to the ruin, taking a step, sword in front of him, looking to one side, looking to another. At once, he turned and stepped out, shaking his head. His brows were drawn low over his eyes, knit together in deep confusion. "I swore I heard something."

A shadow shifted atop the store.

Aleksander had a mere moment to shout his warning before it stumbled forward and fell from the eaves, right onto Varek.

"Homunculi! Above you!"

Chapter

TWENTY THREE

THE CREATURE CRASHED DOWN ONTO VAREK, letting out a wild, pained scream. Its bulging eyes tore around in its skull, searching for the creature it inadvertently used to break its fall.

With a shout, Varek shoved the thing off him and rolled to the side. He was already covered in thick black blood. "It's hurt!" he shouted.

Aleksander rushed forward as it stood, gnarled, clawed fingers scraping wildly through the air. That was when he saw the massive, oozing gash in its chest. It was deep. There was no way it was made by a sword. This was an axe wound. He'd seen one only once, when the palace woodcutter had slipped on a hot day and missed his mark, lodging the blade in his shin. Deep, shattering, and utterly improbable to heal. He'd made it—lost most of the use of his leg, but he made it.

This thing, with such a gash in its chest where Aleksander could see clearly the torn, pulsating bundle of meat that was its heart—there's no way it would live even if Varek hadn't swung his blade down a moment later and severed its head from its spindly neck.

Everyone stood still a moment. Varek frowned at his shirt, trying his best to brush off the ichor and only succeeding in staining his hands as well.

"We need to get to Duke Elmere," Carissa said. Her face was grave, determined. In this moment, she looked much like her mother during event planning or a council meeting. Nothing could dissuade her or throw her in any way. "*Now*."

The notion made Aleksander nearly smile. She was already becoming a queen, already so natural at taking charge and fixing awful situations.

But he didn't. Not only because of where they were or what they now knew was the cause of it. But because he didn't expect her to have to take on that role so soon.

"I..." Iscah tottered forward, pale complexion leaning towards green, "I want to collect some...samples. First. If that's alright, Your Highness."

"Make it quick," she said, straightening her back and turning to everyone. "Demir, scout a path. Make sure there are no more homunculi in the area. We leave as soon as you return."

He nodded, unsheathing his sword and rocketing into the sky. Dust and ash burst into a cloud around them. It settled slowly in the midday light.

Iscah knelt beside the homunculi, face screwed up into a pained grimace.

Aleksander was thankful she didn't mention how the skin on the face still held its color in varying shades of tan, brown, and gold. He was doing his best not to think of it even as his gaze ran over the bodies nearby.

Did this creature come from any of you?

She plucked a small knife from the small bag attached to her hip and got to work trimming off a few bits. It was slow work, especially since she stayed at arm's length from the creature. With a kick, it rolled onto its back, and Iscah gingerly sliced off part of what looked like a lung.

"*Min-fe hira!*" She screeched, pulling her hand back and giving it a strong shake.

"What's wrong?" Varek was by her side immediately.

"Nothing, but...*agh*, that smarts." Tears welled up beneath her fluttering lashes. "*Mother* and all the Kutsalyot."

A chuckle rumbled from Varek, despite the concern etched deep into his brow. "Watch your language, you still have something to lose."

Iscah shot him a glare before shaking her hand once more and retrieving the knife from the corpse. As the metal blade retreated from the gaping chest cavity, a blue spark snapped between it and the flesh. The creature jolted, and before Aleksander had time to move, Varek drove the point of his blade down into its heart. More purple-blue streaks edged up around his blade, and he pulled it free, the already deteriorating ventricles snapping off, taking the heart with it.

"What was that?" Carissa breathed.

Varek's eyes were narrow. They didn't move from the organ impaled on his sword. No more blue flashes were seen—at least, not by Aleksander—and the man shook his head. "No clue. You're the mage."

"And you're Ölmesuz," she countered.

He shot her a look before flinging his sword out to the side. With a graceless squelch, the heart flew off and into a pile of rubble. "Do I look like the magically inclined sort to you?"

"No, but you were the one who gave me the most advice on my notes when I started trying to figure out this whole ordeal. I figure the lightning coming from the homunculi would be related..." She trailed off, eyes growing wide. "Oh, *that's* how they do it."

Aleksander furrowed his brow. "How they do what?"

"They're manipulating the elements. *That's* how they get around the Flow's greed."

"So they're Rodzjiekim?" Iscah stood and wiped her blade off on a kerchief before stowing it in her hip bag. "That narrows it down, at least a little."

Carissa shook her head. "No, it doesn't. I've never seen— never even heard—about Rodzjiekim being able to control lightning. But *somehow* this sorcerer has been able to work around the greed of a spell by doing what the Rodzjiekim do."

She plucked the bundle of organs and tissue from Iscah's hands and nodded. "I'm going to go think about this. I'll...I'll figure something out."

Varek shook his head as he watched her go. "That woman doesn't know when to quit."

"No. But if she's right, this could be huge," Aleksander said. "Not just for what we're doing, but for magic as a whole. If a human figured out—"

"Figured out how to bypass the toll magic requires? To create a mockery of life and wield the Flow with no consequences?" The man's laugh was bitter. "You forget what my people learned from trying that."

Iscah nodded solemnly. "It's not meant to be an easy or accessible thing. We Ölmesuz were gifted that knowledge but it still brought..." She stopped, her head snapping to the left.

Varek followed raising his sword.

A deep, low snarl broke through the ruins.

Aoife was back in Aleksander's hand without a thought.

"Stay back, kid," Varek shifted his feet. "Leave them to us."

"No." Anger jolted through Aleksander. "I can fight, Varek."

"Not as fast as us. And it sounds like there's a lot of them."

Without another word, Aleksander bolted past them and around the bend of what seemed to have once been a clothier's. With a yell, he sliced Aoife up, diagonally across his form. Screams from the two homunculi echoed as he carved into their bodies with swing after swing, only for them to eventually drop and reveal five more.

Dread swept through him.

Before he even had time to react, gusts of wind blew past him on all sides, and when his eyes refocused on the scene, Varek and Iscah were driving cut after cut into their necks, their arms, their legs. Soon, they lay in a mostly still pile, with an occasional finger twitch and zap of energy from one body to another.

"How did we never notice that at the solstice?" Aleksander muttered.

An exhausted Varek shrugged his heaving shoulders. "How

should I know? I wasn't there."

Iscah's ears twitched, and she sheathed her sword. "I don't know what that was, but I keep hearing things."

Unease crawled up Aleksander's spine. It had been there since he set foot in the town, but now...

"Yeah," he breathed. "Yeah, we need to go."

Varek glanced around, an uneasy, self-satisfied smile on his face. "Told you it was a bad idea to stop here."

TWENTY FOUR

*T*HE REST OF THE JOURNEY TO Duke Elmere's estate and the city surrounding it known as Lauklin was had in complete silence. Demir had circled the town as Carissa commanded, reporting back accounts of two more homunculi—both horribly wounded, both near death, just as the first had been. Bunc had steered the horses around the ruins, and not even Demir deigned to fly. As the carriage rattled on, Aleksander could see the shadow cast by his wings on the road as he sat atop their coach.

Iscah thumbed the Aramerk, her gaze directed out the window. After Carissa had stopped using it, she'd returned it to the Crafter for safekeeping, in case there was a time when they would need it again. And now, the first time out of Iscah's pack in days, acting as a source of comfort, Carissa couldn't stop herself from glancing between the world beyond their windows to the small, golden disk flipping through her friend's hand.

Aleksander couldn't stop himself from glancing between the passing world outside and her. Whenever that thing was out, even if it was just moving from pocket to bag or bag to box, he'd grown accustomed to checking Carissa's behavior. Like any addiction, just knowing it was there was a temptation. Holding it was another level entirely. Frustration tugged at his neck. Varek was watching Carissa as nervously as he was. But Iscah did nothing to stop it, to stop her. Didn't she care? Regardless, he kept his mouth shut. Kept his eyes trained on the scenery. Counted the mile markers along the road, counted down the distance to Lauklin. And finally, the farms became more frequent, the pastures became closer until there were two shepherds in the same field, two houses within the same view out his window, then more, and more. There, in the distance, his heart swelled.

Atop a hill, overlooking a valley that led down to the sea, was Elmere's Keep. Its parapets topped with fluttering flags, the buttresses and stone glowing in the fading sunlight, it looked like a hall in heaven, ready to welcome the weary and downtrodden.

But one thought entered Aleksander's mind as he gazed about the castle's windows, a thought he had not allowed himself to dwell on and had at one point entirely forgotten to revisit.

He would get to see Genoise.

THE GROUP WAS MET WITH open arms by the duke's servants and guided to a hall filled with private baths. Upon entering and separating from the others, Aleksander conceded that Iscah was right—they all did stink. Days of travel, plus the awful blood that lingered on their tunics and soaked through Varek's had done a number on them. The hallway down to the baths was all polished limestone and candles flickering on elaborate silver sconces. Between the candles were heavy blue drapes, fringed with gold tassels, drawn back to show an open bathroom and tied shut to imply one in use.

Aleksander was guided through an open one, and inside the room was full of steam and the lovely scents of lavender, patchouli, and an herb he'd only seen once, grown in the mountains: posheica. It was a small, bushy herb similar to nettle. He figured there had been another name for it at some point, but seeing as anyone only ever got it from Rodzjiek healers who harvested it from the Pozhontecs, the Zekharyan name got lost to time and everyone called it by the Rodzjiek word. Its woody, sharp scent cut through the air. There was an edge to it that wasn't quite licorice and not quite mint, but somehow a mix of both.

Those smells along with the steaming water filling the in-ground bath was enough for Aleksander to drop his shoulders. They ached as he pulled his shirt over his head, folding it nicely though he was certain he wouldn't be wearing it after he got clean.

Soaps lined the edge of the bath—honey, oat, milk, lavender, citrus. He could have his pick of any scent he wanted, and he promptly chose honey.

Scrubbing it over his hair, over his skin, sloughing off weeks of dirt and sweat, there was a feeling of relief Aleksander had never experienced before. In all fairness, he'd never been so in need of a bath before.

Once he was clean, he did not hurry to leave. The warmth of the water smoothed the knots from his back, his arms, his hips. There last time he had been in a place like this was when he was back in Castle Brevindun, preparing to take his oath. Sure, they had baths there, but nothing nearly as luxurious as the ones drawing their water from the spring that ran up under this hill and over into the ocean. When he did finally get out, he found fresh clothes and a towel beside the door. They were from his pack—a burnt orange doublet and dark brown pants. Never the colors he chose, certainly not colors he thought he looked good in, but it had been over a week of traveling, maybe two. Aleksander feared he'd lost count. That, coupled with the sinking suspicion these were the only clean clothes he had left, brought a new form of weariness to his mind.

Varek was waiting in the hall as Aleksander stepped out from his bath. His hair, still wet and now visibly longer than when they'd first met, dripped with citrus-scented water. He too had seemingly been provided with a clean doublet. This the shade of ash, with thread the color of pomegranate skin weaving a star-adjacent pattern across his chest. "Good to see you're done then," Varek grunted, pushing himself off the wall. "Let's go eat already."

"Don't we have to meet with Duke Elmere?" Aleksander sounded much more nervous than he intended, but not seeing the duke meant not seeing Genoise—as well as not getting answers.

"We will. We're just not meeting our new addition yet. He's prepared us a meal in the smaller hall, then allowed us to take a reprieve for the evening. Carissa spoke with him briefly, and hearing our...trials, on the road here, and how long we've been traveling anyways, he decided it is best to let us rest." The man rolled his neck, eliciting a few cracks. "Can't say I'm not glad for it. What I wouldn't give to sit in that garden for an hour or two."

"You want to admire a garden?" Aleksander scoffed.

Varek shot him a begrudged glare. "Is it against the law for a man to enjoy the peace and comfort that nature offers?" he growled.

Aleksander's cheeks bloomed red. "I'm just... I... You don't seem like the garden type to me."

"And what type do I seem like?"

"Uh..." Aleksander racked his brain. "I don't know. Not the kind who enjoys flowers."

Varek sniffed and quickly put distance between Aleksander and himself.

"Sorry," Aleksander called, guilt and embarrassment swirling in his stomach. He didn't mean to upset the man. If anything, he'd only intended to talk to Varek the way Varek talked to him. Granted, he shouldn't be surprised that Varek reacted with annoyance. Aleksander hardly reacted positively to Varek's jabs.

He scuffed his boot along the sone and quietly followed. No words left his mouth. None even entered his mind.

The rest of their journey from the baths to the dining room was in silence, but there, at the table, along with pots of steaming soups, a large salad, and large carafes of wine and water, sat

Duke Elmere, his mother, the Dowager Duchess Elmere, and someone Aleksander had not prepared himself to see for another few months, not until the snow was thick on the ground and candles had been set upon every available surface.

Genoise rose from her chair as he entered, bowing her head graciously. Her dark ringlets were carefully pinned up and away from her face, decorated with diamond and pearl pins, not unlike the style Carissa used to wear frequently.

Before the butterflies in his stomach made him do something stupid, he placed a hand over his heart, bowing deeply. "My Lady Elmere. It is truly wonderful to see you," he said. His voice was much lower than usual. He cleared his throat and rose hurriedly to offer bows to her father and grandmother. "Duke Elmere, Dowager Duchess Elmere." His pulse fluttered in his throat, and as his hand rested atop Aoife, he became very aware of the heinous shade of orange his doublet was and how ill it must make him look. "Thank you for being so kind as to offer us a night of respite. We've had a long journey and—"

"My dear boy," the dowager said, inclining her head at him. "Please, take a seat. You mustn't recount your perilous journey whilst standing in the doorway." A withered hand reached forward, gesturing to the seat beside Carissa—the seat right across from Genoise. It hovered there, waiting.

"Oh." He glanced about, noting that Varek had already entered and was indulging himself in a very full glass of wine and a bowl of shrimp, cream, and potatoes. "Of course, my apologies."

The chair made a deafening screech as he pulled it out. His entire face flushed, as if it was not flushed already, and he uttered a quiet apology as he sat on the lush cushion. He filled his plate with breads, cheeses, and a few vegetables after a glance from Carissa before taking a cue from Varek and partaking in the shrimp and potato soup. It was indeed a rich, decadent meal, and after a few bites, Aleksander realized truly just how little he'd eaten over the last few days.

The Dowager Elmere, to his surprise, took over most of the

conversation. Between sips of wine and around mouthfuls of shrimp, she waved around a ring-encrusted hand, inquiring things about every person seated at the table. She first grilled Carissa on how her family was, how she was faring on this journey, what the plan was, and so on. Once she was satisfied,, she began to interview the other members of the group, working her way around the table.

"You." She waved her fork at Demir. Her eyes, black as polished onyx, narrowed. "How did a Mekartlim come to serve Zekhar?"

After a glance around the table and a sharp swallow that looked to hurt him, Demir launched into the explanation. Among his people, he was a skilled fighter, but his family was poor, and as Mekartlim have little to no power in Zekhar, if he wanted to honor his abilities he'd have to join the Zekharyan military. So he did. The dowager seemed oddly disappointed, as though she'd expected something more miraculous coming from the only man at the table with wings. No matter how many Mekartlim moved into the cities or traveled overhead, they were often treated as rare sights. Certainly, the dowager saw them as no less magical than the Orzei they honored and flew with, when in fact neither the people nor the eagles were anything more than what they seemed. Demir did well to humor her with the story of him flying with Defne. At that, the old woman's eyes lit up, wrinkled lips drawing into a wide smile.

When it was Iscah's turn, she graciously explained her position as a Crafter for the party.

Thin white brows drew together and deepened the wrinkles around her eyes. "Were there truly no others suitable in Duke Halkin's ranks that you had to settle for a Crafter?"

"Iscah is a talented Crafter, Lady Dowager," Demir countered, tossing a glance at Iscah. It did not escape Aleksander's notice, the way her cheeks grew pink at his kind defense. "And she's a skilled swordswoman. She bested Varek in their first match against one another, which even our own Champion has yet to do."

"That's because we often end in a draw. Most of our sessions are training, not actual sparring matches," Aleksander countered. "I'll unarm him one day."

"Oh, if you'd like to partake in more *true* sparring matches against me, by all means"—Varek's grin was nearly venomous —"let me know, your holiness, and I would be *glad* to arrange it."

TWENTY FIVE

IND BLEW THROUGH THE DINING HALL, ruffling the dowager's hair. She regarded it with a grimace and continued speaking with Iscah, who was more than happy to show her the Aramerk and explain how it was used—which drew great praise from the old woman. Aleksander's gaze consistently wandered across the table, where Genoise sat silently sipping her wine and taking small, dainty bites of her meal.

"Lovely meal," he said, only to instantly berate himself for how stupid he sounded. It wasn't as though *she* made it... Why was he directing the complement to her? She was eating it too. Of course she knew it was "lovely." And who was he to use a word like "lovely" to describe a meal?

Still, her eyes shifted up, the candlelight playing in them and making them sparkle. A slight smile shifted her lip behind her glass. "I'm glad you think so," she said, taking a sip of her wine before setting it back down. "We do have a very talented cook. I may have grown a bit tired of the same meals over and over, but if visitors enjoy them, that's all that matters."

"Trust me, these visitors truly do enjoy them."

Genoise smiled, glancing over at her grandmother, and then down at her plate. "Will you be here long, my lord Champion?"

"Just until tomorrow, I believe." A glance at Carissa enforced it with a nod. Aleksander looked quickly back at his plate as Carissa grinned at him, glancing between him and Genoise quickly and with such giddiness he thought she would burst and spew what she felt was happening.

It wasn't what was *actually* happening though, was it? They were friends, and yes, they only saw one another a few times a year, but...

But Carissa was right.

Aleksander felt lighter, happier around Genoise. His stomach flipped and turned, and his heart seemed to skip when she was near and... Oh goddess, he really did like her, didn't he?

His eyes flitted back up to her, sitting there across from him. The candles gilded her skin, made her hair look as though it was silk dyed the richest black possible, woven and piled atop her head. As if in affirmation, his stomach rolled, and not in a way that made him nauseous.

When her eyes met his once more, he blushed harder than he had ever previously.

"See," Carissa whispered, leaning over under the guise of serving herself more of the fruit piled on the table. "I knew it."

"This is only happening because *you're* making me feel awkward about it," he hissed.

Genoise's eyebrows raised ever so slightly in confusion, and Aleksander brushed it off with a laugh and a long, deep drink from his water—which caught in his throat and took his air so abruptly and he nearly spewed it across the table. He coughed into his arm, choking down the rest of the water that didn't wet his sleeve.

"Oh my," cried the dowager. "Your holiness, are you alright?"

Through heaving coughs and eyes blurred by tears, Aleksander nodded. "Just...fine," he choked out, trying desperately to gather himself. When he could breathe somewhat steadily, he lowered his sleeve and smiled a quick, pained smile. "Just down the wrong pipe, I believe."

The elderly woman nodded slowly. "Well, that's why we don't gulp our drinks now, isn't it?"

He nodded. "Yes, you're absolutely correct, madam."

She speared a shrimp, looking pleased with herself, and continued to chatter on with Varek, who was doing his best to avoid her questions.

"And where did you say you're from?"

"Everywhere," he answered gruffly, despite the smile on his face. He waved his wine glass through the air. "I've been wandering the earth so long, I forget where I was born. But what matters is that I'm here now, isn't that right?"

The dowager gave an unamused "hmph" and drained her goblet. A servant was there in moments, carafe in hand, filling it once more to the brim.

Lord Elmere was content listening in on conversations, and thus his plate was clear in no time. "Dessert and evening tea shall be brought to your suite," he declared, pushing himself back from the table. His chair too made that horrid screeching sound, but it did not seem nearly as loud or as awful as it did when it had been Aleksander's chair. "Please, do take your time this evening to enjoy the estate. We have lovely gardens, a library, and an observatory on the roof if anyone is interested in the science and magic of the cosmos. I must now take my leave." A deep bow to Carissa and Aleksander, nods to the rest of the party. "I trust you will find your way through well enough. I've duties to complete before our business tomorrow."

Carissa stood herself, wiping her mouth and placing the napkin beside her empty plate. "I shall take my leave as well. Sleep well, my friends, I'll see you in the morning."

After that, everyone left, one by one, until only Aleksander and Genoise were left. The dowager retired to her room with the help of a footman, though Genoise had offered her hand.

"No, no, you have company, my dear, and you're still eating. Stay," she'd said.

So Genoise had.

Aleksander didn't quite know what to do or say in the silence that stretched between them. Genoise's bowl was nearly empty, but she kept sliding her spoon along the sides and picking up small tastes of the sauce. Was she waiting for him to suggest something? To break the silence?

Or perhaps she just really liked the soup.

"Well," she said, abruptly breaking Aleksander's panicked wonderings about Genoise's opinion of the meal. She stood. Fine hands smoothed out the folds in her gown. The rich lavender fabric complemented nicely with the blue sapphire and pearl necklace she wore, bringing out every flush in her skin. She nodded. "I'll retire to my room, now."

Aleksander stood with her, his chair once again making that horrid sound. He grimaced, she jumped. "Sorry." The curve of his back and the hunch of his shoulders suddenly became very apparent to him, and his spine elicited a series of loud cracks as he snapped upright. "I can escort you, if you'd like?"

"Oh well—"

"Or if you'd prefer, we can take a walk about the garden or the library or the..." His words failed and he smiled. "It's just really good to see you, Genoise."

A smile passed over her lips as well. "It's nice to see you too, Aleksander."

"I'd like to talk, to...spend some time with you, if that's alright." His heart thundered in his chest. Goddess, why did he have to realize he liked her? Couldn't he have stayed perfectly oblivious to his own feelings, allowing their friendship to carry out normally? What was it with this sudden desire to spend time with her?

Her eyelashes fluttered. She hesitated.

She hesitated? Aleksander's heart stuttered a beat. *Is it not easy for her to just say yes?*

"I...I'd like to, my lord, but..."

'But.' Oh no.

She glanced around the room. "I've duties to attend to. And they are not the kind that need company." Her dress swished against the chair as she slid around it, beginning to walk down the long length of the table so that she might cross around the end and exit through the large, ornate doors currently situated behind Aleksander.

He matched her steps, walking with her. "I don't need to involve myself in your duties. I just thought that since we have time—since *I* have time, to relax, we might—"

"Aleksander," she bit, turning abruptly around the table to match him. Her eyes were stern, fixed.

What happened?

His brows drew together over his nose, lips parting as though he wanted to speak but nothing came.

With a sharp inhale, she shook her head. "I've enjoyed your company. You are truly the highlight of a solstice gathering. But this is my father's demesne. With my mother gone, I am the lady of this house. I have duties that cannot be waylaid by frolicking in gardens. That's saved for times when I am meant to be conversing with anyone and everyone. That's saved for solstices."

His heart sunk into his gut. "So you're saying I was just a distraction?"

"I'm saying that you were a welcome, wonderful element of a grand party. You let me escape for a moment. And trust me, the friendship we've garnered is not one I regret or despise. Only know that it stays there. It must." She swallowed hard. "You have your job, I have mine. And they cannot mix outside of the moments we steal at parties."

Whatever awful, pained, gnawing feeling had situated in his chest turned molten. "So we'll never be friends aside from when you're bored at a solstice?"

"Is that not what friendship is like for lords and ladies?" Genoise's smile was sad. It only served to make Aleksander feel worse. "You're the son of Tulathne. You of all people must know what it's like to want to form a true relationship with someone, but have...who you *are*...get in the way."

He straightened his spine even more. It pained his chest, his shoulders, the muscles between his shoulder blades. "Of course," he lied. "I understand." He didn't. He pressed a fist against his heart and bowed to her. "I'll take my leave of you, my lady."

When he rose, she was smiling at him that same, pained, sad

smile. "Goodnight, Aleksander."

"It's Sir Wythane. Or Champion Wythane. If you really want to get the point across, you could also try 'your holiness.'" His titles spewed from his lips, angry and hurt and much sharper than he intended to sound.

Genoise swallowed harshly. Her smile disappeared. "Aleksander, I—"

"Why so familiar?" he hissed. Teeth sunk into the inside of his cheek in an attempt to halt the angry, tearful burning behind his eyes. "People might think we're friends."

Her face contorted. Hurt. Desperate. "I didn't—"

"I'm not listening, my lady. You said it yourself, we were only friends at the solstice, and this, as I'm sure you're aware, is not a solstice," he snapped. "Goodnight, Lady Elmere."

Fury clenched along her jaw before she blinked, willing it away. Genoise leaned back; Aleksander hadn't noticed, but he'd been leaning towards her too. Now, they both stood tall as trees, as distant as peaks on a mountain.

"Then goodnight," she said, walking around him, "Sir Wythane."

Chapter

TWENTY SIX

THEY HAD A TELESCOPE IN THE observatory. It was mostly open air, with a small glass-domed room on the section of the roof that housed maps and books and other things one would easily lose to a rainstorm. Aleksander took his time leafing through star maps and old Ölmesuz books on the planets surrounding theirs before taking one out onto the terrace. It was a beautiful space. Duke Elmere hadn't been exaggerating when he'd boasted their observatory to be one of the most "stunning, thought-provoking places this side of the continent," a comment he'd made after running into a frustrated Aleksander who brushed aside the duke's concern with a quick confession for his desire to see the stars.

Aleksander's fingers rested deftly on the telescope. He glanced down at the map he'd placed on the table beside him, adjusted the gears, and peered through it.

There she was.

The Weaver.

With a deep sigh, he slowly shifted the telescope to the right. There, according to the map, should be a small, glowing, red dot. Caliphus, the Ölmesuz called it. A planet somewhere around their sun that sparkled with red and orange dust this time of year. His eye scanned through inky night, passing small pricks of light from other stars—there.

"Huh," he muttered. It was bright. He could nearly make out the swirling bands of red and orange and gold through the lens.

To Aleksander, the planet appeared like a polished orb of red jasper, the kind the priestesses wore in some of their circlets. A stone of balance, of courage. A perfect gem for the women worshipping the goddess of those things.

A shiver went down Aleksander's spine, and he paused.

Tulathne? Was She here, as he stared at a planet resembling a stone sacred to Her, finally reminding him that he's not alone in this?

The words that circled his mind hit him like a weight. He had been feeling alone. How utterly silly, to feel alone when surrounded by Carissa, Iscah, Varek, and Demir. And Bunc. He'd not been alone since the beginning...so why did this sudden sensation of a presence feel so comforting, as if he'd been missing something for much too long?

"Good evening, my lady," he muttered. "I'm sorry I've been so distant from you for so long. I'm sorry if you distanced yourself for any reason brought on by my actions, though I'm not sure what they are." A deep sigh. The wind shifted around him, and he drew his face away from the eyepiece of the telescope, staring at the Weaver and the small red dot beside her. "I hope you're able to continue to guide me, through all this. And keep me devoted to you."

A movement out of the corner of his eye startled him and he bumped the telescope, knocking it forward and nearly smashing its glass on the stone of the roof.

"I'm so sorry!" The voice was loud, right beside him as another pair of hands gripped the stand and helped him pull it upright.

Aleksander launched himself to the side, banging his hip unceremoniously against the table and scattering the various paperweights of stone, carved wood, and ornate gold that he'd placed on the corners of the map. The parchment lifted up, nearly fluttering away on the wind.

"Oh gods!" The intruder burst forward, hands outstretched, fumbling with Aleksander to regain the map. Long, sturdy fingers grabbed the edge of the aged paper and brought it back to the table. The figure leaned in front of Aleksander, recovering the paperweights and sending him stumbling back. His heel caught the lip of a stone and he fell onto his back with a loud smack.

The wind flew out of him in a tight, agonized groan.

"Wow, I just keep making tonight worse and worse for you, don't I?"

Aleksander looked up. This voice was certainly not one he'd heard before. It was bright, not quite high-pitched but not nearly low enough to be a man's. Her tone sat right in the middle, sounding like temple bells on a summer evening, warm and rich and clear. A hand extended, gripping his and pulling him once more to his feet. "Again," she said, "I'm so terribly sorry."

He pressed a hand to his chest, breathing as deeply as he could, and finally took a moment to see who it was that had caused him such pain by attempting to help him. Dark eyes met his in the firelight, and for a moment, he wondered if it was Genoise, come to apologize. Not that he would accept it. The few embers of betrayal fanned in his chest. But upon taking note that she stood a few inches taller than him with long braided hair flickering dark shades of copper, brown, and red in the light of a nearby candelabra, they faded.

Of course it was not Genoise.

She had made her position clear.

He supposed the presence he felt wasn't Tulathne then, but this girl.

Sharp features made soft by a full-lipped smile and round, long nose took him by surprise. Thick lashes mostly shadowed her eyes. Brows clenched together at the center of her forehead made them even darker. "Are you alright? I really didn't mean to startle you."

Aleksander coughed sharply, taking a step back from the girl. "I'm fine."

As though she realized what she was doing, she moved aside, gesturing for him to take up his place by the telescope once more. "All yours," she said.

Slowly, eyes on her, he shifted back into position.

"What are you looking at?" she asked, leaning forward, peering over his shoulder and glancing at the map on the table.

"Caliphus," he said. "And the Weaver."

Those full lips pursed, and she nodded. "Ah yes. Caliphus."

"You don't know what Caliphus is, do you?" Aleksander asked with a raised eyebrow.

Her dark gaze dipped to the map. A finger jutted out to point. "It's that. Right there."

Aleksander chuckled, placing his eye back on the viewfinder of the telescope and adjusting it so the planet was once more in view. "Here," he said, stepping aside.

She took his place, pressing her eye to the viewfinder.

He cocked his head to the side, taking in all he could of this strange newcomer. Her hair was loosely pulled back into a thick braid that ended just above her hips, loose wisps coming loose fluttering in the evening breeze. A strong arm reached forward, covered mostly by the sleeve of a flowing white gown, to steady the telescope. "Do you come up here a lot?" he asked.

She shrugged, adjusting the lens. "Often enough. I like looking at the stars. Never pulled out a map before though." A long, relaxed breath drifted from her mouth. "Gods, that's pretty."

"Isn't it?" He turned his attention back up to the sky. "Only glows like this a few times a year. Lucky I was here, else you'd miss seeing it."

"Oh, I'd see it, just not through this. I always worry I'll break it." She stood up, dragging a hand beneath the eye she'd looked through the scope with and down her cheek. She turned to him, smiling. That same hand extended. "I'm Elspeth."

"Aleksander." He took her hand and shook. Those long, elegant fingers that had draped over the dials with such delicacy moments before wrapped around his hand with frightening strength. "What brings you to Elmere's Keep?"

A thick eyebrow raised. "I could ask you the same thing." A finger hooked around the shoulder of his doublet, tugging lightly. "This is fancy wear. What are you, a lord's son?"

He laughed. "Sort of." The moment the words left his mouth, he wondered why he didn't tell her the truth. It wasn't as though she wouldn't know who he was if he told her.

No, there was something else.

Maybe it was the fact that he'd just lost the ability to have moments like this with Genoise. But Elspeth, so far, hadn't given any indication that she knew who he was. Which meant he didn't need to perform, live up to, or awfully fail to meet whatever expectations she'd have for the Sword. Aleksander leaned on the parapet beside the telescope and crossed his arms, tilting his head to the side and allowing a comfortable, genuine smile to part his lips.

"You didn't answer my question though." He nodded towards her. "What brings you here?"

She answered his grin with one of her own, wide and daring. "Oh, like I said, I like looking at the stars."

"Are you the daughter of a lord then?" A glance at her dress, and he noticed for the first time that what he'd first assumed was a loose, flowing gown was, in fact, her nightclothes. His cheeks burned, and he immediately averted his eyes back up to her face.

Her answering laugh echoed off the roof, like a clap of thunder over the mountains. "No, no. Nothing of the sort."

"A servant then?"

She shrugged. "I suppose that's one word you *could* use to describe me. I was born to a mother who had no way to care for me, and so she dumped me off in Lauklin as soon as I was old enough to not need her. Got taken in by a family working for the Elmere estate, and now I do the same."

The night air swirled around them, filling the silence with the warmth of late summer and the chirping of crickets. Her gaze swept out over the town, and when she met Aleksander's eyes again, he swore the stars themselves were singing in the darkness.

"My family gave me up at a young age too," he said. "Sent me to... Well, they sent me where they sent me. Doesn't matter. But I've been training since I was five to be a swordsman. So like I said, may be in fancy clothes, but I'm not *exactly* a lord's son."

Those dark eyes scanned his face, thick lashes fluttering. A satisfied smile turned just the edge of her lip, and she directed her view back out to the night sky. It made his heart skip. It almost felt as though it was trying to lean out of his chest to get a better look at her.

"I'm here to watch the stars. That's my honest reason. No matter where you go in Zekhar, they're always the same. Their stories are fun too, but I didn't learn them until I got older. I used to look at whatever stars I wanted and come up with names for them. I couldn't read for the longest time." An arm extended, pointing to a cluster that Aleksander immediately recognized as Liadain, Alesathne's wife who perished at the hand of the original Scourge. "That was always 'arrowhead' to me."

Aleksander snorted. "That's Liadain," he said, walking behind her to the book on the table and flipping through until he found the page on her. In the illustration, you could clearly see the drawing of a woman with her arms slightly out to the side, face up to the heavens. Glancing back at the stars above, Aleksander had to admit, "Arrowhead" made sense.

"Yeah, but look." Elspeth reached over, outlining the shape of an arrowhead. "That's what the stars look like."

"I see what you're saying, but you're still wrong." He watched as the shook her head with a silent laugh and looked back through the telescope. "Do you want to see my favorite constellation?" He didn't know why he'd asked, but suddenly he was gently pushing her aside and fitting his eye to the viewfinder. The telescope swiveled silently on oiled joints until the Weaver was once again in view. Stepping back, he smiled. "There."

Taking her place again, Elspeth peered through the scope. "Oh yeah, the sideways dog!"

A startled laugh burst from Aleksander. "What?"

"It looks like a dog but if it were standing up!" Elspeth said, as if that made it any less ridiculous.

"It's the Weaver," he said, leaning on the parapet. "Y'know, like Fate?"

"I know." She shrugged. "But when I was ten, someone said it looked like a dog and that's all I think about now." She pulled back from the telescope, staring up at the woman in the stars with her own two eyes and nothing in the way. "I've always liked that one though."

Aleksander smiled. "Me too. After a rough day it's a comfort to find her."

"Exactly." Elspeth's eyes raked down his form. "Have you had a rough day? Anything you want to talk about? I'm a stranger, so you know nothing you say truly matters to me."

Yet another laugh burst from his chest. How could it be so easy to converse with someone he'd just met? Even with Genoise it had taken time to gain such a smooth rapport.

Perhaps it was the stars sending their aid.

The weight on his shoulders became oppressive as he acknowledged it for the first time in a while. With a wandering gaze, he began, "Eh, it's nothing. Just got a lot on my mind." He intended to stop there and closed his mouth. Forearms resting on the parapet, he peered out over the keep and all the lands beyond, dotted with lamps and torches. The town itself made a sort of constellation, created by all the stories of those living there. "A war is coming," he muttered. "I've no clue how to stop it or how I can fight in it. Not like I don't know how to fight, but just...how do I fight *this*? There are so many people counting on me, and... Well, fighting real things isn't like fighting against other soldiers in a ring. They don't hold their killing blows. And today I found out..." He stopped himself, glancing at her. "Never mind."

"No." Elspeth bobbed on her feet, draping herself on the parapet beside him. "No, please tell me. I love listening to all sorts of drama that affects people other than me."

"Trust me, this complaint is a lot stupider than the others."

"And now is a time to let out all your complaints, stupid or not, so"—she waved a hand towards him—"by all means."

Aleksander blew out a long breath. "There was this girl I'd known for a while, and... I kind of liked her," he began, shuffling his feet, entirely refusing to make eye contact with her. "But it seems that she only saw me as a distraction from her duties. Not even really a friend."

A pause. Then Elspeth cleared her throat. "Was it Lady Elmere?"

His head snapped towards her, voice quivering. "What? No, what makes you think—"

She held up a hand. "Son of a lord—'or something.' You look about the same age as my lady. And I know for a fact she just finished dinner with..." Her face paled, eyes drawing wide and jaw slackening. "Gods, you're him, aren't you?" There was no question in her tone, though the sentence was certainly phrased as one. Her eyes seemed to vibrate in their sockets at the speed with which she scanned his face, his chest, the way he held himself—the sword at his hip. "Oh, you are."

Anxiety bubbled in Aleksander's chest. "Yeah," he whispered.

Elspeth's shoulders began to rise and fall rapidly as her breathing shifted. "Oh gods, I'm awful. I can't believe I... And I'm in this, and you're... Oh gods." Her hands flew to her face, covering her mouth and her throat. "I'm so awful. Oh gods." Frantic hands fluttered as she pushed back her hair, batted openly at the air. Finally, one settled by her side, and she slammed the other in a fist against her heart, bowing at the waist so her back was nearly parallel with the floor.

"Champion Wythane, I'm so terribly sorry for the intrusion." Straightening, she fixed him with an earnest stare. "Then you absolutely were praying to Tulathne when I startled you, weren't you?" Before he could even nod or shake his head, she took a step back. "I'll take my leave, your holiness. I'm so sorry for the intrusion. I'm really so sorry."

He turned, reaching out a hand and opening his mouth, but

both his feet and his tongue refused to act as she quickened her pace across the rest of the roof. Her pale nightgown flapped in the breeze, and the dark rope of her braid snapped against her back with each step. At the doors of the covered observatory, she paused, turned, and flashed a smile. "If you'll allow me though, thank you for the conversation. You're... I needed to..." Rapid blinks cleared away whatever was left of the sentence. She nodded again. "Have a good night."

The sound of the door slamming echoed over the rooftop terrace, as her laugh had moments before.

Nothing but the night wind wrapped around Aleksander.

It felt strangely cold.

Chapter
TWENTY SEVEN

"WELL," VAREK GRUNTED, PLOPPING DOWN ON the chais beside Aleksander and reaching forward to fix himself a steaming mug of tea, "you look terrible. Didn't sleep well after all that pampering, did you?"

The early morning light danced through the sugar crystals he poured into his cup, the tea itself looking thick and rich as liquid bronze while it swirled in the ornately painted clay mug. The curtains off to the right of them on the veranda fluttered in the breeze, bringing with them the sweet scents of lilacs and hawkweed from the garden.

Aleksander shot him a sideways glance and raised his own mug to his lips. "Thank you, Varek, for the lovely complement."

"I'm just saying, we're meeting the new addition in mere moments and the bags under your eyes look as though you'd spent *another* week on the road."

Varek was not wrong in his assumption. After his encounter with Elspeth on the roof, Aleksander had stood in the darkness for a minute longer, rolled up his map, and returned to the wing he and his companions were given as quietly as he could. Varek had been asleep—Aleksander could hear his deep breathing drifting into snores every so often—and Carissa, Iscah, and Demir's rooms off the main suite were all silent, adding to the notion that they were either not there or already asleep as well.

He'd taken the last slice of raspberry tart from the table in the center of the main room before going to his private quarters where he lay on the bed, staring at the ceiling, painting out constellations in his mind's eye and doing his best to trick himself into seeing them on the blank ceiling.

Even amidst all that, his mind continued to circle back around to Genoise, the end of that friendship, and the moments he'd shared with Elspeth before she'd realized who he was and startled. Aleksander had, in the wee hours of the morning, just as the sun began to rise, conceded that Genoise may have had a point, much to his own disappointment. One's station and duties apparently did get in the way of forming meaningful relationships.

Regardless, he shrugged and sank deeper into the cushions, allowing his eyes to drift shut.

Across the way, Iscah leaned forward, pouring more tea for herself. Behind the sofa she'd perched on, Demir rested his forearms, chattering quietly with her. His wings were tucked close behind his back, though there would be the rare moment where they'd twitch or rustle with repositioning or the movement of his torso. Occasionally, her laugh or his comment would float over to Aleksander, and he'd open an eye to see her cheeks pink, smile wide, and a matching expression on Demir's face.

Carissa, who had perched herself in the chair nearest the fluttering curtains with her notes and her own cup of tea, sighed deeply. The mug clattered to the stone end table beside her, along with the papers. She smoothed her hands on her skirt and raised her chin to the wind coming in off the bluff overlooking the sea.

Aleksander pushed himself up from the sofa and meandered over, bumping her shoulder with his hip. "Did you sleep?"

She didn't look up at him as she answered. "Yes. After a long conversation with Duke Elmere's advisor."

"What?" Iscah perked up, leaning over the back of the sofa. "Why did you need to talk to her?"

Carissa shrugged, shifting in her seat to face the rest of the room. "I wanted to know what they knew about the town. I'd talked with Edrun yesterday when we arrived, but he told me to ask Advisor Musgrove about it to know more."

"What did you learn?"

"Nothing, really." Her fingers danced along the rim of her mug. "It wasn't a particularly important town. It had been named Teallach. They were agricultural, mostly. The last time anyone had had contact with Teallach was when they'd sent word to the guard of the town, right after the solstice. It had been standing then. They don't know when it was burned or how. Or even why anyone would bother."

"We know why." Varek's voice was quiet. "The homunculi are proof enough."

Demir's face crumbled into disgust. "The lord here doesn't even know when a portion of his own fief is destroyed?" He looked down as Iscah's hand circled his wrist. She offered a small smile of condolences, her eyebrows drawn into a small peak on her ashen forehead.

"Remember, Demir," she said softly, "they are not like us."

Tension shot through Aleksander's jaw.

"What's that supposed to mean?" Carissa snapped.

"Iscah means," Varek grunted, stretching his legs out on the coffee table and sipping his tea, "that the nobles in this world have never looked at the land and the people on it like we do. Zekharyan nobles, especially." His cup paused against his lips. "Your family most of all, Your Highness."

The word denoting her title was nearly spat across the room to her. It struck Aleksander to his core, and his heart seized as Varek's eyes darkened, locked on the princess.

Where is this coming from?

"Remind me, Varek," she barked, "what have *you* done to help the people of Zekhar? Oh no, you were assigned to kill them, weren't you? In fact, how many of your *own* have you murdered over the centuries?"

The drooping ears flattened back. Aleksander could hear his

teeth grinding together from across the room. "Remind *me*, my lady, who gave me those orders?"

The rage in Carissa's face was entirely unmasked. It burned on her cheeks, in her eyes, the way her lip curled to bare the blunt, perfect teeth of a well-fed, well-cared for royal. Aleksander put his hand on her arm to stop her from screaming at him, charging—doing whatever she deigned to do in this situation.

"Carissa," he whispered.

She didn't answer him, only opened her mouth to fire more venom at the towering mercenary across the room. "If you hate my country and my family so much, Varek, why are you here?"

Wood squealed against tile as the sofa scraped back under the force and speed with which Varek stood. Iscah stood with equal haste, pressing her flattened hands against his chest, holding him back. Varek did not even look at her. "Do you have time to hear six hundred years of history?" He held up his hand, fingers tense. "No, sorry, you're too busy making the same mistakes as your ancestors."

"Varek..." Demir's tone was warning. His hand extended slowly towards the man, still held at bay by the silver woman.

Was she even doing much? Aleksander wondered.

Or was Varek letting her hold him back?

"I am loyal to the vow I made with the First King"—the man's voice rose—"but that does not mean the bargain I made with your father does not stand. I do not do this for you, and I will *never* do anything for *you* that goes against that bargain. Never forget your people's part in all this! For centuries!"

"Varek!" Iscah shouted. Her fingers curled into a strap on his doublet, shaking the man's body as she yanked him towards her. "Leave this," she hissed. "The Zekharyans have wronged our people in the past, yes, but that is no reason—"

"You could not *fathom* what Zekhar has done to me." His eyes were wild, words a silent snarl directed only to Iscah. A hand closed around her wrist. "What they have *taken* from me."

The door opened with a creak, and Iscah's grip released. Her face was red, breathing ragged. Terrified eyes darted to

Aleksander, begging for help he had no clue how to give, just as the clicking boots of Duke Elmere crossed the threshold.

"Ah!" A grin spread across Duke Elmere's face, faltering as his eyes met Aleksander's, then Carissa's. It fell further as he took in the panic in Demir and Iscah's faces—and the violence writhing in Varek's. "You're all here." He cleared his throat. "That's good."

A tug freed Carissa's arm from Aleksander's hand. His fingers ached. How hard had he been holding her back? "Duke Elmere," she said, nodding. "Good morning. Thank you for your hospitality and kindness over yesterday and the following night."

He waved his hand. "Oh, think nothing of it."

"Aleksander." His name was muttered from across the room. Varek twitched his head nearly imperceptibly towards the cup of tea on the table as he sat back down. "Come drink your tea."

Carissa didn't look at either of them. Her still-burning eyes remained fixed on the duke.

"My lord duke," Varek said, wiping his face to that placid, judgmental glare that seemed to be his resting expression and reaching for the tea service on the table, "could I pour you a cup?"

Despite the way he felt more like a deer approaching a lion as he went back to his original seat beside Varek, Aleksander took his mug in his hands and stood beside the Ölmesuz.

He couldn't bring himself to sit.

"Oh no, that's kind of you, Sir Varek, but I'm afraid I'm not here for tea."

"I'm not a sir, my lord."

The duke kept talking, ignoring Varek's comment. "Might I introduce you all to the warrior I offer into your service?" He stepped aside and extended a hand, ushering in their soon-to-be new addition.

Aleksander's fingers spasmed, nearly dropping his cup.

A pair of large, sharp eyes rested immediately on him. Gone was the hesitancy, the shock they'd held last night. Gone was the darkness in them too. In the morning light they glowed just as

Caliphus had, like polished red jasper. Her braid now circled her head, a dark auburn halo, and instead of a nightgown, she was clad in full plate armor, complete with a sword hanging by her hip.

"This is my best and brightest, Elspeth D'orde."

TWENTY EIGHT

*E*LSPETH'S EYES LATCHED ON TO ALEKSANDER'S and refused to budge. A lick of a smile twitched at her lips, and she raised her head, hand to heart, bowing as she had the evening before. "Champion Wythane," she said. Her tone was measured now, not the loose, casual speech they'd shared in the observatory. When she had again risen to her full height, she turned and met Carissa's gaze with a grin and a matching bow. "Princess Wythane. An honor to meet you and serve you."

Aleksander's throat felt thick, his fingers numb. This was more than shock. This was...

Well, he wasn't quite sure.

The silence between them stretched on, daring anything to be the first to break it. His eyes darted from hers for mere moments, taking in the change in her appearance that had occurred purely through a shift in the light and her clothing. Her eyes were still as large as he'd made them out to be the night before. Wavy tendrils licked at her cheeks, a warm shade of reddish brown that insinuated she'd spent most of her life beneath the sun. Or perhaps she was just blessed with that from birth.

"My lord, is everything alright?" Lord Elmere asked.

This nudged Aleksander back to the present, instead of

where he'd gotten himself lost—a space born of his own mind and those two, rich, red eyes staring back at him.

"Of course," he said, nodding briefly to Elspeth. "I do believe we met briefly, Lady D'orde."

The same smile he'd seen on the terrace appeared. In the daylight, two bright fangs peeked from those thick lips. "I do believe you are correct, your holiness."

A Rodzjiek soldier, Aleksander thought. *Back at the solstice. Genoise had mentioned a new Rodzjiek solder our age.*

As the sun fluttered through the curtains and danced on her hair, a memory surged forth—that shade of hair flying after a slicing blade against a window looking out into a dark night.

If he imagined her in an officer's uniform...

"Is she not...young?" Carissa said, her voice unexpectedly biting.

Aleksander's head snapped towards her, mouth opening to... to what, defend her? The person he hardly knew? Carissa had a point, Elspeth was only his age, that much was clear. And yet...

"I may be young, Your Highness, but I have been training on the sword for years." Elspeth turned on her heel to the princess. "Since I was three, in fact. I assure you, I'm as skilled as any other soldier you've amassed to your cause."

Varek snorted. "I'll be the judge of that."

Elspeth met him with a wicked grin. "I do hope that's not *just* talk."

After a moment, Varek threw his head back and laughed. Heartily. *Loudly.* Iscah jumped at the sound, nearly spilling her tea all over her clothes. The shift from the man of fury moments earlier to the man before them now was startling. Part of Aleksander thought it was a strange dream or all a joke, but the joy that persisted in Varek's eyes said otherwise.

"I like this one," he said, still laughing. "Oh, I do like this one." He strode forward, clasping Elspeth's forearm in a soldier's greeting. His grin stayed firmly on his face, any trace of his previous aggression gone. "Varek Kasajb, at your service."

"Elspeth D'orde, at yours," she returned.

As their hands parted, Varek turned to Lord Elmere, who looked as shocked as everyone else at the sudden, intense display of true emotion given by the Ölmesuz. He nodded, the dying rumbles of laughter still bouncing his shoulders and quaking from his chest. "You've chosen well, my lord."

Nervous and still visibly shaken, Lord Elmere smiled. "Yes, well, I'd said at the meeting that I knew just the person for the job. Now, if you have any more questions before—"

Aleksander extended his arm, to Elspeth, hand open to receive hers. "Lady Elspeth D'orde, do you swear yourself to the goddess Tulathne, and your life to mine?"

The room fell silent. No longer did the soft sips of tea echo, nor the shuffling of fabric, metal, leather. Only the curtains flapped in the breeze, and they seemed to have fallen silent along with everyone else. Her expression had fallen to neutral once Varek's attention had left her, and at this, her eyes squinted with the beginnings of a smile.

"My lord Champion," she said slowly, her voice that familiar rich, lilting tone that somehow managed to carry the warmth of last night into today. "I don't think those are all the words. Or, honestly, any of them. And I don't see a priestess around... Don't we need one of those?"

"I am myself as much of a servant of Tulathne as any priestess. In fact, my words probably carry more weight than theirs." He pushed his hand forward, still waiting.

There was an entirely unreadable expression on her face as her eyes flitted down to his hand, then back up to his own. The ghost of a smile she'd allowed to pass earlier returned, and she raised her chin, looking down her strong nose at him. Her hand raised; she clasped his.

Aleksander adjusted his stance, fixing her with as serious of a look as he could muster despite the overwhelming flutter in his chest. He had spoke to this very girl last night. Had lamented after he had gone to bed that she would not be able to stick around longer, with her easy smile and lighthearted words that had offered the exact level of comfort he had needed, and—until he thought all was lost—had helped him momentarily move on from whatever he'd suffered due to his conversation with Genoise.

And here she was. Standing before him. Planning on joining him—on joining all of them. For the foreseeable future of this endeavor.

Carissa had been right. They needed a fifth spirit.

Something deep within Aleksander knew it the moment her hand met his. They could not go on without her.

The oath came to his mind disjointed, but after a moment, he gathered them into the rough approximation of the vow he'd recited with the others before the priestesses. "I, Aleksander Wythane, the Sword of Ages and Child of Tulathne, swear today to guide you with the light of Tulathne, both on the fields of battle and off. You are my charge, and in return I am yours. My body is your shield, my arm your sword. This I swear, and promise you my life."

Elspeth inhaled deeply, then recited it back to him. "I, Elspeth D'orde, swear today to follow you in the light of Tulathne, both on the fields of battle and off. You are my charge, and in return I am yours. My body is your shield, my arm your sword. This I swear, and promise you my life." The smile broadened, and she spoke further. "As sure as the sun in the sky, the fire in my bones will warm you, protect you, guide you, and burn those who touch you."

He blinked sharply at the alteration, the addition he had not expected throwing off whether this was the end or not, whether he was supposed to respond or let it go. A quick glance to Carissa, who strode forward. She'd taken the ribbon from her hair, letting most of it fall loosely around her shoulders, and wrapped it around their joined hands.

"It's not sealed unless there's a binding," she said, guiding each of them to grab the ends of the ribbon and pull. In the absence of two swords to spin and return to their masters, a knot formed in the ribbon, elegant and ornate, the kind a girl would tie into her ribbons on the summer solstice. Carissa frowned.

"Well that's going to take some work to undo."

Demir came forward, clapping Elspeth on the shoulder. "Wonderful to meet you, D'orde."

Aleksander dodged the man's wing, barely managing to keep Elspeth in his view as Demir moved in to greet her.

"Please," she said, "call me Elspeth."

The Mekartlim nodded, his wings twitching. "Very well, Elspeth. You may call me Demir."

"Demir."

His grin widened. Standing to his full height, Demir scanned the room. "Well, what now? We've all the 'spirits,' as Lady Carissa is wont to refer to us."

Those thick, dark brows closed over Elspeth's eyes. "What?"

"It's a long story," Aleksander said, coming to Elspeth's elbow and guiding her further into the veranda, out of the cluster that had begun to form in the doorway. "Lady Carissa is a seer. She had a vision that five spirits came to join me in this battle. The first was Carissa herself, then Varek, then Demir, Iscah, and finally..."

Her head cocked to the side. A single fang flashed in a smile. "Me."

Aleksander grinned. "Exactly." But his grin faltered, and he looked over Elspeth's shoulder at Carissa. "Uh...what *do* we do now?"

Her spring-green eyes flitted around those with her, eyelashes fluttering, lips moving but no sound coming out. A broken "well... I mean now... We, uh" was all she managed before pressing her lips together. "You're not going to like it, Aleksander."

Cold leeched into his stomach. "Carissa, not again."

"I think I was using it wrong last time," she hurried to explain. "I was using it to amplify my seer abilities when I should have been using it to amplify my actual intentions." Her hands clutched one another before her chest, extended ever so slightly as though she were pleading for his approval.

He supposed she was.

"Aleksander, if we don't do this, if we don't figure it out... Who's to say what could happen?"

"Figure what out?" Elspeth asked, turning to face Carissa.

She swallowed. "There's a sorcerer we're trying to find. They formed homunculi, which only appear when the Scourge has faithful followers who take the time to learn the correct method for creating them."

"Supposedly," Varek huffed.

"There was an attack on the royal family's residence on the summer solstice. By those homunculi. We need to find their creator, interrogate them on what they know regarding the Scourge—who it is, if possible—and...kill them."

Elspeth held Carissa's gaze for a very long time before blinking. Her head rose in a slow nod. "I remember that."

The princess shifted on her feet. "It may be best for us to return home. To Castle Brevindun, to the capital. I can confer with the ladies there, the priestesses—my father too—and we can see what we can do. You can all train together—with Varek. And when I finally figure it out, we can go after them."

"Or you could keep trying while we go back." Elspeth shrugged.

"No," Aleksander interjected. "No, we need her home and safe."

Something not unlike a snarl tore from Carissa's throat. "I told you, Aleksander, I was not using the focus as I should. I can adjust how I use it."

A gentle hand rested on Aleksander's arm, and he startled. Iscah's bright eyes drooped with concern. Her words were steady as she expanded on it in terms Aleksander could somewhat manage to understand. "She's right, my lord," she said. "She was using the Aramerk to bring her own energy back on herself. She needs to use it to bring her energy into the components."

"I was selfish," Carissa said softly.

For the second time that morning, the room fell silent.

"I am sorry," she said, taking slow strides towards Aleksander. "I saw something that frightened me, and instead of trusting you and doing what I was supposed to be doing, I damaged myself in an attempt to prove myself wrong."

He shook his head. "We've already covered this, Carissa. I know you're sorry. I've forgiven you."

"Yes, but the damage I did and the...the way I set us back?" She shook her head. "Ever since we passed that village I've been thinking that if I had just trusted you—trusted *Her*..." Her fingers found her pendant once more, tracing the etching of the woman in the silver. "Maybe I could have seen something of that...tragedy...instead of my fears over and over again."

The way she held herself almost made Aleksander smile. She was nervous. It was obvious by how she fiddled with the pendant and held her other arm around her torso. But her expression was purely her mother.

Oddly enough, Aleksander found himself missing the queen.

Muscles tensed along her jaw, and she raised her chin. "I'm not letting that happen again."

His shoulders tensed involuntarily, sensing the stare of six pairs of eyes on him, waiting for a response.

Varek was the first to break the stare with a deep sigh. His hands flew over his head, waving in a frustrated manner at Aleksander. "Why don't we just go, Aleksander?" he huffed. "If we go, and she figures it out while we're on the road, it'll be that much easier to follow whatever type of trail she finds. And if not, then she can get help from the ladies when we get back to Castle Brevindun."

As much as Aleksander hated to admit it, as much as he had stuck himself in his remembrance of the promise he made to Janek to protect Carissa and see that she takes care of herself, Varek was right. The true waste of time would be to hold off on trying anything until they got back.

And after seeing those ruins...

He cleared his throat. "Fine." A shaking hand raised his mug. "May Tulathne guide our steps forward."

Chapter

TWENTY NINE

OURS PASSED, THOUGH THE GNAWING PAIN in Aleksander's chest did not, no matter how much he wished it would subside. The wind off the coast was warm, ruffling his hair and filling his lungs with sweet, salty scents. He sat on the steps to the keep's main manor, watching as Duke Elmere's attendants outfitted the party with an extra horse for Elspeth, a pack, and fresh provisions for the whole of them. Iscah and Carissa talked by the carriage. Iscah's quiet apologies were dripping with earnestness as she poured them out to the princess, despite Carissa's assurance that Iscah was not at fault, it was she who responded wrong. Earlier, Varek and Carissa exchanged a glance and a nod, then carried on as if their spat had never occurred.

Whatever the circumstances around Varek's bargain with her father were, it was becoming increasingly clear that, while it caused tensions, the bargain was nothing to challenge or take lightly.

Demir's hand rested on Aleksander's shoulder as he settled himself down onto the spotless stone steps beside Aleksander. "Are you alright?"

Aleksander glanced at him out of the corner of his eye. "Of course I am. Why wouldn't I be?"

"With the argument this morning...and now us moving off so soon. You seem on edge." He adjusted his bracers. "Nervous."

Aleksander blew a snort from his nose. "Well, can you blame me if I am?"

A matching chuckle rumbled from Demir's chest, and he turned to see the man offering a calm smile. "No, of course not." After a moment, he turned back to the scene before him. Elspeth swung up onto her horse and shifted in the saddle. "I know there's a lot going on that you probably didn't expect, Aleksander. And I'm sorry you've been misled to believe this would be smooth gliding for you. But...know that while our opinions may differ, we agree on one thing."

"And that is?"

"That Zekhar is special, and the people are important. And that we all need to do our part to protect and better whatever we can."

A weight settled heavier on Aleksander's shoulders. Demir was right. That was something they all had in common. It was something that joined them. Yet...

He sighed deeply. "Why is it all on me?"

Demir's brow furrowed. "Why is what 'all on you'?"

Aleksander waved his hand towards the group. "This. You all. I... We have everyone from Carissa's vision and yet if hers and Saoirse's are at all valid, then it won't..." He stopped when a hand rested on his back.

Demir smiled. "Look at them, Aleksander."

And he did.

Elspeth's horse shifted back and forth, but the way she sat on it was commanding, sure. Carissa was checking things over, and Iscah was right beside her. Varek waited, his hand gently smoothing the mane of one of the mares.

"If you're scared of what could happen to us," Demir said, "then know that each of us entered into this aware of the risks. And know that everyone who has joined you is a skilled fighter. Just like you. You are not responsible for us. We are looking out for each other."

"Except I am," Aleksander whispered. "It's because of me that you're brought into this. And if you die..." He trailed off, shaking his head. They were fighters, that much was true. But when it came down to it, Aleksander saw past the armor. Carissa was a woefully underprepared mage-in-training, desperate to protect her people with no clue as to how. Varek let his frustration and hatred get the better of him, and egged people on into a frenzy he may one day be unable to beat. Iscah... She was a Crafter. Varek threw that match, Aleksander was sure of that, and though she wore armor similar to Elspeth's, it rested on her shoulders like a costume, not something she was meant to wear. Then there was Elspeth... She was his age. When they met on the terrace she was laughing about stars and how haughty Genoise could be. He'd never even seen her hold a sword. And Demir, a capable soldier who swore himself to the service of of a goddess he didn't even believe in.

That wasn't even getting started on himself. He had been trained for this, that much was true, but he hadn't been prepared. He'd learned how to wield a sword, how to fight, how to bargain and play the part of a courtier. No part of his time in the castle, in the training ring, prepared him to see those bodies in the village or taught him how to push down the nausea and panic. He wasn't Alesathne. He was called by the same name, maybe he even had his soul, but...for the first time in his life the statement rang loud in his mind.

He wasn't Alesathne.

If he was, this wouldn't be happening.

He couldn't breathe when he ran, his neck ached from the constant tug of his armor, and the first promise he'd made before beginning this journey was one he utterly failed to keep—to protect Carissa from outside threats *and* herself.

How many more promises would he break over the course of it? The notion made his hearing go fuzzy. And yet, when he met Demir's gaze, the icy chill that had been sitting in his bones for the last few days slid away, ever so slightly. Here was a skilled, experienced warrior, putting his faith in Aleksander. Openly.

The ringing in his ears faded.

Perhaps all was not as lost as he thought.

Aleksander nodded. "No," he said. "You're right."

A sly grin slid across Demir's face. He nudged Aleksander with his elbow, rising to his feet. "I know I am." A breath later, and he shot himself into the sky.

Climbing into the carriage, with Iscah, Varek, and Carissa, who sat still, rolling the Aramerk in her fingers but not using it, Aleksander breathed a deep sigh.

Carissa's eyebrows rose, a silent question if he was okay, if he was ready.

Aleksander nodded.

Child or not, ill or not, inexperienced or not, Aleksander was still Alesathne.

Even if the face staring back at him in the fogged carriage window was just his.

THIRTY

NIGHT SWIRLED AROUND THEM LIKE INK in water, muffling most sounds and causing people to instinctually quiet themselves on their own. Clouds covered the sky, which was made even more difficult to observe by the thick plume of smoke coming up from the fire they had made and prepared dinner on.

A day of non-stop travel was, apparently, useful. They'd made it past the charred town once more, where Elspeth had forced her horse to walk beside so that she might see what had happened. When she rejoined the caravan, lifting the visor on her helm to address Aleksander through the window of the carriage, her eyes were not just glistening from the still permeating smoke. Now she stretched out beside him on her own bedroll, armor off and tucked into a trunk. Without the plate, her outfit was remarkably similar to Aleksander's—a loose cream blouse and brown pants, paired with leather boots and a belt to hang her sword.

"What?" he asked. "Not bringing your nightgown out here?"

She laughed her chiming laugh, stretching her arms above her head. "It's in my pack, but you're crazy if you think I'm wearing that while camping in the dirt."

His own laugh answered hers. Demir's eyes raised from his

station over the kettle by the fire, a smirk breaking his lips as Aleksander's eyes caught his and darting between him and Elspeth, still on her back, staring at the sky.

The boy's brows furrowed in a confused response. Once more, Demir glanced between him and Elspeth. Aleksander shook his head, squinting at the man.

Demir sighed, raising from his hunched position and propping himself up on one arm, the other resting lazily on his bent knee. "Elspeth," he called.

"Yes, Demir?" A single hand raised above her head, tracing swirls through the smoke.

"Would you care for some tea?"

Her head popped up for a mere second and bared that fanged grin. "I would love some."

Aleksander followed her finger, watching as the smoke curled around it and danced off into the night. "Are you doing that?" he whispered. She had to be. There was no way the smoke curled that perfectly through the cracks between her fingers when they were this far away from the fire.

"Of course. Didn't you know Rodzjiekim have fire in our veins?" Her other hand raised to join in, and she wove a swirling, beautiful cloud over them. "It likes us. Answers to us."

"I thought Rodzjiekim could control all elements," he said absently, eyes wide and mouth agape at the patterns above.

"Maybe there are some who can, but I've only known fire. The other Rodzjiekim I know have also only known fire. Fire, smoke, and mist." Elspeth waved her hands and the cloud dissipated, floating to the dark ceiling of sky with the rest of the smoke rising from the fire.

The burble of hot water pouring into a cup caught Aleksander's attention, and when he turned, Demir was holding out two cups full of a rich, golden elixir. "Magnolia tea," Demir said. "To help you sleep."

Aleksander took both, handing one to Elspeth who propped herself up on her elbows in order to drink. The first sip he took flooded his senses with an earthy, grassy taste, like the smell that came with scuffing his knee along a field and staining his pants green, though it settled on his tongue with a delightfully floral, buttery taste. Warmth radiated through his fingers, up his arms, and into his shoulders, while simultaneously traveling from his mouth and swirling in his throat, chest, and head.

Elspeth breathed a heavy, relaxed sigh. "Wonderful," she murmured, casting a quick glance and nod at Demir. "Thank you."

"Of course," he said, raising his own cup. "After Her Highness struggled all those nights ago, I made sure to keep the magnolia at the top of our tea box."

"Speaking of"—Elspeth sat tall, scanning the camp—"where is the princess?"

"Here," the weary voice called.

It took every ounce of control Aleksander had not to let guilt settle back in his stomach.

Carissa stepped from the carriage, head bobbing and eyes half-lidded after a day of exhausting work. The entire ride had consisted of her poring over her notes with Iscah, refining their strategy, and, in the last hour or so as they found a spot to stop and began to set up their camp, reacquainting herself with the Aramerk.

The entire time, Aleksander had repeated to himself like a mantra that it was different this time, she wasn't using it on herself, she was getting used to it so she *didn't* use it on herself. Yet the bags beneath her eyes and the stumbling footfalls that sounded as she made her way to the fire did little to bolster that this new trial was, in fact, different.

"Are you going to attempt anything tonight?" He hoped to Tulathne she said no.

"I plan to." Carissa scooted her feet beneath herself, graciously taking the cup of tea immediately offered by Demir. "Once I get something in me."

"Might I have a look over your notes?" Elspeth inched forward. "I don't know magic the way you do, but...who knows, maybe something will come to me."

Carissa passed the stained notebook to the girl, who leaned forward and peered through squinted eyes and furrowed brows at the smudges on the page.

"Can you even read that?" Aleksander asked. "Every time I look it's like...another language."

"It is." Elspeth flipped a page slowly. "Have you tried soaking the rune sticks in the water, or in any way physically connect them to either the earth or the flesh?" Her eyes left the page, flickering with thought. "All I know is, to do my...thing, I have to kind of feel the energy of whatever I'm working with. The smoke, the fire...whatever it is."

A moment passed, and Carissa downed her tea, tottering to her feet and picking her way through the camp back to the coach. Bottles clinked, paper rustled, and when she emerged, the princess's arms were full of various items. Her bag of runes hung at her hip as she placed down the bowl, filled it with water, and tossed the sticks in. In her fingers was the only bottle left of homunculi flesh from the solstice, already beginning to melt and decay. An awful, nauseating smell wafted over the cap a she uncorked it; Aleksander thrust his nose into the crook of his elbow, and Elspeth let out a horrid gag before covering her own.

"Sorry" came the apology from behind her arm, eyes watering and bloodshot.

Carissa grimaced as she poured it into her hand and flicked chunks into the water. "Goddess, that is awful."

"Why are you *touching* it?" Demir shouted through the rag he'd pressed against his nose and mouth.

Not responding or even acknowledging him, she held the Aramerk in one hand and fished the runes out of the bowl with another. Raising both parallel to her shoulders, Carissa closed her eyes.

A great, heavy exhale came from Elspeth, and Aleksander fought between whether to watch the girl beside him or the woman in front of him. Each time he glanced back at her, Elspeth leaned farther forward, her eyes wider, darting all over the scene before her, almost as if she saw something no one else did. Gooseflesh pricked up along her neck, her forearms, her clavicle. What was she experiencing that Aleksander was not? Likewise, each time he glanced back at Carissa, her brows drew closer and closer together, lips tightening against her teeth, eyes flicking beneath lids being held shut. The muscles along her neck twitched, standing out in thick, sturdy lines from her jaw to her clavicle. Around the Aramerk, her fingers curled into claws. They did not clamp down on the device. They caged it.

"Show me," she breathed quietly. "Show me."

On the other side of the fire, Iscah and Demir leaned against one another. The soldier's wings rustled, spread, and contracted in nervous tics. Iscah, latched on to his arm, didn't so much as blink, her tea long forgotten as it rested on her knee, steadied by three gentle fingers.

"What is she doing?" Varek's voice was low as he came around the side of the carriage, steps slow, unsure.

"Channeling." Elspeth's voice was miles away.

The man's face contorted into confusion, frustration, and back to confusion. "What do you mean, channeling?"

"Shhh." The Rodzjiek's hand fluttered up, waving absently at him. "Let her focus. She's almost got it."

Blankets rustled as Varek took a seat beside Elspeth. Even seated, he towered over her, her small frame seeming like a child's beside him. Varek leaned towards her, keeping his eyes on Carissa. "And what, exactly, is she channeling?" he whispered.

Elspeth shook her head. Unmoving, she continued to watch whatever it was that had captivated her attention. "Something. I don't know, but"—sparks snapped in her eyes—"it's beautiful."

Over her head, Varek's eye turned and caught Aleksander's, more relaxed than ever though...inquisitive. Almost scared, had Aleksander not known the man better.

A low rumble began in the back of Carissa's throat. Her nails cracked against the focus as the cage of her bones drew ever tighter around it. Her other palm, still holding the runes, began to twitch as though she was pulling back from a fire.

"Carissa." Iscah leaned away from Demir, moving to stand.

"Don't move." Now it was Carissa's turn to sound far away, as though her voice had to travel through a valley, over a river, and through the very stone of the mountains to get to them. A snap as a nail broke.

Aleksander's heartbeat came to a roar in his ears. "Carissa, stop. Come back."

"No, she's almost got it," Elspeth's eyes glowed. Truly glowed. Not like Caliphus, not like a polished stone—but like a torch had been set alight and her skull rested over it. Her voice rumbled in her throat, low and dark. "Don't interrupt."

Along the backs of Carissa's hands stood tendons and veins like black and cream ropes, pulling at her skin, desperate to spring free.

"Elspeth, I don't think this is—"

"Leave her!" she barked. The shout rocked through Aleksander's body. The flames in her eyes began to lick through her pupils. "Trust her."

The rumble had shifted to Carissa's chest, and a sickening feeling reached down Aleksander's throat and took tight hold of his stomach as he clocked exactly what that rumbling was.

It was *her*. The rumbling wasn't anything that was happening from the magic. It was *Carissa*, growling and straining against whatever it was she felt, whatever it was she endured.

"Carissa," he repeated. His hands shook.

She did not respond. No one did.

"Carissa."

Again, nothing.

Another crack from the hand closing over the Aramerk, but it was sharper, not the sound of a nail snapping. No, it was a sound Aleksander was sickeningly familiar with, though he knew it from its reverberation through his own skeleton to his own ears.

It was bone.

"Stop, you have to stop!" Scrambling against the blankets, the grass, he tried desperately to get to her.

"Aleksander, no!" Elspeth growled, catching his shirt in one hand.

He stumbled against the sudden interference, his chin slamming against the field's floor. Blinding pain split through his skull. It made it hard to focus his eyes, but he fought against it. He needed to watch her, needed to make sure—

The rumble in her chest built to a scream, and her eyes flew open, chucking the sticks into the fire. They snapped, still dripping from being submerged in the bowl. That awful stench of homunculi burned and filled the air.

"Damn it!" She stood, throwing the Aramerk too. It clattered against a rock, and Iscah flew from Demir's side to gather her creation to her chest. Tears streamed down Carissa's face as she yelled again, nothing but pure agony leeching from her very bones. "Why can't I do this?" Her hands crumpled in on themselves, nails biting in to her palms, and pressed against her chest as another wail broke through the night. The princess sunk to her knees, forehead to the grass. Sobs racked her body.

Panic flooded out from Aleksander's being. No longer was he scared she would die or hurt herself. No, now he was merely scared that it would never work.

"Are you alright?" His voice was raw. How loud had he been yelling at her?

Her face lifted, eyes flooded with fury and grief finding him. "No." She stood abruptly, kicking over the water bowl in the process. "No, Aleksander, I'm not alright." Before he could rise to take a step towards her, her hand flew up, shaking, but firm. "Just...leave me," she hissed.

Sorrow clawed at his throat.

There was so much...rage? Hatred? Darkness... There was so much *darkness* in her gaze. Whatever she had touched, whatever she'd seen...

Grief situated itself in his chest.

Whatever she had touched was not something she would recover from. That much was clear by the wild look in her eyes, the tightness in her features, the whites of her eyes that entirely circled the iris, clear and glaring in the darkness of evening.

And it wasn't even worth it.

Carissa stalked back to the carriage, climbed inside, and slammed the door shut.

No one moved for a while. Not until Demir cleared his throat. "Your holiness," he said, his voice barely carrying over the crackling of the fire. "You're bleeding."

◊ ✳ ◊

THE CUT IN HIS LIP ached. It was deep. Apparently his teeth almost went straight through. Elspeth's face was flush as Demir cleaned it and cauterized it, leaving Aleksander with the constant taste of charred steak and an uncomfortable lump of hard flesh just on the other side of his lower teeth. But at least it had stopped bleeding.

Head hanging, Aleksander put his whole being into scrubbing the blood off of the collar of his shirt. All he had at his disposal was the remainder of Carissa's spell water and a handful of ash from the fire. Varek had tossed it on the white linen without a second glance, insisting it would get it cleaner.

So far, Aleksander thought the man just wanted to punish him for what he'd done by interrupting Carissa's attempt.

Bits of ash stuck under his nail, and every time he attempted to pick it out, he somehow only got more stuck.

Elspeth lowered herself beside him. "I'm sorry," she whispered. "I didn't mean to—"

"It's fine," he bit. Her guilt was the least of his worries right now, even if he felt his stomach pinch with rage at the memory of Elspeth trying to stop him from helping her. "Don't even give it a second thought."

Grass shifted beneath her as she tugged her knees against her chest. "I... She was just so close."

"She was hurting herself," Aleksander muttered.

"But she was *so* close."

"But she has a *family*, Elspeth." The words came out like

◊ 224 ◊

venom. By the way her eyes widened, they hit like venom too. Still, he couldn't stop himself from bearing down. "She has a husband, and parents, and a title, and a crown to bear in a year. War or not, Scourge or not, she needs to get back to them. To *him.*"

She needs to stay with me.

Time crept by with an aching slowness as he scanned her face. Her lips were pressed flat between her teeth, points of fangs symmetrically altering the shape. Those eyes no longer burned with whatever innate fire had sparked. No, the silent tears rolling down her cheeks had done well putting them out. He sighed. "I promised him I'd keep her safe." He flicked the boar bristle brush towards the carriage. A speck of frothy ash and water flung with it. "*That* is not safe."

Across the fire, Demir and Iscah slowly resumed the conversation they'd been having before Aleksander's outburst. Their own voices were nothing but whispers now.

"Safe or not..."

Aleksander lifted his head, startled to hear Varek's rumbling bass and not Elspeth's voice calling out to him.

The man sat up on his bedroll, a block of wood and a small knife in his hands. A curl of wood peeled free, and with his thumb holding it to the blade, Varek flicked it into the dying flames. "Family or not"—his eyes were on his work as he continued—"she knows her duty here. Yes, it is frustrating. Yes, it is dangerous. Believe me, Janek and Clauden and Lenore know that as well. But all of them know what she has to do in order to protect her people." Finally, the glowing gold of his irises caught in the firelight behind a curtain of mussed hair. "I wonder, *Alesathne*, have your circles in and out of our world caused you to grow soft and change your relationship with your duty?"

"Alesathne" hit Aleksander square in the chest. It didn't feel right. That same voice from earlier cried out from deep within him that he was *not* Alesathne. That he was a boy, and that was his sister, and she was *hurt.*

Faster than ever before, that cold Presence curled around his spine.

"No," he spat. "Never."

All he had in him fought to push it away, to ignore the chill and the absence it brought with it. To ignore, once again, how *nice* it was.

Varek raised a brow before setting aside his carving and rolling over on his mat. After a minute, his voice floated over to Aleksander. There was no judgement, no malice in his tone. Instead there was something Aleksander thought he'd never hear in Varek's voice. "Give it some thought."

Comfort.

Aleksander's reflection stared back at him in the mirror. It was winter now, and no matter how much wood he piled on the fire in his room, nothing seemed to cut the unearthly chill that seeped through the cracks between the pane of glass in his window and the cut stone around it. His hair was shorter. The way he usually wore it before the trip.

Goddess, that was months ago, wasn't it?

He dragged a bone comb through it, carved intricately with lilies and stars, the same pattern as his screen.

A sharp, whistling blew through, and he shuddered.

"Do you want me to draw your curtains?"

He spun to see Elspeth leaning in the doorway, dressed in an elegant gown. For a moment, he blinked, not entirely sure what he was looking at. It was in the usual Zekharyan style that he'd seen Carissa wear time and time again, not to mention Queen Lenore and countless other women he'd passed at events. But the rich, dark blue fabric felt...wrong. Not that it seemed the wrong color on her, though it did, but that it seemed as if she wasn't even truly wearing it. It appeared on her body more like a dress placed on a doll than anything else. Crushed velvet, they'd called it at the modiste's. At least that was what Elspeth had said. The sleeves were tight against her biceps but fanned out at her elbows, draping to the floor and layered on the interior with wispy, fluttering fabrics of gold and silver and lighter shades of blue.

The only thing that seemed normal about her was the slight twist to her lips that showed one fang and brought blush to her cheeks.

"What?"

"Your curtains," she repeated, nodding her head towards the window. Indeed, his curtains were pulled back, and the heavy fabric was usually one of the key components to holding heat in his room during the winter. Without waiting for a response, she strode over and tugged them shut, casting a glance at Tulathne, still in Her same pose on his tapestry. "You really don't feel Her anymore, do you?"

Aleksander's brow furrowed in the mirror as he dragged his comb through his hair, letting it curl along his cheekbones and just above his brows. How long it had gotten. "What?"

"She's left you. That's what you fear, isn't it?"

"Of course." He picked up a tin of cream, lid clacking against the glass as he opened it. "I...I try my best, but I don't...I..."

"Are you even Her son?"

A jolt of heat ran down his spine. It felt like lightning. At the window, by the oratory, where Elspeth should have been...was no one. The curtains were drawn, still swaying, but she was just *gone.*

"Elspeth?" His chair made that same horrendous screech against the ground the same way it did when they were at Duke Elmere's Keep.

"Yes?"

Again, he spun, finding her leaning in the doorway, in the same position she was in moments before. She unfolded her arms, armor sounding against itself. "Aleksander, are you alright?"

"But..." A glance back at the window. "Never mind. I must be seeing things."

A soft smile appeared as she stepped forward. "My lord," she whispered. "It's understandable. You've a lot on your mind." A gloved hand lifted, brushing hair back from his forehead with a feather of a touch. Her smile flickered in and out of focus. Her voice raised from its normal warm tone to something much nearer to Carissa's bright, measured speech. "Might you want some magnolia tea?"

"I hear it does wonders for sleep" came the low rumble from behind him.

Varek perched on the end of his bed, cup in hand. He gave Aleksander an incredulous look. "Wow, what a way to greet a guest. Wipe that snarl off your face before I wipe it away for you, *hira*."

"You don't get to talk to me like that," Aleksander bit.

The man scoffed, raising himself from the bed. "Fine. When I'm in your house, it's your rules, right?"

"This isn't my house. I just live here."

The phrase sunk like a weight in his gut. No, no, that wasn't true. This *was* his house... In fact, didn't having a house just mean having a building where you lived? He had a house. This was his house.

"Whatever." The Ölmesuz pushed past him, pausing in the doorway beside Elspeth. "Regardless, reconsider that outfit. It's a little to gaudy for a battle."

Two pairs of sabatons clanked against the stone as they retreated from his room.

Aleksander looked down at the robes he wore. Rich, thick swaths of fabric draped over him in a way mean to mimic Tulathne's gown in her iconography. He strode to the mirror and took in the full image of himself.

There he was, dark hair streaming down his shoulders, braided and decorated with gold cuffs. A circlet on his head with a glittering red jasper stone centered on it, breaking the pattern of pearls and sapphires.

He frowned.

They had a point. The fur collar was a *bit* much.

Aleksander unclasped the fur and folded it neatly, intending to return it to his trunk at a later time, but his hands froze as he folded it.

He didn't have black hair.

Peering in the mirror again, he frowned. No, that was him. He'd always had his Mother's hair, and those piercing, golden eyes.

No, he had blue eyes.

Frustration bloomed along his collar bone. He didn't have time for this. He couldn't spend all day tearing apart his room to look for the right color eyes. He was already late for the solstice as is. He couldn't show up even later.

Wrong eye color it was then.

Pulling on his boots, he strode towards the door. Beyond stretched waving, green fields, reflecting the sun in the late morning.

"Look who finally decided to show up," Varek spat. "The god-son himself."

"Shut up, Varek." His voice was deeper than normal. Oh, that's right. He was Alesathne.

Aleksander was just asleep.

A laugh rumbled from his chest. "*That's* why my eyes aren't the right color," he said, "I'm not myself."

"So now you're openly admitting it?" Varek hissed.

"No," Aleksander—no, *Alesathne* shook his head. "No, I'm just saying I'm dreaming right now. This is a dream."

Varek's eye brows rose. He passed a cursory glance over Alesathne. "Well you'd better hope so. Draw your sword."

"I don't have my—"

"Draw your *sword*, Aleksander."

A jolt of fear shot through him. The sun glinted off of Varek's sword, raised, ready to strike. "I don't understand." A weight tugged at his hips, drawing his eyes from Varek's. There, on his belt, wrapped around *Aleksander's* hips, not Alesathne's, was Aoife. Trembling fingers reached for the grip, but he put his hand back down at his side. "No, Varek, tell me what's going on."

A huff blew from the man's nose, so hot it steamed in the

crisp air.

The leaves began to shift, turning shades of red and gold. Beneath his feet, the grass dried and crunched under his boots.

"Aleksander."

It took everything in him not to look in the direction of the voice. To fight to keep his hands by his side. To refuse to partake in whatever this dream was becoming.

"Aleksander!" she yelled.

Carissa. He saw her, there, in the corner of his eye, hair unbound, shimmering pale gold that fluttered in the wind.

"We have to go," she hissed, a thousand voices speaking at once. "Aleksander, *look at me*." The bright image dancing at the edge of his vision swirled, becoming large, dark. Ravenous.

"Well?" Varek adjusted his grip on his sword. "Make up your mind. Are you fighting *her* or me?"

His mouth opened, but no words came out. His tongue clicked against his teeth, throat opening and closing, air squeaking out, but no words. Breaths came quickly, stacking on top of one another, trying desperately to sort out the order they should be inhaled and exhaled in. Aleksander only choked.

The darkness came closer, and he turned, momentarily.

It was the Scourge again. Just like before.

"Alekskander," it whispered. "You need to get up. You need to get away."

"This is a dream," he croaked. "I've got to wake up."

"If this is a dream," the thousand voices spoke as one, soft, melodic—comfortably, eerily feminine, "then why are you bleeding?"

It had a point there. He was losing too much blood. It pooled at his feet, staining his new green tunic, dripping off the sword that stuck through his chest.

"Hm," it mused. "Poor little boy. Dreamers don't bleed, do they?"

The sword made a horrible, sucking scrape as it pulled from between his ribs.

Oh, now he felt...*very* lightheaded.

Around him, the world spun, until he landed face-up on the ground, staring into Varek's eyes.

"Don't pretend to be someone you're not."

Tears dripped from his eyes, down the sides of his face and into his ears. Goddess, getting stabbed *hurt.* "Get off me," he croaked.

"Get up." Varek stood, knife dripping Aleksander's own blood onto his chest.

"What do you *want* from me, Varek?" Every sob convulsed his chest, sending jolts of pain through the gaping hole in it. "Why do you hate me so much? Tell me, why do you hate me?"

"Get. Up" was all he got as a response.

A strangled scream worked out of his chest as he tried to flip onto his side. The pain ricocheted around his body, heart pumping fast to circulate adrenaline.

If only he could tell it to stop so he didn't bleed out in this field.

The grass was trampled now—brown, dead, smeared with blood, and trampled.

Around him, a wicked, powerful wind blew, nearly blotting out all sound with the force of its roar.

"Aleksander." The misty image of the Scourge knelt next to him. A spindly hand brushed the tears from his cheek. "Aleksander, get up. Please."

"Get off me!" His throat was raw, truly raw, as though he'd been screaming for hours.

"Please, Aleksander you need to get up!" It was desperate. Smoke swirled as the glowing void depicting eyes flitted around, head raising. "Take him," it said. "He's not listening to me."

Wetness dropped onto his cheek when it looked back down.

Was this creature...crying?

"Please," its voice wavered, echoing with Elspeth's, Iscah's, Demir's—and finally deepening into Varek's. The mist coalesced, and the eyes dimmed back to that tawny, banded gold.

"Kid, come on," Varek snarled, one hand patting his cheek and the other patting Aleksander's chest.

"Get off me." Sobs racked his body, curling him in on himself.

"No, no, not until you wake up! Come on, kid, come back to us. We need you."

He tried to roll to the side, but was met with awful resistance. His eyes, blurred with tears, sprang open, studying the sky. The clouds drifted away, and, somehow, so did he.

High in the sky, Aleksander looked down at himself, bleeding out in the field, with Varek's hands on his face. Even Varek looked up at this other-Aleksander.

"What are you doing?" he asked.

Aleksander shrugged, heart stilling, floating farther and farther away with the clouds to wherever it was they were going. A piercing, wailing wind cut through the scene, making bleeding-Aleksander and Varek look around, both faces stricken with panic.

"I think I'm waking up."

◊ ✳ ◊

THE FIRE WAS DYING, BUT he could still clearly make out the relief on Varek's face as he blinked back into the world. "What's going on?"

"Thank the gods," he breathed, hoisting Aleksander to his weak, wobbly feet. "It's Carissa. She—"

A sound echoed through the camp that curdled the blood in his veins.

It was never wind in his dream that he heard whistling and howling.

It was screaming.

Chapter

THIRTY TWO

NOT EVEN TAKING A MOMENT TO gauge his surroundings, Aleksander was on his feet, bolting for the carriage. The door was flung open, a pair of wings protruding as Demir wrestled a thrashing, screaming Carissa from the bed she had made on a bench out of her bundled bedroll and a blanket. The whites of her eyes were all he could see beneath the fluttering lashes. Spit trailed down her chin as she continued to scream, hands flailing blindly and savagely.

"Lay her down!" Iscah said, pulling some sort of chain out of her the pack she'd brought, now open with most of its contents spilled onto the ground.

"What are you going to do to her?" Aleksander's hand wrapped around the woman's bicep.

With a glare and a strong tug, she freed herself. "I'm going to try to wake her up."

"She's not dreaming," he shouted after her, still stumbling in his half-awake state. "Look at her eyes—she's having a vision."

"It's both," Elspeth breathed. She stood by the fire, entirely stock-still, once again unblinking as another scream tore through the camp. Nothing but her eyes moved to look at him. "It's both. I think it worked."

Iscah's hands pressed down on Carissa's hip and shoulder,

rolling her onto her back.

"Hold her." Despite the wavering tone, her words still managed to come across measured and sure.

Demir knelt beside the convulsing woman and bared his weight across her torso, hands pressing down into her shoulders. With each toss, each scream, each surge of the princess's body, his wings flared wider, wider, until they were giving small backwards flaps to hold him to her firmer. The wind coming off the powerful appendages stirred the ashes, sending some of those still alight onto the dry grass.

Elspeth waved a trembling hand over them, not daring to take her eyes from the scene playing out before her. The embers died to grey ash.

Two hands snagged Aleksander's biceps, pulling him back from the bundle of chaos mere moments before Demir's wing flung open in the space he had been standing. It was sure to have knocked him back and the wind out of his lungs had Varek not forcibly moved him.

"Just say here." Varek's cheek was pressed to the top of Aleksander's head, both arms wrapped around him in a tight, unmoving embrace. His breathing was unsteady, but his voice was slow. "She'll be okay. Iscah and Demir have her. Stay here. Stay safe."

A tear rolled down the boy's cheek. "But I—"

Varek's hold tightened, locking down the arms that continuously tried to reach out and claw the rest of their body free. "You're fine; she's fine. Don't make me knock you out, kid. Work with me here."

His fingers dug into Varek's forearms, finally relaxing in their attempts to fight their way free. But they still clenched around the muscle there that felt like ropes beneath fabric and skin.

Across the way, Iscah untangled the gold chain, holding it as it draped between her hands above Carissa's shaking form, and stopped. Her chest began to rise and fall rapidly, amethyst eyes scanning the faces of anyone looking back at her. "I...I can't do magic," she said. "I..."

"I'll do it." Elspeth was already moving forward, bare feet not bothering to pick around the rocks and sharp grasses at the campsite. Her hair was out of the tight braided updo she'd worn all day, and now it hung in a single braid down her back, frazzled and stuck with leaves and grass from a night on the ground. She dropped to her knees at Carissa's head, taking the chain from Iscah. Her own chest began to rise and fall at the same pace as Iscah's. "What do I need to do?"

"It's a thought-breaker," Iscah said, eyes wide and unable to stay on one focal point for too long. "Or, at least, it's supposed to be. Place it over her forehead, find your way through her dream, or vision, or...whatever it is, and...wake her up."

A hard swallow traveled down Elspeth's throat. She adjusted her knees, lifted the chain, laid it gently on Carissa's forehead, and shut her eyes.

Almost instantly, Elspeth's features warped from concern and fear to immense suffering. Her brows drew to a peak in the center of her forehead, lips pulling back to bear a pained snarl. Even her strong nose scrunched up between her squinting eyes that were just starting to produce tears.

Varek's arms clamped down again as Aleksander's struggle began anew. "She doesn't know what she's doing. She's Rodzjiek, not a mage!"

"She is all we have, Aleksander," Iscah snapped, panic and anger and desperation swirling about her face all at once.

Elspeth's head tilted to one shoulder, then the other, as if she was looking at a situation from multiple angles.

That roar started to rumble in the back of Carissa's throat again, though this time it was joined by the same rumble coming from Elspeth. Snarl ever widening, she tilted her face down, tears dripping from clenched eyes on to the cheeks and forehead of the other girl. She'd wrapped the chain around her fingers, as if it was one you'd use to cut cheese or as a garrote wire—and now, it bared down onto Carissa's forehead, so strongly Aleksander could start to see Carissa's skin purse up around it.

"Elspeth." Her name was but a desperate whisper on his lips. The rumbling grew. Elspeth's arms shook.

A great gasp flew from her chest, the chain snapped, and Carissa's body fell still.

All was silent.

Demir slowly folded his wings, lifting himself off of Carissa's prone body. Varek's arms relaxed and Aleksander fell forward, knees too weak to support himself as his heart pumped blood and adrenaline around his body, like it needed it to survive, like it wasn't making his head float and his lungs seize.

Carissa's chest shook, not with a scream this time, but a sob.

"Carissa?" Aleksander dragged himself forward on his hands and knees, pulling fistfuls of grass with him as he made his way to her. "Carissa?"

She continued to shake with sobs, but her eyes were open, looking around through pools of tears, but *open*.

Relief flooded through Aleksander as he wrapped his hand around hers. She tucked it close to her chest. "You're okay. Hey. Hey, Carissa. Everything is okay," he crooned, pulling her into his lap the best he could, only to end up with her shoulder and head resting on his knees, one hand over her chest and the other in the dirt beside his knee.

Elspeth's body thudded to the ground beside him, her back pressed against his thigh as she curled into the fetal position. Her hands clasped tightly together, Aleksander could barely see the blood dripping from thin slices on her fingers.

"Elspeth," he breathed, reaching his free hand over to her. "Are you okay?"

"I'm fine," she croaked.

Aleksander's throat clenched. She did not seem fine. Her hands shook, still clutching the chain stuck into her skin. Her breathing was too fast, too shallow. He brushed his hand off on his pants before gently touching her back and rubbing in slow, rhythmic circles. Slowly, the tremors in her arms subsided. Keeping a firm grip on Carissa, he leaned over Elspeth and worked his fingers into hers, untwining the chain. It pulled from her skin with a sickening wet sound. Strings of thickening blood stretched and snapped as he pulled it further. At last, the chain fell loose and swung in his hand. The links, he observed, were almost woven, like one would do for a necklace. Strings of gold, copper, and silver seemed to be carved with something—the design was far too small to make out. Especially with the blood coating it.

"I'm sorry," Elspeth said, pushing herself to her knees. She kept her fingers raised, out of the dirt. "I didn't know how else—"

Carissa shook her head, rolling it from side to side in Aleksander's lap. "No, don't be sorry. You did what you had to." Her voice broke. She sat up with a heavy sigh. Sloppy movements guided Carissa's hands to her face, swiping at her cheeks every which way to clear the tracks of tears. Fingers threaded through her hair, she smoothed back her curls, now frizzed and wild, and took a long, deep breath. Her eyes, exhausted and bloodshot, traveled to everyone in the group, coupled with a nod. "Thank you. I'm sorry."

No one moved.

"Demir," she said, her voice airy and distant.

He met her gaze. "My lady?"

"Do you have any more tea?"

The smile he gave did not dissuade the concern burning in his eyes. "Of course, Your Highness." He hurried off to rattle through the carriage, digging out a bottle of dried leaves and setting the kettle beside the fire once more. The embers beneath it sparked brilliantly in the darkness as the metal weighed down on it, shifting side to side as the water within sloshed. Elspeth returned the ruined chain to the Crafter, who offered a small smile and her reassurances that it wasn't a great loss, and in turn offered the girl her thanks for taking it upon herself to engage with the item when even the Crafter herself would not.

"We Ölmesuz...we understand magic. But it is a common belief among our people that we are not to be wielders of it. In fact, it's frowned upon in Ölmesuz society." A lilac gaze studied Elspeth. "You Rodzjiekim...you understand it, right?"

Elspeth's nose wrinkled. "I don't know if I'd say 'understand.' We feel it. I can tell what needs to be done by how it feels going through my body."

Iscah nodded. "And the mages learn how to sacrifice to the Flow because they cannot feel it the way you do. But we? We understand magic as though the Flow itself is speaking right to us." Her gaze turned to the chain in her hands. "When I Crafted the thought-breaker, I saw the gold and the copper and the silver asking me to make it into this. It showed me how to weave, what to inscribe upon each link. It wasn't clear, but it was enough." Her eyes again flicked up to Elspeth, the group. "Having that power? The ability to speak to magic like it were a friend, to have it tell you what to do..."

"It's too much for one person to ever wield," Varek interjected. "Whether we're 'meant to' or not."

The Rodzjiek girl's eyes narrowed, trying to piece together what they were saying. "I...I think I understand," she finally said.

Iscah shrugged. "You do not need to. You just need to know that you are meant to, and we are not, and that is that." She slid over to Carissa and took her hands, studying the way the fingers on her right hand hung at odd angles. Carissa winced as the Crafter moved them into position and began to bandage them. "I'm so sorry, my lady."

A smile broke Carissa's face. Tired eyes sparkled at her friend, even as her weak voice broke and wavered. "Don't apologize. Your creation worked. You should be proud."

Bubbling filled the camp as Demir began to pour the boiling water in to their mugs.

"Has any Ölmesuz ever tried?" Demir asked, "You know, to actually wield magic?"

"Absolutely," Varek said. "And you want to know what became of them?"

Aleksander shook his head, the tone of Varek's voice was enough for him to guess. Yet Demir nodded.

A strange, pained smile stretched across his face. "Ever heard of the Lunatliyot?"

"Please." Carissa's voice was stronger now, though her hands still shook as she held her tea, free from the steadying presence of Iscah's hands or Aleksander's arm. "Enough of this. We drink our tea, calm our spirits, and go to sleep." A long, deep sip punctuated the silence. "In the morning, we head west."

"The Untamed?" The map of the kingdom appeared in Aleksander's head. From where they were now, west was nothing but forests, streams, the occasional lone hunter's cabin or single-family farm. That is saying nothing of the stories. The Rodzjiek said something called the Dzera roamed the forests and the mountains, and the Orzei—they valued low-population areas to live and hunt. Throw in the stories of giant wolves, deer with fangs, and the unmapped terrain that could drop them into a cave or who knows what they could encounter. "Carissa, I don't think—"

"It's not ideal," she said, raising a hand and breaking through Aleksander's thoughts, "I know. But that's where the homunculi came from."

"Do you not remember the stories?" he said, his voice rising. "Do you *want* us to get lost for eternity? Or mauled by those deer? What about a cave system? There are so many, we could drop right into one." His whole body quivered with nervous energy. "We'd be lost to the earth for who knows how long— maybe forever!"

Carissa exhaled slowly, pressing her lips together.

"None of us want to go through the Untamed." Elspeth's hand found his and delivered a reassuring squeeze. "Believe me. But I saw it too. In Carissa's dream—or vision, I suppose. It was abstract, but we saw a path laden with corpses and posheica." She flashed a grin, tear-glazed cheeks glistening in the fading firelight. "They're in the foothills."

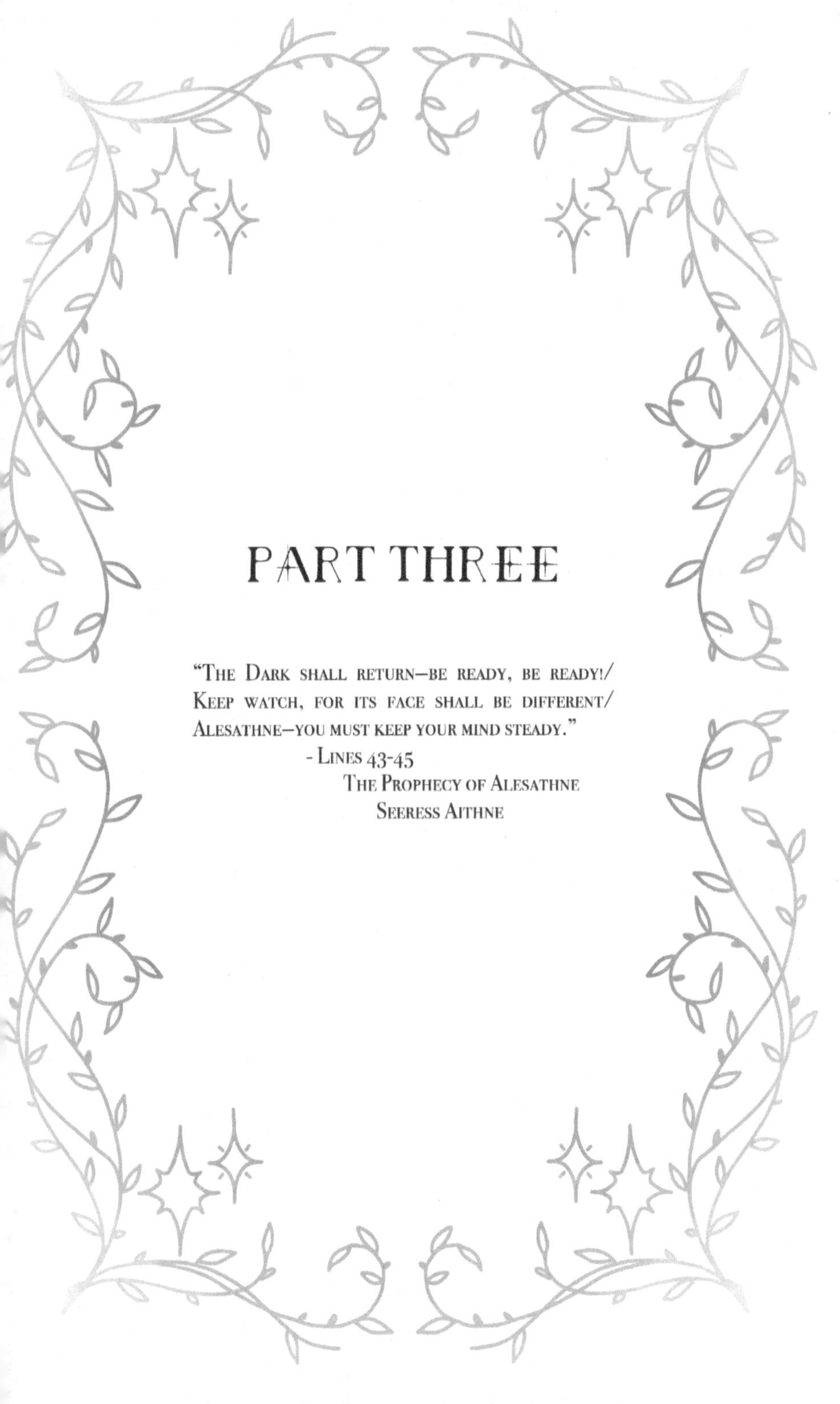

PART THREE

"The Dark shall return—be ready, be ready!/
Keep watch, for its face shall be different/
Alesathne—you must keep your mind steady."
- Lines 43-45
The Prophecy of Alesathne
Seeress Aithne

THIRTY THREE

THE MOMENT DAWN BROKE THE FOLLOWING morning, Carissa had woken everyone up, packed the camp into to the back of the carriage, and shown Bunc the way she wanted to go. The way which was, in fact, not a path that had anything remotely drivable for a cart, and caused everyone to abandon Bunc and the two mares pulling the coach at the edge of the forest so they might continue on foot.

Everyone picked their way along the deer trail, pushing aside ferns and low-hanging branches. Aleksander and Carissa led the charge, Aoife slashing down branches and vines in the way.

Aleksander's pack weighed heavy on his shoulders, but not as heavy as the apology he'd not voiced. Elspeth had done nothing but try to help Carissa. Her sabatons clanked along rocks and roots only a few paces behind Aleksander. Hours earlier, her hand had clutched his as Carissa caught her breath, her head on his shoulder. Part of him wondered if there was the necessity for an apology or if the moments of mutual support and comfort after Carissa's nightmare vision had been enough.

"Is there any time we're able to stop?" came Demir's panting. The man had been forced to change his travel plans in the sky due to thickening foliage. Now his boots clunked along, tripping over the same roots and rocks Elspeth, Aleksander, and Carissa avoided. "I'm not…used to this." Wings tucked tight to his back, every step posed a new obstacle for him. He took extra care to make sure no feathers snagged on any protruding branches.

"Sooner we get through," Carissa answered, hauling herself over a fallen tree, "the sooner we're safer and the sooner we're one step closer to finding and killing the Scourge."

"We can stop for water in a minute," Varek's voice echoed up from the back of the group.

"We're not stopping!" Carissa shot Aleksander a look. He sighed.

It had been like this most of the time they'd been walking. Someone would ask something, Carissa would oppose it, and both would look to Aleksander as the deciding factor.

Craning his head around his shoulder, he shouted back to the group, "We walk until the sun's above us! Then stop for water and lunch."

It was getting exhausting, bartering for Carissa and the entire rest of the party. At his call, everyone groaned—Demir and Carissa the loudest, as neither of them had been sided with. Varek, shockingly, remained silent. Aleksander simply adjusted his pack and brushed a lock of hair out of his eyes.

Their boots tramped along the paths, hour after hour drawing exhaustion deeper into their bones, weighing them to the earth more with each step. Carissa's dress was hiked up to her knees, her hair tied up as best as she could even as sweat threatened to melt it from her very skull.

A screech echoed off the trees behind him, mingling with metal on rock. Aleksander's blood ran cold, and he spun just in time to watch Varek grab Elspeth's arm and drag her out of a hole. It had caved in around her left foot, dropping her clean to her hip. Deep within the earth, stone, stick, and foliage crashed into a cavern.

Aleksander's breath hitched in his throat as he tried to slow it. "You alright, Elspeth?"

Watery, wide eyes flitted up to find him. Her chest heaved as she freed her arm from Varek's grasp, nodding her thanks to the man before responding to the boy a few paces ahead of her. "Yes, I'm fine."

He nodded back, frantic, the reassurance swirling through his head, doing its best to convince him she was telling the truth —even as she grunted when she put weight on the leg that had fallen through earth.

"Check your footing," Varek reminded the group, stomping twice. A hollow sound reverberated through the trees. "We're in some of the foothills. Caves are starting."

With each passing moment, Aleksander's gaze shot to the sky, praying to discern the bright glow of the sun over his head. Alas, it came on too slowly.

Every snap of a branch, every gasp, every sound that was not the steady footfalls of him and his companions sent panic straight to his head. His mind swam with all the stories he'd ever been told, and his vision buzzed with heat and fear.

When the time came that his eyes truly did behold the sun directly above the group, his knees nearly buckled from relief. As much as he'd wanted to continue on, as much as the compromise had, ultimately, been his own opinion on the matter, the moment he'd declared it he'd wanted to take it back and side with Varek and Demir.

"We'll stop here!" he called, bag tumbling from his aching shoulders. Propping it up against a rock, he undid the clasps to find the dried meat he'd packed. Before abandoning the wagon, they'd all divided up the food and supplies. Aleksander had the meat and flat bread, along with tools to make a fire. Varek had the dried fruit, medical kit, and cookware. Demir carried nothing due to his wings, nor did Iscah—her shoulder bag stuffed with Carissa's notes and her own inventions weighed enough. Even Carissa herself did not carry anything. Elspeth's pack sloshed along on her back, stuffed nearly to the brim with water skins.

She knelt beside him and took one out, offering it to him without a word.

He took it. The water was still cool, thanks to the shade of the trees and their positions against one another in her bag. A small stream dribbled down his chin and neck which he hastily swiped away. Sighing, he handed the water skin back to her.

"Thanks," he gasped, head swimming even more from the rushing chill that permeated his throat and lungs as the water settled.

Elspeth grunted, pressing the mouth of the skin to her own lips and drinking as deeply as he had.

"Gods, you two, save some for the rest of us," Varek snarled, snatching another from the open bag and passing it to Iscah. Leaning against a rock, chest heaving, she was even paler than usual.

"Are you okay, Iscah?" Aleksander croaked.

Her ashen cheeks were flushed a brilliant red, along with the tip of her nose and two small spots blooming on her forehead and chin. "I'm alright, your holiness. Don't worry about me." She shoved a strand of mottled silver out of her eyes.

It was strange, Aleksander thought, to see the woman so disheveled. Even when they'd been traveling earlier, she'd managed to keep her hair looking like plaited metal. But now... now it was just sweaty hair that had fallen from her braid. Varek being disheveled was normal—from the way he tied up his hair to the scars that cut along his jaw beneath his beard, to the beard itself. Aleksander had never met or even seen another Ölmesuz man with one. But Iscah? She was, somehow, synonymous with Carissa—pristine, calculating, careful. Not panting, sweaty, tired, and chugging water like she'd been deprived of it for days.

"Can I have some of that meat?" Elspeth asked, her voice no longer cracking as it had on their walk. She finished tightening the strip of linen on her hand. Honey from a jar she insisted on carrying seeped through the weave.

"What is that?" he asked, taking another bite.

She squinted at it. "Honey wrap. Prevents infection, so it's good for wounds. I've had it all day." Opening her hands, palms up, Aleksander noticed the wraps for the first time, tied tightly over her fingers where the chain from the evening before had sliced her. Her fingers wiggled. "Can I have some meat?" she repeated.

"Oh." Aleksander's cheeks flushed and he dug in his pack. "Sorry, yes, of course."

Elspeth took the strip of venison from him and smiled, sinking a fang into it. The meat tore beneath the point so quickly, so fiercely, Aleksander gulped. "Thanks," she said.

"No problem."

He eventually passed out more meat to the others, some only having a piece or two. Demir took four, and Elspeth took three. They sat together, backs to a rock and a tree, munching on meat and the dried raspberries Varek had pulled from his pack. The Rodzjiek didn't say anything. Hardly looked at him, in fact. A nervous itch tugged at his throat, behind his eyes. Every small sound she made, his eyes darted to her. The urge to say something would hit, but no words would come, so he'd open his mouth, shake his head, and close it again. It was different than when he would get this way around Genoise. He needed to say something. It just wasn't something he knew how to start or even say properly. Aleksander adjusted in his seat for what felt like the fiftieth time and cleared his throat.

"I need to apologize," he said softly.

Another tearing sound as she bit into the jerky. "For?"

"For how I spoke to you after Carissa attempted...well. You know." He stuck another raspberry into his mouth. The concentrated sweetness almost sour on his tongue as he chewed, he shrugged, focusing on the dirt that had pressed into his knees. "I was wrong for going off like that. You had only just joined, and you were trying to help, and I—"

"Hey," she interrupted, shaking her head, "you don't need to worry about that."

His eyes rose to hers, and she raised a brow.

"You're right, you *shouldn't* have spoken to me like that. But that doesn't mean I don't understand *why* you did. That doesn't mean I haven't already forgiven you without you needing to ask."

A breath soared out of him. "Then you do forgive me?"

"Of course." She snorted, leaning back against the boulder

behind her.

A heavy pause filled the air, punctuated by the soft, pillowy crunch of another dried raspberry between Aleksander's teeth.

"And?" he said.

Elspeth looked at him. "And?" she repeated.

"And? Aren't you going to apologize now?"

Her eyes went wide before a bellowing laugh shook the very trees around them. "What?"

Aleksander, however, was not laughing. He fixed her with a stare, tendrils of frustration curling around his throat. "You need to apologize too."

"For what? Trying to help?"

"For encouraging the princess in something that could hurt her," Varek shouted from across the small clearing they'd settled in.

Elspeth's mouth froze in an open, gaping grin; giddiness faded from her eyes. "What?"

"You were trying to help her, yes," Varek continued, his cheek bulging with a mouthful of half-chewed venison, "but you do not know her. You are new, and though you are as equal a member of this team as any of us, remember that you've spent the least amount of time with any of us. You don't know Carissa's limits, and you certainly don't know how hard she will push herself for results. She'd do it even if it meant her death."

The girl paled, mouth closing sharply. Her jaw tensed.

"Regardless, thank you for your help. But you need to apologize for overstepping at a time when such unmitigated encouragements could have truly cost her."

"Not to mention"—Demir's face was downcast, voice low —"you caused Sir Wythane to bite through his lip."

"Not all the way," Elspeth snarled. That same, bright fire that had been alight in her eyes on the night they were discussing appeared again, though this time it was as though she felt it, and blinked it away quickly. Aleksander mimicked the deep breath she took, stilling his own racing heart. He slowly released his grip on Aoife—when had he reached for her?

"I'm sorry," she gritted out, "that I caused you both pain. It was not my intention. Princess"—her eyes landed on Carissa—"please forgive me for encouraging you to do what could have hurt you. I didn't know."

Carissa nodded, dropping her head against her raised knees.

Elspeth's eyes landed on Aleksander. "And I'm sorry for making you trip and bite your lip."

A flicker of amusement loosened his tongue. "That didn't sound very sincere," he said with a smirk.

To his surprise, Elspeth smirked back, without a hint of malice. "If you remember, I tried to apologize right after it happened. That's when you went off on me."

Smirk spreading into a grin, Aleksander nodded. "Then I accept your apology."

An hour later, once everyone had eaten enough and drained one and a half skins, packs were re-tied and situated on shoulders that had thankfully gotten just enough reprieve to groan beneath the weight of the leather straps instead of scream.

The sun was hotter now. Midday passed and so it had shifted, allowing its rays to stream directly through the canopy ahead of them, right into their eyes.

"How close to the peaks?" Iscah croaked.

"Us or the sun?" came Varek's reply.

"The sun."

Grunts and "hmms" came from the man. After a minute, he answered, "About three hours."

Three hours and they could rest. Three more hours and the heat would be mostly gone. Carissa would likely try to push everyone to keep walking, keep going, but who knew just how far the location of the vision was. It could be days away, for all Aleksander knew. Neither Carissa nor Elspeth told him anything. They had simply pointed, and everyone walked.

"How much farther?" The words were quiet, only for Carisa, as she trudged along just behind him.

"We're getting close. I can feel it." A tug on his pack as she steadied herself over a slippery root. "Can't you?"

Aleksander shook his head. "I don't know if my 'feeling' works like that."

He searched his body for any sign that he could, any strange sensation along his spine, his mind, his arms—even his feet. If there was anything that felt amiss.

All he found was that small swirl of cold at the base of his skull.

He'd not noticed it for hours.

Chapter

THIRTY FOUR

NIGHT FELL MERCIFULLY WITHOUT INCIDENT. ALEKSANDER had stalked off into the woods with a small hunting bow Elspeth had carried with her, nabbing no more than a single rabbit. It wasn't much, but there were no complaints as everyone took turns peeling freshly roasted meat from the spit over the fire. Any hot food was welcome as the summer evening chill settled through the forest.

Demir, as usual, made tea for everyone. He'd stuck it in a corner of Varek's pack, and when he'd dug it out, the man groaned, chiding the soldier for adding unnecessary weight to his burden.

"I don't think you'll say it's unnecessary when you're able to sleep tonight," Demir said, procuring a small pot and pouring some of the water from the half-full skin into it.

In lieu of their usual mugs, which had been deigned too heavy and large and had thus been left on the carriage with Bunc, they sipped their tea from tiny wooden cups no taller than Aleksander's palm. Still, it was enough. Soon Carissa and Varek dozed off on the beds they'd made for themselves—Carissa's out of fallen ferns, pine needles, and a cloak she'd kept tied out of the way the whole journey, Varek's out of a boulder he propped himself up against.

Iscah curled up next to Demir, whose wing folded in ever so slightly to shield the both of them. His arm looped around her waist, his face pressed against the back of her neck, Aleksander watched as their lips moved through a quiet conversation. A lazy, quiet smile fixed on Iscah's face, and she wiggled back more, taking his hand from her waist and interlacing her fingers with his against her chest. Demir's eyes fluttered shut, followed quickly by Iscah's, and soon her soft snores filled the camp.

Aleksander couldn't help but smile. The image of the Ölmesuz and the Mekartlim reminded him so much of when Carissa and Janek had slowly begun that shift from friends making the best out of an arranged engagement to two people who genuinely loved one another.

On a night not so unlike this, the three of them had gone out into the gardens with a bottle of Lenore's favorite wine and leftover sweets from a dinner where they entertained visiting courtiers. Aleksander had not been allowed to partake in the drink, though the older members of the trio had shared a few glasses before they'd all lain in the grass and discussed the stars, their hopes, their dreams, and their fears. It was all painfully young of them. The oldest was Janek, and he had only been seventeen at the time. Carissa was fifteen, and Aleksander was only eight. Even that young, Aleksander had seen a shift in the way Carissa and Janek looked at one another. They'd all fallen asleep beneath a half moon, and when Aleksander woke later in the night to a chill, he'd found them curled together in a pose not unlike the one Demir and Iscah were in now.

"They're sweet together," Elspeth said, her voice low and rumbling from a day of exhaustion.

"Yeah," Aleksander agreed. "They remind me of Carissa and her husband."

"Oh, right. I forget she's married." Her neck craned towards Aleksander. "Why isn't he here?"

"A very arbitrary reason," he confided. "He wasn't in the vision she'd had."

Elspeth frowned. "So he had to let his wife go out alone?"

A shrug was his response.

"If my husband weren't allowed to go with me someplace, I'd riot," she huffed.

Aleksander's eyes narrowed. "You want to have a husband? I thought you were a soldier."

"I am." She straightened her back and cast a look at him down her nose. "But I didn't ask to be. I'm also fifteen. I don't want to be doing this all my life, and when I've saved enough money I want to move to a quiet village. I don't think I want to do that alone." Posture relaxing, she took a sip from her tea. Aleksander was sure it had gone quite cold by this point. "I could stay in the guard, build a life for myself, but...that doesn't feel right to me." She glanced over to him. "Don't you want to settle down some day?"

Aleksander's eyes fluttered to the sky. Didn't he? He supposed so. That was one thing that had stopped him from taking the priestly vows Caoimhe had tried to get him to recite that first morning this journey started. Priests were confined to a life inside the temple, serving Tulathne, practically married to Her and Her service. It was the same with the priestesses. They'd sworn themselves to Her as maidens swore themselves to noblewomen, to stay chaste and pure and there for Her in all things, to the end of their days.

That kind of life did not appeal to him. Some part of him, deep down, past all the stuff that had piled inside him about his position, his duty—all the stuff that made him Alesathne, he figured—was just that: the desire for more. A family, now that Elspeth mentioned it, did not sound particularly awful.

In fact, it sounded like a soft ending after what was sure to be a grueling few years fulfilling the prophecies.

He met her eyes, glowing in the firelight, merely reflecting. The same warmth he'd felt on the terrace returned, when Caliphus sparkled through the telescope like the flames now dancing in her eyes. Aleksander much preferred that kind of glow to the one that seemed to come from within. He smiled. "I never gave it much thought, but...yeah. I suppose so."

Her own lips curved in a matching smile. It was soft, warm. "I'm sure you'll get to."

"You too," he said. "So long as I have any say in it."

She laughed. "What, so you'll choose my husband for me once all this is done?"

"No." He shook his head, the warmth in his chest turning to an ache. "I'm gonna make sure you live to choose your own."

That glow wavered, Elspeth's smile dipping from her face only to come back forced. Strained. "We'll be fine, Aleksander. Remember, it's our job to protect you."

"But—"

"Go to sleep." She waved her hand, adjusting her legs beneath her. "I'll take first watch."

"Are you sure?"

She nodded. "Sleep well."

Jaw flexing, Aleksander fought against himself to listen to her. Eventually, the logical side won, and he curled up on a bed of moss and fallen ferns, the song of a crackling fire and crickets playing a unique lullaby, just for them. Occasionally, a chirp from a nightingale sounded through the forest or the distant shout of a fox. Eventually, it all silenced as he drifted into a blissful sleep, entirely devoid of dreams.

The notice that he missed his prayers, yet again, didn't occur to him once.

◊ ✹ ◊

Sound came back slowly. The fire had died as he took a deep breath, eyelids fluttering open into the still-dark night. Crickets hummed. A few fireflies danced above the rest of his sleeping comrades.

"Don't move" came the whisper.

Whatever calm had settled on him in those hours of sleep vanished. Every muscle in his body went rigid, his heart thumping violently in his chest.

"What is it?"

"Sh." The soft, slow hiss of a blade sliding free from a scabbard preceded Elspeth's movement. Fallen foliage on the forest floor crunched against itself as she stood, her knees creaking audibly with the movement. She moved so carefully, so slowly, it took Aleksander a minute to actually track that she was, indeed, standing, and was, indeed, walking towards the trees.

"I'd stop there, if I were you" came the rumbling voice.

A gasp whooshed from Elspeth's lungs.

Every fiber of Aleksander's being strained against the instinct to turn, look, help. Eventually, his instinct won over.

All the breath left his body when his eyes landed on whatever it was that was speaking to Elspeth.

It was tall—so, so very tall. And large. Over the body of this *thing* was a thick cloak of leaves, cast in dancing shadows from the flickering, dying fire. Elspeth's shoulders rose and fell rapidly with hyperventilating gasps, sword loose in her fingers, dropped down by her side.

Its head cocked at her, a carved wooden mask covered its face. It was long, similar in design to any one of their faces, any *normal* face, aside from the two openings where bright, gold, glowing eyes could be seen. As its head tilted, branches moved above it.

No, not branches, Aleksander realized.

Antlers. Long, reaching antlers, each rivaling the length of a single one of Demir's wings. Moss—or lichen, perhaps—draped from them.

It studied Elspeth. If it had become aware of Aleksander's consciousness and stare, it had done nothing to let him know it noticed him.

"What are you?" Elspeth squeaked.

"Are you not one of mine?"

The voice was deep as the roots of these trees, rumbling over itself the way rocks clattered over one another in a rockslide.

One of mine.

Aleksander had only heard stories. He assumed Elspeth had

too.

But neither of them second-guessed the name that came to their minds. The name only she was brave enough to speak.

"You're the Dzera."

THIRTY FIVE

HE DZERA. SPIRIT AND PROTECTOR OF the forests. Known to lead people astray and get them lost in caves or trapped in rockslides. The few who had seen it and returned alive were mad for however many days they had left.

They never had many.

Its leaf-cloak rustled, bending down so its face was mere inches from Elspeth's. Her breath curled around its mask like steam around a pot lid.

"You did not answer my question, child."

Her fingers flexed around the wrapped leather handle of her sword. "Am I supposed to? Or was it rhetorical?"

A deep laugh rolled forth, shaking the branches and causing the leaves to whisper against one another.

Aleksander's hands itched to reach for his sword. Every second that slipped past, he dug his fingers into the leaf litter beneath him, mind settling on the pattern of his breathing and flicking every so often to the question of whether the Dzera could see the remaining flames reflecting on his eyes. It began to move. He closed his eyes, not tightly, but loosely, allowing them to flutter, as if he were having a dream. As if he were so deep into sleep that not even a creature whose height rivaled the oldest trees in Zekhar, whose mere presence felt like slowly being encased in a tomb of moss and vines, could wake him.

"Look at your companions," it said, tones trickling over one another like a spring. Aleksander felt the presence shift around the camp, the voice moving with it. "I see none other, aside from you, that bear fire in their bones. Tell me"—it was over by Iscah and Demir now—"do you think I would call the one who prefers the sky one of my own? Or either of them who were born from Time's favorite friend?"

A hot breath blew against Aleksander's ear. It smelled of decaying logs and fresh wildflowers.

"Do you think I would call those who are not even from these lands, who think me to be a demon, one of my own?" Small, clacking sounds echoed, like a tree getting ready to snap, or branches knocking together. "So answer me. Are you one of mine?"

"Yes."

"And what is the Daughter of Fire's name?"

"Elspeth."

Again, that laugh. "Oh, perhaps I was wrong. I have never known one of your kind to answer to such a foreigner's name."

Fallen pine needles cracked beneath her shifting feet.

Aleksander was sure the creature could hear how fast his heart was racing, and if not, it certainly heard the way he struggled to steady his ever-quickening breaths.

"I was not raised by my mother. I was given up and adopted by a Zekharyan family. They named me Elspeth."

"But it is your name, is it not?"

"It is. I answer to it." A pause. "I like it."

The forest fell silent. All Aleksander heard was the crackling of the fire, Elspeth's breathing, the sticking of her sweaty palms on the leather of her sword's grip, and a great, yawning silence. So great, in fact, that it nearly buzzed in Aleksander's ears.

"And what, might I ask," the Dzera rumbled, "is the Daughter of Fire, carrying a foreigner's name, doing in my forest?"

Goddess, please do not tell it, Aleksander begged silently, *Don't say anything. Come up with a good response, a good lie just nothing but—*

"We are here to search for a sorcerer."

—that.

Branches clacked and creaked. "A sorcerer?"

"One that has been using the dead to create abominations in the name of the Scourge. The Scourge is a monster from—"

"I know who the *Scourge* is, girl." A sudden sharpness entered the Dzera's tone, cracking and snapping and cutting to the bone in the same way a snap of lightning does. "I've been here since before Tulathne—long before She bore Her doomed child, and cursed that individual all now wait to watch bleed." Aleksander jumped, and did not open his eyes. A long pause, and for a moment, he feared it had spotted him.

Then the Dzera spoke once more. "What will you do when you find this sorcerer? I hope not congratulate him on disrespecting the dead."

"We're going to kill him."

Wind blew through the camp, and suddenly, the sounds of crickets returned. Fireflies buzzed, mosquitos whined, the fire snapped louder, and somewhere in the distance, a fox screamed.

"Good." Aleksander nearly threw himself into the fire at the hot, breathy whisper spoken directly into his ear. "You'd better."

His eyes flew open, but all he saw above him was Elspeth, kneeling by his side, her face blank and eyelashes fluttering as though she needed to blink but was too scared to.

"Go back to sleep," she said, her voice breathy, shaking. "It's gone."

Sitting up and away from her, he dragged his gaze over her face. "Are you sure? I've been out for a while. I can take watch if —"

"I said, go back to sleep." In one swift move she was back on her feet. A few twirls of her blade as she scanned the forest, and she heaved a sigh. "I'm fine."

◊ ✳ ◊

THE CRUNCHING OF HER BOOTS on dirt, dried leaves, pine needles, and anything else that made sound on the forest floor circled the camp for the rest of the night. Aleksander slept fitfully, waking to her blade swishing through the air, only to discover her wheeling it about at nothing. Not once did she speak to him. Not once did she wake up another person. Not once, at least while he was awake to witness it, did she even sit down.

By the time morning broke, she'd already pulled handfuls of meat and berries from the respective packs and laid them out on a kerchief for everyone to take their share. The fire was doused, and as soon as Carissa woke, Elspeth nodded.

"Off we go."

Aleksander did not dare bring up what happened the night prior. Not around the others, not when questions would be raised and fears would be stoked. They'd made it a day without seeing anything. He could keep himself quiet long enough to let them believe they'd made it a second day without anything as well.

But every moment he got, he'd cast a glance back at Elspeth.

No matter how tired she appeared, how haggard her hair became or labored her breathing, she'd match his gaze, fear and awe burning in tandem within her eyes.

The second day passed similarly to the first. Aleksander mitigated conflicts and cleared a path through the thickening flora, they stopped for lunch and didn't speak, then continued on.

Sometime in the afternoon, Varek had called everyone to a halt. Iscah's ears twitched, following whatever sound it was Varek had also picked up on. They'd simultaneously dropped to their knees, motioning for everyone to do the same. A growing roll of near-thunder echoed through the forest as an entire herd of ten to twelve deer bolted through the trees only feet away. A large male led them, his antlers broad and jagged, dripping with peeling velvet and dying the usually polished bone with fresh blood.

From his lips protruded two sharp fangs.

Aleksander watched them, only to be drawn away from the scene by a huff from Elspeth. With an open smile she ran her tongue over her fangs and winked, as if to say, "Hey, not so different from them, am I?" Aleksander's heart pounded too much to laugh in response.

Iscah eventually asked if Carissa was still going in the right direction. Aleksander breathed a sigh of relief at that—the trees all looked the same to him, and a part of him wondered if the encounter with the Dzera last night had cursed everyone and set them on the wrong path.

Both Elspeth and Carissa confirmed—yes, they were still going the right way.

Night fell. Demir made tea. Varek and Iscah claimed watch. Elspeth bedded down beside Aleksander, both of their swords easily within reach.

Carissa fell asleep fast.

"She's wearing herself out, isn't she?" Varek muttered.

Aleksander blinked up at him from the cloak he'd pulled around himself, eyes already beginning to blur and unfocus from oncoming sleep. "We all are."

"Hmmph."

For the first time in days, as Aleksander focused on the fire they'd made that was smaller than usual and consciously slowed his breathing, his eyes fluttered shut. A prayer formed in his mind.

Watch over us tonight, he began, *Tulathne, my lady. May my dreams and the dreams of my companions be in aid. Let no troubling dreams come to any of us, nor any ill omens. Keep the Dzera from our place of rest, and any others hidden in these trees that may seek to do us harm.*

Protect us. Watch over us.

Give us peace.

When Aleksander awoke from with a start from his third dream of the night, panting and drenched in sweat—this one being particularly unnerving in that the Scourge had been trying to crawl under his skin and destroy him from within after flaying the skin off of everyone else—he could not say he was shocked that his prayer didn't work.

Ever since the solstice, nothing had seemed right.

He lay back down, assuring Iscah that it was nothing, he was fine, it was just a nightmare. Almost no light broke through the canopy. Aleksander could only make out one star.

Closing his eyes, he ran his awareness down his body, trying his best to seek out anything that could give him comfort.

He wasn't shocked when he found that swirling, cold presence again.

Nor was he shocked when it was that, not the now-scarce warmth of Tulathne's presence, that wrapped around him and lulled him to sleep.

Chapter
THIRTY SIX

Clouds covered the sun the next day, so no one complained too much when Carissa overrode Aleksander's calls to rest, drink, and eat in favor of getting there. No one except Demir, though Aleksander was sure it was mainly discomfort. He had not flown in days and his wings were always kept tight against his back. If Aleksander had not been able to stretch his legs in days, much less walk, he'd be ornery too. Regardless, the heat was lesser, and for the first time on the entire journey, there was no sweat trickling down the back of Aleksander's neck. He had not realized how much he hated the feeling until he was free of it.

The princess had become silent. Fierce determination radiated from her, and even Aleksander, who had gotten used to questioning her, had fallen silent. He caught glances of her in the corner of his vision, her stern features, tightly closed lips, furrowed brows.

"What's wrong?" he whispered, helping her over a log.

Her eyes flicked to his, then to the path ahead. "We're almost there," she shouted. "I can feel it."

"Praise the Kutsalyot" came Iscah's sigh.

"We'll find a place to leave our packs and go the rest of the way with just our weapons."

"What?" Demir's voice picked up.

Aleksander closed his eyes, a futile attempt to shut out the new variation of the same argument he'd been sorting through the last few hours.

"So first you don't want to stop, and now we're just going to abandon our packs? Do we at least get to eat first?"

"We eat when we're done," Carissa spat.

"We'll eat before we leave the packs!" Aleksander countered, grabbing the princess's arm and dragging her a few feet ahead. "What is going on with you?"

"I'm not talking about it."

He rolled his eyes. "Not this again."

She caught him with her good hand and dug her nails into his arm, forcing him to a stop. Something burned deep within her eyes. Whatever it was, it made Aleksander's heart lurch into his throat. Never, in all their years together had he seen such panic in her eyes—not even when she was caught climbing the fence to the vineyard, not when Janek went out to assist a neighboring kingdom with a battle, not when Lenore went through yet another dangerous, unviable birth.

Carissa's eyes shone with a primal, ancient fear.

His stomach dropped.

"Yes," she hissed. "*This* again. But this time it matters, because this time, I know when it's happening and I *will* stop it if I can." Her nails dug deeper. If there was blood seeping through his sleeve after she let go, he wouldn't be shocked. "Trust me. I'm going to try something when we're out there. I swear we're a half hour's walk away at most, and when we get there...keep Iscah near Elspeth."

Aleksander's stomach dropped. "What?"

"Keep. Iscah. Near. Elspeth. Trust me."

He nodded, rapid, erratic blinks blurring his vision. "Alright."

Carissa's throat bobbed with a hard swallow. She released his arm—thankfully, there was no blood—and turned back to the group. "We rest here. Drink up, eat your fill. We're thirty minutes out."

Iscah's nose twitched. "We're closer than that."

The princess's brows pressed closer together. "Why do you say that?"

Her amethyst eyes sparkled as they darted between Aleksander and Carissa. "I can smell the homunculi. They're rotting."

◊ ✳ ◊

Varek tore at a strip of jerky. Pack now free from his shoulders, he and Aleksander both watched as Demir strung a rope through them and hoisted them into a tree. Far enough from bears, deer, boars—anything else that might seek to steal or otherwise destroy their goods.

"Do you think we're ready?" Aleksander asked. He didn't know why he asked it. The silence permeating this part of the forest, the way Iscah and Varek's noses kept twitching in discomfort and disgust—it made him uneasy. A dried slice of apple crunched between his molars, and he lightly danced his fingers over the hilt of the sword at his hip.

A snort from the old man. "Why would you ask me such a thing?"

"To get your opinion."

Across the way, Iscah wrapped Elspeth's hands, raw from carrying the pack after the chain cut in to them a mere handful of nights ago. The honey wraps, though, seemed to have done some good. Thick scabs had formed, and she seemed to be in minimal discomfort.

"We're as ready as we can be," the Ölmesuz said softly. "Everyone here is skilled. We'll be fine, and if we aren't, well"—a wink at the boy slumped against a towering oak—"that's why I'm here, isn't it, your holiness?"

It was. They all knew that, Aleksander knew that. For Tulathne's sake, he'd known this was coming from the time he was five, and the moment Janek said he was being replaced, Aleksander hadn't batted an eye.

Was Varek really the last line of defense? Is that why he was here, really?

Did Clauden, Lenore, even Janek... Did they all think so little of him?

The chewy, mushed apple slid uneasily down Aleksander's throat. "Yeah," he muttered, "it is."

"Do you want to... I don't know"—Varek waved his hand sporadically through the air—"ask the blessing of your goddess on the final leg of our quest or something?"

The boy's brow furrowed. He should, shouldn't he? That's why Caoimhe wanted to bless him, wasn't it? So he might bring blessings to the rest of them further down the road? He shrugged. "Wouldn't have thought a non-religious man like yourself would be so encouraging of such a thing."

"I may not be happy with the gods or most of the people that serve them, but that doesn't mean I don't accept their help if it's offered to me." An elbow clad in leather armor nudged Aleksander, nearly making him topple over. "Even if it's from your Zekharyan lady."

"What do you have against Tulathne?"

Aleksander's voice was small. Meek, almost. It didn't startle him, the soft tone he unexpectedly adopted. It just made his soul reach out further than it had previously, hands open and grabbing for anything warm, anything answering—anything there.

"I know you're Ölmesuz and not a lot of you worship her anyways," he continued, "but why do you hate m—Her?"

All the air in Varek's lungs hissed out in a slow, tight exhale. "Kid, there's a lot I could say. And all of it would be true— nothing but my own experiences and opinions. But there's a time and place for it. Now? Here?" He nodded out at the rest of the group, at the woods around them. "This isn't it. And I don't *hate* you. Or Her."

A burning crept into Aleksander's cheeks. He hadn't meant

to say "why do you hate *me,*" but after the events of his last dream, it just slipped out. Almost. He thought he'd covered well enough. Evidently, he did not.

Varek shrugged, eyes playing about the flickering leaves in the canopy. "I just have...issues. With some aspects of this whole deal. With some of your followers."

"They don't follow me. They follow Tulathne."

"Oh, believe me, kid." That golden gaze locked on Aleksander. The boy braced for a scolding, but Varek's lips hung open, unsure. They closed. A sigh blew through his nose. "Believe me"—his tone dripped with pity—"they follow both of you. And I've been around long enough to see what that does to people on both sides of that relationship."

"Everyone ready?" Carissa shouted, standing. In her palm, tied there with a strip of fabric from the tourniquet in the medicine bag, was a small golden device. Aleksander quickly caught the triangular protrusion that identified the Aramerk.

Varek threw the last handful of dried fruit into his mouth, nodding. "Whenever you are, Your Highness."

The group stood, checked their weapons, and Varek leaned down to adjust Aoife, his face hovering inches from Aleksander's own. "Listen, kid," he muttered. "Doesn't matter what I believe. Only matters what you believe, and what you do with that belief. There." He stood back, arms folded across his broad chest, tired eyes scanning Aleksander's form. He nodded. "How's that feel?"

Aleksander shifted, taking in the difference to what Varek had done versus how Aleksander usually secured Aoife.

It felt as if nothing had changed.

"Fine," he said, his wrist resting on the pommel.

Varek's eyebrows rose. "You think *you're* ready?"

"Aleksander!" Carissa waved him over. "Let's go!"

His bangs flopped stiffly on his head as he nodded, heavy with grease and sweat and days of being unwashed. "Yeah" came the quiet reply. "I think I'm ready."

The old soldier nodded, beard twitching with what Aleksander could only assume was a smile he refused to let stay very long. "Let's go."

Chapter

THIRTY SEVEN

T HEY MUST HAVE STOPPED FOR LONGER than Aleksander'd thought. As they continued on, the sky grew darker, the air colder. The chilled presence Aleksander had begun to find comfort in seemed restless, zipping up and down his spine, sending wave after wave of goosebumps up over his arms, his neck, his back.

After a moment, Carissa stopped. "We're almost there. I can feel it."

"I think I can too," Aleksander muttered. Waves of panic began to rush over him with each vertebrae the presence swirled around, ebbing and flowing like a tide in his body. It was like the solstice only much, much worse.

Beside him, Iscah pulled to a stop, fastening a kerchief over her nose and mouth. Behind her, Varek had already done the same. The subtle smell of lavender and citrus floated on an icy breeze to him.

The princess turned around, her face a mask of calm. The "normal" Carissa—to everyone that wasn't Aleksander or Janek.

"You've got something to say, huh?" Varek's muffled voice came from behind the stained black kerchief, lowered even more to match the quiet tone of everyone else. "Alright then, out with it."

A nervous smile licked her cheeks. "Only this. Today marks our first step in a timeless battle. Our first moment to make our mark. Not only will we win, we will take this win with us onto every battlefield going forward." Her hands rested, clasped together, in front of her. She was controlling the shaking in her fingers so well Aleksander wondered if he was imagining the slight tremors he saw. "Now, listen up. Demir, I'm going to need you in the sky. I don't know how thick the foliage is, but I saw a field when I dreamed of it. I'm hoping that much is accurate. Iscah, Elspeth, take the left. Stick with one another." A glance to Aleksander. "I need you to watch one another's backs. Varek—"

"I'll take Iscah," the old Ölmesuz said.

Carissa blinked. "No, I said—"

"And *I* said I'll take Iscah." Leather creaked as he folded his arms once again, staring down at the princess. In the dark leathers, hair tied back, kerchief obscuring the lower half of his face, Aleksander suddenly could see this man not only flying through a battlefield, taking down enemies left and right, just like Janek said, but creeping through streets, sliding into houses, castles, estates, and executing whoever he was paid to. They'd mentioned once that he was paid to work as an assassin, and that thought only came back to Aleksander now. Sure, he'd seen him fight. He was fast, skilled, quiet. But the weight of those attributes had never hit him until this moment.

How many lives has he ended over the centuries?

"And why are you questioning my choices?" Carissa said, mimicking his stance.

"Because it's a stupid choice, Your Highness."

Carissa's mouth hung open in a rage.

Varek raised his hand to continue. "Iscah will not be able to fight properly if she's tasked with keeping Elspeth safe, nor Elspeth with her. You saw us fight. Ölmesuz move fast. Much too fast for you humans or the Rodzjiek. Let me watch my own."

Burning green eyes found Aleksander. "Well, Sword of Ages?" she snapped. "What's your opinion?"

All eyes turned to Aleksander. His heart thundered in his

chest, but for the first time, the deep breath he forced down his throat stilled it. Not much, but enough. He raised his chin. "Demir, you're attacking from the skies. Iscah and Elspeth will keep to one another, but not at the expense of their own lives. If something calls for them to break apart, they will. Carissa, stay in the tree line. You can't fight, and you *know it*. You've got a dagger and that won't be enough, especially with your hand broken. Varek." His eyes landed on the old man with the drooping ears, and his heart flickered a precarious beat.

Varek met his stare with pride in his eyes, but beyond that was a look so intense, it nearly scared his heart into stopping all together.

"Varek, do what you see fit," he said. "I trust your judgement. I only ask that you stay by me at the beginning. Once fighting ensues, you're free to make whatever choices you think are necessary."

A single eyebrow flicked up, and the man inclined his head. "My gratitude, Sir Wythane."

He responded with a stern nod. Whatever thread it was that held him in such a sure stature and mindset tangibly began to fray and he cleared his throat, raising his hands, palms to the sky. "Tulathne, Lady of Balances, Peacekeeper, I come before You as Your son."

Upon realizing what was happening, Carissa closed her eyes, her hands falling open in the same manner as Aleksander's. Demir bowed his head, closed his eyes. Iscah bowed hers, but did nothing beyond that. Her lashes fluttered as her eyes flicked over the various images on the forest floor. Elspeth put her palms up but kept them low to her sides, as though she were unaware of whether or not she was allowed to do it as well as them.

Varek met Aleksander's eyes and nodded.

He continued. "I come before You as Your Sword. Today, we prepare to take into our hands a battle that has been waged for millennia, over and over. Grant us strength, speed, and courage to do what is right. Open our minds to the knowledge You want us to gain. Fortify our steps, and swing our swords with us. May every blow dealt today be dealt by Your hand. For these things I thank You, and for these things I pray."

Carissa's eyes opened, clearer than they had been in days. "That was lovely."

He shrugged. "That was all I could think of."

"It's all you needed." Her gentle, affirming touch swept down his arm. Aleksander leaned into it, patting her hand in return. Casting a glance around the group, he watched as Iscah muttered a soft, quick prayer in the Ölmesuz language. As she drew it to a close, her eyes flicked up to his.

A smile smile turned his lips, and she reciprocated.

"Let's get going," Varek huffed. With a toss of his head, the mist floating through the canopy and gathering on his hair flung free in small droplets. "If we stall any longer, Demir's feathers will be too waterlogged to work right."

"If this is a storm, I'll be fine," Demir countered, shaking his wings open slightly. "We Mekartlim were built to surf on storm currents."

"Is that true?" Iscah leaned back and ran a gentle hand down the front of his wing, inspecting the feathers there.

He twitched with a laugh. "Alright, maybe we weren't *made* to do it, but it's a favorite pastime, nonetheless. Flying in storms isn't easy, but it helps us go faster." He laced his fingers through hers. She met him with a brilliant—albeit, nervous—smile.

The group trudged on through the darkening trees. Mist stuck to Aleksander's face and weighted down his hair even more, though part of him was glad it was cooling. No nightingales sung. No crickets chirped. Only the occasional croak of a tree frog come out to take in the storm filled the air.

It was not long at all until Carissa motioned for everyone to get down behind a line of brush. In the dark, fading light, past the tree line—that was where Aleksander saw it. Bile rose in his stomach at the sight of the small village. Like the one they'd passed through a week or so ago, it wasn't exactly a *village* anymore. Rubble lay scattered out past the boundaries of what appeared to have once been a stone wall encircling the town. It was old—most of it decayed, now sprouting new vegetation and fungi. Ground was dug up outside the wall. Though the image before him was shifting into different shades of grey rather than the greens and browns and myriad of other tones one would come to expect from such a scene, he could still make out the cracked, half-buried stones that marked graves.

Empty graves.

"This is it," Elspeth croaked. A shaking finger pointed at the only building still standing—a hut, with smoke rising from the chimney. "After that night, I'd recognize that cottage anywhere."

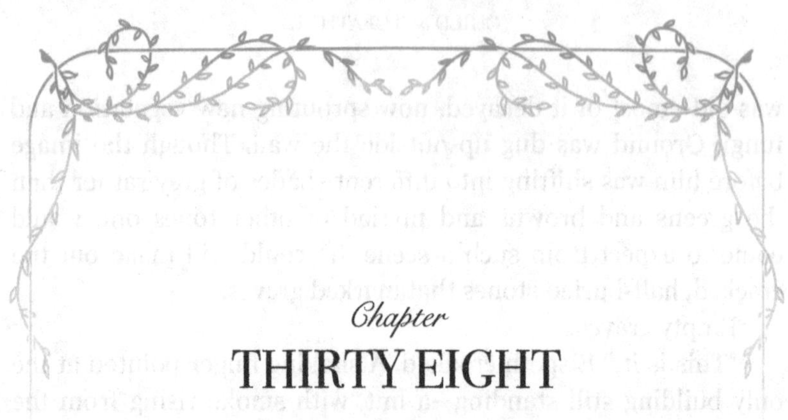

Chapter

THIRTY EIGHT

ITHIN MINUTES, ALEKSANDER WAS SOAKED TO the bone through his armor. The light plate he'd been wearing ever since they left Bunc and the horses had done a good job nearly cooking him as they walked. Dried sweat stuck his base layers to his skin on cooler days and at night, but now all that was mingled with icy rainwater from the mountains in the west. His gorget cut into the back of his neck, pressed at an awkward angle by the blue-grey stones of the cottage he now leaned against. Overhead, Demir circled, catching updrafts of warm air and riding the currents provided. What had begun as an overcast day and mist had turned in to a downpour with lightning and thunder, just as the Mekartlim had said.

Rain pattered on his face as he watched the nearly invisible silhouette of the man's wings against the churning sky. Varek's arm pressed against his, the great, dark sword held out and to the side ever so slightly. Aleksander turned his face to the Ölmesuz, who nodded towards the front of the cottage, where Elspeth had just scampered up the steps through the mud, all the way from the edge of the forest.

A knock on the door hardly traveled through the rainy afternoon, but it echoed just enough to reach Aleksander's ears. His breath caught.

"She'll be fine," Varek whispered, "Just get ready."

He nodded, adjusting his grip on Aoife.

Within the cottage, a slight clatter sounded, followed by heavy footfalls. The latch shifted, the door creaked...

"Who—"

Elspeth's crying cut off the deep voice. "Oh, thank the gods!" she sobbed, "I...I didn't know if there was anyone out here, please I... My horse, he... We got caught in a stampede. The deer, they..." Again, more crying.

Aleksander's throat tightened at the sound. It was an act. They'd planned before taking their places that Elspeth would act as bait. She was the smallest girl, if only by a few inches. Besides that, she was the youngest. After throwing on the nightgown she brought in her pack with Aleksander's doublet, a short, tattered overskirt torn from Carissa's own gown—which now hung about her knees—and rolling in the mud for a moment, the soldier had turned into a remarkably realistic child, thrown from her horse after a freak stampede.

Still, her cries tugged at every string in Aleksander's chest. He blinked hard at each sound, as if that could somehow still his emotions and press his will back into a place he could control it.

"Please," she sobbed. "Might I just... Please, do you have a fire going? It's... I'm so cold."

A moment of pause.

"If it's too much trouble, I can—*hic*—I can go to someone else. Is there anyone else in town? Your house was the first I saw. The rest looks—"

"Fine, come in." The voice was stern. Measured. "I'm all you'll find out here."

"Oh, thank you." Her crying resumed, followed by the click of her boots on dry wooden floors. The door swung shut.

"She's in. Good." Varek shifted, nudging Aleksander forward as he pushed closer and closer to the front of the cottage. "Now we wait."

The rain continued to soak in. Muffled conversation floated through the single-pane windows and the worn door, painted a pale shade of blue—that is, *once* painted a pale shade of blue. Most of it had worn off. Chips flaked in the grass around the cobblestone stairs.

"And your horse is where?" the voice asked.

"Oh, thank you," Elspeth muttered. The sound of a cup sliding across wood reverberated in the windows. "That smells delicious. What's in it?"

"Herbs. And your horse is where?"

"What kind of herbs?"

An exasperated sigh. "Look, miss, I'm trying to help you. Drink that up, and move along. Where did your horse fall?"

The clacking of a cup hitting a table. "Oh, in the forest. I'm not sure how far off. It wasn't a real trail. I was trying to find a short cut. I'll show you, if you're willing."

"Drink that, then we can go."

Aleksander's stomach flipped. What if they were wrong? So far, this person just seemed to be a hermit, frustrated by a random girl showing up at their door. Nothing so far seemed—

As if the presence he'd learned to live with had grown hands and tugged on his spine, Aleksander's attention shot out past the cottage to the nearest decaying building—on top of which, two homunculi crawled and sat, picking nothing out of their teeth, hissing at one another and clawing for space. They had the same thin necks and grotesque, bulging eyes as the first one Aleksander ever saw. Easy to kill. Though that knowledge never made them less terrifying.

His armor clanked as he whipped his head back around, pressing his back to the stone foundation.

Luckily, the pounding rain seemed to be enough of a barrier that neither the creatures nor their creator heard.

"What?" Varek hissed. Rain dripped from his nose and soaked the mask over his face.

"Homunculi," Aleksander breathed. "Two of them."

The man shifted his gaze skyward, catching Demir in his swoop, sword gesturing in the direction of the two. He nodded, shifting forward. "We've handled worse."

Aleksander jutted a hand out to stop him. "We. Don't. Move. Not until Elspeth is out. And safe."

Rustling came from the window right above them. Both flattened as much as they could to the cobblestones. "I fear the rain won't let up. Would it be possible to get my horse in the rain? I...I swore I saw something in the woods. Something terrible, and I...I don't want it to get my horse."

Aleksander could see Elspeth nearly pressing her face to the glass above them, scanning the tree line, eyes pausing far too long on the spot where Carissa waited. Demir swooped again, and her eyes darted up to catch him before moving back to the darkened trees.

"What did you see?" the man asked.

She turned, looking back at him, her wet, muddy locks of hair pressing against the window. "I...I don't know. It was..."

"What. Did. You. See? There are a lot of things in these woods, girl," he hurried to explain, "I want to know what I'm going to be dealing with."

"It was... I...I don't know how to describe it. It looked..."

"She's either gonna describe a homunculus and get herself killed, or come up with an awful lie and get herself killed," Varek said, shifting past Aleksander to crouch beside the stone porch. "Either way, I think it's safe to say this was a stupid decision and we may be screwed."

Elspeth kept talking. "It had this awful mask with...massive, burning eyes. And antlers, and...gods, it was so silent but so *fast*. I...I don't know what it was."

The Dzera.

At the mere mention of the creature, Aleksander's eyes flitted to the forest and what lay beyond, heart racing, thumping against the iron around his chest. There was little relief when he could not pinpoint the two ember eyes that would alert him to the Dzera's presence.

"Hmmph," the man grunted. "I know it well. That *thing's* been getting in my way far too often. Come." The door creaked open in the direction of Varek, blocking him from the man's view for mere moments.

He stiffened, sword raised to be nearly flat against his face.

"We'll take care of it and then you can be on your way."

"Thank y—" Elspeth's words cut off. She stood on the first step, peering out towards the village.

Towards the homunculi.

She couldn't just pretend she didn't see them. They were loud, large. Disgusting. Anyone seeing them for the first time wouldn't ignore them. Aleksander's heart pounded so fiercely in his chest it actually hurt. The arteries in his neck strained against his panic.

Don't move, she'll be fine. Don't move. Don't.

"W-what...what are those?"

The shoulder Aleksander saw drooped.

"Damn it."

Elspeth whirled, slipping down the steps, nearly falling flat into the muddy grass waiting for her. She did not make eye contact with Aleksander or Varek—or Iscah, waiting on the other side of the cottage. "Oh *gods*, what—"

"Miss, I need you to answer a very important question now." A sharp, whining crackle buzzed through the rain droplets still pattering down on Aleksander's pauldrons. "What god do you pray to?"

Elspeth's eyes flashed. "What?"

"What *god* do you pray to?"

No, Aleksander's mind swam. That voice. Measured, careful, the words he spoke, the *way* he said them... A sharp hiss curled around the back of his mind.

Traitor.

"T-Tulathne," she breathed.

A heavy sigh. "That's what I thought."

The door slammed shut. Rain soaked through the man's hair quickly, a sandy blond dusted with grey. He wasn't built like a man used to hard labor. His forearms were soft, sleeves of his white shirt rolled up neatly to his elbows. And his pants were tailored. Exactly to his measurements. The seam down the side, with gold, embroidered vines.

Aleksander refused to be sure. He refused to say his name, even in the private confines of his own mind.

The man's shirt began to soak through, stained with grey splatters in various shades, from nearly white to nearly black.

Ichor.

A short, huffed sigh as he shook his head. In his right hand, electricity wove itself through his fingers. "I do apologize, my dear. But I'm afraid I've got to kill you now."

Chapter
THIRTY NINE

AREK AND ISCAH SWOOPED IN, NEARLY silent in the downpour—though not silent enough. The man spun, toppling down the steps, gritting his teeth at them as the three stopped, weapons raised and ready to strike whenever an opening presented itself. Elspeth slipped back further, drawing her own sword and pinning him in another direction. Aleksander's heart dropped to his feet. The man's eyes were wide, glancing between everyone. Aleksander's lip curled into a snarl.

Traitor. Traitor. TRAITOR.

Lord Terrell stood slowly, brushing off clumps of mud. He still wore his lord's signet on his pinky. "I see now. The girl was a trap. Playing on my empathy, right?" He raised his chin, steel encasing his features. "Now do tell me why you set one before I run you through."

"You know," Aleksander growled, standing and leveling Aoife right at him.

His dark eyes scanned Aleksander. It took a moment as he registered the armor, the crest of a balance with the center pole being the very sword pointed at him now. When he got to Aleksander's face, his eyes crackled with those purple-blue sparks, grin vicious. "My lord Champion," he bellowed, "I never thought I'd see you so soon! Be honest, are you surprised? Did you know it was me, at the festival last month?" When Aleksander did not respond, he threw his head back in a bellowing laugh. "This is too good! Just *wait* until the Scourge hears about this."

"They won't get the chance." Aleksander swished Aoife through the air, flinging water this way and that, slowly taking his place between the traitorous lord and his front door, between Varek and Iscah. He cocked his head to the side, drawing on what it felt like to be Alesathne in that dream. If he was him at some point, he could be him again—bring that energy back to this world through more than his actions. "But out of curiosity, do you know where my old friend is? Or, perhaps, what *their* name is this turn? You're already familiar with mine. It's only fair we even the playing field."

The lord spit on the ground, electricity crackling at his fingertips. In this moment, any trace of courtly decorum left. He hardly seemed like the man Aleksander knew at all. "Oh, wouldn't you *love* to know."

"That's why I asked," Aleksander hissed. Fury bloomed in his chest. Weeks ago Terrell had laughed at Carissa's jokes. Years ago he'd offered a toast to Aleksander after his vows. He'd been at every solstice, every court gathering. Lord Terrell had eaten at the same table as him more times than Aleksander could count. And there the wretch stood, soaked to the skin, eyes raging, *begging* for a fight. Openly siding with the person wanting to burn his country—his *people*—to the ground.

And Aleksander waited. He could lunge now, but...no. That wasn't *fun.*

This man burned a town to ash.

This man not only killed members of his court, but innocent children. Just so he could have the bodies necessary to build these monstrosities.

A fire burned in Aleksander's stomach. His knuckled turned white around Aoife. He gripped his sword so hard it hurt.

For a moment, he wondered if this is what Alesathne felt the first time he encountered the Scourge or one of their followers. This rage. This hatred. To come face to face with someone who willingly admits their desire for total destruction of peace, of life —

And at the same time, he felt fully himself. Not as a god, not as the Champion—but as Aleksander. Raised in the palace around the people he saw get killed. This was not Alesathne's rage.

This was his own. And it was more than enough to give him comfort with the notion of severing the lord's head from his shoulders. Of making him cry and beg for mercy. Of making him bleed.

Terrell didn't deserve to simply die.

He deserved to *suffer*.

For a moment, Aleksander was glad he did not know the man better. If he had, he might not be able to give him exactly what he deserved.

Striding forward, Aleksander pressed Aoife against Lord Terrell's chest. The traitor's smile did not waver. "So you admit," he asked, voice so unexpectedly steady, "that it was you who created these homunculi and set them upon the castle at the summer solstice. You admit that you're a traitor not only to me but to the royal family of Zekhar and the whole of the country. That you *do* serve the Scourge."

"I serve whoever rids the earth of Tulathne and Her scum of a child," Lord Terrell spat. "I serve the Death of a Thousand Ages, not only because they will destroy this country and raise a new one, a *better* one, but because they will rid the world of all mention of your lying *goddess*." His smile faded momentarily. Long enough for Aleksander to pause.

"And, of course, you."

Light exploded. Aleksander went flying.

He slammed against the door, caving it inward, throwing him against a table and into a pile of splintered, stabbing wood. Outside became a flurry of activity—metal against metal, cracks of lightning, and the hideous screams of homunculi.

Hundreds of them.

Their cries filled the air as he stumbled to his feet, the ache in his back nothing as he fought for air. Pain shot through his legs, his arms, anything he tried to move. His head pounded. He blinked, wobbling to his feet, trying to clear his vision from the sparks shooting through it. Windows and doors and walls formed roughly through his splintered vision. Counters full of vials and books and—

No, none of that mattered. Where did she go? Where was—

Aleksander heaved a sigh as the glittering pommel came into focus.

Aoife sat near the door, splintered blue slabs atop her.

Each touch of his fingers against the wood sent bolts of pain up his arms. To lift Aoife would be torture.

A scream echoed outside, followed by a burst of flame flying past his face.

His fingers tightened around the grip, and he ran.

Floorboards creaked under his weight, under the heavy, repeated thuds of his feet. Catching the doorframe, he stopped himself. The scene before him was not one he had prepared himself for.

Sure, he'd spent time thinking about the battle with the sorcerer. He'd imagined a few homunculi.

Not this many.

Iscah and Elspeth found each other and fought back-to-back. The silver-haired Ölmesuz spun this way and that, severing limbs and hacking off heads of even the toughest homunculi. Elspeth summoned flames from the fire in the cottage. They whipped around Aleksander from the candles and hearth behind him, avoiding him so carefully yet tearing through the soft, decaying skin of the monsters around her before the rain sent them hissing away.

Above, wings flapped wildly, sounding like wet sheets after being hung up on a clothesline. Demir did not have long until they gave up. The water would be too much, and he'd be on the ground. Just like the rest of them.

As Aleksander's eyes scanned the scene, searching for the sorcerer, his eyes fell on the Ölmesuz man, soaked to the bone in black blood and rain.

Varek was a whirlwind. Ichor spewed like a fountain from where he fought, cutting down creature after creature. Aleksander's blood chilled. He had been going easy on him; he knew that from witnessing his fight with Iscah. But this Varek before him, the one launching off of one homunculi to spear another and whip the body around to take out three more—this was the man Janek had imagined when he first told him about the warrior, when they were lying on the floor of the great hall, staring at the painted ceiling. When all of this still seemed far away.

He stumbled down the steps, clumsily plunging his sword into one homunculi that took a charge for him. The bulging eyes swung wildly in their too-small sockets, teeth gnashing as it fell forward, pushing the blade further between its ribs. A gurgling, sucking noise sent black blood spewing out of its mouth as Aleksander retracted the blade. It fell aside with a single kick, only for two more to show up, clawing at one another to get to him first.

Severing one's head from its body, he slammed the hilt of his sword into the other, sending it stumbling to the side with a roar.

Another slice across its chest, spewing blood across Aleksander's breastplate, it fell back, ragged nails scraping at the wound, convulsing in pain.

There—a flash of purple light ahead of him, as Demir pulled up.

There stood Terrell, swinging his dagger wildly, eyes crazed. Purple-blue lightning crackled around him, within him.

He staggered back to undisturbed ground and dug his hands into the mud. Even from far away, Aleksander watched as his veins glowed within his arms, his neck, his face—then down into the earth it went, lashing out all around him. A small distance to the sorcerer's left, the ground began to shift. A skeleton crawled out of it, shuddering, bone-pale in the evening storm's light.

Flesh stripped clean from the the fallen creatures around him, slithering with their own minds towards the shuddering bones, leaving the shattered corpses in piles in the mud.

Bulging eyes took their places in the dirt-filled sockets, torn tendon and decaying muscle wrapped around bone.

Aleksander nearly vomited at the sight, but one thought came clear into his mind.

So that's how he does it.

Chapter

FORTY

SCREAM RIPPED FROM HIS THROAT, propelling him forward and shoving the nausea farther down. Now was not the time for that. Each swing of Aoife either felled a creature or disabled it enough for Aleksander to keep pushing. Blood dripped down his face, mixing with rain and sweat beneath his plate.

"We kill him," he shouted over the din, hoping someone would hear him, "and he stops creating the homunculi!"

"Understood!" came the two voices—Varek, to Aleksander's right, and Demir, swooping above. With each beat of his wings, more water rained down on Aleksander and the creatures he battled through.

Demir wobbled in the sky—Aleksander's breath caught in his throat—one wing folded, and Demir fell.

"Demir!" Iscah screamed, slashing aside two homunculi and breaking from Elspeth.

The smaller girl's eyes widened—she, who was without armor, who was supposed to stay with Iscah, now was swarmed by homunculi.

"Elspeth!" Aleksander's cry was hoarse, but it carried.

In the absence of the other woman, Elspeth's cuts became wild, frantic, slicing superficial wounds into the creatures—

enough to give them pause, send them back a few steps, but ultimately only served to anger many at once. They converged on Elspeth in a writhing, howling mass of blood, bile, and flesh.

Aoife severed an arm reaching towards Aleksander, his foot kicking in another's knee just as his blade came down again and speared through the thing's open mouth and out the back of its head. His eyes flashed between the fading sea of homunculi—most collecting around Elspeth and Varek—and the group mere paces away where Demir had fallen, characterized by shouts and the ringing of metal and flashes of necromantic lightning.

A cry echoed from Elspeth, ripping his attention from the fight before him. Blood trailed from her brow, down her cheek. Her eyes blazed with live fire, flames licking around her eyelashes. Foamed spit and rainwater dripped from her open fangs, a roar driving each strike she made with her sword. It grew in volume, contracting her muscles around the weapon, curving her shoulders in. Dark ichor spewed onto her clothes, into her hair, down her face. Ten fell at once. Blackened, decaying organs and intestines spilled onto the muddy ground.

Bile rose in Aleksander's throat, but he couldn't tear his gaze away as Elspeth's hands erupted in flame.

She flung one outward, and with it, fire consumed the five racing up to her left. Spinning again, she ran her hand along the flat of her blade, coating it in flame before she buried it into the heart of a greater homunculi. The flesh caught instantly, and it fell. She wrenched her blade from the creature and looked up, meeting Aleksander's frightened gaze with a feral, wild grin.

Whether he truly wanted to or not, he returned it.

"Go!" she shouted, spinning the flaming blade in her hand, "Varek and I can hold the rest of them off. Finish this."

Mud squished beneath his boots as he turned, racing at full bore towards the winged man doing his best to dodge the blows and shocks from Terrell while unable to take to the sky. Desperate huffs blew from Iscah's mouth with each strike. She dove beneath Demir's wings. The pair moved like dancers around the sorcerer.

Aleksander couldn't help but admit it—Terrell was good. True, he had no armor and fought with a hunting knife, his creations, and what little bursts of electricity he could spare, but he moved nearly as fast as Iscah.

For a man past the midpoint in his life who Aleksander hardly saw without a chalice of wine in his hand, he was formidable.

Entirely unbidden, Aleksander's thoughts momentarily shifted to his heavenly Mother.

Tulathne, if there were ever a time for you to answer my prayers, now would be it.

Raising Aoife, he launched into the air, screaming as he brought the blade down.

It connected.

Steel sliced through skin, muscle, catching on bone—but he drove it further. Even as the man screamed. Even as electricity snapped up Aoife's blade, to the handle, into Aleksander's fingers. Shocks vibrated and clawed up through his forearms. Still, he held.

Demir whirled around, flinging out his wing and catching the man's jaw with the strong edge of it.

His forearm ripped from Aleksander's blade. The sickening crunch of shattering bone turned Aleksander's stomach, but he pushed it down, shifted his feet, and watched as Demir drove his blade through the man's ribs.

A sharp gasp was all he got in response. Mouth full of rainwater and blood from his pierced lung, the traitor's eyes rolled over to Aleksander. "I'm not the last, *Alesathne*," he croaked.

"No," Aleksander panted, eyes blurring with the effort of breathing. His chest burned. Still, he slashed his blade down Terrell's cheek. The man let out a pained scream. "I know you won't be the last. But you will be a message." He laid Aoife's edge against the lord's throat. "And you will not be blessed with another life if I have anything to say about it."

In one swift stroke, he pulled. Tremors reverberated up

Aoife's blade and into Aleksander's hand as she severed skin, cartilage, bone. Thick blood spewed forth. It was different from the necromantic lightning, different from the way a homunculi felt. It sickened Aleksander.

With a spat curse, Demir tugged free his blade. With that final support now absent, the sorcerer fell, face first, into the mud.

Aleksander dropped to his hands and knees, emptying what little was in his stomach as wave after wave of nausea overtook him. The blood, the sound, the way it *felt*—

He'd gotten used to killing homunculi. Whether they were people at one time or not, they were something entirely different now. It *worked* differently.

The man on the ground beside him... He was a human. He had been a member of their court.

And Aleksander had killed him.

His body heaved, even as fighting continued behind him, slashes of metal on bone, through flesh. The burning of homunculi corpses was an affront to his senses, and his eyes watered as still his body tried to rid itself of all that it had gone through in the last few minutes.

The only thing to pull him from his state was Demir's hand leaving his back and the man's panicked voice screaming Iscah's name, over and over.

Aleksander lifted his head.

Wings flapped wildly, hanging at odd angles, spraying blood with each movement. Demir's boots slipped in the mud as he raced towards the Crafter, standing stock-still as a homunculi slid off her blade and onto the earth. Her eyes fluttered, and she dropped.

Gritty mud stuck itself beneath Aleksander's bracers as he crawled forward, thick and stinking of already-rotting corpses. "Iscah?" His voice broke at her name.

Demir's hands cradled her head, silver locks matted with sweat, rain, and mud. As Aleksander got closer, he noticed that was not all there was ruining Iscah's metallic waves. Among the black and brown sludge came a pooling, growing red.

"Iscah," Demir panted, pushing away strands of hair stuck to her forehead, her cheeks. "Iscah, *aşkım*, stay with me, Iscah." Tears mixed with rain, streaming down the man's cheeks. He pulled down her kerchief. A muddy, bloodied thumb passed over her cheek, trying to clear the dirt there but only adding more.

Lavender eyes rolled beneath fluttering lashes, each movement growing more and more lethargic, the effort becoming greater. Gurgling breaths, uneven, ragged, sputtered from her lips.

Aleksander's heart pounded as he dragged himself beside her.

A ragged, dirt-packed gash ran across her neck, all the way up to her ear. Blood dripped from it onto the mud beyond.

"Iscah?" His voice cracked. "Demir, what happened?"

The man didn't respond. Tears continued to fall, his eyes refusing to leave Iscah's.

Squelching steps preceded Elspeth's drop beside Aleksander. She smelled of smoke and rosemary and sweat and death, but Aleksander only pushed down the following wave of nausea and slid aside as her soot-stained hands reached over the woman's throat. Trembling fingers hovered above the wound.

A sob broke free. "I...I'm not a healer. I can't..."

"Iscah!" The cry echoed from the tree line, panic lacing the scream. No one looked to see Carissa's approach—Aleksander just trusted it was her.

Iscah took a ragged breath, blood bubbling at the corners of her mouth. Finally, her eyes found Demir's. Cracked, bloodied, and pale, her lips curved through her pained breaths, moving so slowly Demir shook his head, shushing her as one would a crying child.

"It's okay," he gasped out. "It's okay, *aşkım*. You're going to be okay."

She shook her head, nearly imperceptibly.

Elspeth's fingers dug into Aleksander's gorget, pulling harshly in an attempt to steady herself as sobs wracked her body.

"I was supposed to stay with her. I was supposed to stop her. I-I'm not a healer. *Gods,* why am I not a healer?"

Aleksander's hands patted along the ground until he found her thighs, moving further to wrap around the girl's waist. "It's okay," he whispered.

Iscah's fingers, interlaced with Demir's, fell loose, still pressed against his lips. The light faded from her amethyst eyes, dull in their wake, framed by lashes caked with rain and tears.

Aleksander began to shake. His mind swirled. This couldn't be happening. This was not happening.

But...it was. *She* was, wasn't she?

His hands gripped Elspeth's doublet, both slick with whatever viscera they'd encountered. In turn, her arm wrapped around the back of his neck as she sobbed into his shoulder, body shaking as much as his.

Tears tracked their way down his cheeks.

Not Iscah. It couldn't be. She didn't deserve this.

Iscah, who didn't even believe in his goddess, who didn't even believe in him or this quest, yet went along anyways... This was not the ending she deserved. Away from her family. Away from her home. Away from...everything. Covered in guts and ichor and bleeding from a gash not unlike the one he'd delivered to Lord Terrell moments earlier.

Whatever Demir had said days earlier about everyone knowing the price, everyone deciding that whether they believed or not that this was a way to better the world—it didn't matter.

She didn't deserve this.

His head began to buzz and float, the sobs and erratic breaths taking their toll after such intense fighting. Her face was all he saw, distorted and blurred, eyes open, staring into nothing. A hand reached forward and closed them.

Heavy arms encircled him and Elspeth. Demir placed his forehead against hers, his tears dripping down on to her cheeks.

A low, lilting melody began to rumble through the clearing. The words were indecipherable to Aleksander, full of sounds he'd never heard spoken and guttural consonants that somehow felt like staring at a candle dancing on its wick in an otherwise dark room. The voice serenading them—serenading *her*—broke as it continued, louder and longer, the once strong notes wavering and cracking over the field.

A funeral song.

Aleksander closed his eyes and leaned his head atop Elspeth's.

There, in the rain and mud, Varek held them and continued to sing.

Chapter

FORTY ONE

THE FIRE WAS ALL ALEKSANDER SAW. Licking over logs, popping at the slightest touch of rain that had not yet dried from whatever wood they'd thrown in.

He had not spoken in hours. Not since they'd wrapped Iscah's body in a sheet from Terrell's linen basket and laid her to rest with whatever they could scrounge from the mostly preserved cottage. A single bottle of wine was placed beside her head in the muddy hole Demir dug, alongside fresh berries and a handful of feathers.

A measly grave, Varek had commented, for someone who deserved to be buried like royalty.

For a moment, Carissa had considered burying the Aramerk with her. Varek voted against it. It was never meant for Iscah; it was meant for someone who could use it. Crafters never made things for themselves.

A crow yelled from a branch, breaking the intense focus he'd kept on the images dancing in the flames.

Across the camp, Carissa smoothed the rumpled feathers on Demir's left wing, water washing out the dirt that had begun to stick in the wound. He'd broken it. Aleksander hadn't noticed when they were kneeling in the field together, but the way it hung along the ground, the awkward angle it fell at. He should have. The princess's fingers were careful and sure as she tied a clean bandage from their pack around the fracture.

"I'll heal," he'd said. "Breaking a wing is just like breaking a leg—except I still have those."

No one had laughed. Not even Demir. His eyes focused far away, no matter who he was speaking to. Especially if he wasn't saying anything. He regarded Carissa with a harsh glare whenever he dared regard anyone.

He didn't look at Aleksander.

A day of walking passed, and nothing but the *drip, drip, drip* of water working its way from the top of the canopy. Their packs were soaked when they found them the morning after. With the downpour, they'd done their best to clear the debris of the door Aleksander shattered when he was thrown through it and wrangle blankets and pillows from other small rooms in the cottage. A few extra logs on the still-burning hearth, and they all slept in a pile before it. The fire lasted well past sunrise. While their clothes weren't entirely dry, they were, at the very least, warm. They'd ransacked all the notes the lord had kept in the cottage as well. Somehow, Carissa had convinced herself they would find information on the Scourge's identity and whereabouts, but all they found were old blasphemous scriptures and prophecies, notes on the homunculi, and a list of towns to reach out to for resources and possible allies.

Carissa tucked them away to show her father.

As they stopped walking for the night, their camp was made on damp earth with only a few stolen blankets to keep them entirely out of the elements.

"I'll take watch," Elspeth muttered, fingers dancing over her brow. Above her left eye already bloomed red and purple bruising. It was a miracle it wasn't swollen to the point of blinding her.

"No, I want you to sleep." Varek's voice was just as tired as anyone else's. Dark circles of grief and exhaustion deepened his eyes, heavy lids accentuating the age lines there. Regardless, his jaw set, an exasperated glance casting at Elspeth. "I'll take watch."

"Why don't you both take watch?" Carissa sighed. "Varek takes first, Elspeth takes second."

"Because," Varek said, measured frustration beginning to leech into his tone, "it is summer. Nights are short. We will be up at first light and moving, it doesn't make sense for two people take watch." He looked at her. "Also, because I said so."

No one gave much of a fight. Elspeth tried again to barter for first watch, saying that Varek needed the sleep as much as anyone else.

"I've been on this earth for centuries. One night awake isn't going to kill me" was all he said before jutting a finger towards the bed he'd made for her. "Lie down."

Sleep came in fits. Images of the Dzera, the Scourge, the homunculi and their creator swarmed his dreams. And the sounds...

Screams. Snarls. The slice of Aoife through Terrell's throat.

Aleksander bolted upright, slick with sweat. Each breath was painful, his whole body straining to slow them down, to even them out.

"Go back to sleep, kid" came the weary, whispered admonition. "Everything is fine here."

Varek's back was hunched. His hands were still, void of their usual fidgeting around a block of wood and a paring knife or that small book he'd been working his way through. They wrapped around the hilt of his sword, chin resting on the pommel, eyes staring out into nothing but dark trees and an empty night.

For the first time in days, Aleksander wanted to speak. Everyone else was asleep—everyone but him and the one man who could answer his questions. And there were so many answers he wanted, so many questions he'd been waiting to ask. The question that came, however, was not the one he expected.

"Why did you throw the match against her?"

Varek somehow grew even more statuesque than he had been.

"I saw you do it," Aleksander continued, pulling the blanket up around his shoulders. The chilled night air was getting to be too cold. "I've fought you enough over the last few weeks that I know when you're deliberately losing."

"If you'd been watching closely, you'd have noticed she caught an error I made," he sighed.

"An error you *purposefully* made. It was easy to avoid, Varek. You and I both know that." Wind rustled through the canopy. "Why did you do it?"

A long moment passed.

"We needed her. And I was going to do anything I could to make sure we got her." The man cleared his throat, voice catching. "She was a worthy opponent. I know she would have earned her place anyways, I didn't *have* to throw it. But I did. Just to be sure." Varek's gaze turned to Aleksander, full of sorrow. Of anger. His chin quivered, and the eyes Aleksander had hardly ever seen any emotion in were shimmering with pooling tears. "And don't come at me saying it's my fault—I know it is."

Aleksander's racing pulse stuttered to a stop. That wasn't—

"My only comfort comes from knowing she's not alone anymore." He blinked sharply, turning his eyes back out to the forest. "Our people live alone often. But that doesn't mean we should."

"She wasn't alone," Aleksander whispered. "And it's not your fault. She had us. She had Demir. And I'm the one who chose her in the first place." His pulse picked up again, starting his blood along a slow, slogging pace through his veins. "I was the one who chose a Crafter. I was the one who made her come out on the field with us..." He heaved a deep sigh and lay back, staring through the canopy. Neither action offered any of the relief he was hoping for. "Now that I think about it, she should have stayed and defended Carissa if any homunculi went that way."

Varek grunted. "Then I guess we're both to blame."

Wind rustled Aleksander's hair. He followed its source through the trees. There, a distance off, still as a stone, looming as a mountain, was a figure with branching antlers and two fiery eyes.

He met its eyes without so much as blinking. "Yeah. But at least we killed that son of a bitch."

To one side, the Ölmesuz laughed. To the other, the wind rustled, and the sound of water skating over pebbles on a shoreline trailed on the breeze as the Dzera laughed too.

"Yeah," Varek said. "It may be a step towards war, but he had to go."

The Dzera seemed to nod, its glowing eyes flashing in agreement.

"Sleep, kid," Varek said, adjusting his seat. Aleksander watched as he relaxed his sword by his feet, digging a block of wood and a small knife out of his pack. "Still got a few hours until dawn."

When Aleksander looked back, the Dzera was gone.

FORTY TWO

THE NEXT FEW DAYS WENT ON nearly silently. The exchange between him and Varek in the middle of the night was never repeated—not with Varek, not with anyone else. What was said was said, and that seemed to be all the words anyone needed, whether they heard them or not.

As the trek continued, however, Aleksander found himself unable to look any of his friends in the eye. Everyone but Varek—though when he did share a glance with the old man, the weight that had begun to dissipate thanks to the chirping birds and the slowly reappearing sun settled again. His only solace was in the way Varek's shoulder's slumped when his did, as though he were not carrying this weight, this grief—this guilt—alone.

Carissa's fingers clutched the Aramerk all the while. Aleksander tried not to look at them often. The way they turned white at the knuckle but viciously red on the pads and beneath the nails sent a nervous shiver across his back.

He half expected, alongside cracks of branches and twigs, to hear those already battered nails snap further against the ornate, filigreed, gem-inlaid focus, requiring further bandaging like her other hand.

The princess was not alone in her silent distress. Demir wobbled on uneasy feet, unsure how to move with the loss of use in his left wing. He held it close to his back, folded up with the wrappings Carissa had tied in an attempt to stabilize it for the journey home. Bloodshot eyes never met Aleksander's, and Aleksander didn't blame him. Each skittering of rocks, each frustrated grunt or sigh caused the boy to whip his head around, only to watch the warrior he'd traveled and fought with this last week—or maybe its was 'weeks,' he wasn't sure at this point—stumble, with gritted teeth and clenched fists.

His own body ached. Each step was agony, not to mention the pain breathing caused. Aleksander was sure he'd cracked a few ribs.

Elspeth kept by him. Silent. She never made an attempt to talk, never looked his way, though Aleksander noted maybe she did, but he never noticed because he never looked at her. The only way he was certain of her constant presence as their aching legs and burning feet propelled them at a steady pace over the uneven terrain was the occasional light brush of her fingers on his elbow, shoulder, or even the palm of his hand.

Once, she caught his hand in hers, and delivered a quick squeeze before pulling back and not even acknowledging what she'd done.

For hours after, he still felt the warmth of her hand in his.

Their days were simply that—walking, stopping for food or water, never to talk, walking some more, making camp, arguing over who gets watch, and then waking up and repeating it. Their food was running low, and they'd made it to their last water skin, but somehow everyone agreed that it didn't matter at this point. Their fates were in the hands of the gods now.

Then, one early morning, Aleksander caught something on a nearby tree—a sword cut. *His* sword cut, when he'd first slashed a way through the thicket for them.

His eyes raised, feet speeding along.

At this, his companions spoke.

"What is it?" Carissa's panicked tone cut through the early morning fog. They'd broken camp before dawn, just when the sky began to lighten to a discernible shade of blue, though it had been only a few lighter than the ink of midnight.

He didn't answer.

Boots tumbled along behind him, keeping pace. Varek called out, telling him to slow down. Even Demir asked what was going on, if Aleksander was alright.

Aleksander pushed forward through low-hanging branches, thorned bushes tearing at his pants, until he saw it, until he smelled it.

The fire in the clearing crackled with low flame, only more than a stone's throw from the road that cut through Zekhar from the northeastern coast all the way to the capital and the castle. Beside, bathed in watery blue light, lay Bunc, small sword loose in his hand as he dozed near the two horses they'd left days ago.

The man's shoulders were hunched, his worn face somehow even more worn.

"Bunc." Aleksander's voice cracked.

One of the horses nickered, stamping her feet and tossing her head as he approached, surely smelling of death and sweat and any other manner of rotten things.

The crashing of a body through the forest's edge startled Bunc awake, his dazed, glassy eyes scanning wildly, sword still loose in his grip.

Aleksander had never known this man beyond his name. He'd worked for the palace for years, driven Aleksander and Carissa to countless meetings, events, and on shopping trips in town. He'd carted them to and from the temple, only a few minutes' walk from the castle but when you had an entire day of swordsmanship followed by nights of theology, history, and studying, hopping in a cart and being driven the five minutes to the front steps of your home was a relief.

Yet he threw his arms around the man, waves of relief and thankfulness mixing with all the other complex emotions he'd been carrying the last few days. One image cleared in his mind.

It was of Bunc, his face younger and much less weathered. A thick, dark mustache was neatly trimmed and sat on his upper lip. He held the reigns of one of the horses pulling their cart in his leather gloves. They were rather new, not yet cracked and worn. Bunc let Aleksander pet her. He told her about her. This was...outside Aleksander's house. His family's home. The day King Clauden and Mother Saoirse came to retrieve him and begin his preparation. It was not his father who had comforted him that day, as he cried, his hand in a strange woman's, led away from the only home he'd ever known. The only life he'd ever known. No, his father had stood with his mother on the steps, her eyes glassy and his shining, talking with Clauden. Saoirse had passed him to Bunc, waving her hands and confessing that she wasn't good with children. It was the driver who picked up the crying boy and started telling him all about the mares that drew the carriage. Their names, their temperaments, how one was a grandmother, and wasn't that interesting?

His anger flared at the memory. Perhaps his parents hadn't regretted leaving him.

But Bunc had welcomed him. He'd taken Aleksander's hand in his, guided it to the mare's black velvet nose, and traced the outline of a star that sat between her nostrils. It was the first and only time Bunc had been so personable with him, but...

Aleksander clung to that memory with both hands. He clung to Bunc too. It seemed he couldn't pull himself deep enough into the driver's chest, couldn't shrink himself enough to be held, but still, he tried.

"What's the meaning of this, my lord?" Bunc's voice shook, but Aleksander heard the sword *thump* into the dirt. A moment later, strong arms encircled him, one hand rubbing soft, comforting circles on his back.

Everything in Aleksander's chest exploded. His body wracked with sobs, the shoulder of Bunc's expensive coat soaked with tears in mere moments, Aleksander did nothing but cling to him and cry.

Where the others were didn't matter. If he'd lost them in his haste to get to to the fire, he didn't think of it for more than a moment.

Not when Bunc gently stroked his awful, filthy hair, and quietly murmured, "Well, now. You're alright, my boy. You're alright."

Chapter

FORTY THREE

NIGHT AFTER NIGHT OF THE SPARKLING, shimmering reflections cast on the ornate walls and curtains had begun to make Aleksander's head spin. That was to say nothing of the constant ringing in his ears from the band, the company—the sheer noise of it all.

Weeks traveling—for it had, indeed, been weeks, despite how jumbled the memories from them were—had caused him to grow accustomed to the silence of a woodland evening. Not one filled with courtiers constantly finding him in a sea of finery and asking him to regale them with tales of the adventure he'd just returned from. The first tales of their Sword had finally happened, and they were champing at the bit to be among the first to hear them.

He couldn't count the times he'd forced a smile over the last three nights, recounting how they fought Demir before they knew it was him or the homunculi in the burned village. That one always earned a sympathetic look. To see a village destroyed, how awful. Innocent lives lost, how sad. The courtiers' sympathy faded quickly. They'd never seen such horrors. Part of Aleksander wondered if they even truly cared.

When it came to the story of Varek fighting Iscah, he left out the part where Varek let her win. Whether the man had been telling the truth or just trying to make Aleksander feel better, the low voice saying, "I know she would have earned her place anyways, I didn't *have* to throw it," echoed in his mind. She was a skilled Crafter—a fact he made sure to tell them when he mentioned how much her focus, the Aramerk, helped Carissa—but in the end, she had fought as fiercely as any of them. She deserved to be remembered as both a Crafter and a Warrior—by him, by these people, and by the generations beyond when their portraits were inevitably added to the part of the ceiling above them that had not been painted with images yet, but instead had empty circles, ready for new tales, new Swords.

Ready for him.

His throat tightened when he mentioned her death. He didn't mention how he still felt awful for not seeing it, for not being there for her, for focusing solely on the traitor and only looking her way when Demir cried out.

The courtiers often bowed their heads for a moment of silence at her death, displayed shock at Lord Terrell's betrayal, then continued on sloppily with praise and thanks and "blessed be Tulathne for keeping our young Lord Wythane safe." The air was always irrevocably shifted towards discomfort after that.

As much as everyone knew these events meant the coming of war, and everything that war brought with it, no one ever seemed ready to talk about death.

One woman, an Ölmesuz he'd remembered from the summer solstice, with hair not unlike the silver waterfall that had been coiled upon Iscah's head, short bangs curled to bounce against her equally pale forehead, raised a glass after the seemingly mandatory moment of silence after that part of the story.

"To Iscah Hatenepta," she said, meeting his eyes and not daring to break it with so much as a blink. "For all she has done for us, and all this world has lost. May the Kutsalyot welcome her with open arms."

His throat closed in a desperate attempt to shut off the tears that had already begun to sting his eyes and nose. Yet, he too raised his glass and nodded. "Her words were a light in the dark, and her presence a comfort, till her last breath."

Tears welled in the Ölmesuz woman's eyes. The other courtiers had begun to peel away, called by other dignitaries or other duties, or simply put off by the emotion of it all. The few that lingered watched the exchange with an air of respect and pride for this show of emotion. It was not truly real to them anyways.

She took a sip. Aleksander did too. When she lowered her chalice from her lips, she passed it to her left hand, the right reaching out and placing a firm, reassuring squeeze on Aleksander's forearm. "May the Mother bless you," she whispered.

He nodded. "You as well."

With a curtsy she excused herself, and Aleksander found himself alone for the first time in three days.

As he scanned the ballroom, there was not a single person he saw who he had not talked to, received praise from, or given a blessing to. Varek and Elspeth were scattered at opposite ends of the hall, still sharing their stories best they could. A few forced laughs from the Ölmesuz man and stuttered explanations from the Rodzjiek girl who had clearly never been given this kind of attention before found his ears through the churning din. Demir had posted himself on the terrace, giving room for his wings. A healer had properly set the injured one, but due to the length of time between the injury and the setting, she had confided in the royal family that she was unsure it would ever heal back to full strength.

None of them had the heart to tell him yet.

Whenever Aleksander contemplated drawing the man aside, sitting him down, and breaking the news, all he saw was the tiny shape that was Demir darting through the skies above them with an Orzei. The flush in his cheeks and the sparkle in his eyes after he landed. The joy at being who he was.

Demir needed to know, that much was for certain, but not now. He'd endured too much for right now.

They all had.

Aleksander continued his survey of the room. Elspeth's eyes caught his through a gap in the crowd and he took a step towards her, only for courtiers to sweep through the space and whisk her to the refreshment table, set on hearing more from her over a drink or two.

A pit settled in his stomach. His eyes finally settled at the front of the hall.

There, on the dais, sat Carissa. The bags under her eyes were still dark and heavy, but her cheeks were not as wan as they were before. She smiled when her eyes danced up to her husband, seated on the arm of her throne, fingers interlaced with hers. Her injured hand rested in her lap, wrapped and set with clean linens and splints. Janek kept a constant commentary going—something Aleksander had seen him do for her many times. It gave her something to focus on that was not the chaos before her.

She'd told Aleksander once that all she needed to do was hear the sound of her husband's voice, and all else would fade away the moment she willed it. With the vacant look in those grey-green eyes as she scanned the hall, passing over him without so much as a pause, he knew she had, indeed, willed everything else to fade.

As he approached, a hand rested on his shoulder. A gentle push beckoned him to turn around.

"How are you?" Varek asked. He towered above him, clean and styled. His dark hair was washed and styled in a series of braids, and sectioned curls were pushed fully back away from his face and over his ears.

Aleksander blinked up at him. "I'm fine."

He grunted, folding his arms over the embroidered doublet that was nearly twenty times fancier than what he usually wore. "I'm getting tired of these parties. Thinking about going off to my room, not talking to anyone for a few days."

"Hm." Aleksander nodded, his eyes flitting around the room.

"I'm sure everyone will be fine if I sneak off," Varek said, narrowing his eyes.

"Yeah." The word dragged out slowly. "I'm sure it would be fine."

Varek cleared his throat. "Listen, kid." He shifted from foot to foot. "You need to know you did well."

A weight dropped onto Aleksander's shoulders. It had been there for the last few days—ever since they saw the cottage, even before that—but now he *felt* it.

"What we did out there...what *you* did... It's not easy. But you were made for it, that much is clear. Iscah would be proud of you, and..." His eyes scanned the room before falling back on the boy before him. "And if it means anything, I am too."

The burning that erupted behind Aleksander's eyes was not what he expected.

Varek paused.

He should answer, shouldn't he?

The tightness in his throat suggested otherwise.

"Anyways," the Ölmesuz continued, rolling his neck. "These courtiers are draining. In all my centuries, I've never gotten used to events like this."

Aleksander wanted to back up the conversation, tell Varek that he shouldn't be proud, that Aleksander didn't do well. That he caused a death and killed someone and was causing more harm than good.

But something stopped him. Maybe it was the earnestness in Varek's eyes he'd never seen before. Maybe it was the fact that, for a moment, Aleksander didn't hate him.

But he sniffed, rolled his neck, and shot Varek a side-eye. "How many centuries is that again?"

Varek huffed and a smirk appeared on his face. "As if you'll ever get me to answer truthfully." A moment passed and he pressed his fist to his heart. The bow he delivered was slight, small, but earnest.

I think that's the first time he's ever bowed to me.

"I'll leave you, your holiness." The man straightened, offered a final, small nod, and disappeared into the hallway.

Blowing out a heavy breath, Aleksander spun slowly until his eyes fixed back on Carissa, still seated on the dais, still staring out at the gathering with a blank, reserved expression.

Janek gave him a hesitant smile on his approach, which broadened the moment Aleksander reciprocated. "How are you?" he asked. His hand stayed interlaced with Carissa's, thumb bumping back and forth over her knuckles.

Next to him, Aleksander finally noticed how thin Carissa had gotten. How stern her face had set.

Aleksander shrugged. "Doing as well as I can." He cast a nervous look to the princess, still focused so deeply on seeming as though she was surveying the crowd, but surely was lost in her own mind. "Carissa?"

"Hm?" The vacancy disappeared as her eyes fell on him.

He'd spoken to her only briefly, the first night they'd spent back in the castle. After both had bathed and dressed in clean clothes, she'd shown up in his room. They exchanged pleasantries, as if they were no more than two courtiers meeting one another after a long stretch between the solstices. Then, she sat on his bed, leaning against his shoulder.

"Do you think Tulathne will forgive me?" she'd whispered.

"For what?"

A long moment passed. "For everything."

"Everything" had an incredibly broad connotation. And even with that, Aleksander could not pinpoint one single thing that Carissa would need forgiveness for. Still, he'd wrapped his arm around her and nodded against her hair. "Yeah. I'm sure She will."

It was as though, in that moment, every bit of frustration, tension, and awkwardness between them had been entirely dissolved, as though it never had existed in the first place.

Now, she looked up at him, and smiled. "Oh." Her voice was still distant. "Aleksander. I didn't see you come up."

"I didn't expect you to." He shifted on his feet, glancing back out at the crowd, then back to her. "Do you think they'd be upset if I left?"

Her finely shaped brows furrowed. "Are you alright?"

No, said every nerve in his body. "I'm fine. Just... overwhelmed, I guess. It's been three days of this and I'm..." He sighed, letting that weight he'd finally felt moments earlier stoop his shoulders and curve his back. "I'm tired."

She nodded, hand flying out to catch his own. "You go. Rest. I'll draw the festivities to an end soon...or my father will. He seems to have had enough of this as well."

Aleksander followed her gaze.

Though she said the king was tired, it certainly didn't look that way. Clauden stood in the near middle of the fray, Lenore on his arm, laughing heartily and toasting to something Duke Kallendrine said.

A few paces behind them, Aleksander caught Elspeth refusing a dance from a lord's son. He half debated following her as she escaped out into the dim light of the terrace, but even a single breath was becoming heavy in his lungs.

Turning back to Carissa, he nodded. "Thank you. I will."

WITHIN HOURS, THE NOISE OF the party died. Aleksander lay, unmoving, on his bed, staring at the ceiling, gauging the amount of partygoers still present by how many coaches he heard pull up and leave. By the time the sky was entirely dark and had been so for a long while, all the carriages that had been stationed in the lot to the left of the castle were gone.

The only sounds audible were his own breathing and the flickering of the candle on his vanity.

Tulathne, still and stern as ever behind her fluttering veil, reached out from her place on the tapestry in his oratory.

He hadn't prayed since getting back to Castle Brevindun. In fact, he'd done his best to avoid making eye contact with the woven image of the goddess. Tonight was different though. He felt his attention being almost poked at. Whether it was his own desire for connection and answers or Tulathne Herself, he didn't care. He didn't have the time or the energy to figure out what was driving him.

He only stood, donned pants and a dressing gown, and made sure his door closed silently behind him as he left.

Chapter

FORTY FOUR

THE GRASS WAS COOL UNDER HIS feet, wet with evening dew. He hadn't noticed he'd forgotten shoes until he'd stepped onto the chilled stone of the front steps, but it didn't deter him. The lights of the temple were visible, and so he began the walk, cutting through grass so as to save time and to save his feet from the sharp stones littering the road.

The Great Temple of Tulathne was always open. This was the first time he was entirely grateful for it. The building was tall, with stone pillars holding up an overhang decorated with fabrics and streamers and flowers—no doubt praising Her for his safe return. The white stone steps up to the open oak doors were spotless save for a few petals that had already begun to fall. Their pale blues and oranges flickered and flashed against the marble in the catches of torchlight.

Inside, the vaulted ceiling, hung with chandeliers, was dark. Past the pews and the open spaces for gathering, at the front of the temple, flickered the only light—three oil lamps set out around the front of Her statue. Her head almost hit the ceiling, and Her hands were both held up, elbows tucked to Her waist, one palm facing Her, the other facing the congregation.

She seemed almost alive in the flickering lamplight.

For the first time in months, Aleksander knelt before Her.

His eyes fixed on the one flame dancing before his face. It rose from a wick stuffed into a clear glass lamp, with a beautiful geometric pattern etched into it.

He breathed out and closed his eyes.

"I'm sorry," he whispered.

The goddess did not respond.

For what?

A shiver ran down his back and he startled. He hadn't heard anyone, not actually. There had just been a...*feeling*. A feeling of a question.

He'd heard the priestesses mention such a phenomenon. When deep in prayer or meditation they said they *heard* Her, but not really—that She spoke through notions, feelings, thoughts that popped into your head with no warning or coercion.

Heart pounding, skepticism and confusion threatening to drown his thoughts and derail his prayers, he pushed forward.

"For what happened. To Iscah. I'm...I'm the one to blame."

Sorrow and...pride, almost, flowed through him. The warmth he'd begun to associate with Her presence danced down his spine.

It's okay, She seemed to say. *You'll do better, and you did well regardless.*

He shook his head, pressing his forehead to the stone before the statue. Open eyes stared blankly at the ground. "Am I even supposed to do this?"

At this, he felt nothing. The warmth stayed—but just barely.

The chill stood out against it. Not just the chill in his knees or forehead where they met cold stone, but the one within.

It felt...strange. To have both of them in his body at the same time. Strange, but not wrong, not entirely.

Blowing out another breath, he lifted his eyes to the face of the goddess, towering above him. For the first time since the concept was introduced to him, Aleksander let the notion—the fear—settle in his bones. "Am I Alesathne? Or are they right? Everything I've heard of him, of those before me...it's not me. I don't think he's me."

"What brings on these doubts, my lord?"

The old voice cracked softly, actually in the space, not his head. He skittered back from the statue and scanned the darkness beyond. In the shadows stood a woman, hunched. The white-grey cloud of tight curls cascading down her shoulders was the first thing he made out.

"Mother Saoirse," he breathed. "I'm so sorry if I disturbed you."

"No," she laughed, stepping into the firelight. "No, my dear, you could never disturb me." Her face was wrinkled, yet nearly glowed from within. People said she was hundreds of years old, but everyone knew humans don't live that long. Still, for the first time, he understood in this moment why they said that. Beyond the visible signs of age, the seeress held an otherworldly stature about her. Similar to Varek, he noted, though not as world-weary.

His heart sank at the thought, at the parallel drawn between his own grief and the cloud that seemed to be settled over Varek at all times.

Another stitch of guilt tugged through the muscle beating behind his ribs—right alongside Iscah's death, the way he let Carissa destroy herself, and that town burned to ash.

How could he allow himself to add another loss to the man's life?

To any of their lives?

"You sound discontented, Alesathne. Worried, even." The thick tones of her lilting accent, still holding elements of old Zekharyan, soothed him as much as the use of that name disgruntled him.

She had never once used his real name, not in all the time he knew her. "Aleksander" never existed to Saoirse. It never frustrated him—not until now. Alesathne had not buried Iscah. Alesathne had not seen those bodies in the town. Alesathne was not the one kneeling before the statue of his mother terrified, guilty, and desperate. Alesathne would not have those problems.

No, in this moment he was sure he was Aleksander. Soul of a

demigod or no.

Yet all he did was swallow sharply and stand, offering a bow. The old woman bowed back. Then they both stood there, waiting to see who would speak first.

"I'm... I've seen a lot in the past weeks, Saoirse," he said, unsure of where to start but figuring he'd sort it out as he spoke. "And now I'm...sad, I suppose. Sad and maybe grieving... confused, and... I don't know." Maybe he had been wrong about figuring it out as he spoke. Aleksander backed up, sitting in the first pew and staring up at the goddess. "All the other Swords had time. The youngest before me was well into his twenties, older than even Carissa or Janek. And they were all good at what they did. They didn't have doubts and I..." His gaze flitted to her with a sharp exhale. "Why didn't I get that time? I have so many people looking at me for help and I always have but it's different now, and I... Saiorse, why do I—" His voice broke. "Why do I have to make these choices that determine the fates of people I care about when I don't even know..."

Don't even know what? His thoughts went blank. He shouldn't have to qualify this with such a statement. He should have just left it as "why."

That was all he wanted to know.

Why.

Saoirse stepped forward, head bowed. "The ways of our Lady are...strange. I've been on this earth too long to pretend otherwise. I've *seen* too much to pretend otherwise." She laughed at this. It was a soft sound, rolling through the temple like a soft spring rain. "But I'll say this. Do you want to know why we believe you are Alesathne? Beyond the alignment of the stars on the day of your birth?"

He nodded.

"It was because when we came to get you—King Clauden and I—we saw a boy who was mitigating an imaginary argument between a snake he'd found in his mother's flowerpot and the flowers themselves. And when that boy decided the best course of action was to move the snake, he did so. It bit him, when he picked it up, but he still handled it with care and released it into a nearby grove."

Aleksander blinked at her. "Okay?"

She turned her face towards the statue. "It may sound stupid, but that's when *I* knew. Because beyond being the one to slay the Scourge and protect Zekhar, the Sword is a force of change." Saoirse turned back to Aleksander, fixing him with a stare that called him to attention. "We've never had an age of the Scourge and the Sword that did not result in massive changes. For good, mostly. Sometimes for bad. But even in the bad, there was good. And I knew in that moment, that you were someone who would take the good with the bad and do what you could to make things better. And in all your years here, living among the royal family, studying among my sisters"—her bones creaked as she eased herself onto the pew beside him—"I have only seen you prove me right. Zvezda has told me as much."

Aleksander's head snapped towards her. He never thought the healer told anyone about what he did. Hundreds of names came rushing back to him—Emery, Robert, Baird, Kelsey, Saul, Graciela...Clair. If Saoirse knew about him funding their treatment by Zvezda, did she know about their recoveries?

Did *any* of them still draw breath?

His tongue fell thick in his mouth. He didn't speak.

A heavy sigh echoed as Saoirse sat back, folding her dark, withered hands in her lap. "Bad things have already happened. You lost someone you were supposed to protect, and I can't begin to imagine how painful that is." Her eyes turned to him, a bright, icy blue. "But do you want to know something else? The world has begun its shift. Since news of Lord Terrell's death began spreading, we've heard more and more whispers. Those loyal to—or even interested in the Scourge—are gathering. But alongside that?" She smiled. "Alongside that, our people feel seen by you. Heard. They've vowed loyalty and support in any way they can." Her eyes fixed once more on the statue before them. On the way the carved marble glistened and danced in the firelight. "I've seen nothing but visions of a new Zekhar. A brighter Zekhar. Where we do not live in fear of the Scourge. Ever again."

Aleksander's brow furrowed as her smile widened.

"*Never* again. And it's all because of *you*." The brightness on her face tripped. "I've seen bad too. Do you remember my oracle?"

"Yes."

She nodded. "Hm. Well, it still stands. Only some of it has been fulfilled and truth be told, I fear for how the other parts will fare when translated into our world. But Aleksander." His heart tripped at his name. One withered hand took his, patting it assuredly. "Anything a seer has foretold can be interpreted a multitude of ways. And I believe, whatever the true outcome is, that you will do *good*. Not well—though you will. But *good*."

He sat there, soaking in all her words. He'd met the seeress briefly over the years. She had always seemed...terrifying. Aloof. Ancient, with her dark skin and unearthly eyes, her tall stature and firm mouth. And yet, sitting beside him now, his hand in hers, that gentle smile and the reassured hope in her eyes...

Aleksander wondered if this is what it was like to have a grandmother.

Finally, he nodded, breaking whatever trance he had entered, and stood, bowing to her. "Thank you, Mother Saoirse. That... helped."

She nodded. "I'm glad. Now." She stood once more, slow but sure on her feet, and caught a coil of curl in her knobby fingers, twisting it as she spoke. "This is a lovely evening. And I don't think you've had nearly enough time to enjoy Tulathne's world in the last few years. Do me a favor. Come back tomorrow, and tell me which flower in the garden you like the smell of the most. And maybe which constellation you see the clearest, if you think that far."

A smile lightened his face, and while that warmth from Tulathne had long since passed, a different warmth had taken its place. A better warmth.

"I will, Saoirse."

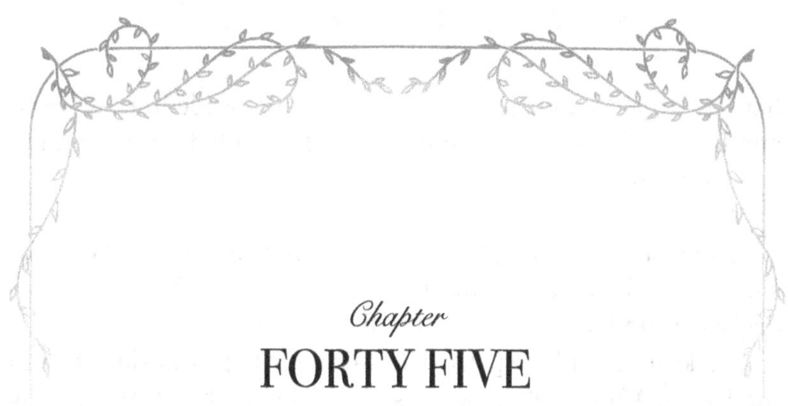

Chapter

FORTY FIVE

EVEN JUST APPROACHING THE GARDEN, HE was already sure he knew the flower he'd tell her when the sun rose. Lilacs. There were so many in the royal garden, their scents cut through the air better than any perfume. As he approached, passing by few torches, a voice slowed his steps. He couldn't make out the words, but the speaker...

"Elspeth?"

She turned, mouth still open from whatever she was saying. The girl sat in the center of the courtyard—one of the many in the expansive garden—on a stone bench. The legs were etched with different flowers—marigolds, dahlias, roses, and forget-me-nots made the bench itself become part of the garden, not just a place to sit in it.

"Aleksander." She scanned him up and down. "How are you?"

He took stock of himself before he answered. His body ached. The ribs he'd broken shifted as he breathed and he still grimaced when he beheld the mottled bruising along his torso when getting dressed, but over the course of the last few days he'd gotten used to the sharp jolts of pain.

"I'm...I'm actually okay, Elspeth. How are you?" He scanned her face, tense and still darkened above her eyebrow and along her jaw from the injuries she'd sustained alongside him. Without another word, he sat beside her. Elspeth scooted away. It wan't just to give him space. It was—

"What's wrong?"

Auburn waves shook, cascading down her back, over her shoulders. The smell of rosemary was strong on the breeze that drifted around her. "Nothing, I'm fine."

Aleksander didn't speak. The pair hadn't spoken since before the battle. After...well, after was after. No one had walked away the same.

"They kept asking about me," she muttered, looking down at her hands. "About who I was, who my family was. They were... disappointed that I wasn't raised in Rodzjiek culture. But"—she shook her head, meeting his eyes—"in a weird way? Like I failed them by being raised by Zekharyans. I've been to court before. I was at the solstice. But today..."

He rolled his eyes. "Ignore them. I've read tales of when Ölmesuz first joined the courts. They were seen as decoration, not actual members. But that changed. And it'll change again."

"I couldn't give them explanations. For my magic." A bitter laugh followed. With no warning, Elspeth stretched out her hands and let them burst into flame. Heat flared sharply and Aleksander jumped, nearly falling off the bench. "I don't know *how* I can do this. I didn't even know we *could*. And they were so fascinated and kept asking and I was just as shocked as them. And when I..." Turning back to him, her face paled. The flames died immediately, leaving her palms bare and unharmed. "I'm scaring you."

Though his heart pounded, he shook his head. "How could you scare me?"

"Your face." She flicked a finger up at him. "You look at me now and see the...*thing*...I became on the field, don't you? I saw how much I scared you then. All of you." Her words began to jumble together, and all Aleksander wanted to do was reach into her mind and untangle them for her. Smooth a hand down her face. Force her to take a deep breath. "And honestly I scared myself. I've never done that before and when I did I just felt such...gods, I don't know. Just such fury, such fear, and suddenly, my bones felt like they were on fire and I just *had* to get it out. And yet I'm scared because it felt necessary, and *gods*, what kind of person feels good after doing something like that? I'm—"

His hand closed around hers, and the rest of her words died on her tongue. It was warm beneath his palm—not hot, not as though it had been on fire moments before, but warm. Soft. Slowly, his thumb bumped over her knuckles. "You're okay. I'm not scared of you. You scared me, yes, but that does not mean I fear *you*, El."

She blinked at the name and glanced down at their hands. "Are you sure?" Her eyes flickered as they rose once more to his.

He nodded. "Absolutely." An unexpected panic began to churn in his gut. "If anyone should be apologizing, it's me."

Thick brows dropped over her eyes. "Why?"

"I'm the one who came up with the plan. And it got Iscah killed." He withdrew his hand, peering out at the flowers, the bushes, the starry sky beyond. A fresh, cool breeze blew through, bringing with it the scent of lilacs and rosemary. Elspeth was silent as he took a deep breath. He focused on the air floating through his nose, his throat, his lungs. He noted the way it smelled—the freshness of late summer and the sweetness of the flowers. "I'm not equipped to do this. Tulathne... She's pulled away from me, I think. I don't know why, but that's just what I feel. And as much as Saoirse gave me good advice and I'm... comfortable with my duty, regardless of Tulathne's constant guidance or lack thereof." He glanced at her. "I would understand if you don't want to be a part of this anymore. If you feel uncomfortable being a part of this weird"—he shook his head—"whatever you want to call it. Team, regiment, party, inner circle, council."

"I'm a part of your inner circle?" The excitement bloomed and refused to fade in her eyes, no matter how hard she pressed her lips flat to try and hide it. "Like a king's right hand or something?"

He fought back a smile. The brightness in her eyes brought a new spark to his soul. "I mean, that's what I consider everyone who went on this first expedition. You were all there for the start of...everything. But like I said, if you or Demir or even Varek want to—"

"Let me stop you right there," she said. "Who did I vow myself to?"

Aleksander's brows furrowed. "What?"

"When we recited that oath together, who did I vow myself to?"

The fragmented, half-forgotten words circled through his head, even more disjointed than when he'd recited it to her. He shook his head. "Tulathne?"

"You." Elspeth's gaze was steady, locked on his face. "Tulathne was mentioned, but I vowed myself to *you*. 'I swear to follow *you*, my body is *your* shield, my arm *your* sword.'" She grinned, fangs sharp and shining. "'The fire in my bones will warm you,' remember?"

Another round of guilt settled in his stomach despite the joy and peace fighting to light up his chest. "You shouldn't, I'm—"

"You're what, inexperienced? Scared?" She leaned forward, her hand resting on the side of his face and turning his eyes to hers though his gaze kept wandering out into the evening. "Aleksander, we all are. But I've seen more of Zekhar in the last two weeks than my whole life, and I don't want to give up this freedom I've found serving you. I'm scared too. But you wanna know something? I think you can do this. And I'll be beside you for it."

Somehow, regardless of the tumult occurring throughout his entire body, spirit, and mind, regardless of the fact that he wanted to stop her and explain that it wasn't just that he was scared of the war but scared of who he may not be, Aleksander smiled. "I'm giving you an out. Formally. Do you take it?"

"No." Elspeth did not hesitate. Her face was stern, serious. "This is gonna be rough. And painful. And we're gonna lose more people, I'm sure of it. But ever since we talked on that rooftop and I realized who you were"—she smiled back—"I don't know, you...you give me hope for all this. You're not who I was taught the Sword of Ages would be. You're so much better. And so much more than just the Sword." Her eyes slid to his cheek, now resting in her hand, and pulled back.

Blush burned instantly in Aleksander's face.

Her long lashes fluttered with erratic blinks. "Anyways." She surveyed the sky, scanning until she fixed on one image. Aleksander didn't need to ask to know what she was looking at.

He'd found the Weaver the moment he'd stepped outside.

"I think she's got good things in store for us," Elspeth whispered.

Aleksander studied the girl beside him. Hair unbound, draped in a dressing gown not unlike his own, shoulders hunched and soft face turned up towards the moon. The image of her here and now was unlike any other he'd seen of her. The mystery astronomer, the soldier, the bait—a girl. Just a girl he hadn't known very long but already knew the constellation she liked most, the oil she massaged into her scalp every night, even some of her fears. Already, she was imprinted on him in a way he didn't quite understand.

"I think if we'd met under different circumstances," he began, not quite sure how his sentence would end, "we'd be really good friends."

She smiled. "What do you mean, 'different circumstances'? We could be friends now."

He shrugged, shifting in his seat. Genoise's words came floating back to him. Lord Terrell's face flashed through his mind. "I'm the Sword of Ages. That kind of position isn't one that works well with friends. Only allies, and even that is...tricky."

Lips splitting further into a grin, she rocked to the side, knocking his shoulder with hers. "Oh, come on. What's a friend but the truest ally you'd get? An ally not only on the field of battle, but through the fields of life instead?"

Aleksander laughed at the flowery language she spewed, and

she responded in kind.

Elspeth had a point, however; he had to acknowledge that.

"Maybe," she continued, voice low, leaning towards his ear yet still surveying the garden before her, "that's a stupid concept, and you should have friends because you deserve friends."

He leaned back slightly, taking in her countenance. The air around them was not exactly warm, but he felt as comfortable as when he was wrapped in quilts beside a fire. He supposed Elspeth was that fire, that bright warmth that could sustain life just as easily as take it.

In that moment, he knew—her fire would only ever sustain him.

After all, she'd sworn it to him, hadn't she?

With a cockeyed grin, he jutted his hand forward. "I don't believe we've met."

Her nose and brows scrunched up, smile still on her lips.

"I'm Aleksander Fylan." His family name tripped off his tongue. He'd never used it before, only read it in his own records. It settled in his bones as much as Elspeth's presence. As much as that chill that he no longer hated.

The soft features of the Rodzjiek girl relaxed, smile becoming more radiant and yet more subtle than he'd seen it ever before. Her hand raised, taking his. "Elspeth D'orde. A pleasure."

They sat there for a moment, hand in hand, grinning at one another.

"Hey." Elspeth squeezed his hand. "Do you happen to like astronomy?"

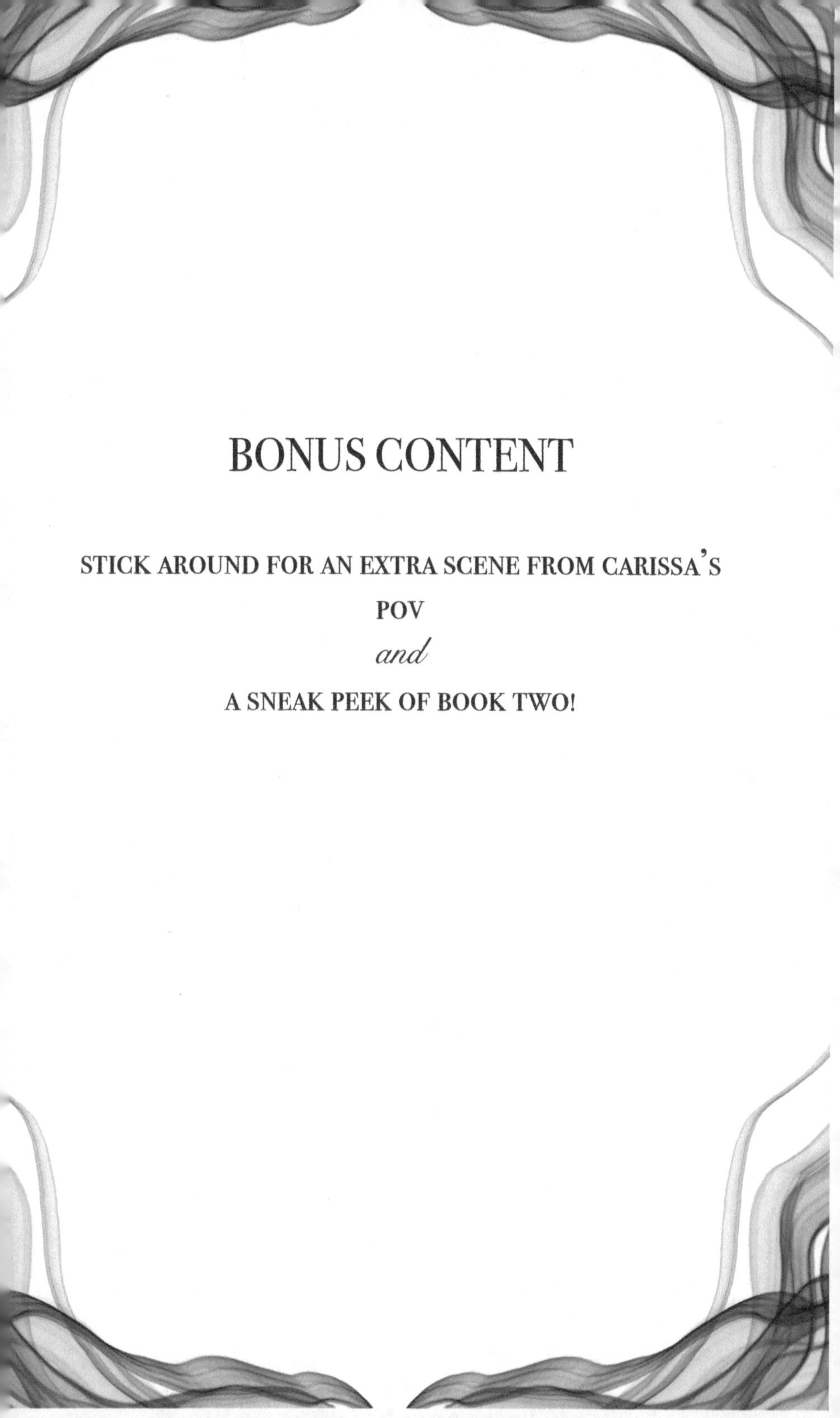# BONUS CONTENT

STICK AROUND FOR AN EXTRA SCENE FROM CARISSA'S

POV

and

A SNEAK PEEK OF BOOK TWO!

Chapter Twenty
CARISSA'S VISION

THE ARAMERK WAS COLD BETWEEN HER fingers. Goddess, how it was cold. No matter how long she held it, no matter how she often blew slow, warm breaths over the metal, it always stayed cold.

Her shoulders shook from that last one. The images were fresh in her mind—the skin stripping from her brother's body as he screamed, slithering along the ground to join up with other discarded scraps of flesh to create a whole new kind of monstrosity.

A tear dropped onto her hand.

No. This was not going to happen.

Tulathne, she thought to herself, repositioning the focus in her palm, *show me the* truth. *Not whatever you need to warn me of. Show me the inevitable.*

A slow, deep pull began to radiate from her chest into her arms. It was exhausting. Painful, almost. But she continued; the more she let the Flow have its way with her, the deeper the visions. And the deeper the visions, the more she could learn.

The more she saw, in all ways "seeing" could be interpreted.

She felt herself begin to float back. Her vision blurred as her eyes rolled back into her head, covered by fluttering eyelids. Cold rushed her body—

And she was standing in a field. The same field as before. Carissa rubbed her collarbone, trying to ground herself in the vision—if she didn't have the pendant of her goddess, then she would stay aware of the fact that this was not reality.

No metal chain twisted beneath her palm. Just warm skin and a frantic heartbeat.

She'd learned the trick as a child, when the visions became so overwhelming she lost herself and had to be dragged out of it by the priestesses. For some reason, her amulet never followed her into this realm.

The wind shifted around her, carrying with it a putrid scent of rotting flesh—the homunculi. When Carissa's vision focused, she centered on the four people with her. Varek's muffled orders echoed through the dreamlike space. Iscah stood, sword at the ready, beside the princess. Her face was gaunt, her eyes empty. She hardly looked at Carissa—instead she focused on the hoard of creatures swarming towards them in a wave.

Demir stretched his wings to her other side. He winced, lips quivering. At the homunculi? At something else?

His eyes were...green. Strange, they aren't normally—

"Carissa!"

Her face snapped towards the sound, where she saw Aleksander crying. He knelt in the grass, face red, eyes bloodshot. Dark, wispy tendrils of smoke circled his throat, his wrists, his ankles. They shackled him to the ground.

"Aleksander!" With no further thought, she sprinted towards him. This was how it always started—they were together, they saw Aleksander, and then...

The dark figure appeared beside Aleksander, a hand reaching out to grab a fistful of his hair. Rage flooded her senses. Of course, Carissa had never been able to make it to him before the figure appeared, why would now be any different? *Goddess* if she had just been able to—

No.

Springy moss and grass halted her approach. She drew a deep breath, slow and steady; then another.

Emotion clouded the visions. This wouldn't help.

She watched as the figure extended their hand—but instead of taking a fistful of Aleksander's hair and forcing him to stand, instead of flaying him and creating a new monstrosity, it gently cupped his chin.

Slowly, he rose to his feet. His eyes grew wide, blinking rapidly, not leaving the burning embers that sat in the shadow-sockets of the Scourge.

"I see," he muttered.

Carissa's heart raced. *What?*

This was not what she'd seen before. This was nothing she'd seen, ever.

The mist-shackles around his wrists fell away, and he stood. Some strange countenance fell over him, and she watched as he clasped the shadow-figure's hand. The two faced her.

"Aleksander—" her words flew away in a violent wind. The two rose into the sky, and from all corners of the earth, her people screamed.

It tore through to her heart. Panic beat a terrified, desperate pace against her ribs, and her hand again slammed flat against her collarbone—still no pendant, no chain beneath her palm. She pressed harder, not breaking the contact that proves one thing above all else—*this isn't real.*

"Oh" came the deep, echoing song. It looped around her, dancing in the flames that licked from every corner of her country. Trees burned, villages were swallowed whole. Aleksander smiled down at her from his terrifying space above the land. "Oh, my sister. But it is."

Her hand pressed to her chest and suddenly, there was the metal. It bit into her palm. Every muscle in her body was fatigued and even just keeping her hand by her chest sent tremors down her fingers. It dropped into her lap with a heavy *thump.* Her shoulder sagged. Every bit of skin felt too tight and too loose all at once. Her fingers twitched around the Aramerk.

No.

No, that was not all. That was not real.

She swiped a tear away. Tears were useless right now, they didn't fix anything, they didn't prove the vision to be some sort of horrid manipulation meant to break her resolve. That's what it had to be—a trick, somehow sent by the Scourge or her own worst fears to wear her down. They certainly weren't rational.

Her heart beat too thunderously in her chest. Each pulse was near agony for her drained body—as much as the Aramerk helped channel her visions, it made the Flow greedier. Carissa took a deep breath. It clawed down her throat and as she swallowed she was shocked there wasn't blood in her mouth.

Aleksander...he would never. All of that was a lie. It had to be.

Even as her body screamed, she repositioned herself and closed her eyes.

"Tulathne," she whispered, "show me the *truth.*"

Again, she fell into oblivion.

A Sneak Peek of
Book Two:

LIES OF THE GODDESS
BY LILA SAMSON

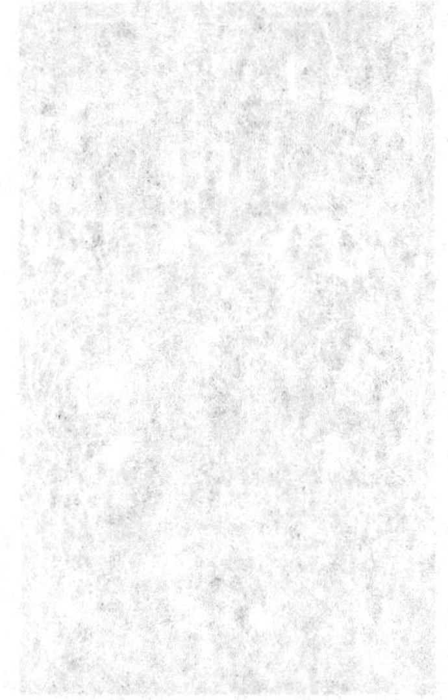

THE NIGHT SKY ABOVE THE SMALL cottage was clear. Not simply in that it was devoid of clouds, but that it was devoid entirely of stars. A full moon was the only object shining its light down on to the small village, on the sleeping and wakeful alike. She watched, silently, as a young woman stumbled into her home at the edge of this village; so many matters of this world had become tiresome to her, but as she rose, great and glowing behind the mountain, the moon couldn't help but be fixated on the scene unfolding before her.

The young mother pressed her hands against her back as another wave of pain rolled through her. Clattering steps issued along the boards of the porch until she reached the door, already sweating from not only the heat of the day but the strain of the child now attempting to kick its way out of her. Inside, she filled a pot of water and placed it on a dying hearth. Her counters were full of herbs and talismans—different medicines she'd used all throughout her time while her baby grew.

There was no room aside from the floor for her to set out a bowl, a blanket, or even a place to lay the child once it was here.

No midwife would be coming. The child had sullied the mother, unwed as she was. No one in town was going to care should either of them live or die.

The woman knelt on folded blankets, lifting her skirts and doing her best to feel for the position of the baby. She knew nothing about what to do. She was a healer, a setter of bones and remover of curses; there was nothing she knew about midwifery aside from what she'd seen when her sister had given birth years ago.

Her sister. How did she fare? It had been so long since—

A scream ripped from her throat, pain coursing through her pelvis, her back, her legs. Folded arms rested on a bench, her forehead pressing in to the embroidered fabric of her sleeves and the wood beyond.

She counted the seconds. One. Two. Three. Four. On to a

minute when another round passed, strong and sustained; blood flowed down her legs onto the blanket. Her grandmother had woven it. Her mother had been swaddled in it. How fitting then, that the family that abandoned her was what would be influential in cradling her child moments later.

Provided she made it that long.

Gods, she had not even had time to weave a bracelet of red nettle thread for the child. How would they be safe when—

Pain shot up her spine, and her mind emptied of all thoughts but one: *breathe*.

Everything was on fire. The mother counted her breaths, the minutes, the pace of the whole thing, slick with sweat and still wearing her layers of clothes after a day in the marketplace. Glancing up, through the window, she saw the moon. For a moment the pain faded—then it was blinding.

Curling up on hands and knees, she screamed as a contraction tore through her. Knobby joints and wiggling fingers sent nothing but pain through her cervix.

What was it her sister did? She went limp—with each contraction her and their mother and a midwife had held her up, and her sister had relaxed her whole body. It made birth easier, she'd said—her niece had slipped right out with little to no effort.

Can't do that now, she noted, and bore down along with another contraction.

She pushed, squatting best she could, hands slick with sweat and blood cradling a small head already full of hair.

Moaned prayers echoed through the small house. Aside from her pain, the only sound was the wind softly whistling through the window that never fully closed, and the cracking of wood in the hearth.

One final push and her child slid free, screaming and hot.

Resting her hips on her heels, pain still pulsing through her though not nearly as awful as it had been moments before, she wrestled the squirming newborn from her skirts.

Tears flooded down her cheeks—no longer caused by pain or fear, but instead rapt awe at the beauty of the child in her arms.

Covered in fluids and red as the dye used in Rodzjiek embroidery, her daughter shook with cries, tiny hands clenched in fists, toes the size of a lentil balled up, only to stretch out and ball up again.

The mother fell back against the bench, holding her girl to her chest.

In the sky outside, the moon paled; she was overjoyed at the safe delivery, yes. But something was wrong. She felt it in the shift of the cosmos just as she'd felt it a few nights prior, when a woman had birthed a boy at the foot of the mountains the moon hovered over now; and whatever it implied, this new mother would be powerless to stop it. The moon had seen it often enough, though millennia always stood between the girls destined to bring a curse to the land—whether they wanted to or not.

The lack of stars in the sky, the night as it was—she was strong, this new addition to the continent, but would she be strong enough?

Still, the two clung to one another.

Little body and face now clear of fluids, cord cut, the mother wrapped her newborn in a swath of soft, worn linen. The dark hair on the little one's head stuck up in odd directions, and she squinted at her mother through puffy eyes, the rich irises glowing in the firelight.

Shaking fingers smoothed out the creases on her wrinkly face. For the first time in years, the mother breathed a prayer of thanks. Thanks for a safe delivery. Thanks for her strength.

Thanks for the child, and please, any god who is listening, give her a good, long life.

Let no one hurt her.

The mother's eyes drifted to the moon and the space past, where she caught a faded glimmer of a single constellation.

Please, she whispered—to the stars, to the woman within them, *please let Czelsawa be given a good fate.*

ACKNOWLEDGEMENTS

THIS BOOK WAS A SIMULTANEOUSLY a long time in the making and a very short experience. The plot itself came to fruition after I jotted down a few ideas, a few questions, and stewed in some music for a few days. Aleksander and Varek and everyone possessed me, and it was a need to write that bordered on insanity. Ask my mother—I'd meet up with her and talk about this story as if it was one I'd read, not one that was living inside my head (her words, not mine.) The concepts in it, however, are ones I've been stewing over for years. I do think I needed to write this book—not just because the characters and the story begged me to write it, but because I needed to put pen to paper about the topics both in *Child of Tulathne* and all subsequent books in the trilogy. So thank you to everyone who joined me on this journey—and now it's time to get in to the specific thanks and the specific yous.

First off, obviously, I need to thank my parents. Thanks mom and dad for raising me on stories of adventure and wonder, of drama and strife and love and hope. You guys always encouraged me to read and write and act and watch things that sparked my creativity and brought me joy. Mom, thank you for encouraging my reading and my writing and all my interests, even if you had absolutely no clue what was going on with them. Honestly, it's fun to re-explain *Lord of the Rings* to you every time we watch it —it gets you invested and involved, and I get to be a little nerd about it. And thank you for sitting through conversations about this book where I continuously hemmed and hawed over whether or not to share certain aspects of it with you, and thank you for being excited when I did. We both know I'll change things and you probably won't remember it anyways. Dad, thank you for reading to me when I was little and introducing me to fantasy when mom thought it was stupid. I hope you enjoy this adventure as much as our trips to Mordor. And thank you for being patient with me and letting me keep my little secrets from you until the book's release.

Thank you to my husband, Elijah. You are my best friend, the love of my life, and my inspiration for so many things in so many ways. I am beyond grateful for your encouragement and support in my writing endeavors, even if you don't read nearly as much as I do and struggle to get through anything actually written. I was so nervous for you to read my writing for the longest time because you're the person whose opinion I value the most, and when I finally let you read you came back with encouragements and valid criticisms that truly helped shape the story into what it is now. I love you more than you can fathom.

Thank you to my little grey boy, Winston, aka Winnie the Poop, aka aka-ka Beeper. My nights of writing and editing would have been much less eventful and, admittedly, enjoyable, if it were not for you choosing to lay right on my arms as I typed, or at least on my lap, making me reach around you at strange, awkward angles. In fact, you're doing that as I write this very paragraph, purring as loud as a car engine. And in that same vein, thank you to baby Grand Duchess, Taka, my husband's elderly and crotchety ex-feral cat, who for some reason only loves women and my husband. Thank you for laying on my back, my chest, my arms, or any available space while I spent night after night editing in bed. The love of one's pets can not be understated in the discussion of encouragement and positive mental attitudes.

I've also got a big thank you for my bestie Emily, who stuck with me when I said I was gonna write a book in 2015 and then did, got an agent and almost had a publishing deal, and then scrapped the whole thing after nearly a decade or so of working on it. Look, Em, I actually finished it this time! And I know you didn't read the beta copy—that's fine. This one is much better anyways.

And of course, nothing but massive thanks and love for everyone who helped my book come to fruition. To my fantastic editor Hannah VanVels Ausbury, thank you for coming in on the tail end of this project and making it that much better—I hope we can work more closely on many more books to come. And to my beta readers, Cameron, and Lily. Your excitement and feedback is more than I could have asked for. You got me hyped up and thinking, and this story wouldn't be what it is without you!

I also want to put out a thank you to TikTok—it's likely going away as I write this, but I found so many fantastic independent authors there whose works encouraged me to publish my own, as well as a new friend and writing companion in Lauren Cole (if you're reading this and you haven't read *The Day of Sun*, get to it, it's fantastic).

Another well deserved thanks goes to everyone and everything that inspired this book and the characters within: Suzanne Collins for *The Underland Chronicles*, FromSoftware (specifically because of *Elden Ring*), JRR Tolkien, C.S. Lewis for *The Chronicles of Narnia*, NotQuiteIcarus on TikTok, *The Legend of Zelda: Breath of the Wild* and *Tears of the Kingdom*, the general existence of theological debates and discussions, *Dungeons and Dragons*, Sara Raztressen for *The Glass Witch*, "Soldier, Poet, King" by the Oh Hellos, cryptids and other eldritch horrors, and the rich cultures of Poland, Türkiye, Ancient Egypt, and Medieval England who served as heavy inspiration for the Rodzjiekim, Mekartlim, Ölmesuz, and Zekharyans respectively. I feel like I'm missing some, but that's a good start.

And, last but not least, thank *you*. Yes, you. I am honored you read this far, and I hope you liked what you've read. If you didn't, hey, no big deal, not everyone will. But you still read my story, so thank you. And to those of you who read it *and* liked it? Thank you, thank you, *thank you*. You've no idea how much it means to me, and I can't wait to continue this journey with you.

Lila Samson is a Minnesota born-and-raised author and artist. Stories were a part of her life from a very early age, in the form of audio dramas, books, her own writings on printer paper, and her father regaling her with stories around the dinner table and campfires. With countless books crammed in her suitcase for roadtrips to the North Shore, it was there she found her love for fantasy thanks to her battered copies of *The Chronicles of Narnia* and her father's box set of *The Lord of the Rings* on tape.

After writing for a decade and then abandoning her first novel right before publication, she finally makes her debut with *Child of Tulathne*, the first in a YA Fantasy trilogy.

She currently lives in Minnesota with her husband and their two cats. You can find her on TikTok at @lilasamsonauthor and on Instagram at @shelvedbylila.

www.ingramcontent.com/pod-product-compliance
Lightning Source LLC
Chambersburg PA
CBHW011410310726
48972CB00011B/2920